NEVER MIND THE GOLDBERGS

NEVER MIND THE GOLDBERGS

MATTHUE ROTH

PUSH

SCHOLASTIC INC.
NEW YORK TORONTO LONDON AUCKLAND SYDNEY
MEXICO CITY NEW DELHI HONG KONG BUENOS AIRES

b"h

ISBN 0-439-69189-3

 Published by PUSH, an imprint of Scholastic Inc., 557 Broadway, New York, NY 10012.

12 11 10 9 8 7 6 5 4 3 2 1 6 7 8 9 10 11/0

Printed in the U.S.A. 40

First PUSH paperback printing, April 2006

First printing, February 2005

CHAPTERS

01

HAVA KICKS THE NEW YORK HABIT

The last day of school was when I really lost it.

I'd spent my whole life watching people through a screen, an invisible cellophane coating on the world. Talking to my friends was like reading from a script. I always knew what they were about to say, what tone of voice they would use, and how they wanted me to react. I guess I was just born different.

Of course, if you'd asked my friends, they wouldn't have known what you were talking about. They would've told you I wasn't capable of holding *any*thing in.

But — when you're a seventeen-year-old Orthodox Jewish girl with purple-and-burgundy-streaked hair, ripped denim skirts that come down to your ankles, and death rock T-shirts — you don't look like you're holding back. I had this friend last year who decided that she didn't believe in G-d. She ran away from her parents' house and lived in a squatter house with a pack of hippies, eating ninety-nine-cent bags of potato chips and beef jerky. She came back a month later, still atheist, just not as loud about it.

That wasn't me. I still believed in G-d. I just didn't believe in other people.

I mean, some days, I felt like G-d was the only one who believed back at me.

I was two periods away from summer break. In our Prophets class, I ruffled the pages of my textbook through my fingers, the same way I did every day, only louder, because today I didn't care.

Rabbi Greenberg's ears perked up. His head shot toward me, eyes like a hawk. Flipping pages pissed him off severely, a physical act of blasphemy, worse than passing notes or coming late to class. Rabbi Greenberg was the principal of our yeshiva. He had this speech about how every single word of the Torah was G-d's gift to the Jews. He always checked that we paged through our books from beginning to end.

I pinched all my fingers in the book at once, like a glove. Raised ink slid against my fingertips. My nails eased into the horizontal crevice of the spine.

We were reading the story of David and Jonathan. Jonathan's father, Saul, the King of Israel, sent an army to kill David, and Jonathan was the only person who could save him. The king's troops were running all over Israel with knives and scimitars, and Jonathan finally hid David inside a cave for a few days. At first I thought that was really shitty, to abandon him, and in a ratty cave at that. But I guess it wouldn't have been that bad. You could sit it out and leave the world alone for a few rounds.

Today I imagined there were caves hidden throughout the yeshiva hallways.

Some days I dressed like a glam-metal punk rock diva, and

some days I toned it down so I wouldn't get another lecture. Since today was the last day of school, I'd let my fractured fashion sense run wild. If I were a boy, today would be my Marilyn Monroe drag-queen day. Since I was a girl, I went for the layered look in a big way. We had to wear long skirts but I had three going at once: a denim one down to my ankles, a bright green plaid knee-length skirt over it, and a maroon polyester miniskirt over that. I had on a hoodie that I kept pulled halfway over my head, to where a tiara would fall. And a Metallica T-shirt (*so* over them, but the statement must be made) with a picture of bloody I-don't-know-whats peeking out from the V-neck of my hoodie.

I leaned far back in my chair from exhaustion and heat. I was already finished with this day. I don't know why it wasn't finished with me yet.

I let the pages fall against my fingers, fanning them again and again, a sigh of air on my hand. I closed my eyes and imagined what it was like to be free, no walls, no adults breathing down your back.

Rabbi Greenberg taught only one class a year. It was always Prophets. In the hallways and in assemblies, whenever anyone fell out of line, he would repeat the same word in a library tone of voice, "*Osser. Osser.*"

He'd say it again and again, that single Yiddish word. It was one of those untranslatable words, like "Forbidden. Forbidden." or "Asshole. Asshole." It had the power to drive you insane.

Everybody's Prophets books were open to the same page. The class looked like twenty-six identical little icons on a computer desktop, except for me. There were two hours left before summer started.

To the Rabbi, it might as well have been a year.

"David and Jonathan shared a beautiful friendship," he said. "The Sages teach that a love that is not founded on selfishness is the highest form of love. When Jonathan hid David in the cave outside Jerusalem and told his father that David had been killed, he went against his family and his kingdom. There was nothing for him but the love of his dearest companion. And yet that was enough. Hava Aaronson, flipping the pages of a holy book is *osser*."

I stared out the window. In early summer, New York always looked like it was sweating. The sun was yellower than it had ever been, orange almost. Like a campfire. It reminded me of caves.

"Hava. *Osser*."

I heard my name. I snapped back into reality, and David and Jonathan and all the caves in my mind evaporated.

"He's *so* keeping us after class," moaned Rechama Zeitstein, loud enough for everyone to hear.

I stared at Rabbi Greenberg head-on. I felt a breeze on my hand and realized I hadn't stopped flipping pages.

"*Osser. Osser. Osser*."

The class breathed heavy. I skimmed the pages with my nails, one by one. I pursed my firm, defined, Clairol Fetish mahogany-pink lips into an O and blew a narrow cone of cold air down at the back of my palm.

"*Osser*, Hava. *Osser. Osser. Osser. Osser*."

I flinched.

I didn't stop. I couldn't, now.

"*Osser, osser, OSSER!!!*"

The table in front of Rabbi Greenberg gave one final earthquake rattle. His hands gripped the metal edge. They shook hard.

Before I knew what I was doing, I stood up.

My skirts flapped against the edge of my desk. They made a noise like a whip. I felt the dead air of the class as I rose up from the level where everyone else was sitting. I took a breath.

"It's not *osser*. My dad flips through books all the time. English and Hebrew ones. It's some obscure rule you found. It's just one more way you think you can control us. And you're so full of yourself, I wonder why nobody ever stuffed *you* in a cave."

Now nobody was breathing.

Twenty-six pairs of eyes opened wide. I squeezed my sweating palms.

Everybody waited.

"Osser."

Rabbi Greenberg said it again, after a while.

But the fire had gone out of his eyes, and his face looked like ashes. For the first time since I'd started at Rashi Yeshiva High School — maybe for the first time ever — Rabbi Greenberg's voice sounded hollow and empty. The unspoken threat behind his warnings was harmless.

"Oh, shove it," I said. "Flipping pages is not a law. And also, Jonathan and David were gay."

I looked back at my fingertips. They pulsed the same beat as my heart. I'd fired my shot and it hit a lot deeper than I ever thought it would.

Now all I had to do was get out.

I snatched up my knapsack with one hand and my Bible with the other. I let the door flop closed after me. The bell rang as soon as I cleared the classroom. Doors opened. Kids started to flock through the halls. I felt the crowd swallow me up. I wondered idly about going to next period.

I thought about going home instead.

No. One more class and everyone would be out. And my last class of the day was Yiddish, which was my favorite subject, although I utterly sucked at it.

I expected a messenger from Rabbi Greenberg's office to meet me at the door and drag me to his office. I walked in, slid down deep into my seat, held my breath, and didn't let go. I bit my bottom lip until I could actually feel the blood move to the other side of my mouth.

Our Yiddish teacher, Mrs. Teitelbaum, was young and kind of pretty. She had a toned-down hip look, the kind of beautiful person who tries not to stand out and ends up standing out even more. She wore modest crew-neck sweaters, flowy poetry skirts, smart-looking hats that no *goyim* would guess she wore to comply with the religious mandate of covering her hair. She looked like a rock star. She grew up as a Satmar Hasid in Williamsburg, Brooklyn, and became Modern Orthodox when she married an entertainment lawyer from Philadelphia. Her Hasidic family had declared her *nifter*, that she was dead to them, and they had not spoken to her since. The whole Modern Orthodox community knew her story and sympathized tremendously. All the kids in our high school thought she was sort of a hero, and all the adults treated her charitably. I breezed into class a minute ahead of everyone else, even Gittel Glassman, who wore glasses like Woody Allen and sat in the front row in every class. Mrs. Teitelbaum looked at me proudly but said nothing.

Neither did I. One blowup a day was enough.

Mrs. Teitelbaum had a special lesson planned for our last day. "Since I really don't expect you to learn anything new today," Mrs. Teitelbaum said, sliding her long-skirted hips along the front of the classroom like she was ice-skating, "we'll have a review of previous material. Now, Yiddish is the best language in the world for what, class?"

"To insult people in!" replied the class in one voice.

"Good, good," said Mrs. Teitelbaum. "Today we'll practice some creative ways to say things to people who get on your nerves — or, rather, to someone who might *hak a kain tsheinik* at you."

The class burst out laughing.

My fingers tightened into knots. I could feel trouble in the air. A messenger was totally gonna come into class at this moment, probably Emily Cohen, with a note from the principal to kick me right on out of school and probably Mrs. Teitelbaum, too, in the process. For harboring a fugitive.

We drew numbers to pick our conversation partners. Fruma Goldstein, whose skirt was one inch longer and two sizes tighter than every other skirt in school, strode up to my desk with a disgusted look on her face.

"Deal with it," she hissed.

Fruma Goldstein was the most popular girl at Rashi High. Her father, Rabbi Goldstein, ran the biggest synagogue in Riverside Heights, and also wrote a series of books on Jewish living that became crossover bestsellers among the secular population. Their family was very observant. In first grade, Fruma made the biggest deal of which kids' houses her father said weren't kosher enough to eat at. In ninth grade, I went out for about five minutes with this guy that Fruma liked, and she told everyone that I smoked on Sabbath.

The next week he started dating Fruma, not for too long and not with any enthusiasm. But Fruma had that kind of pull. When all the lots were drawn, Mrs. Teitelbaum smiled weakly at me. She didn't know the details, but she had grown up Hasidic and she could smell problems on the wind, even inside a building. She closed her eyes and said a psalm to herself as everybody worked.

"Oh my G-d," Fruma said. "I can't be*lieve* what you pulled last period. Aren't you afraid you'll have to go to a new school next year?"

That was exactly what I was afraid of. Hearing the words from Fruma's mouth made my stomach drop one level.

"Anyway," Fruma continued, "let's not diverge. Would you like to start, or should I?" She had her notebook out and everything. She was really going to do the assignment.

"I never smoked on Shabbos," I said. "What were you thinking? I don't even smoke during the week."

Fruma flipped her book open. "I won't even pre*tend* to know what you're talking about, Hava," she said.

I glared.

"*Was machst du, Frau Aaronson?*" Fruma read from her notebook. "*Du bist ein chazzer. Ein grosse rotte farshtuppen chazzer.*"

A *chazzer* was a pig. Fruma's Yiddish wasn't even challenging: *You are a pig* is what she said. Fruma was insulting me, but she couldn't even pretend I was *intelligently* insultable. *You are a fat red stuck-up pig.* She just had to use small words.

"And where the hell do you get off talking about people smoking on Shabbos, anyway?" I said.

"Do you want to do this work or not, Hava?" Fruma hissed below her breath.

"Look, it's the last day of class, right? And you won't have to talk to me again for three months. And you are so fake that I can smell your brains burning. And nobody likes you, they're just afraid of you. And *you're* a *chazzer*. And also, *Sie mater*."

"My mother? What about my mother?"

"Jesus, do you not get anything! It's an expression. Your mother your mother your MOTHER!" This was beyond *me*, even. Two outbursts in one day. I was kind of afraid of myself, and kind of curious to see where I'd go. My desk was shaking.

Emily Cohen burst into the room at that second. The whole class shot their glares away from me and my sudden outburst. "Sorry I'm not in class," Emily said to Mrs. Teitelbaum. "Rabbi Greenberg wanted me in his office to xerox some Talmud stuff. Also, he just got an emergency phone call, and he says for Hava to come to his office immediately."

Shit.

Being in trouble was nothing new for me. I guess I had always been that kind of kid, the one who never quite fits in, the one who has to party on her own terms and bring everyone else down with her. My mother was always asking if I was doing it on purpose, did I want to stop being Orthodox. Actually, that's the last thing I ever wanted. I thought I was the only person I knew who really understood what G-d wanted. When I got in trouble, it was just me proselytizing.

I exited the classroom like I was playing a role in a movie I'd already seen. The students' heads panned out the door, following my steps. Mrs. Teitelbaum cleared her throat and started a group conversation. I decided I could just nod in the rabbi's office and pretend to listen, and then I'd stand up and waltz out the second the bell rang.

I knew I probably wouldn't go through with it. I wouldn't diss him. I'd wait until the rabbi finished speaking. Today was the first time I'd ever actually raised my voice. Even now, my lungs felt bloated and stretched out. Usually, I was so fucking polite. Even when I was totally justified in blowing off people, I didn't. Sometimes I ignored rules, but only when it was safe.

So when I was told to go to the rabbi's office, I went. I was curious. I wanted to see what he'd do to me. The only part that didn't make sense was the phone call, but I wasn't up to that yet. In the headmaster's office, Rabbi Greenberg looked even more displeased than usual. When I stood there and cleared my throat and waited for him to say something, even just that word *osser* again, he just looked up and shook his head. Not angrily but sadly.

He looked down at the desk.

I followed his gaze.

The phone was off the hook. Rabbi Greenberg nodded at it. I felt so jumbled. I was sure G-d would be on the other line, *Thou Hast Sinned Against Thine Anointed High School Principal*, and I would be left with nothing to say. Even Catholics have Hail Marys. Jews only have guilt.

"This movie producer," Rabbi Greenberg said. "He asked for you by name."

I picked up the phone.

"Hava?" the voice said, smooth as milk.

My spine shivered. I already felt like he was trying to sell me something.

"What do you want?"

"We're casting a new comedy pilot for next spring's network television lineup. We've seen your résumé and we're very impressed with your acting career, and if your schedule's free, we'd like to fly you out tomorrow for a shoot."

I fumbled.

"I — I'll have to ask my parents."

"Hava?" My father's voice chirped in.

I bit my lip. Three-way calling.

"You know your mother and I have been after you to get a summer job."

"I'm missing my Yiddish class, sir," I said into the phone. I couldn't think of anything to say. I could feel myself losing ground, spinning out of control. I hated not being in control. And this phone was taking over — this blank, anonymous phone.

Somehow, on the other side of this country, there was a gazillionaire producer on a cell phone, pacing in the confines of a home office, staring out at his pool from atop his Beverly Hills sundeck, breathing in the same static that I could hear right now.

I thought about the possibility of another New York summer, working a stupid job, spending every night at stupid PG-rated romantic comedies with the girls in my class.

I breathed low and hard. "I'll just see you on Monday, is that okay?"

I got home before my parents. My room felt smaller than it ever had — Björk and Sleater-Kinney posters, splatter-paint spots of purple and red and yellow paint on the walls, my twin bed narrowly crammed next to the wall, between my sole window and the amp for the electric guitar that I'd bought and never learned to play. Buying it was my one bratty move as a ninth-grader, the same year that Shira made her parents take her to Laos, and Fruma got a $200 haircut for the first day of school. At least my rebellion was punk rock. My compact hibernation chamber of a room looked like an underwater cabin on an ocean liner, all my worldly possessions crammed in like it was my only space in the universe.

And, after 8:35 the next morning, it wouldn't even be mine anymore.

That night we all went out in a big big way. It wasn't that I didn't have any guy friends, but when we went out at night, it always started out as a girls-only evening. In our neighborhood, all the kids our age knew everything about one another, but girls were just closer. I knew the boys' names and birthdays, but I knew the girls' pulses. We went everywhere together. We did everything together. Even Fruma and me, who loathed each other, we did that together, too. I could tell you the last time each girl had a date, a haircut, or a late period.

The other girls could tell you the same things about me, but they probably wouldn't waste their breath. I'd always been the weird kid. I liked different books, watched different movies, eventually started wearing different clothes. Somewhere along the way, I'd decided that I wasn't the lame one. They all were.

And so I'd spent the first half of high school trying to ignore the rest of my class. But greatness got lonely. When I started talking again to the girls in my class — who all wore their hair in braids and never figured out how to make long skirts look anything but frumpy — I think I forgot how to really communicate with them. I wanted to talk about the homeless problem and the meaninglessness of life and how I always felt so horny even though there were only stupid-looking khaki boys with monkey haircuts to flirt with. The other girls *liked* khaki boys. When I talked about the boys I liked — skinny, T-shirted boys with spiky bleach-blond hair and fabulous style — everyone called them *faygelehs.* We were dead air, stuck together like we shared a deformed umbilical cord that would never fall off, joined by virtue of not having anywhere else to run.

We were all Orthodox. I guess that was something.

At dinnertime, Shira and Meira picked me up at my parents' apartment. Plastic fans whirred at full blast, and we all wore shirts with sleeves that cut off at the elbows. On the way to the subway, the street vendors sold melting ice out of refrigerated trucks, blowing stray jets of harsh, cold air in our faces when the doors swung open. Elementary-school kids thumb-wrestled on the stoops outside their apartments. Everything was uneasy, like the city was about to bust out with a dance number. Shira stopped to stare in the music window of Gottlieb's. She always did. After tomorrow morning, I might not see Gottlieb's again for a year.

Except in Hollywood, they call a year a *season.*

"Why did they want you for this thing, anyway?" Shira asked me. She was wiry, mouselike, and always sounded anxious.

I shrugged. "I don't know what the deal is. I just say *yes* and watch what happens. I think it's a sitcom about Jews, something like that."

"Do you think you'll even be back in fall for Greenberg to hate you?" said Meira. "You'll get a tutor out there for teaching you between episodes. That's what they do in Hollywood. It's the law. You're gonna be so rich you can hire another girl to take classes for you. Except you'll have to bribe the tutor not to notice. 'Cause, you know. Class of one. I wonder if you'll learn Talmud on the show. Do you think they'll use a real Talmud or just a prayerbook and think people won't notice? Since it's in Hebrew and nobody knows Hebrew? Hey, will they hire you a Hebrew language coach, do you think?"

I rolled my eyes and walked faster. "I already speak Hebrew, Meira."

"You never know. Maybe he'll be cute. Plus, the studio will be spending a lot of money on you. You shouldn't turn down anything they offer."

"Stop bothering Hava," Shira said matter-of-factly. "The trainers in Hollywood are all *faygelehs*, anyway. And I'm sure Hava's thought about this all already." She squeezed my arm confidently.

I hadn't. I panicked. I kept thinking in New York terms. Everything would fall into place when I got there. My flight would land, my car would pull up, some business-suit chick who talked like a bank commercial would explain what I had to do, and then I'd do it. I was counting on ignorance as a weapon.

Shira and Meira laughed at my suddenly frightened face, grabbed my arms, and pulled me down into the subway. We took the brown-brick stairs two at a time, passed under the sign that said Downtown Trains, and slid our fare cards through the turnstile. Shira and I agreed that at the end of the night I'd give her my subway pass. I loved going to the Village and always bought a monthly. Shira never left the Jewish ghetto where we lived. Maybe with me gone, and having no responsibility but summer, my pass would turn Shira into an extrovert. A hipster extrovert.

The restaurant was double anchovy jam-packed. We squeezed past families and couples in line. Some of our friends were holding a table at the back of the restaurant. We couldn't see. Shira called another girl on her cell phone — "Are you REALLY here? How far back?" — and stayed on the phone till we found our place, a long, straight banquet table at the end of the bar. It was the last night of school, so everyone was coming out. We slid into the three empty chairs in the middle. I was next to Fruma.

I looked around to switch seats. The table was already overstuffed. There was no way out.

Fruma smiled.

It made me squirm. She had that crocodile look down to a science.

"I guess you don't get to stick around for Greenberg's vengeance after all," Fruma said. That was her way of starting a peaceful conversation.

"I'm coming back in fall," I told her. "And you know Rabbi Greenberg. He's an elephant."

"Hava. Startle me more. Was that you caring?"

"That's me preparing," I said.

There was a mushroom pie just out of my reach. I was feeling the need for an incredible mushroom fix just then, but someone had already passed me a slice of Hawaiian and I felt really stuck-up asking for something else. But I wanted that peppery shiitake chewiness, not the rubbery feel of leaky pineapple squishing between my teeth. The roasted mushrooms on the mushroom pizza looked cata*stroph*ically good. It sat wedged in the middle of the other table — mostly boys — which was pushed up against our table. It was a segregated, sublimated flirtation.

I sat in the groove between tables, squashed in the center. Shira and Meira planned for tonight to be just a girls' night, but somehow the guys got hold of our scheme. Fruma and her boyfriend, Shmuel, had probably leaked it. They were always looking for opportunities to hang out without looking sleazy. Sleazy, among Orthodox Jews, means hanging out alone and holding hands in public. Shmuel sat directly on my other side.

I sat back and watched. Guys and girls spoke with elaborate hand gestures, boys reaching into each other's personal space, girls giggling in silent agreement that would be called immodesty if the giggles were actual words.

We weren't supposed to touch boys who we weren't related to — it was called being *shomer negiah* — but almost none of us followed it strictly. We wouldn't hug in public or jump on each other, but as the night ran on, everybody would slink away. First the official couples, like Fruma and Shmuel, followed by maybe-couples, like Shira and Lev, who didn't have a perfect practiced eye for finding safely abandoned doorways to sneak into and make out. They would be fumbly and awkward and sometimes even apologetic as they left.

Now Fruma and her boyfriend were discussing their plans for Shabbos, Meira and Shira were arguing with the other girls about a new line of modest clothes ("clothes that want to look like Banana Republic but they can't stop looking so *Jew*ish"), and the boys were talking about sports. Despite all the conversations, I realized that every person at the table, directly or indirectly, was watching me. Rafael said something to me and I went, "Why are you looking at me like that?"

Everybody — absolutely everybody — heard.

Fruma cleared her throat. She offered up a comment about Jewish clothes stores but everyone was so tense that their mouths were frozen.

Nobody knew what was going to happen.

Lev's forearm shot awkwardly toward Shira's forearm. I bet they were touching palms under the table.

I eyed the mushroom pie, easier to reach since two boys had gotten up to leave, but still not close enough.

The silence hung for a second.

From behind my seat, a high, awkward male voice rang out over our collective embarrassment, "I'm *beyond* ready for Hollywood. But, *mamish,* I don't think it's ready for me."

Moish? I mouthed.

Across from me, Meira nodded confirmation.

"Not for long," Moish said. He sauntered up to the table, draped one palm over each side of my seat, and surveyed the crowd. The guys at the table halfheartedly fished for extra seats.

"Six more days," Moish told everyone proudly, "and my life on this coast is toast."

He looked around, waiting for it to sink in.

"Moishele," said Fruma, patiently and condescendingly, "what are you talking about?"

Moish was caught off guard. "I thought you knew," he stammered. "My cousin in L.A. just got married. But her lease goes till September. So I'm going to spend the summer hanging out on the Sunset Strip and working on my career."

Moish was wearing all black that night. Not a surprise. He

went to Rashi High, too, in the boys' building, but he took different classes from the rest of us. Slower classes. Hebrew and Talmud and chemistry were not skills that came easily to Moish. He wasn't dumb. He was just incredibly awkward.

Moish hung out in the Village, too. Except he went for the straight-up weird look. It was partly his black turtlenecks and odd hats, but also, when you talked to him, you felt like he spoke a language that only eighty percent overlapped with your language. Sticking out from beneath his black pullover and black vest would always be his ritual fringes, which we call *tzitzis*, white as printer paper, killing his fantasy of being the consummate post-pomo intellectual. We all thought some secular college would pay him loads of money one day to be the token Orthodox Jew on staff. But what he really wanted was to be a performance artist.

"What career?" Fruma demanded. "Heresy?"

"I'm gonna make a movie," Moish informed her and, by proxy, the entire table. "It's the total anti-L.A. experience. I'm calling it *Hollywood Movie* and it will be absolutely live, with no actors. It's ultimate realism."

Moish stood in front of the seat they'd found for him, looking pleased and expecting a barrage of admiration.

Freddy Gellar was the first to break the silence. He asked Shmuel about the Mets.

I felt vaguely annoyed at the boys for dissing him like that. But I was every bit as pissed at Moish, for just not getting it. Moish and I were the only two hipster refugees in our entire school. I'd learned to act wild in my head and act socially acceptable around school. Subtlety, poise, and showers twice a day. Why couldn't he?

Poor Moish. Maybe Hollywood would be best for him. Nobody here seemed to get him, and he had all the chameleon skills of a purple elephant.

I slid back in my seat, listening to Fruma going off on secular music. "Rap songs," she said. "What, do they think they don't have to *sing* anymore?" It was horrid and a little funny. Across the table Meira was telling Moish — who was in the lower-level Talmud class and missed my entire fiasco that afternoon — about my impending Hollywood superstardom.

". . . So the network ordered thirteen episodes, and Hava is the last-minute replacement for the Angsty Teenage Girl part because their first choice got pregnant or something, and there was a whole potential tabloid scandal that lasted about twenty seconds, but nobody even knew who she was, and anyway they'd had Hava in mind the whole time." Meira looked divinely proud of herself. "She flies out tomorrow morning, and they film all summer long."

"But —" Moish's lower lip trembled. "Sitcoms usually film in fall — and what about summer break, and your job at the deli, and I was supposed to be totally by myself, and . . ." he stammered. "Hava, are you really selling out?"

I wanted to tell him it wasn't selling out if there was an adventure attached. I wanted to tell him how this was the first time that I was excited about anything, *any*thing, in over a year.

Instead, I intoned my mantra of the week: "It's not what you're selling, it's what you're buying."

"Is that from Psalms?" Moish asked.

"Yeah, totally," I told him. Actually, it was a quote from a Fugazi song, searing electric guitars, soaring primal drums. "Absolutely, it is."

After dinner, the whole crew headed for the movies together. It totally baffled me that I was hanging out with these people. I figured it was nature. It was as much my choice as what color eyes I was born with, or who my parents were. Ignoring the Jewish kids was tantamount to ignoring the world outside my head. The Village, punk rock music — even Ian, my only real secular friend — they were all illusions. The day I was born, fifty of my father's friends held his hands and learned Talmud for my safe delivery, and a hundred of my mother's friends breathed in unison with her and kept warm smelling salts burning to add richness to the air she breathed.

I wasn't gonna turn out like that, one gear in a chain.

But I wasn't ready to leave it, either. Not yet.

Fruma and Shmuel slipped out of the movie early, just before the sex scene that you knew was coming. Ultra-Orthodox Jews did that at secular movies. Shmuel had already slipped his yarmulke off so he wouldn't disgrace Judaism by looking like a pious boy watching a secular movie. Ultra-Orthodox Jews did that, too. Fruma got someone to tap my shoulder down the row. She blew me an air kiss. I smiled stately, remembering suddenly that I wouldn't have to deal with her again until autumn. Maybe never.

Two o'clock that morning, I sat on the roof of my building, palms digging into the gravel. I looked Ian square in the eye. My eyes were wet and red and I couldn't see cleanly through them.

"It's not about being punk rock," I said. "You *know* I don't care about that shit. I'm not gonna sell Barbie dolls to anorexic beauty queens, or tell people to listen to Britney or shit like that.

I'm just gonna be me. Maybe if girls see someone like me on TV, they'll believe someone who isn't ditzy or blond or preternaturally skinny can be popular."

"Or someone Orthodox." Ian chewed on a toothpick. His mohawk glowed bright against the full moon.

"Exactly," I said. "Maybe all the marginal minorities will start getting press space, too."

"Not Jewish, Hava. I said Orthodox."

"So?"

"So there's a diff. What you are isn't an ethnicity. It's a choice. And you can be Orthodox and punk rock and riot grrrly on your own, in high school and in your bedroom and when nobody's watching you, but TV is one big-ass magnifying glass."

"Yeah, I'm gonna miss you knocking on my fire escape, too, Ian."

"Just remember the little people who treated you kind, when you're big and rich and giving away Oscars," Ian said, fake-poking the air next to my belly.

"I'll buy you every Beastie Boys CD ever," I said. "Cross my heart."

Ian said nothing and gazed up at the stars, as if to find the exact horizon where summer breaks.

I sank deeper into the gravel.

"Ian," I said, "I'll never be punk rock like the people on our walls. I don't want to be. I'm afraid of losing myself in myself. Have you ever seen Hollywood on the news? I read about this one teen actress who saw so many airbrushed pictures of herself on billboards that one day she flipped completely, started ripping them down with her teeth. I think she made it most of the way down Sunset Boulevard before the cops started in on her."

Ian smiled at me, this big goofy smile that was reassuring and called to mind every shared memory we had since we were six months old, crawling up the apartment building stairs together. We always raced. I always won. He always knew which records were the best, though. I was just slick; he was intuitive.

"Ain't no way, dude-o," he said, sinking comfortably into a fetal ball against the brick wall. "Look at you. You pretty much grew up in a cult, and you're more of a nonconformist than half the bands on Lookout. You're uncorruptible."

"But am I uncorruptible against myself?" I said. The city behind that brick wall looked bigger than it ever did. Usually it was small, an ocean of lights that you could walk on. Tonight the buildings loomed tall over our heads like they could crush us. The Empire State Building glowed green and blue and white, a soft summer pattern. By the time I came back, the lights would have a whole different motif.

"Tonight at the restaurant there was this piece of mushroom pizza. I wanted a piece so fucking bad. I forgot to pack lunch, and Dad hasn't made me lunch since we fought last weekend, and I hadn't eaten all day. I just wanted one slice. I couldn't force myself to do it. It was so fucking weird, Ian. I sat there and stared at it all night through all the other kids talking. I wanted to reach over Shmuel and grab it. Even when he left, I couldn't. It broke too many boundaries. I didn't want to look that desperate."

I swallowed. It felt even worse when I thought about it then. I was afraid to look desperate. Hungry. Fat. I hated the way my cheeks puffed out when I chewed and I didn't want that to be the last image of me on everybody's minds. I was going away. This was the last photograph before television. I worried I'd never be three-dimensional for the kids in my class again. I looked at Ian like he held the world on a pendulum. I wanted him to tell me everything was better.

He blinked lamely.

"It's better that way, Hava. Cows die for cheese."

Ian was a vegan. I think he only did it as an excuse to behave like an asshole toward non-vegans. The wall was making brick-shaped indentations on my lower back. I pulled my hoodie over my head. I felt like building a cave. I shut my eyes hard.

When I opened them a second later, Ian was kneeling in front of me. "Hava," he whispered, "I was pushing your buttons. I'm sorry." His voice was soft like an electric razor's purr.

"I should sleep. My flight leaves in four hours," I said. The words felt weird.

Ian looked at his hands uselessly. "I know you don't touch boys. But if you did —"

The moon was a shade of blue that seemed to say *I'm Not Telling,* and the roof was quiet like a dream, and at the same minute both of our arms pulled each other in tight, this hug that not even Rabbi Greenberg would say was laden with sexual content. We held each other so hard, like sisters, and only for a moment. It was tight the way you squeeze your eyes closed. We stepped back, blinked at each other lightly. He smiled reassuringly. When his body moved, metal chains sang.

"I should go to sleep," I said again.

"You should go get pizza," Ian told me.

I looked at him.

"You don't have much time left in New York," Ian said. "Where the fuck else can you get mushroom slices at three a.m.?"

"Every Beastie Boys CD," I re-promised him. "Even the side projects."

02

STARDUST IS A POLITE WAY OF SAYING DANDRUFF

I was kicking it around the East Village at the beginning of junior year, early October, dead in the middle of Indian summer. I had just bombed a Gemara test big-time, and Shira and Meira were bumming with the popular kids. I was bored with them, and too grouchy to talk to anyone. Who needed to hang out with Orthodox kids, anyway? Not me. I could swear there was a much bigger world than the New York Jewish ghetto. It was out there somewhere. In New York, every corner I turned, there were more Jews. Yuppie Lawyer Jews and Hasidic Jews in black trench coats and Young Adult Mother Jews who looked my age and did nothing but tote around babies all day.

So I went to St. Mark's Place, the punk rock mecca in the Village. It was far enough away from home to feel like a different universe, and a different universe was exactly what I needed. Where boys had mohawks instead of antennae, the pierced and tattooed kids looked like beautiful outer space cyborgs, and absolutely everyone sparkled. You could always find them on St. Mark's Place. That street was their home.

But that day, even St. Mark's was deserted.

I felt like punching a hole in a wall. Strangling a puppy. Doing permanent damage.

I bought a bottle of Elmer's glue and dribbled it slowly over my fingers. I massaged my fingertips into each other, blew on them to dry, and peeled off the glue. I sat on the stoop of Trash & Vaudeville for a while. On a good day I could last an hour sitting there without getting kicked off by irate salespeople. On a really good day, a rock star would trip over my legs. Then when Meira and Shira were talking to me again, I could tell them, and Meira would get awed and demand the whole story. Shira would say, "Who cares? Secular music is ridiculous, anyway," but I'd know she was jealous, too.

That day some guy caught me busting on the stairs quick.

"I'm tying my shoes, asshole," I said. The guy sighed melodramatically and put his hands on his hips. He waited on the stairs for me to finish.

I wasn't lying. My shoes were untied. But then again, they usually are.

And, just to spite him, I went in.

I'd never actually been inside Trash & Vaudeville. I hadn't seen more than the exteriors of most stores on St. Mark's Place. I just liked the punks who hung out there, and most of them had never been inside any of the stores, either. The stores were a backdrop, what volcanoes were in the days of the dinosaurs. We were the teeth and claws. We were what people paid attention to.

Inside I walked around dizzily. I thumped my backpack

onto the counter and the salesguy slung it into a cubby. The sun was going down on the street, but inside they'd cranked all the lights up to high. The air conditioner was set on freezing. Racks of clothes protruded from the walls on diagonal slants. They made me feel like I was tripping. I think. I'd never tripped, but if it made you dizzy and unsteady, like the wood planks on the floor were turning into a series of balance beams, that's what it was. I gripped an orange MEN AT WORK–style jacket for support.

Instantly the clerk was at my elbow. It was the same prissy dillweed from the stoop. "May I help you with that?" he asked me snidely. I think he was just waiting to peek down the V-neck of my wallet and see the perilous absence of cash and/or credit cards inside.

I slid my eyelids half-open to look superior and bored, and I slid the words out of my mouth all biley and puslike.

"Just. Brrrowsssing."

And then, perkily, I added "But thanks!" as a knee-jerk reaction. My parents brought me up too well.

I crossed the aisle to the sign that said BARGAIN RACK, enticed by the thought that maybe I could afford something here. The bin was filled with bondage bustiers that I would never wear. A necklace of red grapefruit-size ball gags was giving me nightmares. I backed away — straight into a display of police uniform shirts lined on a display rack like dominoes. They toppled forward in a slo-mo undulation that spilt across the perimeter of the store. Me, the jackwad clerk, and the lone customer in the store (a pretty lady in a white petticoat who may or may not have been Ani Difranco) watched uniforms tumble in a quiet grace that pervaded the absolutely silent atmosphere of the store.

I knew I should apologize or run. The door was half an aisle away. I could dash out and never be seen again. Instead I was transfixed. The uniforms, falling, looked like an army of paper soldiers going to bed. They collapsed atop one another and it was such a nice, easy feeling, everything tumbling over, a really beautiful chaos. The shirts tumbled to the ground softly, the dim clink of metal button against button. I sighed.

"Why the hell is it so quiet? If you're going to be all punk rock, shouldn't you have music playing on some big-ass speakers?" I said quickly.

Then I realized exactly what I'd just done.

My pulse throbbed with adrenaline.

I felt myself swivel on one leg like a pendulum. My entire body hovered into position. One foot came down hard on the wood planks, and my body catapulted into running position.

"Your backpack —" the clerk called out.

The wind was in my face. I could taste the street on my tongue, just a set of stairs away.

I leaped as I hit the steps. I felt my body catch, fly, and hang in midair. My hands flat against the wind, one leg flung into the sky. I closed my eyes. I always thought flying involved merely throwing yourself to the ground and missing.

Then I felt my body slam hard into another body.

For the next few seconds I couldn't think anything. I may have blacked out from embarrassment, and the next thing I knew I heard a scream that, curiously, turned out to be a wail of delight. I looked at the man, confused, expecting him to yell at me hysterically for being an offensive kid. I climbed up, and the man and I were pulling each other to our feet, brushing the New York street dust off ourselves, and he squealed again.

"What?" I demanded, annoyed, but *very* curious as hell about that inhumanly flamboyant squeal.

"Your hair!" he cried. "It looks like an intersection of Audrey and *Spiders*-era Bowie, by way of, oh, I don't know — Ella Fitzgerald, maybe?"

My hair was a piled-up mess, spiky ends sticking out from a little bouffant pulled in a lopsided bun. That month, it was dyed orange and teal in even stripes, which I admit looked pretty amazing, but it was definitely not worth accolades from an actual real-life East Village queen.

"Uhh —" I struggled to my feet "— thanks." And I tried to walk away.

"Don't be ab*surd*!" the man shrilled, pulling on my arm. "You think I'd dare let you knock me out with hair like that on my way into a place like this? I *must* take you in as my consultant. Are you running somewhere?"

"Only to Hell," I murmured.

The man fixed his eyes on me and reaffixed his arm to mine. I felt a little uncomfortable, but he was gay, so that didn't really count, right? I sighed and fired a tentative smile at him.

"Don't worry, gorgeous. Hell isn't going anywhere for a while."

And he took me in.

We breezed through the aisles, holding torn concert shirts and leather necklaces up to each other's chests half-jokingly. He swept everything from my hands and deposited it in a pile on the counter, murmuring "Don't worry about it" in a way that I thought people only said in movies.

Long story short: This guy was a producer for this little off-Broadway play. It was called *UnCaged: John Cage Unplugged*. It was a musical about John Cage, the avant-garde composer, and his fictional adolescence as a geeky rebel. This guy wanted me to play the sympathetic teenage girlfriend of Young John Cage.

It was billed as a "nonmusical" because John Cage did all these revolutionary things like composing a symphony that was four and a half minutes of silence. On the first day of rehearsal, I asked, "Shouldn't we call it an *un*-musical?" and the other cast members stared at me like I'd stuffed worms up my nostrils. I didn't understand the plot cause it was written all avant-garde, but I deadpanned all my lines, muttering like I was talking to my parents or something, and then yelled my soliloquies. The director fell back in his chair, happy.

The nonmusical aspect of the play called for all cast members to wear Walkmen playing static loud in our ears, which meant we had almost no onstage interaction and had to rely on lipreading for our cues. Our lines were inevitably unsynchronized, uncoordinated, and screamed maniacally.

I told my dad when I arrived home from St. Mark's. We got back at the same time. He was a paramedic and worked these monster eighteen-hour shifts. We raced each other to the kitchen (he won), threw the groceries out of his hands, and started chopping vegetables. We threw them in a vat of water and I told him about the play. I was sure he was gonna say it wasn't kosher.

Instead he asked, "So do you want to do it?"

I shrugged. "I dunno," I said. "He's cool with Shabbos and everything. But it's still weird, you know, to go onstage and pretend to be someone I'm not."

My father wiped his knife off, sat down, and looked at me with his big blue eyes. "Hava," he said, "*everything* is about faking it. In English, you make up stories to tie the themes of different novels together. In Torah study, you do the same thing, but for real life." He took my Chex Mix from me and hunted for pretzels. "Litvish rabbis say a blessing before washing hands. Hasidic rabbis say the blessing after washing. And who's right?" he asked. "They both are. People don't just follow rules, they *decide* to follow rules. But once we do, we follow them and stick with them." He grabbed some curry powder off a shelf and sent a cataclysmic amount flying into our soup. "So maybe faking it isn't so fake after all."

The show opened on the first chilly Friday in November, although my debut came a night later, on Saturday, after the sun had set and Shabbos went out. My mother was anal about me getting there on time and wanted us to take a taxi to the theater, but I walked instead.

I left the apartment some time around midafternoon, after we'd finished Shabbos lunch. I walked straight through Central Park, going the long way down any path I could, taking every underground tunnel I could find. The city shot by in the background.

I felt cool, like I didn't need New York but it still kept following me around. My parents' best friends, the Grubers, had come over for Shabbos lunch, and they were all over the play, asking the most yuppie questions they could dig up ("Is Hava getting elective credit from the school for this?" and "It's not like that *Rent* show with all the drugs, is it?").

My parents seemed totally unperturbed by the show, even the dance number at the end of the second scene where all these West African dancers did a piece in the background and

Young John Cage had his first pubescent sex fantasy. I watched from behind a black curtain, stage left. They were right below me. Meira and Shira, who had by then decided to let me back in touch with their social lives, were a few rows back. They whispered cataphrenically during the whole first act. Mom and Dad looked positively on top of the world.

I came out and delivered my first line in a pristine whine — "If nothing in the world matters, John, then why do you keep looking down my shirt?" — and I got this moment of total clarity. For a second I didn't question the fact that I hadn't felt in character for one moment, or that they'd sold me as this utterly weird pseudo-Buddhist fawning-girlfriend-type chick. The audience was only a random assortment of four hundred people watching me, waiting for me to say a line, and when I said it — taking my time, much slower than I had during rehearsals — I felt like I had control over the words. Even though somebody else wrote them, I could make them mean anything.

The show was professional and all, but when you got down to basics, it was one big joke. Who knows what John Cage's life was like, anyway? Not the scriptwriter, that's for sure. And not the West African dancers. I learned just how far you could get by faking it. You could make a play about Moses starring Madonna, and if she could say "Let my people go" with any enthusiasm at all, she'd have the audience eating out of the palm of her hand. As Young John's girlfriend, I deadpanned my lines constantly. I said them without grace or focus or feeling. Sometimes, just to be mischievous, I forgot them entirely.

The audiences loved it.

That went on for four months, through December, over Chanukah, and into January. Our run was extended twice. The first few weekends, we played to snotty intellectual crowds. Then we got written up in the *Times*, and the mainstream Broadway folks came. We played to packed houses solidly throughout the run. But during a snowstorm in early February that stranded us in the theater way beyond our scheduled rehearsal, the director called us together, like a camp counselor. He said that the whole trip had been fun, but he wanted to end on a high note, and he couldn't see us getting much higher.

It was true. Rocky Samborra (Young John Cage) and I had shared a cover of *Time Out New York*. We'd wowed our friends enough; now vacation was over and it was time for school. I'd get my nights back to myself, to do whatever it is I did with my nights before I was acting five days a week.

Funny, I couldn't remember.

Our last performance was a two-hour ovation. We hit every cue. We shone as though the stars inside our heads had all suddenly gone nova. With no sense of attachment to our script, we could screw around with it and embrace our roles with total abandon. I felt my brain grow that night, like I was learning all these things that would soon revolutionize my acting career. How to pass a line to someone else. How to flub a line well, so not even the other actors were thrown off. Music cues. Actor cues. The slow, deliberate movement of reaching for a prop onstage, which was different entirely from movement in real life.

The cast took the stage crew out for drinks, and at the end of the night I tried to sneak past my parents with tequila shots knocking around my stomach. I had enough trouble coordinating my feet. They smiled knowingly, not saying a word, not even to tell me they loved my show (there was a waist-high Hallmark card outside my bedroom the next morning). And when we closed up shop that night — I turned around on my way out; already, they were starting to break down the cartoonish backdrops — I thought, well, that was my acting career.

And then I got this call on the last day of school, and before I knew it, I was flying to Los Angeles.

03

AT LEAST WE OWN HOLLYWOOD

"This is your new city," Shira O'Sullivan said.

The limo cruised past a white-and-blue road sign, NORTH HOLLYWOOD CITY LIMITS. I saw a blur of roadkill and speed limit signs in the window. Palm trees flew by. The driver, in wraparound shades, looked an '80s kind of cool. Shira O'Sullivan reclined like a movie star in the backseat. The stores looked like Gilligan's Island huts with '50s cocktail-glass writing on the signs. You could still vaguely see the airport, silhouetted in dust clouds behind us.

We were in Hollywood, I told myself.

I lived in Hollywood.

At the airport, the driver had met me with a sign. I nodded at him coolly. He walked me outside, pulled the wraparound shades from the pocket of his jacket, and slid them casually over his eyes. Dry, temperate air brushed my cheeks. The periwinkle-blue parking garage was silent and cool. It was so spacious after sitting in the plane for hours. Palm trees swayed docilely in the distance.

The car was a sleek, black affair that seemed to swallow the light around it. I reached for the latch on the front door. The driver waved me off and opened the back door instead.

Shira O'Sullivan smiled up at me.

Her face was shaped like an isosceles triangle, with a narrow chin and sharp, buoyant eyebrows and lips. She wore her business suit like an army uniform. The driver stood back and cleared his throat. His hand splayed the back door wide open.

Shira leaned out. "Hava," she said my name slowly, like I was a baby, "people like us don't *ride* in the front."

She looked at me impatiently.

I toyed with the strings of my hoodie. I wanted to argue. A, it was my limo, so I could sit wherever the hell I wanted. B, who the hell was Shira O'Sullivan? I was the actor. I had luggage to put away, an apartment to choreograph, and a new, wild Los Angelic life to start.

I decided to humor her. I mean, there were worse things than being treated like a celebrity. I slugged my bags in the trunk and followed the driver's white-gloved hand like an arrow. The backseat was leather-coated. Shira O'Sullivan smiled at me again, politely, running her accountant eyes over my slouched frame. She reached into the sleek black minibar, extracted a Coke, and cracked it open for me. Her fingernails were longer than my fingers.

I said a prayer over the Coke and sipped it as Shira fired information at me and noted my reactions with beady blackbird eyes. What forms had I filled out? Did I have previous work experience in Hollywood? Did I go to clubs at night, or did I stay home? Shira was my talent coordinator, manager, and au pair all at once. She was like a translator, except everyone was speaking English. I tried not to be afraid of her.

The limousine cut a ninety-degree turn off Santa Monica Boulevard, ducking off a traffic-stuffed boulevard and past a shopping mall. We swerved past another blue sign, entering another city. I didn't catch the name. "This is your new neighborhood," Shira said.

"And this," after a pause, "is your new street."

I took a final gulp of soda and tried to look bored, but my eyes fixated on the boxy white apartments. One of them was mine.

Welcome to Hollywood, Hava Aaronson.

Welcome to the next level.

The limo slowed as we pulled up to a Spanish-style three-story apartment complex. I leaped out before the car stopped moving. I could feel Shira's skinny shoulders flinch, a microscopic gust of wind in the backseat.

The car screeched to a stop. I swung my backpack over my shoulder. I wondered if they'd blame it on Shira O'Sullivan if I got injured. Probably. I grinned, walking away from the limo with a cheerful bounce in my step. The sky had grown dusky, and a clean wind whipped my hair across my face.

Shira breezed past me, key in hand, and rushed up the iron stairs, two at a time. She clicked open a door marked 204 and dropped the key in my hand without a word.

The studio had found my apartment and furnished it for me. There was a geometric compact couch by the window and alien lampshades everywhere, patterns selected by someone with a weird penchant for green and yellow fleur-de-lis. I could just imagine the college intern whose summer job was to furnish bedrooms for actors. I bet they thought they'd be fetching carrot juice for Harrison Ford. Suckers.

Shira's tone was easier and more conversational now that we were out of the car. I listened to her blab about my schedule, the rules of the apartment, not to have parties or tell people where I lived. The bedroom door was ajar. I walked in, surveyed the room, and flopped myself on the bed. It was queen size.

"Hey," I said, "you know, my best friend back home is named Shira, too."

Shira stiffened. Her face contorted. Then she composed herself, huffed, and her voice got all businesslike again. She handed me her card and said, "That's great. Listen, I've got a meeting. If you need anything, here's my cell number." Then she marched out.

Maybe I got too Orthodox on her, I thought.

One year, I worked with a bunch of secular Jews at a summer camp. Secular Jews will freak out sometimes when you use Hebrew words or remark how their name is Jewish, anything that reminds them too strongly of being Jews. They act like you're calling them on a bluff.

Shira hesitated at the door. Her neck straightened. "Be ready by nine," she called over her shoulder. "Carlos will wait outside. Wear something sub*stan*tial, if you can manage."

"You got it," I said brightly.

"Till then, just take it easy," Shira said. She slipped out the bedroom door. Her voice dropped a notch. "Don't look so worried, kid. It never rains in California."

I heard the front door click shut. I flopped over on my bed, drew the Venetian blinds open, and watched Shira O'Sullivan vanish into the limo. I lay in bed and listened.

It started raining as soon as the car door closed.

The patter sounded like tin music notes, tinkling on the windows in tiny drips that echoed through the apartment. I felt so tropical. The limo's ignition revved and, through the mass of leaves in the window, I watched it roll away. I jumped up from my bed, walked around, climbed on the sofa to look out the window. Water spattered against the glass in hard bulletlike droplets. They were crystal-clear, translucent, and pure like the first day of spring.

Like a Hollywood movie.

I rolled over on my bed, suddenly alone. Shira had really buzzed out of here, a puff of smoke and she was gone. It seemed like such a Hollywood way to be. Even if the next twenty-four hours of your life aren't double booked, you have to act like they are.

I wondered if I'd ever be good at that.

I dug in my pocket for my cell. I had to go through all the pockets on one skirt and half the pockets on the one underneath before I found it. The small plastic phone felt reassuring, the one friend I hadn't left in New York. Its ring was the voice of all my friends rolled into one. I tumbled over a few times on my new bed, feeling the hugeness of it. I could turn over twice and not fall over the edge.

I lay in the silence for a moment, feeling the dampness of the air and the post-apocalyptic stillness of L.A. My bags sat in the living room, untouched. Without Shira and the driver, the apartment seemed sparse and boxlike.

I sped through my speed-dial alphabet.

Everybody asked me the same thing.

"Where are you?"

"In my new apartment," I told them. In the City of Hollywood. In bed. The only answer that seemed to satisfy anyone was *Far, far away*. I listened to my mother's voice, and in the background I could hear cars honking, men shouting. Eight-thirty at night, she was leaving work early. As I told her about my flight, she shouted instructions at her intern, her secretary, the doorman. I tried not to mind. The way most mothers know how to cook or breast-feed or tell bedtime stories, my mother was a natural at multitasking. I pulled the phone away from my ear, hearing her shout down a cab. Getting back on the phone, she asked what I could see out my window.

When I told her, "Lawns," she gave a mournful sigh.

"Why do you want to know?" I asked her.

"I want to picture you, Havaleh," she said. "It feels like you're just down the block at Fruma's house. Like you're sleeping over, and soon you're just going to pop back in through your window and wake up here in the morning."

My friends were just as bad. Meira acted like I hadn't even left. I called her cell and woke her up. We talked under the covers, her voice muffled by the blankets draped over her head. She talked for seven minutes and twenty-one seconds without inserting a period, catching a breath, or asking a question about my life. I watched the minutes on my phone tick past. Meira told me about this girl we know who's dating a guy that we never would have expected, and how this girl we used to go to youth group conventions with had just gotten engaged at seventeen years old.

Talking to Shira was even worse. When I asked her what she did all day, she said, "Nothing." Even when I tried to go step by step, she was vacant and boring. She asked all these questions about what my bedroom looked like. She didn't say it out loud, but I could hear the accusation in her voice.

I told her it was eight-thirty and I was at home with nothing to do, and every single one of my friends was three thousand miles away from me.

"Then why did you leave?" Shira demanded.

I didn't know what to say.

Eventually, we hung up and I slumped into the bathroom. There was a regular light switch and a red heat lamp that had its own switch. The sudden red tint threw the place into nightclub lighting. My hair, timid and shoulder-length, was suddenly transformed.

My hair had gotten frumpy since the last time I'd cut it. I ran back into the living room, rummaged through my bags, and fished out my scissors. I stared at myself in the mirror for a second, put Hole on my portable stereo, and when the opening guitar riffs started, my scissors went *swish*.

Time passed. Hair fell. I thought about my family, my friends, all of them asking the same question in different voices.

"Where are you?"

Where was I? I was in this twilight zone where all the clocks said 9:00, but it sure as hell felt like midnight to me.

I woke up early the next morning with shards of hair all over my pillow. I was ready to pray and the TV show was fresh on my mind. I hoped that, in preparing my apartment, some studio lackey had packed the refrigerator full of orange juice (Bed?

Check. Limo? Check. Fresh-squeezed not-from-concentrate orange juice? Of *course* check). I didn't feel like my life was real, but I hadn't felt real since school let out.

The entrance to my kitchen had these vented half-doors, like saloons in the Old West. My television sat on the kitchen table, squarely in the middle. I walked past it and swung open the refrigerator. It was empty. The rush of cool air blew on my face. I turned to face the television. Still slightly asleep, I wondered why they'd left a TV in my kitchen.

The television crackled on.

"Fame, fortune, notoriety beyond your wildest dreams!" it said. "All these could be yours, Hava! And for no price at all! Just for the toil of a summer job and tolerating the adoration of a nation of millions! What do you think?"

I was thinking I should still be horizontal in my bed. The TV faced me head-on like an angry Rottweiler. A sleazy used-car salesman filled the screen. Tweed suit, a curled, greasy mustache, wildly flailing hands that kept pointing right at *me.* It cut away to a montage of adoring preteens and luxury airplanes and awards shows. A weird, slightly older version of me breezed through the montage, looking posh and comfortable as she signed autographs voraciously.

I ran my hand through my hair, puzzled.

My haircut felt gross and furry. Last night, it had seemed like such a brilliant idea. Right about now, split ends and fuzz patches felt a lot less rebellious, and a lot more dumb-ass. Shira O'Sullivan was going to murder me with her bare fingernails.

A theme song drew my attention back to the TV. The sleazy salesman was back onscreen. He watched me, expectant. I looked him in the eye and shrugged.

"Why the hell not? I've got off all summer, anyway," I said.

"Forget high school. Matter of fact, forget the entire East Coast. Why have friends when you can have fans? Every kid in America will run out to buy the same T-shirt as you."

I yawned. "If you're trying to scare me, you're going in the wrong direction. I can handle being famous. Kids who want to be me? It sounds cool. And having a shitload of money, I think I can deal with that." I opened cabinets, found a tumbler, and poured a glass of water from the sink. It tasted awful. I swallowed it, anyway. "And besides, acting's easy. It beats working for Fruma's uncle at Gap headquarters. I'm gonna change the world, remember?"

"Of course I remember. You already went through your teen insecurity crisis, Hava. You think you've got all the answers, how to be Orthodox and cool at the same time. Now you just have to show America. And then they'll accept you and everything will be all right." The television man looked enthralled. Enthralled and satisfied in that used-car-salesman way.

It felt like he'd shot me.

"Stop trying to poke holes in my theory. I'm bulletproof."

"Then why are you still listening?" said the TV man. "Aren't there some prayers you need to say?"

I looked at the clock in the corner of the TV screen, under the station identification. He was right. I was late. Outside, a car honked. That would be my limo.

"Get off my back," I said, hitting the power button. The picture zapped off. "I told you. I'm bulletproof."

I grabbed my backpack and ran outside, thinking I could hit the corner store and grab some orange juice. I scanned the block. I'd forgotten — in L.A., they really don't *do* corner stores. If my block had a corner store at all, it was a couple miles down.

The driver was the same guy from yesterday. He wore short sleeves, no tie, white gloves, and a chauffeur's cap.

"What's up?" I said, sliding in. The knee-length vinyl of my skirt screamed against the leather seat.

"Hrmm. I see your stylist's been working nights." He surveyed the train wreck of my hair in the rearview mirror.

"Now ignore me," I said. "I have to pray."

I started *shockeling* even before I ripped my prayerbook open.

The prayerbook is more a prop than anything else. I know the words by heart, but looking at them keeps them fresh and it stops praying from getting rote. *Shockeling* is that back-and-forth motion of swaying your body above your hips. It's like dancing to your prayers. All the Hebrew verses have these very intense rhythms that sound like belly-dancing music but more hardcore. The words aren't melody. They're a drum section, beating out rhythm into your morning.

I prayed, as much as I could in a car. I said all the morning blessings fast and furious, like a punk song. I got up to *Yishtabach*, which you should stand for but you don't have to; then I did all the prayers before *Amidah*, which are more airy and spiritual, about angels and shit. They climax when you stand and recite the beginning of the *Amidah* itself, only I couldn't stand and the Lincoln was trapped in traffic on Wilshire Boulevard. Skyscrapers ate up the clouds. The driver, seeing me slumped back in my seat after all the prayer dancing, said, "Traffic's like this every morning. They schedule it into the commute."

"Hm-hmm," I said. You're not supposed to talk between prayers, but I'd prayed all I could for now. I guessed I was allowed to talk. I opened my mouth tentatively. "What's the schedule today, anyway?"

The driver retrieved it from a clipboard by his seat and read it to me. "Looks like you're not even acting today," he said. He held the clipboard and read it to me, as though I didn't know how to read, or like I shouldn't waste my eyes on paperwork. I shifted in my seat.

"Eleven a.m., meet with the rest of the cast and staging directors. One o'clock, lunch. Two o'clock, you have a table read. That's where you sit around with the other actors and read straight from the script. Somewhere along the line, you got to find the legal people to fill out forms. That should be the easy part. You just sign your J. Q. Hancock over and over for an hour. Give your brain a rest."

The truth was, I faded out instead of listening to him. I started paging through the back of my prayerbook and reading the Psalms printed after the daily prayers. I rarely did Psalms but they always seemed kinda cool, like extra credit in case you felt like you didn't pray enough.

I don't think I could be Orthodox if I were a guy. Everything's about teamwork and discipline for them. Putting prayer shawls and phylacteries on, praying with a ten-man quorum, scheduling all those board meetings. All the things my father and his friends did. Men have to force the spirituality to come. They don't have the patience to carry around a prayerbook and remember to use it.

But I'm an Orthodox woman — sitting happy, living pretty, and ready to rock out. We pulled up to the Paramount Pictures main gate. Two gargantuan Jurassic Park doors opened and the car pulled into Lot 21. I grabbed my pack and jumped out.

This girl stood on the pavement outside our soundstage, smoking. She watched me with beady, suspicious eyes as I de-limoed. She took a single drag and held it in her lungs for a good strong minute. I stood in front of the car, breathing and idly gazing around the checkerboard of warehouse-size buildings. Only as I passed right in front of the girl did she let out a single, solid breath that came out as a perceptible cone of smoke in my face. Maybe when everyone said that Hollywood eats you alive, they meant that it drives you to smoking. If so, I was *so* completely safe. Her breath smelled like ass. I moved away from the line of her breathing.

"What's up with the hair?" the girl asked. She jutted out her chin. "Failed fashion statement or did someone try to jump you and miss?"

"Oh my G-d," I said. "Did you actually say that?"

She shrugged. She tossed her cigarette to the ground, stubbed it out with one stiletto toe, and extended a tanned, manicured hand at me. "I'm Evie Cameron," she said. "I'm Hindel."

I did a double take. Blond hair, Aryan button nose. She was just about the least likely person in the universe to say a Yiddish name like that.

"*What?*" I croaked.

"Evie Arling Cameron: real name. Hindel: what Middle America will call me for the next ten years. I play the adorably ditzy teenage daughter. Are you stage crew or something?" She once-overed me the way that I was used to guys doing on the street. I'd never felt that coming from a girl before.

"Hava Aaronson. I play the cranky older sister. Where do we pick up our TV names — are they waiting in a folder or something?"

"You're going to be on the show?" Evie sounded incredulous. She checked me out again. Her eyes lingered on my skirt, the Star of David hanging from my collar. For the moment, at least, she decided to believe me. "You're on the show and your agent hasn't told you what your character's name is?"

My agent. Butterflies beat wings against my stomach.

"No," I said. "Things have just been so whirlwind. You know how it is."

Evie eyed me even more suspiciously. "So they're keeping you busy? Yeah, I know how *that* is," she demurred. "Let's go do our paperwork together." A swish of her negligible ass and she was walking through the doors, blood-red Prada purse in the wind behind her.

All day I was consumed by recitals. Not even script recitals. Recitals for being a successful Hollywood star.

First I had to meet all the principals involved, Producers and directors and tanned men in polo shirts who looked like they played too much golf. In hallways and offices, I shook hands with lines and lines of people, people who recognized me in the halls and tossed their names at me like hand grenades. I smiled. I was proper. They didn't talk down to me or ignore me like adults back in New York. They just acted briefly impressed and scampered on.

I remembered that, for these people, my army jacket and band patches were a fashion statement, not a political statement. I mean, they didn't even read the patches.

Eventually, a short, round, completely bald man in a plaid suit and bow tie spotted me sitting in the lobby and grabbed my arm.

"Welcome to Paramount Studios, er —" [*stage direction:* glance at paper for name refreshment] "— Hava Aaronson," he said. The man was pudgy and fat, almost spherical, as though he had too much money and it was rolling around inside his stomach. He told me his name was Mr. Lederhaus, but to call him Howard. He flashed a patronizing grin at me. He was, he told me, a representative of the Producers.

"And welcome to your new life. Or, should I say —" he whispered, in a hushed, awed tone "— welcome to the Goldbergs."

The Goldbergs was what they were calling the show. The last name of my TV family was Goldberg. Nobody told me where it came from, but I figured Goldberg sounded tastefully bland. Jewish, but not *too* Jewish.

"The casting director was so glad you could commit," Howard said. "After Brittany left, we weren't at all sure we'd be able to find someone who could fit the role and manage to convincingly pull off the, ahh, the Jewish part."

"Mmm-hmm," I said. This Howard guy was clean-shaven and bald, but the more he talked, the harder it was to separate him from Rabbi Greenberg in my mind. Shit, even Rabbi Greenberg's *name* sounded too much like this show. I shuddered, imagining him as my father. I nodded and cracked a big, encouraging smile at Howard to show how much I appreciated his explanations. "So what's the deal with this show, anyway?"

"They — *you* — are the everyday normal American family, just a little bit wackier and a little bit Orthodox," he recited.

"Modern Orthodox, of course. Nothing too racy and black-hatted. You'll wear regular clothes — you'll be outfitted in the wardrobe department, you can trash those vampire clothes — but you'll have, oh, yarmulkes and long skirts, too. Just think of it as *The Cosby Show*, only with Jewish people instead of Negroes."

I stuttered a half-formed protest. I didn't even know which part to protest first. It came out sounding like a nondescript question, "*Wha-homina?*"

That was all Howard needed to encourage him.

"Imagine our surprise when we received your audition reel," he said. "You're a brilliant actress in your own right. And, of course, you bring such an air of authenticity and homeliness — *haimishness*, wouldn't you say? — to the show."

"But I never aud —"

"And let me say again what a pleasure it is to meet you," Howard finished, sweeping his hand in the air grandiosely. "The other actors — your new family, ha ha — are just arriving. What do you say, shall we go and meet them?"

I actually didn't say anything. People seemed so cut-scene-let's-move-on around here. And I thought New York people were bossy. Bewildered and culture-shocked, I followed Howard down the hall to makeup.

"We're not going to actually *do* anything today," the stylist said, filing her nails along the comb's teeth and making it hum. "Today we just want to get a sense of what you need, who you are, what kind of look the Producers —" She stopped when she looked up at my face. "Honey, what the hell happened to your hair?"

I shrugged. "It's been going through a lot lately."

"You haven't even started *film*ing yet. People have been *fired* for so much less."

"Really? Like what?" I was all ears.

"Sit down." She plopped me in her swivel chair and surveyed my body with her eyes. I stared back at myself, frayed black hair like a Sex Pistol, my head small and nubby on my shoulders. I wondered if I was supposed to strike a pose. It was the exact same chill as when Evie Cameron-slash-Hindel checked me out in front of the building and I wondered, did every conversation in this city seem like an audition or was it just my life in particular?

The makeup session seemed particularly not like a makeup session. How to Lose Your Individuality in 30 Minutes or Less was more like it. Once in a while, for family dinners, I would smear on lipstick and stick down my hair. But now, suddenly, a stylist was tweaking my eyebrows, plastering my face in white powder and then red powder. I looked in a mirror. I looked unnaturally exaggerated, like a Cruella De Vil version of a woman's face. "What's up with that?" I asked.

"You know how the camera adds weight?" the stylist said. "We're your first, last, and only line of defense against it. It adds ten pounds, we take off fifteen."

I thought about explaining how I was a healthy weight for somebody my height and I was going to be a spokesperson for normal-size women, but I held it. I didn't need to preach.

After all, I was the talent. She was working for me.

The reading room looked like a normal office building conference hall. Wide, movie screen–size windows opened to the street, exotic purple bushes and Africa-style boutiques. Shit-brown swivel chairs surrounded a long coffinlike table. We all sat around it and faced off and checked each other out and inhaled coffee together. Coffee made me feel sufficiently mature. Besides me, everyone was pretty divided into the standard groups, *adult* and *non*. Adults drank coffee. The nons didn't drink anything. Everybody sat with almost preternaturally good posture. The kids' hands rested symmetrically, folded in their laps.

This was how I met my new family.

I mean — my new family, ha ha.

Charles Beaufort ("Call me Charlie, my real kids do!") was my new sitcom dad. His name on the show was Baruch Goldberg. There were so many things wrong with that. There were three different Baruchs in my parents' circle of friends. None of them would ever tell me to call *them* by their first name. It was improper. It wasn't Jewish. Also, Charles looked even less like a Baruch than I did. His face was rugged and sensitive, like a 1970s character actor. He had graying hair in a 50 Most Beautiful People wave, parted on the left and smoothed down like plastic. He was tan, with lizard skin. He wore a brown sport coat and a nondescript tie with a plaid shirt underneath, which looked dorky, but cute. He'd been in movies. I couldn't tell you which ones, but I recognized his face. When he was in movies, the poster was usually a big print of his face. Movies where his shirt always seemed to come off without any apparent reason. Charles — *Charlie* — had a reassuring, jarlike face with a solid jaw and a smile that businessmen would call *killer*. He smiled a lot and when he talked, his voice rang really ebullient and friendly. I liked him and decided I was wary of him at the same time.

Paula Oxnard was the Skipper to Charles's Gilligan. It was scary how she seemed to get along with everyone so instantly and naturally. She dressed like a hip Martha Stewart and talked like a stockbroker. Charles kept dishing out clever anecdotes, all of which Paula had heard before. She kept interrupting him with a voice that crackled. She paged through the script and shot out questions to the writers whenever anyone (usually Charles) veered off topic. Questions like "What's my motivation for lighting Sabbath candles?" and "Where's Mrs. Goldberg's onstage placement here?" and "This scene where I'm making kugel, what exactly is a kugel? Does one simmer it or fry it?" In class she would have been a Fruma.

You already met **Evie Cameron**, but she was at the table, too. She could pass for fourteen — a well-developed fourteen, that is — but I bet she could be mistaken for twenty-two as well. You looked at her and you immediately thought *sweet and wicked*, the kind of sexuality that boys chase after and never get. She wore a designer jumper and her hair in pigtails, but you could tell she was doing the little-girl look as a front, that she didn't *really* go to Catholic school on the off-season. Evie did her makeup with a vengeance and she crossed her legs under her little plaid skirt like she meant it. I think people were supposed to see through the schoolgirl thing, at least partly, so the men didn't feel so guilty about being turned on. She looked like someone had groomed her professionally. Evie and I spent a good portion of the production session rolling our eyes at each other and giving each other exasperated looks. I'm sure she'd been through this before. Hell, I probably recognized her from something on the WB. And I would've known which show, too, if I ever made up my mind to play along and pay attention. Evie had stopped caring, too.

That means we'll get on perfectly, I thought.

Then there was **David Lee Mitchell**, who I decided should still count as a kid, but at this meeting he was a definite coffee drinker. He played Dovid, the studious older brother who went to college across town. That freed David Lee to act in movies when he didn't appear in an episode. He came late, and when he *did* show up, a whole posse of yes-men followed him. Somebody even carried his coffee for him. The guy handed it over whenever David Lee said "Coffee!" and extended his hand in a coffee-size grip.

Most of the coterie vanished when David Lee sat down. Two sharply dressed women stayed behind to take notes. He flashed a *huuuge* smile around the table, "Sorry I'm late. You know, L.A. traffic. I got pulled over by a cop, and he just had to ask about *Mega Force*, and you *know* how cops get when you don't talk about *Mega Force*." He rolled his eyes histrionically. Everyone laughed, even Shira O'Sullivan, who was standing in the back like a playground monitor throughout the meeting.

David Lee looked up across the table. "Jesus, Charlie, is that you?" He ran over and they shared a manly bear hug. Turns out the two of them had filmed a cop-buddies pilot together last year. Each must have totally known that the other would be here, but they had to make a show of it. I guess in Hollywood, if you're ever gonna feel real emotions, you have to hold on to them as long as you can.

As for *Jamie Diesel* and *Corey van Dyne*, they were — oh, I won't lie, I had to look up their names that night; I'd forgotten as soon as they'd introduced themselves. Corey and Jamie were two interchangeably anonymous kids who were anywhere between five and twelve, one slightly older than the other. One was a boy and one was a girl but I couldn't figure out which was which. They played Yoshie and Yocheved, the preteen twins. They sat at the edge of the table and whispered. The wall of execs on the other side didn't seem to mind. I wondered if Corey and Jamie were flirting with each other, or if they were just sick of talking to adults.

At first it was just the actors, plus David Lee's posse and Shira O'Sullivan. I think the execs gave us time alone on purpose, to loosen us up. I was sitting there for a while before everyone drifted in, gradually, not talking to one another. The actors sat patiently, monotonously, like robots waiting to be activated. I stared openly and didn't feel too weird about it. Nobody seemed to mind. I bet they were used to being stared at.

At some point, out of nowhere, Charles started to laugh.

We all looked up. Paula looked startled. Jamie and Corey looked like they thought he was crazy.

"It just hit me, folks," he said. "We're supposed to be a family."

Then he laughed again.

Paula lay a hand on his knee, and then she started laughing too, and so did David Lee. Evie joined in with this laugh that sounded like someone had taught her how to do it. Jamie and

Corey made these faces at each other — *Aren't grown-ups weird?* — and they laughed. I kept feeling more and more skeptical until my cheeks spread wide and it was easy for me to fake the laugh, too. It was so silly and ridiculous that I believed it and laughed even harder.

We laughed. I felt so perfect and fake and *loved*, as though, for this one single moment, I fit in seamlessly. If someone started singing "Kumbaya," I would have sung along. It was the feeling of being stuck on the *Titanic*. We were all brothers and sisters, sharing the sense of being lost. We didn't know what to do but listen to this man and his nervous laugh and then, suddenly, we were our own laugh track.

"One day," Charles told us all, "this will be the first thing you remember. We *are* supposed to be a family, after all. When you act in movies, it's a done deal — there will always be another movie, maybe bigger than your last one, maybe not — but TV series are scripts that last forever. You're not playing a character. You're playing a moment. The audience loves you for building up to the moment, for finally getting to the climax and for *being* that reassuring hug in the twenty-ninth minute. That's why movie stars always want to reprise the same role. America gets crushes on movie stars, but they fall in love with television stars. They go on dates to movies, but they keep coming home to us."

I looked at Evie, who caught my eye at once. Her perfectly plucked eyebrows shot up in question marks. I couldn't tell if she thought Charles was naïve or full of himself.

Nobody knew what to say.

The girl — Corey or Jamie — cleared her throat. Evie reclined. She plucked a mug off the coffee table and cradled it between her palms.

There's this feeling I get sometimes when I think of something and I need to tell someone. It's like a secret, but it's more like a brilliant idea that I absolutely *must* share or I'll explode. And everything felt so wrong, and I needed to ask, and my mouth opened and it tumbled out.

"What the hell do any of you know about being Jewish?" I said.

Everybody opened and closed their mouths without saying anything. We waited the longest time.

Nobody wanted to answer.

"My great-aunt was Jewish," Charles said eventually. "Or Unitarian, maybe. I forget."

"I go to the Kabbalah Center," said David Lee Mitchell.

"We could ask the same thing," said Evie, stirring her coffee with one manicured pinky finger, "about you and acting."

"It's just, I'm the tiniest bit weirded out," I said, rubbing my palms against the mahogany table, "about thinking of you all as my family. Let alone a Jewish family. I don't know anything about any of you. I don't know if you can make matzoh ball soup or sing me to sleep with *zemiros* or be assholically trepidatious about the secular world when, let's face it, you guys *are* the secular world."

I collapsed back into the fabricky pillows of the swivel chair.

Then I heard the sound of clapping. Everyone was beaming at me. They were applauding.

"Bravo, Hava Aaronson," said Howard, walking in and patting the headrest right above my head. He smiled generously. A bunch of men and women in khakis were filing into the room, all in a cluster, easing into the seats on the other side of the table.

Howard cleared his throat. "The perfect cast is like the perfect jigsaw puzzle, all different jagged edges and no two pieces in the same shape. The Producers have asked me to communicate how pleased they are that each of you has chosen to join *The Goldbergs*. We think your jigsaw puzzle is turning out just perfectly."

Not even Charles knew what to say.

"So now we'd like to overwhelm you a little. These are the writers. They're going to observe as we dive right in for a table read."

Scripts were passed out. It was weird to see Charles and Paula and David Lee, those composed, analytical, perfect-posture TV stars, bent over scripts, murmuring lines to themselves like they were memorizing math formulas. It was just like study hall, only nobody was my age. Absolutely everyone but me slipped on pairs of reading glasses. I wondered if that meant I would grow wrinkles faster than everyone else. Probably.

I found my first line and tried to muster some enthusiasm. We only had a few minutes to look it over. The writers wanted us to sight-read the script so it sounded fresh. They wanted the words to flow naturally.

I kept glancing at my character's first sentence, thinking it might change and, somehow, I would be transported into some otherworldly being, a g-ddess of clarity and subtlety who could recite dialogue with such authenticity that everyone could believe I was just another Jewish teenager speaking these lines in my own bedroom.

SCENE 1

Living room, the Goldberg House. Hindel is studying. Shoshana is slumped on the couch watching TV.

MRS. GOLDBERG

Shoshana, I thought I asked you to clean your room before you left?

SHOSHANA

I tried!

HINDEL

She couldn't find it underneath all those clothes.

SHOSHANA

Maybe you should come to the city with me. We could take a one-way trip off the Brooklyn Bridge.

HINDEL

Mooom! Shoshana's threatening to kill me!

SHOSHANA

I swear to you, my room is absolutely spotless.

MRS. GOLDBERG

You and that room! (*beat*) Did you two have a disagreement I should know about?

SHOSHANA

You know – if you're so concerned, maybe you could just clean my bedroom instead?

Oh, it was a regular laugh riot.

Half the scenes were played straight, not a Jewish line in them. The jokes were almost as dumb as my grandfather's knock-knock jokes. We sounded lame enough to be an actual all-American family.

The other half was made up of surreal, Jewish-themed scenes where we used words that normal Americans understood, like *schlep* and *putz*. It made us sound authentic. I felt like we were the first wave of black Barbies, the ones that looked the same as white Barbie dolls except for their skin color. You know, before they replaced Barbie's J. Crew clothes with soul-food clothes and a different-shaped head.

"Maybe you could just clean my bedroom instead?" I said again. I felt like a parody of every stuck-up Jewish American Princess.

Paula, my ostensible mother, read from the script like a Shakespearean actress. She talked unnecessarily haughty, over-acting like crazy. When I replied, I spoke straight-up, like I was just talking. You'd think, between the two of us, she would be the experienced professional. I wanted to pull her aside and lecture her.

"Shoshana?" the director said in a whiny, tattletale voice. He scratched his hair under his beret.

"Yes?" I said. I presumed when he said *Shoshana* he meant me.

"Try to get a little more *feel*ing into the lines. Pretend you're *liv*ing them, not just *say*ing them."

"Maybe you could just clean my bedroom instead?" I repeated, stepping back into character.

"More," he urged.

"Maybe *you* could just clean my bedroom in*stead*?" I said, harder. Focusing on Paula this time.

"*More*," he said.

"*May*be *you* could just *cleeean* my *bed*room in*stead??*" I said. Vacant and melodramatic.

"*Shoshana!*" he said.

"MAYBE YOU SHOULD JUST CLEAN MY G-DDAM BEDROOM FOR ME!"

It usually takes more, much more, for me to lose my temper. By this point, though, I was boiling straight through my skin.

"Keep going!" screamed the director. "Keep going!"

"Now, Shoshana," said Paula, still in that phony infomercial voice, "remember that one commandment in the Ten Commandments?"

"'Rest on the Sabbath and keep it holy'?" Evie chimed in. Her voice had slipped into a brash, sticky Brooklyn accent. She sounded indistinguishable from someone who actually should be named Hindel.

"No," Paula said. "Think, oh, something about honoring someone?"

"Honoring G-d?" I said brightly.

"Perfect, absolutely fricking *purrr*fect," moaned the director. He squirmed in his bamboo-and-fabric seat.

The lines flowed like a pinball game, fast and calculated. Paula and I made eye contact like fourteen-year-olds at a synagogue party looking for a broom closet to make out inside. We had each other's rhythm like lightning.

And then came the scream —

"*Osssssser!!!!!*"

It was a bloodcurdling scream, a voice that was barely

human. It was sharp Lee Press-On Nails across the blackboard of our sanity.

Evie and Paula and I all shot up. Our faces scanned the room.

I saw Evie's face dry up at once. She gaped at the corner of the room. Her eyes grew big and fearful. I followed her gaze and, soon enough, so did mine.

I flipped to the next page in the script. There, in vivid bold black letters, was the last member of the cast.

It was *Baby Goldberg*.

The first chance I had, I ran outside and called Ian.

"There's a cute baby on your show?" he asked me. "But you *loathe* cute babies."

"I know," I retorted. I almost screamed into my cell phone. "Do you think I have enough star pull to get it taken off the show forever?"

"You might want to wait until that landmark character-development episode . . ."

"Yeah, I think I will."

I hung up and looked around. The lot was barren. Huge, wooden doorways and rows of lockers and backdrops scattered around the mausoleum of studio buildings.

My life was so big. I didn't know if I could compete.

By the end of the workday, my palms itched like crazy. I was having fresh-air withdrawal. I hadn't seen sunlight since I'd dialed Ian. The director called it a day, tossed his script on the table, and strode out. The writers in their rigid postures went limp, like ventriloquist dummies, sighing into their chairs. I saw

David Lee and Evie make a run for the back doors. I followed them.

"That was a really masterful performance you pulled in there," said Charles, putting his hand around my shoulder. I thought about telling him that I didn't touch men, then figured that it didn't matter, it was just a one-time grab, anyway. Hands around your shoulder were the equivalent of friendly handshakes when it came to the outside world. We stopped when we got to Charles's car. He grinned good-bye. I smiled shyly.

I watched Charles, Paula, and David Lee zoom out the Paramount arch in their swanky slick coupes. I inhaled their dust tracks with the delicacy of a Hollywood movie maiden. I figured my limo was late, then remembered that I hadn't ever met with the studio people to sign release forms. I wondered if the entire day was a waste.

"Hey." Evie squeezed my hand. "What are you doing tonight?"

"You tell me," I said, slipping on my shades.

"Anything," she smiled. "*Every*thing."

04

FAKE IT WITH FLAVOR

We went to the Roxy and watched bands I'd never heard of. I'd seen black-and-white photographs of the Ramones and Jane's Addiction and Slayer going wild inside the Roxy, tearing up guitar string after guitar string on solos. They danced on the wooden stage planks, gloriously fucking up everything in sight. Back in New York, Ian and I would talk about the Roxy like you'd talk about G-d.

I paid my cover and I felt like saying a blessing. The room was narrow and misty, black compared to the glimmering city outside. Evie strode straight up to the balcony. She leaned over the rail, taking in the action below, folding her wraithlike shoulders forward in a bored hunch. She offered me a clove cigarette. I shook my head. I never smoked. I leaned my head close to hers. Smoke crawled up my nostrils. Unsteadiness swam through my brain. I felt flashbulbs go off. Were people taking pictures of us? Tonight was making me dizzy.

The first band sounded all pop-punk and harmonic —

MTV frat boys — and it made me want to throw up. We got there halfway through their set. I turned to Evie, looking doubtful. My forehead wrinkled.

Evie smiled at me. She thought I was giving her that smug, bored look that celebrities were supposed to use on everything.

The next band was hardcore — slow grinding rhythms and animal screams. I dug them a lot. They were so angry and untalented. I tried to catch their name, but the lead singer roared it instead of enunciating the syllables.

"Come on," Evie sighed. She took one final drag of her cigarette and flicked it off the balcony. The butt flopped down into the crowd below, where I heard someone shout under the furious sizzle of seared flesh. The boys down there crashed into each other even harder. Evie blinked drowsily. "You wanna hit the real clubs?"

"Impress me," I said with a grin.

Outside on the Sunset Strip, we navigated through throngs of well-dressed young professionals. Some wore suits and some wore polo shirts and some were in pristine hip-hop clothes that gleamed satin-white. At first I registered them as overgrown college kids, but my brain hiccupped and I corrected myself. I couldn't think in East Coast terms anymore. I reminded myself that they could be record producers or avant-garde photographers.

Lines wrapped around the clubs and stretched along the block. The street sizzled like a steak on the grill, so shiny and ready to explode. It felt like a movie set. Nothing was real. Billboard advertisements fought for my attention like a Japanese monster battle, epic and luminous. I bumped a woman's shoulder and we both kept walking without turning around, as though apologizing would spoil the illusion. We were all actors. I looked down the opposite side of the street. Men with open shirts and checkerboard pectoral muscles grinned at me, sharing their smiles like secrets. This was where film actors went when they pretended to be the characters they played.

We stopped in front of a single white door next to a ritzy Italian restaurant. Evie pulled out her wallet. She checked the address and nodded. In the space between buildings, I could see the lighted skyscrapers of downtown L.A., glistening.

Evie walked nonchalantly past the end of the line. She set one foot carefully in front of the other when she walked. Her tiny hips swayed. All her motions were deliberate. She looked over her shoulder and shot me a soldier-movie *can-you-handle-more?* look. I set my chin determinedly. I followed her past all the leather-coated boys and minidressed girls.

Three burly guards surrounded the white door. They were the first working-class guys I'd seen all day. They stared Evie down, unimpressed.

Evie tugged on the sleeve of the biggest man there. She pulled him down and whispered in his ear. Despite her diminutive size and developing body, Evie had the absolute biggest lips I'd ever seen. They were full and plump, so commanding, almost hypnotic. The huge security dude nodded. His eyes flickered amusement. He grinned, and then actually laughed. I honestly thought they weren't allowed to laugh.

"What are you waiting for?" Evie pursed her massive lips kvetchily. "Come *on*!"

The unmarked door swung open. I scurried down the stairs, following her.

* * *

The first time I went to a punk show in New York, I had to sneak out under the cover of night, out my window and down the fire escape. I borrowed a pair of pants from Ian because I didn't want anyone at the show to realize I was Orthodox. He met me on the fire escape and our gaudy spiked belts and bracelets clanged all the way down. We were the youngest kids at the concert by about ten years, one of Ian's secret underground bands, and the whole time Ian was afraid that the skinheads up front were going to beat us up. I hung back from the pit, afraid to walk too close to the dancing in case guys started rubbing up against me. But people jostled us and pushed us and before we knew it we'd landed in the mosh pit, those bald kids screaming and hurling into each other. I dodged them. I was so good at dodging them. By the end of the night, they were laughing at us as they danced, and one told Ian he was cute, and I mouthed to Ian *Are they —?* and we watched two of the biggest bald skinheads walking down the street holding hands.

I'd found my outfit for the night at the TV soundstage. I plucked it from between my character's concert shirts and tight leather skirts that made my ass look as big as a Girl Scout troop. Phat Farm, one of the network sponsors, had donated a whole wardrobe to me for after-hours parties. All the clothes looked like lingerie. I mixed and matched and finally settled on an outfit that wasn't too immodest. I swiped a flower-print skirt in horribly clashing patterns — purple and orange, green and yellow — which, together, were almost gross enough to be cool. It covered my knees, but barely.

Knee-high boots made the skirt look slightly more modest.

Posing nervously in front of a mirror in my dressing room, I finally decided that I wasn't exhibiting too much skin to be kosher. The polyester shirt had a collar salvaged from *Saturday Night Fever.* It was designed to exhibit and accentuate John Travolta–style chest hair, not my fatty cleavage. The skirt rode too high on my legs. The shirt went too low on my boobs. I felt like the punch line to a joke that I missed the beginning of.

I felt better once we were inside the club, with fewer people around and the air cool on my skin. The lights, moving like waves, swallowed us up. Frenetic cymbals and deep house music rode up my spine. I felt a tinge of nervousness. In New York, whenever I stayed out past curfew or wore a T-shirt that said something too secular (SUMMER SANITARIUM TOUR; MY BODY MY BUSINESS), I was always half-holding my breath for my parents' right-wing friends to pass me, or for someone to recognize my skirt and hairstyle and nose and call me out as being Jewish. L.A. was supposed to be teeming with Jews.

I scanned the heads of people in the crowd — you do this kind of thing when you're Orthodox — and couldn't find a yarmulke in sight. I exhaled. I kept reminding myself: You don't have to hold your breath, people aren't constantly Jewish. And even if they are, it's a different scene tonight. Secular Jews aren't going to call you out when you're behaving immodestly. Orthodox Jews aren't going to call your parents on you. This is club culture, where there is no right and wrong, just desirable and lame.

A full-length mirror hung by the bar. People made constant eye contact with their reflections, brushing stray hairs when they thought nobody was looking.

"Are you on lo-fi tonight or what?" said Evie. "You're acting like a — I don't know what. You look like you're watching TV."

A woman walked by, balancing blue and purple drinks on a tray. In one liquid motion, she slipped one into Evie's outstretched hand. Evie's other hand popped up, holding a rolled bill between two fingers.

I licked my lips, parched as fuck. By the time I noticed, the drinks lady was halfway across the dance floor. I looked at Evie. "I'm, umm," I stumbled. "I'm just, uh. Don't mind me, I'm still acclimating."

"I know you're new at this, Hava. But I'm *over* hanging out with Hollywood immigrants. I like you 'cause I think you can hang. But if you can't, *please* don't try to."

I really was trying to soak it all in. The walls were made of liquid cellophane and Silly Putty. Metallic diamonds and prisms hung from the ceiling. I'm not sure if there was a balcony but I felt people watching us. Green and yellow and blue spotlights swathed our bodies and swam over the dance floor. My brain jolted like a mad rush of oxygen as people danced over us, everyone looking ten years older than me. Evie was so calm and sophisticated when she danced, surrounded by a gaggle of fratty boys who looked like they wanted to jump her. I caught a glimpse of myself in a mirror, still disguised under unfamiliar studio makeup. *I* looked ten years older than me, too.

"It's okay, really," I told Evie coolly. I strode through the crowd, absently, possessed. "Leave any time you want, I can take care of myself. I'm — *immigrants*, did you say?"

Evie nodded absently, scanning the faces in the room. "Yeah, that's what I said. That pleasant, understanding friend who shows you how to meet a movie star and then rubs your back and brings you breakfast when he leaves in the morning – that's not me. I've been there. I'm not there anymore. I'm not sticking around waiting up for you, Hava. I'll abandon you when I need to."

"You haven't played this game much longer than me. You couldn't have. What's with the immigrant talk?"

Evie sipped her cocktail through a straw. "Geez, Hava. How young do you think I *am*?"

"Fifteen. Not more than fifteen and a quarter, definitely."

"Fuck!" Evie spat a volley of blue alcohol drops across her glass and dress. She bit her lip, collected herself, and dabbed an index finger over each drop on her silvery umbrellalike dress, performing a silent and impeccable cleanup. She was rattled. "Not so loud, 'kay? And how do you get so *right* about everything?"

"Try growing up with seventeen first cousins," I said. "See what it does to you."

Evie nodded. Her face was paler than it was before. The fear in her eyes said *Don't tell anyone*.

The grip that I clutched her hand with said *I got you covered.*

It didn't matter. Evie's guard was up.

"Do you wanna dance?" Evie's voice gained confidence as she talked. "Or we can lounge at the bar and guy-watch. Or I can show you around the place and introduce you to people. I kind of – you could say I know my way around this part of town."

"I'd like to dance," I said.

The floor pounded and it was hard to talk. Massive black speakers focused the baritone inside, toward the dance floor and away from the bar. My ribs shuddered. I had never gone to dance clubs back in New York, unless you counted the mosh pits at rock shows, which I didn't. In pits, you're not dancing, you're wrestling with your own skin. Ian had just started teaching me how to dance for real, club-style dancing, which was understated, subtle, and sometimes even sexy. I liked watching guys stand there, swaying awkwardly to the beat, digging hips into the air as they tried to let go of their inhibitions.

Dancing this close to boys was definitely not so kosher. There were pretty big *shomer negiah* rules against mixed dancing. Literally, *shomer negiah* meant "guarding your touch," and dancing made you look like you were giving it away.

I felt the beat. I swung my hips, contracted my fingers into little fists, rolled them flat and ran them against my body. I swayed with the drums, feeling my heart quicken as the midtempo Motown song mixed rhythms and faded into a faster hip-hop song. Through half-closed eyelids I watched everybody else, thirty-year-olds with five o'clock shadows wading through the swimming pool of swishing bodies, their eyes predatory. It was kind of thrilling. I wondered how many of them I should have been able to recognize. I felt woozy with music, trancelike. Evie had been dancing next to me a few minutes ago. But now I couldn't find her.

I didn't know how to walk on a dance floor. I tried to dance in one direction, scanning the crowd with my eyes, trying to spot her. Faces blew past me. Faces I thought I recognized, faces I wasn't sure I could recognize. When my parents and I spent the summer in Philadelphia a few summers back, people on the street looked exactly like people I knew back in Manhattan and I'd wondered if each city had different people playing the same roles — the balding, mustachioed dry cleaner or the cute oil-slick-haired boy at the corner coffeehouse. Here, it was a wild equation: People I Thought I Knew + Possible Movie Stars + People From the Studio. Where was Evie?

I tried to make the music matter. I was about to give up the chase when a bunch of preppie guys in Izod shirts parted to reveal Evie's impossibly compact body, jamming hard against the industrial drumbeats, filling her body between a sandwich of two guys, short nebbishy know-it-all types whose gluey eyes never left her.

You'd probably expect me to be sick or turned off, but I was fascinated. I'd only met Evie that morning, but I met her as a no-nonsense, untouchable flirt. All of a sudden she was *so* overtly sexual, eating these men alive. At that moment I had so many questions for her. If only I could figure out how to speak.

My stomach slammed into the bar railing, Evie's arm wrapped around mine, three laughing guys (where did the third come from?) surrounding us. They clamored for drinks, asking us what we wanted.

"Cosmo," Evie said, laughing. Her other arm was around one of the guy's waists.

I didn't know what came in a Cosmo. Probably chemicals or preservatives or something. Mixed drinks usually had at least one unkosher ingredient, so to be safe I said "Heineken" in a nonchalant tone of voice.

The guys looked puzzled. Evie shot me an impatient glance. "You want a *beer*?" she said distastefully, as though *beer* was a secret movie-star code word for "human blood."

I shrugged. "I like the way it tastes."

"Baby," said the second guy, who had somehow latched onto

me as his conversation partner in this mixed doubles flirtation, "*nobody* likes the way beer tastes."

"All beer is kosher," I relented. I don't know why, but I just hated explaining things in terms of Judaism. Like I was outing myself.

"Are you Jewish? Hey, I'm Jewish, too!" my new suitor exclaimed.

I tried to change the topic and still act interested in him. He really wanted to find out what synagogue I went to. I kept having flashbacks of him getting animalistic on Evie's ass. Now he was joking and sounding so civilized, asking if I kept kosher my whole life, was I that strict about all the rules. I sipped my beer and listened. "Where are you from?" he asked.

"New York," I said, and the torrent came.

The first guy looked over at me with admiration. "I'm writing this screenplay all about New York!" he exclaimed. "What a wild co —"

"Come on." Evie grabbed my arm, stomping away. "Let's dance."

She stepped onto the dance floor and threw herself into it. Except for her glisteningly smooth and perspirationless forehead, she looked like she'd been dancing all night. She wiggled her hips and shook her arms. She smiled at me.

"What was that about?" I shouted over the music.

"He had a *screen*play," she moaned.

"Which means . . . ?"

Evie rolled her eyes. It was getting to the level where she communicated that way more than talking. "Forget that," she yelled in my ear. "Actors we can talk to. Producers, definitely.

And, if a writer says he's *contracted* to do a screenplay, we can talk to him, too. If they *have* a screenplay, that means they're nothing. Screenwriters. That's, like, *less* than nothing." Evie glanced back at them. "I should have known from the start. They're wearing imitation Dockers."

I burst out laughing. I was shocked, horrified, amused. I decided that Evie might be even more cynical than I was.

Before, when I watched Evie dance across the room, I felt like I couldn't compete, like I was an inferior version of the same software. I shook my body in that I'm-So-White way and hoped nobody would notice me.

But now I watched her and she looked pathetic. Dancing next to me she was caustic, electric, rustling feathers and preening and brushing calmly against my skin. Her body twisted in a way that was sickeningly untalented, like all she cared about was looking good. Evie's voice brushed in my ear. "So what's wrong with that, Hava?"

"Nothing," I told her. "If you want to play that game."

"*Everybody* plays that game. What do you think is paying for your college education?"

Not all movie stars did this. I pictured the reclusive geniuses whose talent fueled Hollywood. I was sure they sat alone at home all night long, reading foreign literature and cracking all the esoteric artistic secrets, the riddles of their lives.

But not really. Talented people always surrounded themselves with crowds: yes-men and groupies and safe people. People who were dull and predictable and safe.

You're so dense, I imagined Evie saying. *We're in the acting business, right? So* act.

The in-my-head world cut out abruptly, and my mind

zoomed wide, facing the much broader focus of the real world. I blinked. The lights were moving fast. We were close to the center of the dance floor. Hardcore house music thudded over the casual trance beats, and people around us were dancing more. Women in boyish haircuts danced with their shoulders bare and breasts vibrating, holding their backs with a rigidly good posture. Gay men swarmed the room, some vogueing with jellyfish hands. The low bass shook between my thighs. I ducked, swung my arms out, wiggled my legs, and made a sine wave with my shoulders.

In a few minutes, Evie was screaming in my ear. "Hava," she said, "what the hell did you *do*? You're a tornado. And I think that gray-haired man at the bar is checking you out."

I blinked. I stopped dancing and stared at her straight on. My body was standing still. Only the alcohol in my blood throbbed.

"That's nice," I said, totally indifferent to the man at the bar, to the dance-floor guys checking me out, to this whole ridiculous and beautiful world. "Come outside with me? I think I'd like a cigarette."

Two hours later, expensive drinks rolled around my entire body. I stared at my cigarette dully, studying with awe the way it burned. This is why I believe in G-d, I told myself. Because somebody set up this entire scientific universe with a set of laws that makes paper burn in such a beautiful and chaotic way.

Somewhere after the second beer, when my head was beginning to sparkle, I decided that plain mixed drinks, like screwdrivers and greyhounds and Cuba libres, were kosher because they were only juice and alcohol, and what could be unkosher about fruit juice or vodka? Men started bringing me drinks. At one point, a teen rock idol watched, openmouthed, his credit card outstretched, and our bartender listened placidly as I actually stood at the bar, trying to explain, "I can drink anything but wine. Nothing with grapes. I mean, some cranberry juices have grapes in them but some don't and you don't *need* to check the ingredients for me but could you, anyway?" The bartender made me a Long Island Iced Tea with two straws. The teen rock idol drank it with me.

Had I stood in the same spot all evening, thinking about G-d? Had I not moved? No, I had totally moved. I'd been in and out of the club a dozen times, smoking, catching a breath of air, talking to guys. I stood outside and watched clamoring clubbers, people who didn't know anyone and who would never get inside. It was already one-thirty. The teen rock idol had told me that, in half an hour, every bar in L.A. would close for the night. I wondered why the people in line kept waiting, doomed to being turned away forever, as lumbering, apelike security guards kept watch over the line.

I leaned against the wall like I did at punk shows, striking a disaffected pose. This time, a cigarette lolled out of my mouth. The entire city of Los Angeles was lit up below me, scattered skyscrapers rising out of the sea of lights, an ocean of one-story houses and Astroturf-lined apartment buildings like mine. If somebody dropped a nuclear bomb on this building tonight, America would go without new movies and television shows for months. I tried to picture a person living inside every one of those house lights, and I couldn't. New York was so big, but finite. Los Angeles continued out forever, to the horizon. The thought was too big for my head. I felt like I could dive into the city, like a swimming pool. I would let the lights crash above my head so I could drown peacefully inside.

I looked at the much smaller red light of the cigarette ember, creeping slowly and constantly toward my fingers. I rolled the cigarette around, testing its uneven burn. A few feet away, an actor that I'd seen but whose name I could not place was throwing Evie onto the waist-high balcony and rolling up her short skirt indiscreetly, his hand clamped on her ass. I couldn't believe it but I was pretty sure they were having sex in public. I wondered how I could have gone this long in my life without smoking even once. There was a cold and empty feeling when I thought about Evie right now. I wanted the warm and comfortable alcohol in my stomach to overtake that feeling. It would render her invisible and obsolete and then it would teleport me home to my bed.

At the other end of the balcony, Evie whimpered gleefully. I tried to ignore it, but outside, the music wasn't loud enough to drown her out. I decided, if I was ever going to leave, now would be the time.

I looked over at her just for a second. Her bare legs were wrapped around the guy's khakied waist, fingers digging deep into his shoulder. Her head was turned to me. Her eyes were wide open. In her pupils was a look of pleading and ravenous hunger.

I took one more drag on my cigarette. It was close to going out, almost nothing left but the brown filter.

I reached over the balcony, as far on top of nothing as I could reach, and flicked the glowing red butt out, like a spitball, coasting on a wind gust until it fell into the sea of the city.

* * *

On the street I checked my cell phone messages. The line hadn't moved and the street was buzzing with cars. My phone glowed an alien shade of green. The last number I had called was Ian's. I hit redial immediately.

"Ian," I said, "I smoked tonight."

"G-d."

There was a stony silence.

"Ian? Are you there?"

"Yes, I'm here," he said. "Hava, what did you smoke?"

"Just a cigarette. Well. I mean, a few cigarettes."

"Tobacco? Like, not pot? They weren't laced with acid or anything?"

"No *way*," I said. "Not at all, Ian! How could you think I could do something like that?"

"Hava, you're drunk. You're utterly fucking drunk and I can hear you slurring your words. I left the hardcore show early to wait for you to call and tell me how rehearsal went. I should be living my life here instead of hanging on to yours. That's pretty fucked up. Don't call me again, okay? I'll call you when I think I can deal with it."

After shows back in New York, Ian used to drop me off at the door to my apartment, then take the stairs two flights back down. He always lingered so we could finish our conversation, which always ended in us going "dum dat DUN DUN dat" to the tune of the songs we heard.

Tonight, I walked home alone.

05

YR OWN PRIVATE IDAHO

During the days, I acted, like my life depended on it.

On camera, I acted as Shoshana Goldberg, sensitive girl trapped in an insensitive family. I was demure when I told jokes, funny when I complained, sweet and sensitive when I spoke to the camera about how Nobody Really Understood. Off camera, I acted like a Hollywood native. I was cold and distant and aloof. Bobby Drake, the director's assistant, chased after me, calling out messages. "Hava, they want you back in wardrobe in ten, your father called the studio and says you aren't answering your cell, and, um, Evie says you left your army jacket in her limo and to stop by her dressing room to get it back."

I stifled a groan.

"And the director says to memorize this thing." He flumped a crisp white script into my arms. "It's the new draft."

For the past few days, since we parted ways at that bar, I'd been trying to avoid Evie. Every time I looked at her, I pictured her on the railing, head pitched back, skirt grinding up her hips. She was so vulnerable and she let herself get so wasted. Every time I replayed the scene, it made me want to cringe.

It made me a little jealous.

I stormed down the corridor to her room. Every time I walked anywhere, I tried to memorize lines. Scene by scene. Line by line. I was a horrible memorizer. I still didn't know my times tables by heart. I had to imagine the scene, think of all the things that my character could say, and then eliminate all the lines except for the one line that was scripted for me. Walking gave me a rhythm to memorize things. And, since I didn't have anything else to do at night, I took long, long walks, reciting line after line. *Shabbos sucks at home!* Stomp. *I hate eating with the whole family.* Stomp. *And why can't we have pizza and French fries for Shabbos dinner?*

I stopped. I was standing at the door to Evie's dressing room.

Even if I wanted to bust in, there was no way I could. The room was stuffed solid with people — mostly guys — standing around Evie, rustling through her clothes, playing songs on her jam box, laughing at stupid things she said.

It was only our first week, and Evie had already managed to score the biggest clique on the set.

I groaned loudly.

A surfer near the door looked in the direction of the offending noise. He stared straight through me, running a hand through his hair. Nobody else noticed.

I couldn't even see Evie.

"Hey," came her voice, deep in the nest of people. "Who knows what's going down tonight?"

A chorus of voices all chimed in with prospective parties. I spied my jacket lying on a chair. I snatched it quick, whirled around, and stormed out.

I stomped past the writers' room, where editors were tossing balled-up papers at one another. One sailed past my head. I winced. Farther down the hall, Jamie and Corey were taking morning lessons with their personal tutor. They were both home-schooled, and because of their families' vigilance, they were stuck with the tutor all summer long. I found the studio entrance, flung the doors open, and walked outside. I felt like taking a cigarette break, only without the cigarettes. A hot-air break. That sounded like something I could use.

I pressed my back into the beige stucco wall. Coldness permeated my T-shirt and into my back. I breathed deep, looking around the studio. A movie was filming across the way. Beside our studio, catering was setting up for lunch. The smells of burning meat licked at my nose, reminding me how I couldn't eat any of the food in this entire studio, since none of it was kosher.

Tucked out of the way, behind some bushes, Charles and Paula were arguing.

They swayed with the slight breeze, glaring levelly at each other. Both folded their arms across their chests and stopped speaking. Charles licked his lips, then opened his mouth gently, as if he were going to ask a question. Fire flashed in Paula's eyes. She opened and closed her mouth, flung out her arms angrily, and started to walk away.

As she left, Charles touched her elbow.

His touch was brief, faint, tentative, sincere. A month from now, women on the subway would probably read tabloids about this very moment. Charles. Paula. His apology. Her blow-off.

But right now, the drama was playing out before my eyes. It was like television. I was too far away to hear, but I read their bodies. Paula shoved his fingers off her elbow, heaved a sigh, and lit up a cigarette.

Charles stared helplessly at his floppy brown Timberlands.

Twangs of pain hit my stomach. It's not the sort of thing I can explain. In a tabloid story, it would be too insignificant to mention at all.

But Charles looked so hopeful and sincere, and Paula had that dull, glazed-over look on her face, the kind you get when you've given up on someone.

In that single moment, I wanted to run to Charles and tell him everything was going to be okay. I wanted to reassure him that he was a good guy.

I mean, I knew I was *shomer negiah* and everything, but I almost wanted to hug him.

"Hey, Hava!" yelled Bobby Drake, clipboard in hand. "Afternoon rehearsal in five!"

I sighed. Without a word, I breezed into the building.

During our rehearsals, Paula and Charles were always chatty, amiable, and energetic. They never made eye contact. They never broke their perfect theater faces. And they never, ever let anyone see their private little war.

I mentioned it to Evie. She blinked at me, bored, as though she'd heard it a million times before. She turned right around to the crowd of production assistants and photographers and editorial interns who followed her around. She pronounced a joke, badly. She always knew how to signal the end of a conversation.

Walking through the studio corridors alone, sitting around people at lunch with no substantial conversations going on, I shrugged it off. I told myself I didn't care. The truth was, though, there wasn't anything else to care about. Without friends, a high school, or a fake ID, my social life was a very big bedroom and a bunch of voices on my cell.

I'd start up conversations with the gaffers, a steady stream of twentysomething intern guys who got fired and replaced every couple of days, but it wasn't the same. The conversations were weak, and they were all about name-dropping. Having a conversation with them was like having a conversation with MTV. They never seemed to hear what you said. There was always too much overt sex in our talks, or none at all. Evie's method of keeping her guys in line, staring at her cocooning chest, kept them coming back, fueled by promises of privacy and genuine interest.

At night I'd get driven back home and I'd stay at home. I read a lot. I studied Jewish Law every day like we were supposed to. I got back into the comic book series I'd abandoned when I was thirteen. Life was finally manageable. When you were friends with people your own age, life got so messy and hard to keep up with.

I started to wonder what my old friends and I actually *did* back in Manhattan, besides going to school. One night two weeks ago, Shira had come over and we'd stayed up till five a.m. I tried to remember what we'd talked about and I couldn't.

But if I spent an hour studying my Mishna Berura, like I did the night after the clubbing escapade and the nights after that, I retained every word. My dad had yelled at me for packing so many hardcover religious books instead of more clothes ("Hava, are you sure you want to do that to your posture?"), but you can always buy more clothes.

With the Mishna Berura, I could spend hours on a single page.

The Mishna Berura is a book of mundane laws. It doesn't talk about G-d and holiness and how to save your soul. Instead, it talks about what clothes are most spiritual to wear and the correct way to tie your shoes and what part of a loaf of bread to eat first. The idea being, these are the bare essentials of living, and the easiest way to live a soulful life was to start with these things. That week, I was studying a chapter on waking up in the morning. You always put your left shoe on first, and then the right, and then tie them the same way. Left-handed people tie their shoes the other way, but put them on their feet in the same order.

During the daytime, I adjusted my poise when the director told me to. We were working our way straight through the first episode and the director called a cut on me. "Shoshana! You're using your body too much," he said. "Move less."

We played it again. The continuity assistant, a preppie guy about my age who took photos constantly, scribbled something down. I could see the chronicle of my life looking like this someday, a big gold-plated book filled with notations: *Hava Aaronson, June 23, 2005 — 10:17 a.m. overacted during onstage panic attack; 1:22 p.m. forgot to redo lipstick after lunch; 3:35 p.m. did not move enough.* Every minute, I found new reasons to yell at people. I breathed hard, inhaling heavily, exhaling slowly, almost not at all. I tried to find that Kabbalah calmness. Paula walked five steps back. David Lee propped his elbows on the dining-room counter. We held our positions like mannequins.

"Action," breathed the director.

We tumbled into motion.

* * *

My talent agent's office sat in the middle of a residential block. Crisp horizontal lawns and pillars flaunted the buildings. A plain white sign on the grass read TALENT AGENCY in unobtrusive, address-size letters. The simplicity seemed like snobbery. I felt very out of my league.

"Hava, honey," said Pearl Stein, leading me through a set of glass doors, "you're doing *great.* On the phone you sounded so concerned, I could almost hear your wrinkle lines growing. Do you want me to reassure you? Most actors think their agents don't pay *enough* attention to them, not the other way around."

Pearl Stein was my agent. She was short, round, and dumpy. She moved fast, like a squirrel. I struggled to keep up.

"I know," I swallowed, walking briskly.

She sat me down in her office. There were walls of autographed pictures, all personalized and made out to her. Bushels of flowers were everywhere. I momentarily panicked. Had I remembered to send flowers when I'd gotten my role? After a second I manifested my overneurotic parents in my head. Of course they had.

"Listen," I said. "I don't mean to take time away from your clients and your business and stuff. I was just feeling kind of unsure. I mean, you placed me in this sitcom and I haven't even really met you in person before, I —"

"*Hava.*"

"Yes?" I was taken off guard. She said my name in a disturbingly Rabbi Greenberg–like tone of voice. I straightened my posture.

"How did we find out about you? Did we pull you off the street?"

"No, Ms. Stein, I was acting in a play in New York. You found me. Then the play people sent you a bunch of head shots and stuff."

"Ah, yes. *UnCaged.* Read the review. Loved it. The studio found you and they wanted you, so we just came in as middlemen. Well, thanks for the commission, kid."

"Umm. Yeah . . ."

"Yes, Ms. Aaronson." Pearl Stein looked ready to sign off on me and toss me back on the production line.

I breathed long and hard.

"So what I really want to know," I said, "is how did I get into this?"

Pearl Stein didn't bat an eye. "We Googled the words *orthodox*, *punk*, and *actor*. We needed someone by Monday. You worked."

"Oh."

Her burned-in makeup smile widened a little.

"Is there anything else we can help you with?"

She was so saccharine and sarcastic. Every gut impulse in my body was ready to stand up, walk out, and hitchhike back to Manhattan.

Instead I leaned forward.

I put my elbows on my knees and looked straight into Pearl Stein's eyes.

"What is my deal with you, for real? Why did anybody think I'd be any good in this sitcom at all, besides the obvious stuff? I mean, we're supposed to be working together, and I don't even know who you *are* and I've barely ever spoken to you on the phone, even, and nobody else is Jewish and I don't think I belong here and I think you need to get me out and who really thinks I have talent, anyway?"

"Is that all?"

Ms. Stein circled something in her appointment book.

"I think so."

"Good." She paused and adjusted her glasses. "We of the agenting world provide a strange service, Hava. We're not the creators of movies and TV shows, and we're not the actors around whom the industry is based. We're like matchmakers. I'm sure a good Jew like you knows about matchmakers. We don't do much — one way or another, without us, directors would still find scripts to produce, actors would still act, screenplays would still get memorized — but we like to think there is still a place for us in this universe. Call it ego, Hava. We know about ego; we see a lot of it around here. We make sure that everybody in an arrangement is keeping their end of the bargain, and that everyone is satisfied with their station. Are you happy, Hava?"

"I think so," I gulped.

"That's what we like to hear. Of course you're unsure of yourself — you're living a different life now. It's like jet lag. Everybody gets it."

I nodded dumbly. I was still nodding when she deposited me outside on the stoop. My limo was there, engine revving, ready to shoot me back to the studio.

Somewhere between the meeting and the next morning, I decided that, the same way everybody else was learning to act the part of Jewish characters, I would learn to act the part of a non-Jewish actor. Or even a Jewish actor. Just not an antisocial Orthodox punk one.

On Wednesday, we dove straight into the material and did a run-through of the opening scene. Then the director stood up, yawned, and called a ten-minute break for everyone.

The cliques assembled and retreated: Jamie and Corey to one corner, Paula and David Lee to their respective dressing rooms, Evie out to smoke as half the crew followed her, all holding out lighters. Charles fetched his pack of Camels and started walking the same way.

I jogged after him.

Charles turned around and grinned at me. It was the kind of smile you could open up to. He stopped in the vestibule, shook out a cigarette, and waited to hear me talk.

I looked into his eyes. They were good eyes.

"I don't get it," I told him. "I feel like a creepy swimsuit model, only I'm supposed to wear the clothes everybody wants to see *and* say the words they want to hear, too. The director and cameramen and the crew just stand around, waiting for me to say something. I spend every night on the phone, and every day in front of these act-o-matic robots. It's *tenuous*, Charles."

"You're lucky," Charles said, lighting up his cigarette. "That's the advantage to being a woman in this culture. Your attention is a valued commodity. When I want someone to listen to me talk about myself, I have to pay them two hundred bucks an hour."

I gawked.

Charles smirked. His eyes creased, but warmly. "That's a therapist, you know."

"I would never have thought otherwise." I smiled innocently. "So what *do* you do at night, anyway, Charles?"

"After this, you mean? I don't know. Acting kind of burns me out. All that partying and gallivanting and stuff in the newspapers, that's mostly the kids, and I don't even know how they keep it up."

He shrugged. His shoulders hunched forward a little, his face grew a few lines and his eyes got a little wider. Within that second, he seemed a lot more distant and, at the same time, a lot closer.

"You're kidding. And here I was, thinking you were *such* the consummate Hollywood *macher*."

He barked out a laugh. "Sorry to disappoint you. I'm the oddball out who likes my privacy. I read a lot. I play records in my house alone. I think about all the stuff I'd never tell anyone else about, because this town is filled with backstabbers and jerks who'll sell you out the first chance they get. Sometimes — and don't you go spreading this around, my reputation among all the swooning women will go to pot — sometimes, I even take walks."

I portended astonishment. "I thought nobody ever walked in L.A.!"

Charles put a finger to his lips. The intimacy of that gesture, just that moment of touching his own body, seemed at once dorky and charming, like an admission that he was someone who it was okay to clown around and act stupid with.

Charles's eyebrows rose. He looked amused, like I'd finally gotten it. "There you go, Hava. You're a genius and an anthropologist extraordinaire. Now" — he aimed his pack of cigarettes back toward the studio — "what do you say we rejoin civilization? I think it's time I started acting like your father."

Charles stubbed out his cigarette and dropped it neatly into the can. He opened the door. I could see a thin sliver of our alternate lives poke through, and his tall, awkward body about to vanish inside.

"Hey, Charles?" I said.

"Yes?" He turned around slowly.

"You can talk to me about your problems if you want. For free."

Charles fixed his look on me for a minute — weary, but bright. His eyes glinted.

"Thanks, Hava," he said.

"Why do you keep calling him Charles?" Evie asked me coldly.

"'Cause that's his name?" I replied.

The boys laughed, a victory for me, even though they had no idea what we were talking about.

Evie and I were in the backseat of a sleek red convertible. In the front seat were Jack and Weston, two guys that Evie knew, who threw around money like nothing and laughed like they were the only ones in the room. We were on our way down the Hollywood Hills.

Trees swooped past us. The hills were blurs of green shooting by the windows. The night sky felt big and close, like we could fall into it.

Evie rolled her eyes. The pause killed my advantage. I had to give a real answer, or I'd lose. I still wasn't sure how I ended up in this car on this night, with Evie of all people. She had a way of taking me on the best adventures and still making me feel like shit.

"He asked us to call him Charlie," Evie said. "I remember, he specifically asked *you*. It offends him, you know. He's a professional."

"It's still weird to call him by his first name. He's so much older and everything." I regretted the words the second they rolled out of my mouth. Maybe non-Jews called everyone by their first name and I could just chalk it up to being raised in a different culture, but not in the minds of Evie and these boys. There was some assumption that, unless you asked to be treated otherwise, child actors like Evie and me were to be treated as adults. One part of that was pretending that you deserved A-list star treatment, even if our names didn't come before the title in the credits.

CHARLES BEAUFORT PAULA OXNARD

in

<u>THE GOLDBERGS</u>

and featuring . . .

Evie, Jamie, Corey, me, Baby Goldberg, and even David Lee were second-tier. As professional as we acted, we were still just kids. Evie stared out the window.

"We're lost, aren't we?" she said.

"We're not lost," Jack grumbled. "We just have to find Mulholland Drive, and it's right off there." The car accelerated with his words.

"So find Mulholland Drive already," said Evie.

We rode the highway for a while. There was silence in the

car. Not that I'd have much to say to these monkeys, anyway. We were just sharing time.

"What kind of party is it tonight, anyway?" Evie murmured.

"The usual," Weston said. "Teen post-grunge bands, ex-breakfast-cereal-commercial kids, dope fiends. What are you looking for?"

"As long as it's not ordinary," she said.

Our freeway connection appeared on a chalky green road sign. We were almost free of each other.

Jack parked on the edge of a cliff, a jigsaw puzzle parking job that barely fit the convertible's frame. Evie and I climbed out over the trunk. The boys brushed past us. We followed the twisted cobblestones around the house to a backyard entrance gate. The backdrop of city swept out behind the hills.

We slipped inside a kitchen that was bigger than my apartment. Suburban Valley kids rammed through us like we were roadblocks. Everyone seemed to know everyone else. I listened in to the different conversations. Kids called each other by fake nicknames, preemptive one-syllable cuts like *Val* and *Sy*. Evie was in her element like a shark in a fish tank, hugging all the guys and smiling demurely at the girls. I watched her studiously. I felt so third-person just then. The guys we came with were gone. I didn't especially care.

I grabbed a beer-size cup, filled it full of vodka, and drank. It rankled my mouth with a sour, repulsive taste. I drank harder.

Girls passed by with identical faces, asking the inevitable Where Is *She* From question when they looked at me. I didn't even try to recognize them. I wanted to walk back outside, but I wouldn't let myself. I wouldn't allow the L.A. skyline panorama to make me feel better. At that moment I hated the idea of lights stretching out in every direction.

I walked outside and found a group of guys making their way to a car. They were heading toward Hollywood. I asked if they could give me a ride.

"Going to the Biltmore party?" they asked.

"Yeah," I said, bored, like it didn't matter.

It was the perfect tone of voice for them to believe me.

The Biltmore party was walking distance from my house, although no *real* Angeleno would have walked home. I did. I slammed the door to my apartment, kicked off my shoes, let the shag carpeting swallow my feet, and ripped out my cell phone.

"Ian," I said, "you need to get me out of here. Los Angeles is like a nightmare awards show, and I'm the only one in my underwear."

"I told you I'm not talking to you anymore."

"Don't say that. G-d, please don't say that, Ian. I need you to be real. This phone is like a walkie-talkie out of hell. And you're the only real thing in my life."

He paused. There was a dramatic silence. I could feel Ian chewing his lip in deliberation.

"Ian, *please*. I need to not be alone. Tell me something that only you can tell me."

He thought.

"Baby," Ian said, "fuck the outside world and that Oscar-ready wardrobe shit. You're a Hello Kitty karaoke singer with lyrics pouring out of a crystal ball."

I smiled. I collapsed onto my bed with my clothes still on.

"Tell me again about our deal?"

"If we're both still single by the time we hit thirty, I'll convert to Judaism and you'll move into my warehouse and we'll get married. We'll make stainless steel Christmas trees one month a year, sell them as modern art, and live like kings through the other eleven."

"Nobody around me understands. Everyone thinks in terms of ratings. TV ratings. Fashion faux pas ratings. I think I'm the only one left in the universe who doesn't dream in surround sound."

"St. Mark's Place is waiting for you, Hava. Today I found a corset on the street outside Trash & Vaudeville. I think someone dropped it on their way out, if you can believe that. It'll look great with a shirt beneath it. I'm sending it to you Monday when I get paid at work."

"You know, Ian, I can afford to buy stuff from Trash & Vaudeville for real now."

"Yeah, but why would you want to?"

I felt the night wind rustle my hair. It smelled like the cologne that Charles wore.

"I'm gonna get through this, right?" I whispered.

"You already are," Ian whispered back.

The next day, rehearsal went three hours into our lunch hour.

"That's enough. Let's cool it for an hour," said the director finally. He rolled his lumpy ass out of his canvas chair, and out of our field of caring. We were done for the day.

Paula turned on her cell phone, which immediately started ringing, and vanished. David faded away to his dressing room.

The weird tutor guy tapped a pen on his knuckles in the doorway. Jamie and Corey ran to him.

Some creepy fuck in a big purple elephant costume showed up behind the scientist dude and held out his paws. Baby Goldberg gave a delighted squeal and crawled over. The dude in the costume lifted him up between giant elephant paws and carried him away.

"You coming, Hava?" Charles asked. He held the door propped open. Evie was already shucking down her first cigarette of the afternoon.

I looked at the main doorway, watched the swiftly disappearing teacher and pupils and baby and purple elephant. I looked back at Charles and Evie.

I guess I'd found my clique.

06

SHABBOS IN FIVE

Today was our first day in front of a live audience. We'd rehearsed the script all week, first at a table, then onstage. And now it was Friday, the last day of our workweek. The Producers promised, through Howard, that the filming would definitely wrap by sunset, when according to Jewish Law, I would no longer be able to work, travel, or use electricity. "Where the hell *are* the Producers, then?" said Evie, and Howard replied, "Don't worry, they're watching." Not even *They're here* or *They're around.* No — *They're watching.*

The other message from the Producers that day, which Howard announced before filming, was this: *KlanBuster*, long thought to be the weakest new show on the network, had been canceled. *The Goldbergs* was now scheduled for a fall premiere.

This was no longer just a pilot. This was the real thing.

Everyone sent up a cheer.

I popped a piece of chewing gum in my mouth. I ground it between my teeth.

At once the baby began to wail uncontrollably, "*Osser-osserosssssserrrr!!*"

"What is with that kid?" said Evie, talking straight to Charles. She held his eyes with hers. She twirled her cigarette around with her tongue.

"Couldn't tell you if I tried," replied Charles, grinning. He put a hand on Baby Goldberg's head. "You okay there, squirt?"

"Aw, shit," I grumbled. I fished the gum out of my mouth. I said a blessing, then popped it back in. Instantly, the baby stopped. "He does that whenever I do something *osser*."

"What's an *osser*?" Charles asked.

"It's in the script," I said. "It's Yiddish. It means anything that's prohibited by Jewish Law. Like cursing G-d or shoplifting or eating nonkosher food. Anything. I think it's the only word he knows."

"You eat nonkosher food that often?" Evie asked sweetly, daggers in her eyes.

"All the time," I lied. "But I know how to fake it with flavor."

The first episode, by the way, centered on my character.

Shoshana Goldberg is about to visit her hip older brother Dovid (that would be David Lee Mitchell, all you *Mega Force* fans out there!) at college in Manhattan. But the car breaks down outside our little Brooklyn townhouse, I sweat and kick and yell (Baby Goldberg on the porch swing: "*Osser!*") and so Dovid drives home to have Shabbos with the family instead.

The real reason I want to visit Dovid, though, is that there's a guy at his college that I have a crush on. The secret comes out at Shabbos dinner, when Dovid accidentally spills the beans. My mom has a conniption, I scream and run out, the guy shows up at the house right before the second commercial break and has to leave, and then Dovid and I fix a silly whipped cream–intensive dessert for the whole family. We get it all over each other's faces. Me: "Do you wanna carry it in?" Dovid: "You want me to take credit for *that*? Go for it, kiddo," and he pushes me into the dining room, funny visual gag, credits roll.

SHOSHANA

I tried to clean my room! Okay, Eema and Abba, I love ya. Now step aside. I have a date with New York!

MRS. GOLDBERG

She has a date?

BABY GOLDBERG

Osser! Osser!

YOSHIE

Moooom! I'm hungry! Can I have some dates, too?

SHOSHANA (*to camera*)

Oy vey, dude.

The studio audience was our final test. We rehearsed all morning, on the set, straight run-throughs of each scene. As actors, our objective quickly became to draw as little attention from the director as possible. Early in the second scene, I got called out for "acting too much" (I didn't even ask). There are two types of time-outs that the director called: when he yelled one-liners of advice that didn't interrupt the action — like "*Smile less!*" or "*More cleavage!*" — and the kind that actually froze the action, so everybody had to wait while the director talked to you.

When I got yelled at, it was the second kind. The director had a snit about this one line. I thought it should sound the way I said it. I argued back. That was my first mistake. A big man in a thousand-dollar suit whose index finger was bigger than my fist walked up and poked me in the chest with that finger. My chest is pretty sizable but to him, it was like poking a toddler, and he said "You. Are. Not. Paid. To. Argue." Then he vanished back into the shadows.

We started rehearsing again.

The Yiddishisms took without a problem. We said *schlep* and *oy vey* and even *osser* and the audience ate it up like starved lab rats. Even with some of the lines that I didn't realize were supposed to be funny, they laughed on cue. Performing for a studio audience wasn't as hard as I thought, but it also wasn't as rewarding as I'd figured. The laughter was tenuous, weak. Charles told me between sets that the sound engineers have hyped-up sound-effect laughter that they add later to make it seem more real.

Lame or not, though, people were still laughing. My first line — "I *tried* to clean my room!" — I said in a loud and kvetchy voice. The audience roared. Caustically. Wildly. It's like when you put ants in an ant farm and they automatically dig the sand into interlocking tunnels. I'd never seen anybody laugh at a sitcom on TV, and here, once we told the audience, *Go for it, you're the laugh track,* they laughed.

And even a seventeen-year-old girl whining about Shabbos cleaning can be the laugh riot of the afternoon.

Shabbos at my house was never crowded like that, six kids and a wisecracking momma. My father managed to get Friday afternoons off, and he was home by noon, frying meats and sautéing onions. By the time I got home, the house was pungent with the smell of carrots and chicken soup. I jumped into cooking, blending hummus, slicing vegetables for salads, and by sunset, when my mom came home from work, we'd have a line of bowls overflowing with greens and reds and oranges, food spilling over the sides.

I was an only child, rare but not unheard of in religious communities. I guess it made me mature faster, but at Shabbos dinner, our family conversation flowed like a talk show, the three of us filling the room with our voices. As much as we ate, we never seemed to make a dent in the food, and Saturday afternoon, as we drifted in from synagogue, we made *motzi* on bagels and piled our dinner leftovers on their spongy surface. My mother would come in halfway through my lunch, frown at my colossal mush of salads in disgust, and then make a concoction of her own. That was Shabbos at my house.

The rehearsals had been a lot less unpleasant than I'd expected. After my initial outburst, I realized how quickly — and how efficiently — they'd tamed me. I said my lines in the tones that the director had fed to me. I was quick to react to the other actors, but not *too* quick. I felt the cameras on me, and I played to them, not looking them in the lens, but tilting my head just so, taking my time with every movement, and not having too many emotions for everyone to keep track of. The biggest part of acting was just to dumb down our movements and simplify ourselves, so when the camera switches between six different actors, the audience doesn't forget what you've been doing for the past five minutes.

Beyond that, it was the same as my first retail job. When the boss was watching, you did what he said. When I could tell that the director was looking at me, or when I knew my line delivery had to be *just* so, I was on top of myself. The rest of the time, I did things my way. I knew what they wanted me to be: a self-involved snob who was at heart a Valley girl. What I gave them was a girl who knew the right buttons to press when her parents were around, and who was a demon waiting to erupt when they weren't.

But if rehearsing wasn't as bad as I thought it would be, the actual taping was a challenge. A scene would start and we'd carry it. There were no encouraging hisses from the director, only the stifled sounds of two hundred people trying to be silent, punctuated by an occasional sharp burst of laughter. Before the shoot, a studio P.R. honcho instructed the audience to keep their laughter as short as possible. From backstage, I was thinking, you're telling people how to *laugh*? The bulge of my forehead wrinkled in disgust. Both the makeup artist and the hairstylist froze.

"Honey," said the makeup artist, "you just added fifteen minutes onto your age. You add fifteen minutes every time you wrinkle that forehead. Do that five times a day and you'll look fifty by the time you're thirty-five."

They both looked venomously satisfied.

The makeup artist dabbed a decisive dash of talcum powder

to the left side of my nose. "I think your left side is shinier than your right," he said, frowning.

"Is something wrong with my face?"

"No. Well, not necessarily. You probably sleep on one side too much. It clogs the oil flow from your pores."

I shuddered. I couldn't believe I could be having this conversation with anyone.

And then onstage.

I stepped onto the set, into the waiting area before I actually went onstage. Paula and Evie were in the kitchen, already in mid-scene, cracking eggs and baking kugels. This teenage kid, lip-synching every line from a clipboard script, shot his finger for me to go on.

I walked through an artificial doorway with nothing on the other side, and I felt plush, unfamiliar carpet sponge and contract beneath my feet, and I was, like, this is my new home and I'm never going to live here. Four hundred people held their breath.

"I *tried* to clean my room!"

Four hundred people watched the Goldberg family talk about my weekend plans. They watched Evie freak out and bitch about school. They didn't release their breath until finally, hours into the production, the director stepped out to explain that there would be an exterior add-on shot of me kicking the car, and then David came on.

The studio audience clapped long and hard for David. I cringed. He looked all wrong for the part. His yarmulke stood up on his head like a teepee. If he really lived in New York, every Modern Orthodox kid this side of Coney Island would have reamed his ass for looking like a nerd.

* * *

I traded lines and lines and lines. It felt so natural and easy, being this person who was not me. I liked having my conversations pre-plotted. The soundstage was a little box where there were no surprises, only retakes. The audience started to fidget eventually, and I didn't blame them; watching this shit must have been excruciating. But for me, it was so fun. Before each scene, they'd hold us in poses for what seemed like hours, testing light angles and sound meters with these little *Star Trek* tricorders that beeped when we moved too much. In that first scene, I nicked a piece of crust from the kugel.

The baby yelled "*Osser!*"

"Shoshana," said Paula, as Mrs. Goldberg, "you'd better start driving into the city. It's almost sunset."

"Why, Mom," said Evie, "is she *driving* you *crazy*?"

The audience didn't laugh like they were supposed to. The director called cut. From somewhere, I heard the writers whispering.

We started from five or six lines earlier. I zeroed back to the other side of the kitchen counter. Evie sat back on her stool. Props ran in with a new kugel, and we reenacted life.

"No point in me sticking around, eh, Mom?" I said. I broke off some kugel crust.

"*Cut!*" The guy with the camera whispered to the director. "The first time, you had one arm folded on your chest. This time it was leaning on the counter. Don't give us more shadows than we need, yeah?"

"Yeah." I retraced five steps. Evie hopped back on the stool. "No point in me sticking around, eh, Mom?" I said again. I felt my body movements, familiar, the way I knew my bedroom in the darkness. The swing of my arm, the tilt of my head when I talked. A scene or two later the director told me my shirt was hiding too much cleavage, could I pull it down where it was before? The line of fabric against the skin of my neck felt familiar. I smoothed it into place.

Lunch break. I unwrapped the kosher sandwich I'd brought from home. Everyone else had steamed lasagna, lathered in strips of mozzarella and gouda, leaves of spinach and tomato peeking out. I was beyond hungry. The cold food landed in my stomach with a hard thud. I bet theirs was performing a tango dance. I consoled myself that it was almost Shabbos. My mother's cousins had called the night before. I was going to get a ride over there after work and do Shabbos up with them.

I finished my sandwich and started on my dessert, this half-assed combination of Reese's Peanut Butter Cups and smashed sandwich cookies from a store on Hollywood Boulevard. I felt pretty pathetic. Evie's eyes were on me throughout the meal. She took a perverse pleasure in watching my culinary needs suffer. Actors are supposed to have an intense control over their bodies, and I could swear she chewed her lasagna extra slowly and demonstratively, packing pockets of half-chewed food into her cheeks, pushing her eyes to widen fully when she swallowed.

I walked outside. We hadn't been outside all day. My eyes hurt from the instant sunlight, and I felt my body contract and shrivel up when it hit my eyes. There was a feathery breeze on my skin. The sun hovered in mid-sky, the way it would for hours. The sky reminded me that it was Friday, and that all this would be over soon.

"Curtain call!" shouted an assistant.

I turned around. It was only me in the yard.

He flashed a cute, boyish grin. "Just kiddin'," he said. "Lunch is almost over. They'll start filming whenever you're ready."

After lunch we shot more David scenes. Those were the easiest, when everybody was so focused on David that I could go on autopilot and have my mind wherever I wanted it. After my fuck-up with the lights, I was feeling every inch an amateur.

When there were only two of us onstage, it moved quickly. Things felt more natural. Even if we weren't having a real conversation with each other, we were pretending so well. He said, "Look, Shoshana, we can't always get what we want."

"Watch it happen," I told him.

He said to calm down and be rational. I said I'd rather be on my date.

That was my screaming moment. I opened my mouth and my lungs popped open, too. I looked at him with such hatred that I couldn't tell the difference between snobby, stuck-up actor David Lee Mitchell and snobby, stuck-up brother Dovid Goldberg. I looked at him and felt such venom and indecision. "What should I do?" I choked, and it felt like desperation with my role, with this whole acting thing.

In the corner of my eye, the audience was grinning with one solid mouth. One woman forgot the rules and started clapping. G-d, I felt beautiful.

I'd nailed it.

"You see now?" Howard said backstage. "That's why the Producers wanted you."

I reached over, took a gulp of Coke, and, feeling the bubbles pop in my mouth, took another gulp. When a three-minute piece of life takes three hours to shoot, your mind starts thinking of time differently. I was so dehydrated right then, and the clean, fresh taste of Coca-Cola in my mouth felt so smooth.

"I thought they wanted me 'cause I was Jewish," I said.

"I don't know. Don't question it, baby. They wanted you 'cause of *you*," Howard said. He patted me emphatically on the shoulder. I winced. "Now, don't smudge your makeup. Curtain call in five."

"Curtain call?" The Coke froze in my esophagus.

"You heard that obnoxious woman clapping, right? We're reshooting that scene once more. Then all you have is the final dinner scene, and we're golden."

"What the hell time is it?" I demanded.

"— or should I say, we're gold-*berg*." Howard chuckled.

I drained my glass and stared at myself unbelievingly in the mirror, like some dark alternate-reality version of myself had possessed me.

Okay, so "once more" turned into three more times and four more hours. First the director wanted us to switch positions, David closer to the audience, and we had to relight the stage. The second time, he wanted us to switch back. Finally: "The same thing," said the director, "only more Jewish," and David Lee's accent went from *New York* to *Noo Yawk*. I compensated as best as I could. Thank G-d the director took my Jewish accent at face value. I don't think I could deal with being a punching bag again.

We finally wrapped the scene, and I needed a breath of fresh air. I threw off my wig and headed to the back-lot door. My hand hit the emergency-exit bar. Another hand landed atop mine, freezing the door shut. I looked up, stage-dazed. It was Evie.

We shared a hostile look. Then, at the same time, we relented, unspoken, like a decision we'd both made simultaneously.

"Why did he want our accents thicker?" I complained. "I spent seventeen and a half years trying to *lose* that accent."

"It's like talking black," Evie said. "My friend Dominique, she grew up in the whitest suburb ever and then she got cast on this, like, *urban life* sitcom. They had to hire an ebonics coach just so she wouldn't sound like a Boston prep school commercial." She shook one cigarette out and offered the pack to me. "You want?"

"I don't smoke," I said coldly.

"Hava, nobody cares if you smoke." Evie breathed in my face. We were inside, the cigarette was unlit, and her breath still smelled like smoke. I tried not to inhale.

"In spite of your newly acquired fame," she continued, "nobody knows shit about you. They might never. You might want to stop believing the universe revolves around you for a second."

"How the hell did you get so wise?" I said. Evie was at once so charitable and so demonic.

She gestured at the outside door. "I need to smoke. You want to smoke?" she said.

I popped open the door.

The last vestiges of light trickled off the clouds. The sun was still barely visible, sinking behind the low-rise houses to the west of the studio.

I froze, one hand on the door, one hand on Evie's box of cigarettes.

"It's Shabbos," I whispered.

MRS. GOLDBERG

There's no time to get to the station, catch the subway to the campus bus, and <u>then</u> get to Dovid's apartment before Shabbos! Shoshana, some things are impossible even for you!

SHOSHANA

Name one.

MRS. GOLDBERG

I just named three.

SHOSHANA

Okay, name one <u>more</u>.

"What's your problem?" Evie was spying on the actors who were shooting outside the soundstage next door. She watched me absently, doing serious surveillance of this one blond preppy guy in the background. Evie always got annoyed when she didn't understand something I said. "Shatnes what?"

"I have to go."

Shabbos actually lasts twenty-five hours, one hour more than an entire day. The Jewish day goes from sunset to sunset — not from morning to night like the secular day — but on Shabbos, we allow extra time on both ends, and so it begins at dusk on Friday night and ends Saturday night at nightfall.

At that moment, it was far beyond dusk.

At that moment, I could rip the director's arm out of his socket. I'd show them what I was like when I screamed for real.

But I didn't.

Instead, I turned on a dime, strode across the lot to the main gate, and walked out.

I checked my pockets for change, my cell, or anything else that I couldn't carry on Shabbos. My pockets were totally empty. All my belongings were in the dressing room. Little-known acting fact #1: Actors onstage never have any nonessential items in their pockets, because it looks weird on camera, like your thighs are pregnant. Of course I already could have guessed that, but now I knew for sure. Maybe I could have carried my keys, if I was inside the *eruv* — there was this thing called an *eruv* that surrounded the Jewish part of town; on Shabbos, you couldn't carry anything outside an *eruv* — but I didn't know whether the *eruv* boundaries surrounded the studio. I'd never thought to look it up.

Maybe because I never figured I would get marooned in the studio on Shabbos.

Little-known acting fact #2: It's easier to get out of a studio than you'd think. The guard didn't bat an eye as I slipped out and waltzed onto the street. The booth-bound security guy, who must have been sitting there practically forever, was watching TV. He glanced over at the TV and made a snide comment about the network's new fall lineup, how none of the shows were worth sitting through.

"You know it," I said, a gleam in my eye.

And then I was on the street.

I didn't know how to get home, just which way the limo turned and which vague direction home was. I knew my cross streets. I saw the Hollywood Hills in the distance. If I just walked a few miles one direction, a bunch of miles in another, I'd get to my intersection.

Then I remembered I wasn't supposed to go home. Miles away in the Pico Robertson district, I had strange, foreign West Coast cousins who expected me to show up for dinner and sleep on their couch. Their address was sitting on my kitchen table.

I breathed hard. The Los Angeles air got clearer at night, but not by much. The stars were starting to swell into existence up in the sky.

I needed to act responsibly right now.

I looked left, looked right. I figured my best bet was to get home, if I could find it. Then I could decide where to go from there. I could always pray alone, and, G-d willing, there was enough food in my refrigerator to feed me through Shabbos.

I decided on the direction where I thought home lay. I walked round the studio perimeter, found a street, and started walking.

Los Angeles was huge and amorphous. No one in L.A. walked; I knew that. The boulevards were long and bright and spread-out. There was nobody else walking on the streets. I'd never felt like such an alien. I knew the trip back home was enormous – it would take me two hours, at least, possibly three or four – but the sun was already setting, and I didn't have any other option. Red tiled roofs lined the East Hollywood pueblo houses, lines and lines of them in a rote order that repeated endlessly as I walked.

After a while, I heard music from a few blocks away, the hum of amplifiers and screeching electric guitars. A few broken notes blared, and then a period of silence.

Since I had to cover the entire length of the neighborhood, anyway, I followed the sound of punk. I was like Hansel and Gretel on the road, stopping every few minutes when the noise stopped, trying to judge direction by the stray bursts of staccato. The houses started looking more Hansel and Gretel, too, as I walked farther into the Latino area and farther and farther away from the white Melrose district.

The guitars were louder than ever as I turned onto this block where all the houses were flamingo pink and minty green with brown trim. A garage door was wide open, hovering in the air. A semicircle of kids smoked on the pavement outside. They all wore leather jackets. In the warm, microwavey eighty-degree L.A. evening, it could only mean one thing.

I wanted to ask them for permission to go in. I didn't. They gave me antsy once-overs. I stared back indifferently. They nodded coolly. I turned around and walked into the garage.

From the outside, you couldn't tell how big the garage was. Forty or fifty kids crammed inside. I pushed my way to the front, squeezing my shoulders between lanky boys in plaid and the preppie girls who are always at these shows, looking so out of place. At the New York clubs, I was like the only girl who actually wore fatigues and band shirts. It's like the sex stereotypes don't apply to punk boys, but people still think punk girls are supposed to look like J. Crew models. In the front, there was a row of girls with mohawks. I stood with them. I was still in my Modern Cosmopolitan Wardrobe clothes, but I hoped they could see through to the real me. The staccato guitar had been getting more and more constant as I got closer to the house. The two guitarists faced each other, right in front of the drummer, and every few seconds they played the same riff. The drummer counted time in the air with his drumsticks.

Ready? mouthed one of the guitar boys to the other.

The other nodded.

Their perfect posture swung into three dimensions. They threw their guitars in the air and ran the scales wildly. The drummer crashed into action on his snare drum. He pounded the cymbals until brass shards flew off the ends. The crowd pounded their heads in the air. Tiny fists beat out the rhythm on my back. We all started dancing. "*¡Caramba!*" somebody yelled out. I gave the rest of the kids another glance. Everyone here was Latino. I wasn't sure whether to be culture-shocked or not. My stomach twisted in a knot with that Am I Allowed to Be Here? dread. Then I realized — it's a punk show. Who the hell can't be at a punk show?

I listened to the lyrics. They were in English.

You say you wanna be sedated/You're the first song I ever hated/ Gimme real music/Gimme rock shows/I hate the fucking radio.

Hell fuckin' yeah.

Everybody started to dance. So I started dancing, too.

Four or five songs in, some mohawk girls had hoisted me on their shoulders and I was alight. Twenty different hands supported me in the air. Camera flashbulbs clicked in the background. My hands flailed, pushing against other palms. I hovered inches from the garage roof, contemplating the fact that this was the first time I'd ever seriously broken Shabbos. Everyone back home had rebelled once or twice. Meira spent a whole month eating cheeseburgers, which were just about the least kosher food on earth. Once I went with her to Wendy's and bought a soda and watched her eat because I was curious. After that, she never did again. She said she felt like she was cheating in a relationship, except it was her relationship with G-d. And I knew I wasn't doing anything literally wrong — I wasn't actually playing music or using electricity or working — but it definitely went outside the holiness of the Law. I was hanging by the skin of my teeth.

I checked my head. I didn't feel guilty. I didn't feel anything.

You could hear how the song was about to end. One guitarist took charge of the song and started jamming, and the band rocked out with him. Like they'd taken hold of a moment and stretched it out, made it bigger and more explosive than any moment had ever been. The speeding drums. The climbing guitar. Keyboards like a xylophone gone wild.

After the set, we all went outside, drenched and drowning in our own perspiration. The kids still weren't talking to me, but I could tell they weren't suspicious anymore. I jammed my hands into empty pockets, plastered my back to the wall, and made myself look cool.

The lead singer of the band came up to me. He asked if I wanted a cigarette.

I'd always wondered where the flame went after you lit a cigarette. The glowing ember looked like the tip of a Shabbos candle. I hadn't been feeling lonely all night. Not until someone started talking to me.

"*No, gracias. No fumo nunca porque soy un straightedge,*" I said automatically. I never used an accent when I talked Spanish because it always sounded like I was trying, and real Spanish people would automatically think less of me.

The only time I really sound genuine, I think, is inside my head.

Shit.

I had to get to G-d.

I smiled good-bye at the band, walked to the end of the block, then turned the corner and broke into a run. Dry wind beat my face. Hair whisked in and out of my mouth. The blocks flew by. I balled my fists and swung my arms into full gallop.

I heard my name in the air, someone yelling "*Hava! Hava!*" and, Spanish still beating in my brain, I thought it was the command form of a verb I hadn't learned. I was still shaking. I changed to a brisk walk. I stared ahead, pretending not to notice, the way you do when you're walking alone in a city at night. With its mile-long rows of houses, Hollywood could look like a suburb, but it was still a city. I still had to watch out.

This six-year-old kid ran past. He stopped, whirled round on one shoe, and stared straight up at me with that ultraserious expression that only kids can make. "Hava Aaronson," he said, "what are you doing for Shabbos?"

I looked down at his gold-and-black yarmulke and starched white shirt.

Oh my G-d. He was a Hasidic missionary.

"How do you know my name?" My mind was zooming in overtime. The studio must have issued an APB on me and called every rabbi in the area. I looked around nervously, sizing up the street.

"That weird boy kept yelling it at you." The kid wagged a trembling finger across the street.

The kid wasn't alone. Hasidim always came out in entire families, like an army. The first person that hit my eye was the Hasidic rabbi, portly and tall, in a black hat and coat. His stomach and beard looked so awkward on the street of miniature pueblos that it almost seemed like there was nothing else.

"No," said the kid, following my gaze. "*There.*"

My eyes shifted.

Standing next to the rabbi, decked out in a black suit with a black shirt and black tie and black beret, was Moish.

07

SLEEPOVER

Moish flung a sleeping bag, bright orange and blue, onto the floor, next to his cot. It shot open like a parachute, froze in the air, and fluttered to the ground in a neat, flat Fruit Roll-Up strip.

I leaned against the wall drunkenly. I felt the room shift. I thought it was an earthquake, then realized it was just my stomach. I tried to maintain my balance until Moish was finished with the sleeping bag. I whimpered inadvertently.

"There ya go," Moish said, flopping a pillow on top. "All the trappings of home, and none of those pesky creature comforts. Beds and tables are overrated, anyway. How do you feel, Hava?"

"Like if I change my elevation, I'll vomit," I said. "Help me sit down, okay, Moish?"

"You — uh, you might not want to sit down in this room, then," he said.

The living room of Moish's cousin's apartment was a decadent, mahogany upper-middle-class affair. The couch was spacious and comfortable. The dining room was lavish. There was real silverware. A chandelier hung over the table, and all the pictures on the walls had frames. The apartment was pleasant, real-world but funky, a place that bridged the gap between us and our parents.

The only uncomfortable room in the house was Moish's bedroom. It was a squalid, furnitureless room where the laundry room should have been. The floor was cement. Two Cure posters decked out the main walls. The window looked out on an alley.

"So you sleep in here, huh?" I said. My brain had cleared a little, and my vision was less blurry, almost in line with my head.

"Sleep, eat, and create. My cousins aren't religious, so I have to make food in here. And since I sleep in here, I don't even get out of bed for a midnight snack. There's my one-piece oven, stove, and refrigerator, over in the corner."

He gestured at the microwave.

"Refrigerator?" I said.

"It gets cold at night."

I nodded.

The night had been a long one. After running into Moish and that eerie Hasidic family (it *was* still the same night, although my brain was having trouble processing right then), I'd tried to play it cool, even though my ears were still ringing with electric guitar feedback and my hands trembled. The rabbi asked me how I ended up in this part of L.A., miles and miles from Jewville. I told him that I hadn't looked at the time until almost sundown. I took a breath before leaving out the rock concert part of my saga.

I'd never actually told a stranger that I was acting in a television show before. The rabbi was baffled and overjoyed. He thought I was some sort of star. He kept calling me that: "Hava, the Star."

The rabbi was from a sect of Hasidic Jews that were called Chabad. He was an outreach rabbi. There were hundreds of Chabad outreach rabbis, all living in neighborhoods without a big Orthodox community. They were on a mission to educate nonobservant Jews about Judaism, and to help all the observant Jews who were traveling through the wilderness of the secular world find food and places to pray.

And, since I hadn't said anything to the contrary, Moish's rabbi friend figured I was a nonobservant Jew who just happened to be friends with Moish.

Walking to his house, the rabbi kept explaining things like the holiness of Sabbath and how Orthodox Jews didn't use electricity or carry outside their houses. I kept nodding. I didn't want to interrupt him.

But, in the middle of dinner, I had to blow his mind by talking about my Gemara class and this argument I'd been studying between two rabbis about carrying on Shabbos. His wife, a timid woman in a tight ankle-length skirt and a glittery bandanna, shot her hands in the air. Among right-wing Orthodox people, women didn't study Gemara. At Rashi High, everybody studied Gemara. My favorite subject in school last year was Gemara.

"That's how we know each other," Moish said. "We were at school together back in the Old Country — you know, in New York."

The rabbi's face lit up. Turns out he studied in New York for seven years, but had never left the Hasidic part of Brooklyn. He was baffled by these modern equal-rights revelations. But he was an outreach rabbi, after all, and he took the news of a co-ed Orthodox school pretty well, considering.

He had the normal Hasidic reaction to unexpected news. He called for a *l'chaim*.

L'chaim means "to life," and it's what Jews say when we toast each other. Non-Jews bang their glasses together, so that the drinks spill from one glass to another in a gesture of goodwill. Historically, it was started by travelers wary of poisoning each other. Because we trust other Jews, we don't clink our glasses, and we shout something at each other to make up for lost noise. That's where *l'chaim* comes in.

So the rabbi started *l'chaims*, and I don't remember if they ever really stopped. At some point I realized how much we were drinking in terms of sheer quantity — between the three of us, we'd finished an entire bottle of vodka, and we were working on another — and I started eating bread manically to fill up my stomach. I was already tipsy. My head swished like an airplane in a storm. I was a jolly drunk, easygoing and trusting, and the whole problem of not having my keys to walk home didn't bother me at all. I mentioned it drunkenly over dessert. Somehow, just as drunkenly, neither the rabbi nor Moish had any issues with me crashing at Moish's.

That was how we ended up in the small room, drunk and without conscience, seeing our religious morality vanish in waves of capriciousness.

"So this is your outpost," I said.

"Just think of me," said Moish, "as the Chabad missionary to the realm of hipster cool."

I walked over to the small window, parting his Venetian blinds with a finger. We were right off a stretch of Melrose Boulevard. Bar lights and neon boutique signs flashed back at me. The streets packed people in like Mardi Gras, migrating from one club to the next.

Inside was Moish's world. His possessions were evenly divided among corners — food corner, clothes corner, stacks of film books. His video camera sat neatly on a tripod. The power was off, but the lens was still aimed directly at his bed.

The walls were covered, ceiling to floor, in storyboards. I moved away from the window, examined them closely. Charcoal silhouettes wrote, sketched, ate, prayed, drank coffee, looked into store windows. There was an inordinate number of panels in which the Moish figures were drawing storyboards. I checked the date on the corners. They had all been drawn in the last twenty-four hours.

"I really want to make it a full second-by-second account," he said. "A movie as long as the entire summer. It might be a new world record. But I haven't decided whether to ignore Shabbos altogether or come back and film it later. Do you think it would compromise my artistic principles to film reenactments?"

"Moish, you could just leave the cameras running in your bedroom. You wouldn't have to touch them. Reality TV is all about, well, reality."

"Yeah — but not on Shabbos. I need to rest on the seventh day. It's the only time I'm not acting."

One space on the wall was a list that was mostly blank. It said CAST OF CHARACTERS at the top, and only two names were listed: *Mosheh Baruch Resnick* and *Hava Aaronson*, with a numbered list and a lot of space beneath.

I gasped. "Moish, did you know you'd run into me tonight?"

"No. But you're the only person I know here, so for sure you need to be in my film."

"And the rabbi?"

"Doesn't count. He's a Shabbos-only character."

"What about all the hipsters and artists around here?"

"If I ever start talking to them, I'll probably learn their names."

Moish's storyboard montages did seem lacking in, well, non-Moish characters. Sitting on his bed, Moish looked sullen and melancholy, even more so than normal. That, I think, was the fundamental difference between the two of us: I knew when to call it quits with the melodrama. And if you asked Moish, he'd tell you that he wasn't being melodramatic at all.

"Moish," I asked, "are you going to keep being Orthodox this summer?"

"Why?" Moish said. "You mean, because I'm three thousand miles away from my family and no one's watching?"

"Yeah," I said. "That."

He looked out the window with sober eyes that were perfectly round, full like moons. "Fuck, yes," he said. "Being Orthodox is the only thing I don't question."

"Why not?" I lay down on the carpet and stared at the ceiling.

" 'Cause there's no possible way for it to be true. There's this invisible guy called G-d who gives us a list of foods we can't eat, asks us to pray to him three times a day, and never talks back. Why the hell would anyone be Orthodox? It's absolute lunacy. There's nothing to keep us from stopping, except that our beliefs are so unbelievable. I once tried to eat a cheeseburger, and as soon as I bought it and realized that I *could*, there was no point in actually eating it. I gave it to a homeless guy on Bleecker Street and walked the eighty-six blocks home."

There was an archaic rule, one that nobody followed anymore, that said that an unmarried guy and girl should never be in a room alone together. Actually, this rule said that if any single boy-and-girl combination did end up in a room alone they were, in Torah terms, assumed to have had sex.

That wasn't what I was thinking about as I lay on Moish's floor that night, watching him in his wavy lost stare. If we could have listened to music, we'd have played Nina Simone or Portishead, music that moved like snails and dust tracks, and sounded older than time. Moish's face was steeped in shadows. Somehow I wished I could pull him together. At that moment, I could totally fall in love with Moish, not because I wanted him at all, but because I thought I understood him totally. He looked so awkward in his black clothes. He didn't know how to behave in black.

I can sleep in any kind of light. Noise is the only thing that keeps me awake. One two-thousand-watt bulb shining at my head, it's no problem to ignore. I just close my eyes and dream.

That's the best way I know to fall asleep, too. That whole week, I had to force myself to sleep, thinking of my real-life life in New York and my imaginary life as Shoshana Goldberg and a third life in the dream world, with even more drama. I thought of people in my two worlds, and imagined them drowsily interacting with one another while I lay there, and soon my fake dreams faded into actual dreams.

Moish left on all the lights for Shabbos, since we weren't

allowed to turn them on or off. Ignoring those lights was no problem for me.

Moish had forgotten to get curtains for his room, though, and the warmth of sunlight poured in, waking him at dawn. It was six or seven a.m., that blank slate of morning when there's still hours before you have to be anywhere. The clap of Moish's toes on the hard floor rustled me in my sleep. The scrape of his morning toothbrush woke me beyond return.

"Hey, kiddo." Moish walked over to my recumbent form. "Where do you want to go today?"

I let out a groan.

"By the way," he said. "What the hell happened to your hair?"

I groaned louder and threw the blankets over my head.

The streets gleamed. Shards of glass beer bottles and aluminum cans made the world shine like the end of a rainbow. I thought of my grandparents in Hungary, reading stories about America, repeating to their parents the hackneyed phrase, "The streets are paved with gold!"

But they knew! Oh, they knew.

That Shabbos morning, the world spun around us. Shrunken Indian grandmothers swathed in saris waddled to grocery stores, clutching empty canvas bags. A dreary bus plodded down the boulevard. Oceans of front lawn sprung out in both directions as we rounded the corner, heading south and west from the Hollywood Hills.

It took three hours to walk to Pico Robertson. The whole time, neither of us spoke. Still sleep-dazed, everything kept reminding me of my dreams — bus kiosks, billboards, restaurant window displays. I dreamed that regular butchers had started carrying kosher meat. To advertise, whole flanks of raw kosher meat were hanging in store windows. My TV show had somehow sponsored it. All the meat was *The Goldbergs* brand roasts, and atop every flank was a picture of my face, a full-color head shot.

The neighborhoods flew by like weird late-night TV commercials, each with its own clashing Art Deco style. The streets got wider and busier. Finally the names *Pico* and *Robertson* intersected on a street sign, the dead center of Jewville. I was ready for the rush.

We waited.

Moish and I exchanged nervous looks. In New York, all you had to do in a Jewish neighborhood was show up on the street, wait twenty seconds for someone wearing a long skirt to pass by, and follow her to a synagogue. It always worked. In New York, we'd walk across the city to a foreign neighborhood and do it for fun.

"Hava, what do you think?"

"Maybe everyone in L.A. drives to synagogue?"

"Whoa. Look alive, Hava," Moish said. "Beard alert."

I squeezed my palms together. I hated Hasidim. Not like the family last night, who were friendly and painless. I'm talking about the groups of twenty guys hanging out together, zealots who think a girl's dangerous if she's not at home cooking. These boys would pick up Moish in a second and strand me just as fast. Or, worse, they'd take me along and not say a word to me all day.

"Hell, no," I said. "I'm not going to be a women's minyan of one."

"Not that." Moish rolled his eyes. "*That.*"

From the other side of the street came a couple younger than our parents. The woman had on short sleeves and the guy's yarmulke was sewn to look like a watermelon. Their wardrobes screamed Modern Orthodox almost as much as their casual, nonmilitary Jewishness. These were our people.

They slipped into a building we hadn't noticed, but which was pretty huge. Right around the corner from where we stood, there were like a dozen different shuls. We followed the couple. The straight-faced black-hat boys went into one building at the end of the block. We followed the watermelon yarmulke people into another. I left Moish at the belly-high wall between the men's and women's sections, air-punched his forearm, and took a seat near the front. The leader prayed fast, the way I like it, where every word comes and leaves with a fury instead of being stranded in a lame, weak singalong. After services I lingered, hoping someone would talk to me. I tried to meet all the other girls' eyes on the way out. They didn't even pass over the crowd. Everyone found their friends like magnets and popped out in groups.

It's no coincidence that, every time Jews go to synagogue, it's followed by a massive meal. Friday night, you can show up at any Orthodox synagogue in the universe and, as long as you look lonely, families will flood you with invitations for Shabbos dinner. On Sabbath, we're commanded to eat three huge meals, and we mix Friday night leftovers with massive new courses, salads, and stews for Saturday lunch. I felt like I was saving up my appetite all week, as though G-d would repay me on Shabbos for all those sad and lonely meals.

No such luck. Moish and I wandered through the meager display of potato chips, cookies, and grape juice after services. People drifted through their own little worlds. Moish gorged himself on a little paper plate of chocolate-and-vanilla cremes.

"What's your call?" I asked.

He shrugged. "You got any food at your place?"

"Moish," I informed him, "my place is even farther than yours. We *could* walk. We'd get there maybe by next Shabbos. And then have to break in, since my keys are in the studio." I flattened my palms against the table, then started twisting the paper tablecloth in swirls around my finger. "Shit," I said, "I wish I remembered where my cousins lived."

"Phone book?"

We left the dwindling crowd of people who were obviously not going to invite us to lunch. It took a while to find a phone booth on the street, since nobody in L.A. walked, which meant no public phones, either. I pulled out the hefty white pages. I sent out a prayer.

My fingers combed the millions of last names. The gravity of our situation started to dawn, and I sank against the door of the phone booth. "This is never gonna work, Moish. My cousin Josh is an entertainment lawyer. There's no way he'll have his home number in the book."

"Maybe it's under AARONSON, comma, J?"

"He's on my mother's side. Her last name is Klein."

I'd just hit the KLEIN entry. There was an entire page of KLEIN J's. I slammed the book shut and thudded it back into the phone booth. "It's a shame it's Shabbos, dude," I said without looking at him. "Starving to death could be the next subplot of your reality movie."

Last night at the Chabad rabbi's house, all the courses had meat. Gefilte fish, chicken soup, salad with chicken slices, mashed potatoes in gravy. I gorged myself on hummus and asparagus and Turkish tomato salad. The rabbi's wife, all timid and nineteenth-century, offered to spoon the chicken pieces out of my soup.

I shuddered. I hadn't eaten a real meal in days. I wondered how far I would go before I ate chicken.

"*Hey!*"

There was a blinding yell like a building on fire. Moish and I twisted our heads. A tubby black-hat boy raced across the street. He ran against traffic. We were in his sights. I felt my body brace. He leaped onto the pavement right before a fleet of neon BMWs coasted through his path.

We both took a step back.

"Don't use that telephone!" he said. "It's Shabbos! You're Jews! I can tell."

Moish touched his beret, self-consciously making sure it hadn't blown off. I blinked. I had about the most Jewish face you could imagine. Plus, there was my Ortho-hip skirt and the time and the neighborhood.

"We were just looking for Hava's cousin's address," Moish replied quickly. I could hear defensiveness in his voice. It was the same voice he got when Shmuel and Fruma would question him about how kosher he was. "We were supposed to go there for lunch, and we can't find them."

The black-hat boy didn't miss a beat. "Well, don't stand at the telephone looking like *goyim*," he said. "Eat by us!"

* * *

We followed him through the streets. I was uneasy the whole time. I kept expecting him to ignore me. But when he told us his name was Yossi, he looked at both of us. Even when other Hasidim walked by, he kept talking in my direction. I don't want to sound too prejudiced; I really did know there were friendly Hasidim out there. I'd just never met any before.

Yossi raved and raved about his mother's *chollint* and apple pies. He talked like a news radio announcer, stopping occasionally to check that we were still listening. I think everyone I met these days spoke like that. But Yossi was so intense. That cliché, hackneyed dialogue that they made us speak on the set all week, filled with *oy*s and *vey*s and *schlep*s, it was like every word came straight from Yossi's mouth.

Yossi, though, was a new kind of Jew.

"You're vegetarians?" he said. "*Mamish*, there's so many vegetarians out here, *boruch Hashem* there should be this many Yids with such *chutzpah* in the whole world, but such a thing as vegetarians is a little *fakachte*, if you ask me, *mamish*, I couldn't survive on it, not so much, but *das ist der veldt*, whatever makes the world work, you know? It's all good. *Mamish*."

"Are you Chabad?" I asked. I wanted to be prepared, if the meal was going to be all weird and outreachy again.

"Naah. I'm a different kind of Hasid, but really, we're all just plain Jews. It's not about the hats so much. We're all brothers under G-d. All that matters is, you wear a yarmulke, that's good enough for Him, right?" He glanced in my direction. "Or for that matter, if you're wearing anything at all."

Yossi burst out laughing.

I bit my lip. Yossi didn't mean anything sexual about that

remark. That's what I love and hate about Hasidim — they're so naïve in a bad way, but also, they're so naïve in a good way. Any other man would turn into a twelve-year-old boy. Not jolly, giggly Yossi.

"Look," he said, "we're all put on earth to do something, right? I figure, none of us knows why we're here. I mean, none of us *really* knows. I pray, I eat kosher food, I try to be friendly to everyone I can. And if that makes a little bit of difference to some other folks, well, why not." He stopped in his tracks. "You don't really want to go to my mother's house, do you? She's having the entire Sisterhood over. It's gonna be eighty-year-old ladies and *chollint* that's thin like soup. Let's hit the yeshiva."

And he turned a corner into a building that looked like a high-school gymnasium and smelled that way, too. The Yiddish writing on all the doors was the only giveaway. A yeshiva was a boarding school for Jewish kids to study Torah, usually right-wing boys, and I don't know how Yossi assumed it was okay to take me inside.

Moish was the one to ask him. "Yossi, are you sure Hava can —"

Yossi cut him off with a look. "I said, anybody that needs help. You need someplace to eat, am I right?"

We couldn't argue with that.

In the main room was a table that was layered with food, piles of it, like burial mounds. Black-hat boys stood all around it, scarfing down cold cuts and challah rolls and egg salad and macaroni. There was no method to the mayhem — boys sat in disfigured configurations of chairs, strewn through the room, some standing up and eating, some talking in between frantic mouthfuls. When they saw me, most of the boys stared down hard at their tables, maybe trying to make me disappear. Yossi started to list their names — "Hava and Moish, this is Yaakov and Yitzhak and Yonasson and Yehoshua and Ezra and Erez and Ephraim . . ." — but had the good sense to recognize a doomed mission as he started. He snagged a cup of wine and made kiddush on it, and we washed our hands and made a blessing on two challahs.

And then we ate.

It was a little bit of hell finding vegetarian food — Hasidim are notorious meat eaters — but we managed to secure a small army of eggplant and egg and hummus-based salads to let ourselves loose upon. I grabbed a full-size challah as big as my arm and began ripping pieces off, savaging myself on the cucumber-dill hummus. My stomach inflated as we ate, as Yossi, between servings of brisket, found more salads to bring us. Moish scooped egg salad into his mouth by the forkful. Somewhere in my head, I worried about some evil stepmother coming after us, we were being so gluttonous and Goldilocks-ish, but gluttony is a sin only in classical Christianity. In Judaism, taking advantage of the good things in life is encouraged. We're a race of martyrs, but not by choice. The two questions we're going to be asked when we get to the Afterlife are, *Did you obey the laws that were given?* and *Did you take advantage of the pleasures that were allowed to you?*

Both those questions have equal weight.

"So what are you doing in Los Angeles?" Yossi asked, toppling contentedly back into his chair.

"I'm directing and starring in an entirely new kind of motion picture experience," Moish remarked matter-of-factly. "It's going to be a movie with a three-month running time. The plot is my life. The viewers will eat when I eat, sleep when I sleep. Uh — except for Shabbos. I dunno about that yet."

Yossi nodded and turned to look at me.

"I, uh, I'm acting in this TV thing," I said. "I live in outer Hollywood. I kind of got stranded here."

"What kind of TV thing?" called a lanky black-hat boy from the next table over. His voice was pointed and skeptical.

"It's just a sitcom. I'm from Manhattan. I got asked to be on this show for a few weeks and I said yes."

"It's not that sitcom about Orthodox Jews, is it?" asked another kid, nonchalantly seating himself at our table.

"My uncle works for CBS and he says he passed on that show like bacon. He says there's no way they can make *The Goldbergs* without shaming the name of G-d."

"Any Jews on TV are shaming the image of G-d," someone else said. "My rebbe says, 'You cannot take down the master's house with the master's tools.'"

"It's possible to look good on TV," called over another boy from across the room. "But they won't let it happen. Jews are easy to poke fun at."

"That show, it's more fodder for the *goyim* to hate us for what we have."

"So what are you gonna act as? Will they make you wear pants? All women on television wear pants."

"Imagine, people in the Midwest will wonder why you don't have horns."

"Will you stop insulting our guests, please?" Yossi's body shook. "Let Hava talk!"

"I'm on *ER*," I said, forcing a big spoonful of babaganoush into my mouth.

*   *   *

Third Meal was the last meal of Shabbos. The Torah, in its overbearing Jewish-mother-like way of dishing out the laws, says that you should eat on Sabbath until you can't eat anymore, and then some. Third Meal was the *and then some* part. We could go to the Chabad rabbi's house and dig on some crackers and fruit salad with them. Instead, we headed back to Moish's place. He unwrapped the key from his belt, I collapsed on the living room sofa, and he foraged through the food corner of his room for enough snacks to sustain us.

We ate pita, pickles, Triscuits, challah crusts, wrinkly mineola oranges, roma tomato moons, and two slices of cold pizza cut up into hors d'oeuvre squares. It was a beggars' banquet, a lavish spread of junk food on a hundred disposable plates. We ate nebbishly, pecking at the fruit and nibbling the corners of crackers. Then Moish went to pray and I sat on the couch, staring out the window. The sun was blazing above the downtown skyline. It was past seven at night, already evening, and the sky was only starting to turn purple and orange and lemon.

Shabbos was getting ready to end.

I thought about running away from the soundstage, not even telling the director I was gone. At first I wondered if they'd yell at Evie. Then I wondered what she'd tell the Producers to make them even madder. It felt like a million years since I'd run away. In the real world, it was barely twenty-four hours ago. G-d made me into a rebel, and I was gonna have to face the consequences.

But right now, early in the night with the sun still streaming over us, I was sure that I was doing all right.

08

THE NEW JEWS

I was not taking any shit from anybody on Monday morning. Chin up, head high, I returned to the studio. Riding there, I argued back and forth in my head. I could be meek and apologetic. I could be an asshole. I was a Jew and they were assaulting my religion. No — I was a star and I had rights. Privileges. Filming couldn't go on without me.

The truth was, they could replace me at any second.

I wouldn't be a star about it. I was going to be civilized. They were wrong. I was right. Things always work out and I did the right thing by walking out and the whole reason I was in Hollywood was a miracle, anyway. That's what I kept telling myself.

The director had gone way over on filming time. He didn't even tell me. It was his fault I was there past Shabbos.

I could sue.

I could leak the story to tabloids.

My hands shook uncontrollably. Yeah, I was not good at fooling myself. I wondered if they'd fire me.

They could do it, too. I was a no-name third-tier actress on a second-tier television show. I realized how alarmingly easy it would be to reshoot all my scenes using a professional actress who'd been playing teenagers since she was born. Real actresses could memorize lines in an afternoon, waltz in, and do the entire episode without retakes. I was the Producers' measure of legitimacy. But this was Hollywood. They didn't *need* a measure of legitimacy.

My limo was the last to pull up. Everyone else was already on the set. In costume. The director glanced at me once and looked away. He said something to his assistant and walked out. There was a bustle that I didn't understand, then the assistant director called on a megaphone, "Can we get wardrobe and makeup out here, please?"

The shoot went quickly. It still took way too long. You could feel everyone's frustration bouncing off the walls in that room. The cameras followed us too lazily. Charles's delivery was a notch too quick. Evie didn't whine as long as she had in rehearsals. The last scene between me and David Lee was trepidatious and rushed. The go-get-'em-girl emotional punch was weak, even by the decaf standards of modern television. The director didn't ask for anything to be reshot. "It's a take," he said impotently, flipping himself off the canvas chair and vanishing into his office.

I looked around for support from the cast. There was none. Jamie and Corey were giggling in a way that I *knew* was gossip, Evie trotted puppily after David Lee, and Charles stood alone on the stoop, smoking agitatedly.

I don't know what I'd expected. Some kind of party, maybe. When we finish a book of the Torah in synagogue, the women spin in circles and all the men do a little dance at the front of the sanctuary. Here, nobody met my eyes. It was lunchtime. The last one out was Paula, who stood at the door a second too long. She met my gaze with an icy stare, folded her arms across her Donna Karan get-busy business jacket, and raised one eyebrow like an evil spell.

Lunch that day was uneasy. Still no kosher food. I asked my favorite production assistant about it. He gave me this look that said, *You just don't get it.*

That was when I got it.

I walked past dressing rooms and felt the blank stares like doors being pulled shut. I winced like they were slamming into my face. The building seemed so cramped. I wanted to walk but there was no place to walk to. I wanted to rage and felt my mind clamming up and trying to behave. I didn't know what I was allowed to *say*, even. You couldn't raise your voice in the hallways. People could be filming.

I squeezed into Evie's room. "Oh my G-d," I said. "Evie, everything's so fucked up and I don't know what to do."

"Get out."

"What?" I blanched. Speed metal songs were still playing in my head. I thought I'd just misheard her.

"Leave my room, Hava. Get away from me."

Yeah. I hadn't misheard.

I went to my own dressing room.

Then I realized I wanted to be here less than anywhere else in the universe. So I went to Charles's dressing room.

The door was ajar. I pushed it quietly and slipped in through the narrow crevice of the opening. Before Charles even turned around, he sensed me in the room. He spoke. "Nobody wants to talk to you, am I right?"

"How did you know it was me?"

"I'm sitting in front of my makeup mirror," he said. "I'm psychic, but I'm not *that* psychic. I know your mind is in twenty different places right now. Drop them, Hava. None of them are important right now."

I collapsed into his stylist's chair. "Charles," I groaned.

"Hava."

I caught his eye in the mirror.

"Do you really mind that I don't call you Charlie?"

He laughed.

Charles's laugh was a full, solid laugh. He was not half-assed about it. His formidable broad shoulders shook in rhythm with the rest of his body. He had a big, tender mouth and a big set of lungs to go along with it. His hair was rugged, always combed in a manner that was supposed to look uncombed. He wore plaid shirts a lot, which de-emphasized his neck and framed his head nicely. He looked like a man in a way that was dangerous and comforting at the same time.

I realized I was staring at him. I asked, "Are you mad at me for leaving?"

He raised his eyebrows. "Do you care if I am?"

I actually did care. It took me a second to realize that. Six snappy replies lined up on my tongue before I said a word. I didn't care what the studio thought. But, for a second, I saw the incident from Charles's — from Char*lie*'s — point of view. You were at the studio two hours late on a Friday night. You had dinner, a lady friend, and two tickets to a movie premiere. You're standing in freeze-frame position for ten minutes while the production assistants shout at each other, *Where's the chick who plays Shoshana?*, before that sexy little Evie girl tells everyone, *Oh, she took off, she thought she was too important for her big finale*, and you're finally off the hook.

Late for your premiere, but off the hook.

I shrugged. "Everybody else seems to."

"Yeah, well, a lot of money got unmade last Friday night."

"Screw the money. They fucked up my relationship with my Creator."

"And now nobody wants to talk to you."

"You're still talking to me."

"I'm too good to you, Hava. I'm just the father. I've got a little too much advice up my sleeve, and you're the only one listening."

I sat there, glum. "You want me to call you Daddy instead of Charles? The tabloids will eat that one up." I looked up hopefully.

"Tabloids? My, aren't *you* full of yourself today."

My face fell even farther. Charles leaned over, put on a sympathetic face, and told me to look alive.

"Chin up, Hava," he said. "They'll listen to you. You're a booming starlet, and you're ready to explode. Heck, you're already exploding. If you haven't noticed, you're the star of this sitcom. Me, I'm just the old guard. Nobody wants to watch a plot that revolves around a charming middle-aged man in a happy marriage. You've got the looks and you've definitely got the attitude and everyone here either looks up to you or is jealous of you, bar none."

I smiled wide at Charles, looking into his eyes. "This constant reification is boosting my ego like hell. I should walk out more often."

"I'm serious, Hava. They love you."

"The Producers hate me."

He shot me a look.

"Evie doesn't love me."

Charles gaped at me disbelievingly. "Evie wants to *be* you."

"We go out to clubs and she ig*nores* me."

"That's because she's afraid of the power you have. Evie's the most popular girl in high school. She looks like a model. She's about to get into a much bigger world with a thousand girls who resemble her exactly. She figures she's going to get eaten alive. And then she sees you. You're an individual. You're hot and sexy and cunning, just like she is, but you do it on your own terms. Of course she's terrified of you. She's not afraid you're going to steal her territory; she's afraid she won't be left with any territory to fend for. She's been working her whole life to be the Sexy Young Thing on a prime-time TV show, and when she finally gets it, she's playing second fiddle to a girl who hit a perfect ten on the first audition. You're the one getting all the play."

"Yeah," I huffed, "but only on-screen."

"Where do you think it counts?"

I thought of our off-screen lives: Evie hitting on movie stars. Evie hitting on drug dealers. Evie and her elaborately structured evening plans, trying to make life resemble an After-School Special. On camera, I was the one with all the dates, while Evie complained about test scores and eating spinach. In our real lives, she was begging the boys to treat her like a queen, bribing them with a taste of her, as I played second fiddle. Just like she wanted me to.

"Oh, Charles," I murmured, "you're so right."

"She wants everything," Charles whispered in my ear. His eyes gleamed. I felt his eyes ripple, running over the length of my body. I shifted, pulled in my breath, listened to his slow, quiet words. "We all want everything. That's why we're here. Hava, to be in your position is to have a considerable amount of power. None of us has ever been where you are now. I can only wonder what it would be like to wield the power that you have. I can only imagine what it's like to touch it."

Charles was so close. I could feel his skin making my body warmer. I didn't want to breathe. I was afraid my breath would hit his perfect face, and he would realize I'm not as beautiful as he thought I was.

I mumbled something dumb, like "Thank you" or "You're too kind." *G-d.* My face was heating up like a nuclear reactor.

A production assistant knocked on the door. We could tell it was a PA because of the knock they used, one of those smarmy *bum da da dum-dum* knocks.

I tried to breathe normally. Charles rummaged for his sport coat in the rack of fatherly clothes.

"Mr. Beaufort? There's a script run-through in five minutes," the PA called through the door. "The director wants to start rehearsing Episode Two this afternoon and just run this week's sched normally. Oh — and you probably want to check out the new *Variety* that just came into the office."

Charles threw on his sport coat and straightened his tie. I fixed my collar, my heart racing. Then something on Charles's desk caught my eye. A small framed round memento of a smiling, middle-aged but attractive woman.

Paula.

"You ready to rock and roll?" Charles asked, fixing his tie.

I threw the door open. "What's up with *Variety*?" I demanded.

The PA looked genuinely surprised to find me in Charles's dressing room. "Hava —" he gulped. "You look way hot — I was — I mean, I just wanted to know if you could sign my copy . . ."

THE NEW JEWS

Hava Aaronson and the rest of The Goldbergs tie TV's first Orthodox family ties

The front page of *Variety* showed me grinning like a buck-toothed baby. It was a solo shot, just my face and torso and a treacherous pink background. My hair was straight and brown, bangs the size of a zip code, echoes of that stupid dead-cat wig. I looked like Miss Everygirl Teenage Yeshiva Student. I was wearing an army jacket — at least *that* looked punk — but underneath was a tank top that made my breasts look like cannon fodder. My hair never looked this clean and straight and retarded. Fuck, I almost looked normal.

The shot was taken straight from the publicity photos for that John Cage nonmusical, and Photoshopped with a pleasant living room backdrop so it looked like an actual photo shoot. It felt so not-me. My face reminded me of seeing some friend from years ago who I'd never hang out with if we met each other now. Magazine covers were something that happened to people with publicity departments and tell-all books and, well, high school diplomas.

The first thing I saw was the poster-size mock-up on an easel.

Behind that was a table, right outside the reading room, covered with copies. Inside the room, PAs and writers thumbed through it, holding their copies high in the air as they read. Twenty identical duplicates of my face stared at me through the doorway. I felt like my dreams were coming alive.

The cast worked their way into the reading room groggily, Mondayishly. They took copies and read them, too, not showing any sign of being impressed. I scooped up a copy and opened to the story. It was just a preview for the new season. There was nothing specifically about me, or about the show, other than the standard blurb:

> The Goldbergs — *The misadventures of an Orthodox Jewish family in New York City. Disorganized religion at its funniest.*

"Not bad, huh, kid?" remarked Charles, leafing through the rest of the fall listings. "First we get bumped up to a fall airdate. Now you're on the front of the industry bible. Pretty good for someone who still hasn't passed her driver's test."

I lay the magazine back down in the stack. I grimaced, heading into the reading room and bracing for the inevitable backlash from my fellow Hollywoodland costars.

I had to wait for that. Fortunately, everyone else's personalities were on hiatus for the rest of the afternoon. Until the clock hit five — until the director decided we were done with our script reading for the day, anyway — my coworkers' delightfully misanthropic Los Angeles attitudes got submerged beneath their delightfully laconic New York characters.

Scripts were passed out, motivations assigned, and we did our read-through. It was mercifully quick. There was a degree of familiarity with our characters now. Evie whined with a refined shrill. Paula's dramatic pauses before her lines were timed exactly with Charles's d'oh-did-you-really-say-that one-liners. Because we'd had to reshoot the end of last week's episode, we didn't get the half day that we would come to expect from Mondays — a read-through, basic comments from the director, occasional breaks for the writers to replace some lines and make us recite other lines with a different cadence, and then an early dismissal.

We still got out somewhat early that day, and when I climbed into my car, the sun still high on the horizon, I said to the driver, "Can you take me to the Jewish part of town?"

"Doin' some research for the part, huh?" he laughed. "Sure thing. I know how you actors are. I'll drop you on Fairfax Avenue, and you can take it from there."

We pulled up to a bakery with blue frosted Yiddish letters in the windows. "Thanks a lot," I gulped, leaping out. I pulled my knapsack off the seat, told the driver not to wait around, and strutted down the street like I owned it.

Cheesy Hebrew wedding music poured out from a music store. At the counter, an elfin woman bobbed her head to the bounce of clarinets. Little Jewish boys with mouselike faces and Digimon backpacks scurried down the sidewalk, pursued by young mothers with more children tucked in their elbows. The sun climbed into my shirt through the back of my collar in a cone. It made my skin warm to the touch, my arms glowing like someone was pressing against them. It was a good day.

I walked along, growing wary quickly. I don't know what I

expected but I don't think this was it. There were Jews all over the place. None of them recognized me, or flocked to me, or made that grin of identification like when you're at a strange subway stop and a guy gets on wearing a yarmulke and, suddenly, you two are kindred spirits. Not only did they not have a real subway in L.A., they didn't have strange neighborhoods either. I could imagine, if you lived in this neighborhood, you stayed here. There was a native Jewish culture here. I was not a part of it. I walked quicker past the electronics stores and schwarma stands, looking for that quintessence of Jewish neighborhoods, the kosher pizza place.

I stopped in a dairy restaurant far down, where the stores gave way to houses, and miles of cars in unbroken lines framed the pavements with pastel and black borders. I was worried I was gonna run out of places to eat. I could have just turned back. No, I couldn't have. I saw those cold Jews with homeless eyes staring at me, reading the length of my skirt to see how religious I was, the pattern of my denim jacket to tell if I was modern or Orthodox, because on these streets, you couldn't be both. It was all about how strict you were. Back home, all the adults were lawyers, and here they were movie producers, but it was the same thing: You trafficked in the secular world all day. When you came home, when you planted yourselves in your communities, you wanted to be with Jews.

There was a giant plastic model of a smiley falafel in the window. Inside, a bunch of solitary men sat at tables by themselves, reading books. In the corner was a Hasidic man with six daughters, none more than two inches different from the last one in height. I'm sure their ages worked like that, too.

"Let me guess. You want falafel," said the girl at the window.

She was short, thin, with long black hair in a ponytail and dramatic mahogany eyes. Her skin was a deep burnt sienna.

"Do you have pizza?"

"Do we have pizza? Do we ever. All anyone ever wants is falafel, though. You really want pizza? You want a family pie?"

"G-d, no. Just a slice or two. Mushroom, if you got it."

I sat at a booth by myself. The pizza tasted like falafel. That's the thing about these generic dairy restaurants — they have one kind of food in a lot of different shapes. I once saw a place in Brooklyn that was, no kidding, a pizza place, taco hut, Chinese takeout, Italian restaurant, and ice-cream parlor in one. Oh, and donuts, too. The donuts tasted a little like Chinese food, and the Chinese food tasted like tacos. That way, you knew everything was kosher.

I'd been eating in kosher restaurants my whole life, hanging around these families and old people that I'd never be caught dead with otherwise, except we ate the same food.

Look: I grew up this way. I'm not doing this to be hip. I'm not doing this to be popular. I might be doing it to be different — when people know I'm Orthodox, they fixate on that, and they don't ask about the other parts of my life that don't fit into a neat little box. Why do you dress weird? Why do you listen to loud rock music? Is your fuck-you attitude just a cover for the inner insecurity that people won't accept you as normal?

I used to think way too much. Somewhere along the line, I stopped second-guessing myself. Last Friday, when I walked out of the studio, I was building up to that moment for half my life. I knew how this world worked. People don't care about you. They don't try to understand you. Unless you're exactly the same as them, or you have something that other people want, you're like nothing.

The whole time I chewed my pizza, my eyes kept darting to the door. I was waiting for a group of kids, my age, possibly slightly older, to come in and occupy one of the giant tables in the center of the restaurant, intended for a Hasidic family of twenty, and start talking about school and bands and how weird it was to be Jews. Tonight I was sick of being the voice telling kids that they weren't alone, that other people out there understood and were listening. Tonight I wanted someone to tell *me* that hopeful shit. Tonight I wanted someone to listen to me.

Yeah, I was on my way to being famous. So what. I had one friend in this whole city, and I couldn't call him because he was filming a movie for the next three months.

I finished my pizza slowly, carried my tray to the trash can, sat back down, and prayed. I still stole glances at the doorway, just in case the dream group of cool Orthodox kids suddenly burst in.

Then I told myself off.

Hava, I said, *they're not gonna come for you if you don't come for them first.*

And with that I grabbed my knapsack, scooted off the booth, and walked up Fairfax Avenue.

A few blocks back down, I came to Fairfax High School. I'd always been curious about public high schools, since I had never actually been inside one. There were several in our neighborhood in Manhattan, but there was never any reason for me to go inside. I always tried to look in their windows, catch a glimpse of the decorations on the walls, just in case there was something inside that I had always desperately needed to see.

Sitting against the black tar-painted fence of the school yard were a couple of boys with the tightest, most geometrically glistening mohawks I had ever seen. One was orange and black and yellow, and one was rainbow-colored. Both were long, uninterrupted fans of watercolor breathlessness.

In my ideal fantasy world, I would be a Japanese princess silhouetted in a backdrop of jacaranda trees, and these mohawks would be my geisha fans when I danced.

I was taking my time gazing into the grated windows of the high school building when I noticed them staring. I didn't mind.

"Check you out," the Halloween mohawk boy said with a predatory grin. His teeth were rotting and his eyes were small black marbles. "Whatcha lookin' for?"

I spot-checked my outfit that day, a mesh of new corporate-sponsor clothes and old Salvation Army ones. To them I probably looked like myself in reverse: a spoiled Beverly Hills girl who just scored a killer scarf and T-shirt from a thrift store on Melrose.

I was not in the mood to justify myself. I told their snotty and self-assured grimaces, "Don't give me that shit. All I want is to find a fun show."

"Whoa," rainbow dude said. "I don't think we listen to the same kind of music."

"Try me," I whispered.

They exchanged glances. I hopped up onto the top of the fence, four feet if it was an inch. I did it seamlessly, and in a skirt. I stifled the *unnnh* exhalation out of my lips, propping myself neatly on my haunches, heels between spikes.

"You're not from around here, are you?"

I shook my head.

"Where you from?"

"East Coast," I said nervously.

They issued the challenge. "Dischord Records."

"Fugazi, duh. Also El Guapo, Q and Not U, Rites of Spring, and Shudder to Think."

"Alternative Tentacles."

"The Dead Kennedys, Pansy Division, Tribe 8."

They exchanged give-me-a-break looks when I said Tribe 8, a girl band, but I still scored. "Epitaph?"

"Bad Religion, Rancid, and — oh yeah — and the Bouncing Souls."

"Fat Wreck Chords?"

"Lagwagon, Propagandhi, NoFX. Who, by the way, my friend Ian's band opened for last week at CBGB's."

"Whoa whoa whoa. When she starts name-dropping, the test may finally end," said the rainbow-mohawked guy. "You won. We think you're cool. Officially."

"Thanks," I said, leaning back against the fence post. Only, of course, I was on top of the fence, and only barely aware of being there. I almost lost my balance.

"*Peligro!*" yelled one of the boys. My left arm was stretched in midair, as though trying to wave myself back onto the fence. I fell to the ground with a significant *whump*. Through rubber Doc Marten soles, my feet smarted like incalculable blisters.

"What's wrong, you don't *habla* the *Español*?" the Halloween mohawk boy asked, baring his teeth again.

"White boy," I said, sliding myself back up to a comfortable perch on the fence, "I'm from New York. *Yo puedo hablar todo que tu tienes* and more; don't be like that."

"What'd you say? I don't really speak Spanish. I grew up in Beverly Hills."

"His mom's the costume designer for MTV2," the rainbow mohawk kid explained. "He likes to act like he has street cred, just 'cause his parents manage half the bands we used to listen to before they sold out. You really looking for a concert?"

"No," I said, letting my feet dangle. "I got sick of being lonely, that's all."

"Hang out here," he said, fishing in his pack for a forty-ounce bottle of Miller. "There's a bunch of kids at a Deftones listening party down on Sunset. They'll trickle in."

We sat and watched the moon rise. Night got cold out here, not just in that your-mother's-worried sense that it did back East, but in sudden and dramatic waves of wind that rustled your clothes and smacked hard against your skin.

Those guys didn't talk. I didn't worry. I wasn't after more friends. The ones I had scared me more than enough. I just wanted something familiar, and if it came in three dimensions, breathed, and smelled like hair dye and dirty laundry, that was fine by me. They were part of the backdrop, not part of the action, and they knew it.

We watched the punk rock kids stumble back from the listening party, some with brown paper bags of alcohol in hand, some with massive hamburger headphones that made it completely unnecessary for them to interact with other people. The kids sat on the ground and the fences and the blacktop inside the school, dangling from the basketball nets.

Yeah, it wasn't much of an interaction. But I could feel why they all came here — why they came to their high school during summer break — without asking. It was the same reason I ended up there.

There was nowhere else to go.

The discovery of Fairfax High electrified me. Just the thought of a bored punk rock mecca propelled me through days of scripting and tepid, traumatic rehearsals like nothing else could. I never learned anyone's name there, even after I started recognizing individual punks from blocks away by the shape and color of their hair.

My driver grew accustomed to the routine. Eventually, he developed a sense of humor about it. He'd drop me a block or two away so nobody had to witness me climbing out of a limousine. One day I ran into the rainbow mohawk kid from the first time around. He was doing the same thing. We exchanged knowing glances, and that was that.

At home those nights, I studied the new script. It's September, the High Holidays are coming, and me and David are learning how to read Torah. David says: "Here's the secret — whenever you don't know what tune to use, just sing the *Gilligan's Island* theme." Poppa Goldberg (Charles to you) passes by my bedroom, eavesdropping. He gets this pleased look in his eyes.

The next morning, at the congregation board meeting, Paula volunteers Charles to read the Torah portion on the first day of Rosh Hashana. Charles isn't there because he's conducting the school board meeting, and he volunteers me to lead the kiddie services. My big problem is, I hate leading kiddie services. Charles's bigger problem is, he never learned how to read Torah.

Now, instead of communicating with his wife like a normal

person would, Charles teaches himself how to sing Torah ("A *three-hour tour, a three-hour tour . . .*") And I, instead of teaching, decide to let the kids do whatever they want to.

Anarchy encouraged. I could almost love this writer. And even though there's a charming resolution, forced moral, and neatly wrapped-up plot, it wasn't as bad as I was prepared for. At the end, the kids all charge into the main sanctuary just as Charles is about to start reading Torah. He reads, absolutely nobody can hear him sing, I'm standing there fumbling in the doorway, and the episode denouements with me and Charles on the outside steps of the synagogue, sitting side by side, both our heads on our knees.

MR. GOLDBERG

I need a cigarette.

SHOSHANA

Dad, you don't smoke.

MR. GOLDBERG

It doesn't matter, it's Shabbos today. I couldn't light one, anyway.

SHOSHANA

Aww, Dad. (*She wraps her arm around* MR. GOLDBERG) You know that Mom doesn't think any less of you, right? And neither does anyone in the synagogue.

MR. GOLDBERG

Easy for you to say. All their kids are

running loose in the main service because of you.

SHOSHANA

Tell you what. You wanna pig out on some honey cakes?

MR. GOLDBERG

You mean the ones your mother baked for the congregation supper tonight?

SHOSHANA

If only we knew the hiding spot.

MR. GOLDBERG

Hey, didn't you hide them?!

SHOSHANA

Race you to the library—

MR. GOLDBERG *sits there for a minute, mouthing "Library??" as* SHOSHANA *runs inside the synagogue. After a second it occurs to him.* MR. GOLDBERG *dashes off in pursuit.*

I stayed up late that night, feeling the lines erode into my brain, slowly, one by one. I found that for every line Shoshana spoke, I had to memorize three more. I had to be ready for the ending of Charles's lines, the beginning of his next line, and anticipate the way that he would want me to say any given line of dialogue. I would absorb a whole page, turn to the next one, and feel all the old dialogue slipping out of my mind. My brain is malleable, easy to absorb information, but even easier to let it go.

I carried on till late that night; the rhythmic pattern of flipping pages and branding keystrokes of dialogue into my head became so methodical I thought I might fall asleep. My eyes dilated. The words all squished into identical black stains on white paper. I noticed the clock; it was past three a.m.

Suddenly, the world felt a lot lonelier. Outside my window, the jacaranda branches sighed in early morning winds. I tried to think of anyone I knew who would be awake now, in any time zone. I couldn't.

Except . . .

Oh. Yeah.

Before I went to bed, I made one last call. I dialed only seven numbers. It was a local call.

The phone rang several times before I heard a voice.

"Hold on, I have to hook up the audio input to the camera. The phone says to plug the blue cord into the X jack . . . oh, X means any jack, I think there's one right . . . here . . ." The line distorted to static and Moish's voice fuzzed out completely. When he came back, there was a weird surround-sound echo quality to his voice. "Hello, Moish Resnick, Celebrity at Large. Do we have your complete permission to record and reproduce any statements you make and disseminate them for theatrical purposes?"

"Damn, Moish, it's me!"

"Hava! Hey! I already have your permission secured. Tell me dirt."

"You're a freak."

"Uh, I think our viewing audience knows that already."

"G-d, Moish. Just talk to me, okay?"

"Sure, Hava, no problem. Just tell me what you need. What's going on?"

"Not much," I said. "Work. It's boring."

"Riiight. Listen, give me something to go on, okay? You're at the top of Hollywood. Something cool must have happened."

I considered. The static of recording devices crackled over the phone lines. I said: "Today at work, Charles said I was the New."

"The New?"

"Yeah, I didn't understand it, either. I said, you mean the Next Big Thing? He said no, that's passé as soon as it happens. He said it like that — *No, baby. You're the New.* What do you think that's all about?"

"Hollywood's changing, Hava," Moish said at length. "I know I'm not a part of it, but anyone can see it. Everything's commodifying. You can't just look hot to be a star anymore. You always have to be mysterious and evasive. Once the public has you labeled and pinned down, your career's got a shelf life. You're like the next phase of that, though. So different that no one can touch you. Unlabelable."

"Mmm. You think so?"

"I do. What are you doing tomorrow?"

"I dunno. Hanging in the school yard?"

"What?"

"Nothing. You want me to be in your movie?"

"Yes," Moish said, instantly awestruck. "Hell yes."

09

ALL THAT AND A BAG OF GLATT KOSHER CHIPS

After that crazy Monday, everything went up. Evie started treating me with a healthy measure of awe, giddiness, and fraternity. The *Variety* story had made her more envious than ever, trying to secure a position as close to my chalice as she could get. She started asking me to parties — not that she hadn't already dragged me along, but now she'd actually call my cell in advance. She'd ask my opinions. "What are you feeling like tonight, Hava — a movie premiere or dancing? Live bands or DJs? And, oh, what kind of eye candy would you prefer?"

Evie even, after much persuasion, agreed not to set me up with guys. I told her about my religious restrictions, that I couldn't date anyone who wasn't Jewish and I probably wouldn't date anyone non-Orthodox. Evie relaxed a great deal around me after that. Not only was she off the hook for finding me suitable (and nonthreatening) B-list dates, but she didn't have to worry about competition for her A-list romantic interests.

"I didn't think you'd go for industry guys, after all," she said gleefully.

Hearing my name out of random people's lips was a shock. Like the first time you hear a new version of an old song, you're just not accustomed to hearing *those* words in *that* voice. I passed by the writers' office while they were talking about "the Hava angle." They said it like it was a good thing. Jews asked me if the studio was treating me all right. Non-Jews asked me if being Orthodox in Hollywood was really that hard.

With a sparkle in my eye, I replied: "Not if you know how to play the game."

Tuesday morning I received flowers from a popular teen movie star who'd seen my cover. Evie told me he was a player; he'd tried to make out with her on the trailers of her old soap opera during the week that he had a cameo appearance. I didn't care. It wasn't like he could get with me. But I was still flattered.

Filming continued under a brisk schedule. We were given the impossible task of filming the first half season, thirteen weeks, in just under eight weeks' time. Most TV casts filmed an episode in a week. And most shows also didn't break for Sabbath.

We started to have interviews every day over lunch. Paula talked with *Glamour*, *Reader's Digest*, and *Harper's Bazaar*. Charles did *U.S. News* and *Playboy*. Evie got interviewed by a few of the teen-beat magazines. My big magazine interview for the day was the *Jewish Forward*. "Don't worry, Hava," Charles told me, "any day now you'll start to despise interviews. Reporters are like piles of shit. Any way you poke them, you'll make an impression. You'll learn to say yes to every question just to finish faster." The interviewer across the table coughed. Howard shot Charles a reproachful glare.

There was one saving grace to that day. Everyone sat down for lunch and shmoozed with their respective interviewers. The smell of greasy French fries and sweet ketchup lingered in the air. I jammed myself into a plastic chair and looked venomous.

One of the PAs approached me. He carried a steaming tin-foil package. I averted my eyes politely. I didn't want to get that rush of salivation and then force it down. He lay the package before me.

"Is that —" I choked.

"Check the label," the PA grinned.

Sure enough, the seal said UNION OF ORTHODOX RABBIS — CERTIFIED KOSHER DAIRY.

I ripped it open and dug in. For the next fifteen minutes, the *Forward* interviewer could barely get a word out of me.

A reporter from *Rolling Stone* followed us each around for a day. On my shift, he asked Jewish questions about everything I did. "Do you have a chauffeur-driven limousine because of Orthodox Jewish prohibitions?" he asked.

"Yeah," I said. "Jewish Law says you're not allowed to drive without a license."

I heard that Jamie and Corey, on the day of their interview, spoke only in a native Yucatan dialect of Spanish. Jamie or Corey — the girl — told me they'd picked it up from a *National Geographic* special that her father hosted. She spoke it for me. I said it sounded like she was making up noises. "Nooo," she denied. She rolled her eyes in that playful, sisterly way that meant yes. Between actors, words were such a small part of our conversations.

Take David Lee Mitchell, for instance. Under that $500

haircut, there was a face that I trusted like gravity. I don't think I had a crush on him. But when I talked to him, he was so understanding and enthusiastic and interested, I was always like *why not?* Whenever there was a stage direction that I didn't understand, I'd turn to David Lee. I wouldn't ask him, because asking would be too simple. I'd just look at him and he'd fix me with one of those go-get-'em-girl smiles. He didn't tell me how to recite a line *complacently* or *eagerly* or *whiny*, the way the scripts said. He just acted confident that I wouldn't mess up.

And usually, that was all I needed.

"Have you thought about David Lee?" I asked Evie later, in the wardrobe department. I draped a Betsey Johnson sundress over my clothes and stared in the mirror.

We were on a mid-afternoon break. Rehearsal was a bitch, everything on a sped-up schedule, and everyone too jumpy to act. Charles and Evie both got saddled with a shitload of Yiddish words in this week's script, and neither could get the hang of the guttural *ch* sound. Finally the director got exasperated, threw his hands in the air, and told everybody to come back in an hour.

Now Evie gave me that look of hers. "Next, please."

"Next dress or next guy?"

"He's my *brother*, Hava."

"Yeah, if you can't tell the difference between TV and reality."

"Are you kidding? I'll get in so much shit. The Producers, whoever the hell they are, will freak. Nobody wants to watch siblings on TV and imagine us making out."

I tried out the mental image.

I could understand that.

* * *

I kept reading the script, and I kept pretending that the stage directions didn't count. *SHOSHANA cries* and *Close-up on HINDEL* and *YOSHIE eats bag of chips.* All those lines that nobody says, the ones that are supposed to be read between the lines.

My eyes kept flying back to the same stage direction. It was written in black and white and it still hadn't gone away.

SHOSHANA wraps her arm around MR. GOLDBERG.

Between readings, I told the director that I wasn't supposed to touch other men. Predictably, he went apeshit. "We got you kosher food, didn't we?"

"That was a totally different rule. I'm not supposed to touch men who aren't my family."

"He's your *father,* Hava."

I could tell this wasn't going anywhere.

I went into Charles's dressing room with my coat and knapsack. Work for the day was done. I was on my way to Fairfax High. Charles was leafing through the script for the next episode, which we'd already been given to start memorizing. Spectacles were poised on the edge of his nose. As he read, absorbing the words, his chin wrinkled like a sponge. I wrung my hands behind my back. I felt so weird even talking about this.

"Charles," I said, "can we talk about the script?"

"We can talk about anything."

He tossed the script onto his dresser. He swiveled his chair around and gestured at the other chair, which I slid into.

"Shoot."

"They want me to hug you."

"In general?"

"Page thirty-four, about halfway down."

"This is in-character hugging?"

"It happens after I let the kids run into the main sanctuary and you're faking the Torah singing and they yell so loud that nobody hears you. You get away with it, then we go outside and have a tempestuous bonding moment."

"I'm remembering the bonding moment. And we hug?"

"So say the writers. But still. I dunno."

"It's that no-touching rule, isn't it?"

"We call it *shomer negiah*. Not like you need to know."

"I appreciate your not wanting to burden me with Jewish terms, Hava, but I do need to know. If we're going to act together. And if you want me to be your friend."

When Charles said *friend,* it had never sounded more true. I wondered how he found a place for himself in Hollywood, this land of changing roles as fast as clothes. He used words like he was the first person to think of using them in a sentence together.

I remembered I was supposed to be miserable. I sunk my chin into my fists.

"So I talked to the Producers — or the liaisons for the Producers, anyway — and they don't get it at *all* and I don't know how to make them realize it's my religion."

"Maybe, instead, you should make them realize it's *you.*"

"What do you mean?"

"Some actors won't do nude scenes. It's a matter of preference. They just let their agents know. When they audition for movies, they just don't take roles that require nudity. The real question is, are you worried about touching someone or are you worried about the Orthodox community *seeing* you touch someone?"

I bit my lip.

There are certain things we do that we do for G-d, and certain things that we do for ourselves. Following the laws, like keeping kosher, I did for G-d. But I wouldn't eat salad in a nonkosher restaurant — even though the salad could totally be kosher — because of the community. We just didn't do those things. It was one part of the secular world that was sketchy ground. So we sidestepped it, ignored the whole existence of a question by simply saying *no*.

Charles took off his reading glasses.

"Whatever the case, it's still okay. You still have the right not to do it." He crouched forward, like he was telling me a secret. "That's the first rule of dealing with execs — you're the one who calls the shots. *They* asked *you* to act. Not the other way around."

"So I just say the word and no more touchery?"

"Say the word."

I felt good. I jumped up, this smile that I would never let my Fairfax punk friends see spreading across my face. Charles looked relieved, too. I was so glad, like we were back to being that *friends* word that his mouth made so appealing.

"Oh, Charles," I said. "G-d, that's so great! That's so — that's so big of you. I could just about hug you."

He raised his eyebrows.

"You know," I said. "If I did that kind of thing."

We both laughed.

Charles's eyes were hazel, like chai tea, wide and willowy. They were little-boy eyes. They were funny and charming and amiable, always like he'd just told a joke or shared a secret. They made him look innocent.

I felt so relaxed right now, like I could say anything.

So I asked, "What's up with you and Paula?"

"How do you mean?" Charles waited a beat, long enough for me to think of an answer but too quick for me to reply. "I know what you mean, and I know why you're asking, Hava. It's okay. I really don't mind saying. It's true, Paula and I did have a relationship once. It isn't the type of thing I normally do — hell, I'll just say it outright, I'd never done that sort of thing before. We enjoyed each other's company socially, and she wanted to take it to the next level. I was flattered. I won't tell you the sentiment didn't go both ways. We got along exceedingly well, Hava. I suppose it wasn't my fault. Things were going so well and . . . eventually I discovered that I wasn't the only person she had this arrangement with."

"And when you were fighting . . ." I don't know why, when someone confesses to me, the first thing I want is more gossip. If one day nobody ever trusts me again, I'll understand. I'm asking for it. I always want more.

"She wanted to continue the terms of our arrangement."

I couldn't stop from looking disgusted. I guess I was a prude, but I still felt horrible.

Charles was like a wounded puppy. I wanted to bring him into my house, show him what a kickass seventeen-year-old boy he'd make. My friends would be all over him. Shira and Meira would agree that he was a stud and giggle behind their palms. Fruma would plead with her father to find out about Charles's family background. Moish would look perturbed that there was someone who could possibly be cooler than he was.

Oh. Moish.

His imagined presence kicked me back to reality. I wondered what would happen if Charles and Moish were to meet.

"I'm sorry," Charles said, rising. "You don't need to know all this. I'm burdening you with torrid details that you've probably never wanted to hear."

"Hey," I said, "I told you, you can tell me anything. I meant it."

"I know. And I'm glad. I guess I just wanted you to know why I've been feeling so inclined to think the worst of people lately, Hava."

I knew what Charles was talking about. I really *knew* it. I think this was the first time — not counting Moish, who was a drug all his own — that anyone in Los Angeles was on the same page as me. Yossi was amazing and the Fairfax kids were entertaining. But when Charles talked, everything made sense.

"Hell, that's okay," I told him. "If I'm not thinking the worst of people, I start wondering what's wrong with *me*."

Moish's film project was in full swing, too. He would walk up to slinky blondes and ask them about obscure *Star Wars* characters like Boba Fett and Greedo. He would talk with middle-aged businessmen about foreign movies. Moish's universe had always been plagued with an unceasing stream of obscure references, understandable only to Moish himself, that everyone else in school always scoffed at.

These people with no knowledge of Moish, though, ate it up like dinner after Yom Kippur. Blondes giggled when he talked about Greedo's difficulty communicating through a reptilian cone of a mouth. Businessmen asked intelligent, thought-provoking questions about the metaphors in Czech surrealist fairy tales. Nobody seemed to mind that they were on-camera. If anything, it enhanced Moish's appeal. Twice in one week, he got asked out by aspiring actresses. (Moish said no to both; one wasn't Jewish and one was Reform. Later he told me, "How am I supposed to date them? They'd never put up with Shabbos, and they didn't even realize that Greedo's mouth was V-shaped, not cone-shaped.")

Sometimes, to get Moish's face on-screen, he handed me the camera and I filmed for him. We did a segment together called "Moish in Reflexivity" (his title) and it used both video cameras at once. After meeting someone, Moish would say good-bye and continue wandering around the city. Then, on the other half of a split screen, I interviewed the person that Moish had just left, asking what they thought of Moish, what was their reaction to his all-black wardrobe and his being Orthodox, and did they think that Moish would really show up at that company barbeque or movie premiere or bar that he or she had invited Moish to. Inevitably, people would invite Moish on a follow-up date to get more screen time.

One night, Moish and I prowled the streets around my house in North Hollywood, where the normal people walk. We plotted our course with a giant foldout map of Los Angeles as big as the floor of Moish's bedroom, looking for a ripe destination. There were eighty-eight incorporated cities in the county of Los Angeles. We could go to any of them. The night felt that big.

"Hava, this is ridiculous," Moish said. "None of these names means anything, and every street looks the same when they're nothing but little pink lines. Where do we know?"

"My neighborhood and your neighborhood and Studio

City," I said. "Oh, and that street with all the kosher restaurants."

"Fairfax?" Moish said. "That's out. We've already done the Jewish crowd. I think we need to include more movie stars."

"Movie stars?" I repeated. The word summoned up daunting images in my head of Evie and her tragic drug-and-luster sparkly clubs. I made a face.

"Movie stars. But *quiet* movie stars. Not the ones at discos. The ones out drinking at normal places, spending a normal night being normal people. You know. Like reality television."

I didn't believe him. I never believed Moish. But I admired how unflappable he was. I quelled my natural instinct to argue with him. I folded my arms at my chest, grinned sportingly, and watched him go at it.

Moish was prone to make a fool of himself, but there was something charmingly old-school about it. Jimmy Stewart had his naïveté and Dick Van Dyke had that ottoman he was always tripping over. Moish didn't trip over anything but himself, but he was so good at it. There was a full moon when we went outside my room, and the swimming pool in the apartment complex glowed green. It smelled like fireflies and cinnamon.

We walked down a random residential street, talking to an actor we both recognized, who I'd seen in movies since I was born. He wore a V-neck sweater and comfortable, worn-in shoes, hands folded on his knees, a smile we could trust. Moish began asking him questions in his usual polite but intrusive way, prodding gently and amiably. They settled into an actual conversation, fast-paced back-and-forth dialogue like an independent movie. This man looked into Moish's eyes and said, "Yeah, of course I'm afraid that some idiot's going to explode a nuclear bomb and we're all going to die. But haven't we always been afraid of that?"

Moish's eyes were sober. His hands rubbed against the fabric of his pants, nervous but comfortable, playing the conversation like a game. He took a breath, let it out, and thought before he spoke. Moish replied, "I think I'm just beginning to realize that I'm not going to live forever." And the famous actor nodded. He understood.

They talked for what seemed like hours. The man ignored my video camera from the beginning, as though every teenage girl walking down the street had one perched on her shoulder. He'd lived enough of his life in front of video cameras. I guess, one day, your eyes just screen them out, the way New Yorkers do to homeless people.

But I realized, watching them go back and forth, toying with ideas like Silly Putty, stretching them and playing with them and twisting them into different malleable forms, that he wasn't. My left eye was closed. My right eye saw life through the camera, a one-inch square of glowing moonlight and flora surrounded by black. He was looking at the camera, playing to it without looking into it, yet at the same time, as I watched him, I could feel him watching me back, like this was all a performance aimed directly at me. I shivered. It was everything I was supposed to know how to do with my acting skills, and nothing that I could actually wrap my fingers around and touch. "I feel like every second counts," Moish said, his voice getting that poetry lilt.

Their conversation felt like marble and wisteria leaves, so smooth and sapless, like it could hang there forever. I felt like a voyeur, sitting there and listening. Maybe this was my redemption for pitching that awful sitcom shit into people's brains: I was being forced to witness the rest of life as a television show in which I was the girl sidekick, only speaking in extreme conditions or to crack a joke. Tonight, everything felt perfect. No jokes needed cracking. We set a mission for ourselves, and we'd accomplished it. At one point, they sat on a random stoop and the elderly couple who lived in the house came to the door, curious. We all looked toward them, shooting broad smiles, and waved gingerly. Startled and probably half asleep, the old couple waved back naïvely.

I felt like I should want to be in their conversation, but I didn't. The same way that I felt neutral about appearing as a watered-down version of an Orthodox girl in order to have my own apartment and my own Los Angeles dream life, I was enjoying witnessing the conversation as a spectator. I could close my eyes and see both points of view, each long-winded story coming to life in my head. Neither Moish nor this man were people I could identify with, the way I recognized myself when Charles spoke. But I could hear their voices. Like characters.

Maybe this is how people learn how to act.

I snapped into reality, the two of them standing up, adjusting their trousers.

"Let's walk a little farther, shall we?"

"I'd like that," said Moish amiably. I zoomed in quick for a close-up of their quietly meditative faces in one shared frame before we turned down the street.

Somewhere, a dog barked. Somewhere music played, and I could hear the muted sounds of people dancing. I listened as we walked. It was the new record by a band I liked a lot. I wondered who I could copy it from, and then I realized, I can afford to buy it. In another few weeks, after the show wrapped, I could probably afford to buy an entire music store.

We crossed a bridge on a deserted boulevard, the freeway below our feet. The opalescent lights of a million cars flashed and sped by. Moish and our new friend talked about Moish's film. Moish was saying that the credit roll at the end would probably take an estimated three hours to scroll, even if he didn't waste half the column space by throwing a bunch of dots and the eponymous words

. . . . as HIMSELF

after everyone's names. "Art is life," Moish was saying, "and in school we were talking about Pop Art, and how Andy Warhol painted regular everyday objects as art. I thought how cool it would be to just build frames with nothing inside, so people would have to look through them to see art. That was how I thought of doing this. But I knew I wanted to do it in Hollywood. Everything's more interesting in Hollywood."

"Yes. Yes, I can see that," said the man who we both recognized from all the famous movies. "That's why I'm afraid I'm going to have to ask you to destroy that tape."

The cars below died down. He was whispering. We could hear every word.

Moish laughed nervously, like his laugh was coming from his lips instead of his throat. "But you know I can't," he said. "Every moment needs to be documented. Even switching rolls of film. This is the story of my life."

The man's voice was still friendly and even. I watched his hand curl into a fist at his side.

"Moish," he said. "It's been a good conversation, hasn't it? I'd hate for it to end this way. I'd hate for you to be on my bad side."

"We — we talked about the world," Moish stammered.

"And it was very interesting. But conversations end, Moish. I'd like my privacy back." He extended a hand. It was strong and calloused and huge.

The cars below sped up. They cut the air with a sound like low whistling. I felt like there was no ground beneath us, like the ground could evaporate and we would simply fall.

"Here — here," Moish stammered. "Here it is."

A sudden slap cut the silence. The man's hand connected with Moish's, with the hand that held the videotape. It skidded hard across the sidewalk.

"No," Moish said. "No. Please, Hashem, no."

The man removed a Zippo lighter the size of his fist. I think he took it from his pocket, but all of a sudden, it was in his hand. He unscrewed the top, shook a generous amount of lighter fluid onto the videotape, then screwed the lighter back together and lit the cassette on fire.

Moish yelped. The actor threw the cassette onto the freeway below us. We watched it shrink and shrink until it hit the ground and its tiny shell shattered. The plastic pieces melted, bubbling as they burned. The air smelled like sulfur and stink bombs and frogs burning. It was orange and yellow and purple, flames licking the concrete sidewalk and the blue-green rose bushes and the milky black night.

10

SOMETHING ELSE, ANYTHING ELSE

MOISH *(close-up, wide angle, eyes and nose only)*: I would just like to apologize to viewers. I mean — I really wanted to make this an uninterrupted account of my whole summer . . . Oh my G-d . . . Oh my G-d. Hava, you talk. I just . . . I can't. I don't know what to say.

(MOISH *walks away from the lens, crawling into a corner of the room. Rolls up into a ball. Faces corner. Shivers.)*

HAVA: *(long pause)* Geez. Moish. What the fuck just happened?

MOISH *(head buried in arms and legs. Muffled)*: Please! Just talk!

HAVA: I don't know what to say. I don't know what to say.

MOISH: *Talk!*

HAVA: I don't know!

MOISH: Dead air is the worst. We can't have dead air —

(HAVA storms off camera. Door slams.)

(MOISH shudders in corner)

MOISH *(muffled)*: I'm sorry. I'm sorry you have to hear this dead air. I don't know if you're there. I don't even know if anyone's still in the theater. . . . I could be talking to a dead audience, row after row of empty seats. But I know there's one person watching. There's gotta be . . . that guy tonight . . . he can afford to turn off the camera. He's sick of being watched. But at least there's people watching. At least he knows he's loved. You can't turn off the rest of the world if the rest of the world doesn't know you *exist* . . . and I need you to know I exist. I'm making this movie, I'm writing a letter to you. You know who you are. Because I'm sick of being alone and I need to know you're out there. . . . You know what my biggest fear is? That the only person watching this movie is my grandkids. That I'll grow up to be an investment banker or a lawyer or a rabbi, and on my graduation day I'll take all these tapes and throw them into a box and bury it in our storage closet. I always want to dream. And if you're looking through your grandfather's old shit and you happen to stumble on this . . . and I never got to make a film . . . just know that I wasn't always like that. *(pause)* I used to dream. *(silence)*

HAVA *(offscreen)*: Moish?

MOISH: Yeah?

HAVA: Are you done?

MOISH: I thought you were leaving.

HAVA: Yeah, well, we're at my house.

MOISH: Oh, yeah.

HAVA: You can stay here if you need.

The next morning, I left Moish asleep on my sofa, the video camera pointed at him, balanced on the empty bookcase.

At lunch, I nibbled at my kosher meal (vegetable lasagna, second time this week) and dashed into the writers' offices, where there was a computer. I wrote up a hurried account of the past evening's activities in my online journal.

As I was about to log off, I saw a remark posted to my last entry, from Triangulary, which was Ian's screen name. I clicked and read. It was brief.

> Sorry Life Sux Hava. I Love You. Clear Off That Sofa, I'll Be There In A Jiff. ((now wait five months before you read the next part: Happy Early Birthday, Baby.))

If I hadn't had anything to worry about before, now would be the time to start.

When I got home from work, Moish was gone, a note on the kitchen table that said *Out Wandering City. Am Resilient as F-ck.*

That part was crossed out. Underneath was scribbled *Am Upstairs.*

Another note, which had blown atop Moish's jacket and camera bag, asked what my plans were for Shabbos.

"Well, what do you think?"

Moish walked in, a half-empty glass of cranberry juice in one hand, video camera in the other. His face appeared right above the note in my hand. He looked fresher, like he'd showered not too long ago, his hair waterily pressed down. He was wearing a BIKINI KILLER T-shirt and my size 40 rave pants. He spoke airily, like he'd just asked out loud what I was doing for Shabbos.

"I think this week really *is* gonna be Friday night with the fam," I said apologetically. "My mom told me off last night. She said she doesn't get to see me for two months, the least I can do is give myself over to her sister-in-law for inspection and evaluation."

"Yawn," said Moish.

"Yeah. It bites. But, you know, they still have control of my paychecks." Which was not entirely true. I mean, the control of my money part was, if you didn't count the big-but-not-big-enough allowance I received each week. My parents were insistent about seeing my family, but I welcomed it, partially because it would be a break from Moish. I was overdue for some Hava time.

"I, uh, I borrowed some of your clothes."

I grinned. My Bikini Killer shirt was a baby tee. It looked good on Moish's slight frame, especially the rainbow letters over his chest. It made his body look less droopy and shapeless, and the non-black coloration brightened his skin almost to the point of humanity. I didn't know what to say about his *tzitzis*, the ritual fringes that stuck out far beyond fashionable length, to the point where the cloth flapped over his belly button in a half-assed manner that couldn't decide whether to hide his inconspicuous outie or bare it for the world to see.

Moish's camera was going again, perched on his shoulder like a pirate's loyal parrot. It was back to normal position, its traditional nesting ground since I first saw him film in L.A. Moish had been sitting on the roof of my apartment building. He was filming pieces of the Los Angeles skyline. He said he wanted to fill in the empty spaces. He said he needed to stop being so self-involved, to show viewers his world as much as he showed himself. Shrouded in my secondhand hipster clothes, it didn't seem like Moish's expansion could be a bad thing.

"What's up with these pants?" he asked. "Not to get all ultra-Orthodox on you. But are they yours?"

Most Modern Orthodox women wore pants. I think Fruma and I were the only two girls in our class who never wore pants. It wasn't a modesty issue. I don't even know why I didn't. Just so I could be a little more conservative. If I was going to wear ridiculous clothes and freak everyone out, the one thing they couldn't call me on was wearing pants. I know it wasn't supposed to make me feel more religious than everybody else, but it did. *Lehavdil.* Like a separation.

I shrugged. "I guess, I'm keeping my options open," I said. "I could always change my mind. And besides, even hardcore Hasidic girls would have to admit, those rave pants are fucking huge. In so many words, I mean."

Moish held up his leg. The hemline of the pants swayed back and forth against the ground. They were far, far baggier than any dress.

"In so many words," Moish repeated, grinning.

Friday at work, David Lee and I planted ourselves on the bed, arranged pillows and papers as though we were studying, and he held the big *Torah Tikkun* book out to read like a poetry portfolio. Lighting was still getting the set ready, and we had a few minutes to fuck around.

"You've got the book upside down," I pointed out. I liked being the authoritative one on the set.

"It's for the blooper reel," David Lee insisted.

"*If* we ever get the episode recorded," the director of photography called snottily. He blew his whistle like a parakeet in heat. "*Miss* Aaronson. *Mis*ter Mitchell. If you please?"

David Lee bit his bottom lip. We shot each other an exasperated glance. It felt nice, super nice, to share the same deadpan look. And especially having our names called out in the same breath. Like I'd finally found someone to make trouble with.

By mid-afternoon, we'd shot most of the script, and the studio audience was getting antsy. The director called it a wrap but told us privately that he wanted to shoot some more scenes again. I checked the backstage clock.

We had plenty of time before sunset.

I carried Baby Goldberg to lunch, where one of his personal handlers clipped him from my hands. As soon as the baby left me behind, he stopped screaming. Evie had already claimed the seat next to Charles, so I slid onto the other end of the cast table, with Jamie and Corey on one side and Paula on my other.

"Are you gonna fuck up the rest of today's rehearsal, too?" Corey or Jamie asked.

They both laughed amiably.

"We both hope so," the other one added eagerly. "This week's been boring as shit. We need some crazy-ass Hava action."

"What kind of words have you been teaching these kids?" Paula said, more spiteful than shocked. I was shocked, too. These felt like the first unscripted words she'd said to me. They caught me completely off guard. I guess I'd kind of expected something less like my mother.

"As *if*, Paula," I said. "These kids get plenty of bad influence without me. My parents complain about movies tamer than the ones the Wonder Twins have acted in." I rolled my eyes.

I turned to Jamie and Corey, waving a finger in their direction like I thought I was supposed to. "And don't say 'fuck.' There's no bad words, just bad people to use them in front of."

Paula stiffened.

Corey and Jamie's eyes lit up, unsure whether or not I'd just insulted Paula in front of them.

"Just be careful with your newfound stardom, Hava," Paula said, gathering up her tray. "You might want to stay at the kiddie table until you know how to swim." And she was gone, finishing her lunch in the privacy of her dressing room.

Charles watched from the far end of the room. He nodded approvingly. I smiled back.

I sat out on the stoop with Charles. He wore a suit coat, a blue-and-red-striped tie. I traced the pleats of my dress with a finger and hugged my legs closer to my torso.

Charles's brow was furrowed. He stared straight ahead instead of looking at me. Cars whizzed by in the foreground. His fingers danced nervously between each other.

"I need a cigarette," Charles said.

"You don't smoke," I told him.

"It doesn't matter. It's Rosh Hashana. I couldn't light one, anyway."

"Aww, Dad," I said. I gripped my bared knee with one tender hand and leaned close. I blinked my eyes big, tender, smiling like I loved him more than anything. I made indirect eye contact with the camera lens. I looked deep into Charles's eyes and I looked past him, straight into the camera, at the viewer, giving every visual cue of hugging without the actual touch. My cheeks swelled, big and smooth and sad. My eyes glowed with longing and blessing and love. I pursed my lips like I was about to give away my last kiss. I wanted to tell Charles everything. I wanted to give him all the hope I had.

"You know Mom doesn't think any less of you, right? And neither does the rest of the congregation." I paused. I counted to three in my head, just the way the director told me in rehearsals. "Heck, half the Jews in there are too deaf to hear you."

"Easy for you to say, Shoshana. You just set your entire class loose in the main service."

"That's okay, Daddy. You still love me."

Laughter.

Fade out.

Cut.

Roll credits.

We were done. It was so early. Especially after last week, everyone felt a little guilty leaving so early. Evie and Charles had one last cigarette outside, and I felt a pang of — what, jealousy? — so I went to join them.

"Hava, you *do* realize that you're a nonsmoker, don't you?" Evie took a long, cool hit off her cigarette.

"I have better ways to kill myself," I retorted. "Hanging with you guys just boosts my ego."

I shot Charles a knowing glance.

"Well, don't drown yourself before Saturday night," Evie said. "You've got plans with me, and finding a replacement this late is *so* passé." To Charles, she added, "Hava only hooks up with members of the tribe. She's such a drag at parties. I almost feel guilty bringing her."

"What's the alternative?" Charles quipped. "Let her run rampant alone? You're safer locking her up at home."

"Now there's an idea." Evie's eyes glinted sardonically.

"Don't you dare," I said. "I might not kiss boys, but nothing in Jewish Law says I can't get as smashed as the next girl."

"Too bad for the boys," murmured Charles.

"Too bad for *Hava*," remarked Evie. She finished the cigarette with an impossibly long inhalation, eyes half closed, eyelashes batting hard and heavy at Charles.

I had to go. If I didn't, I'd never stop playing this game.

All the way to my aunt's house, I kept telling myself, it's a game, it's a game.

I climbed into my limousine. "Is there a long way you can take? Something scenic and racy and overdrive-ish?" I said.

Today of all days, the driver picked up something on my personality, a whiff of danger that smelled like expensive rum. "I can take any way you want," he said, touching the brim of his cap with a salute that was only half mocking.

"Take it," I said.

We zoomed out the gate. The driver coughed up the overdrive. I felt the backseat hum. "Nice," I said, lying my face against the window. We turned onto the freeway. Trees flew past. Cars soared miraculously behind us. The limo picked up speed and when we hit the foothills all the way down Beverly Boulevard, the car nearly soared over the humps into open air.

Friday afternoons are supposed to feel this way. Freer than anything, about to burst into song and rock out. That song was

Shabbos, and when I was feeling good about being religious, Shabbos was the best part of my week. You throw away your keys and your money and you just *fly*.

When I thought about my cousins' house, my stomach dropped. Horribly skeptical glances at my clothes, the unceasing stream of why-do-you-do-this and why-do-you-look-like-this questions. It didn't feel like I was about to start my holiday. It felt like my holiday was about to end.

My family was disastrous. This neighborhood was disastrous. It reminded me of the Jewish ghetto in New York, only without all the cool-looking homeless people and the Puerto Rican markets. Pico Robertson was dreary, middle-class, and *suburban*. I felt like I was being punished for something I didn't do.

As we drove along Pico Boulevard and turned onto the street, I revamped my opinion. There were things I liked about Shabbos here. The Jews in Pico Robertson had their own little houses, which felt more natural than the econo-size apartment buildings at home — like they were living in the world and not stacked on top of it. I loved the Farsi grocery stores and the abundance of tanned, olive-skinned, and thick-haired Sephardic boys on the street, who made being Jewish a culture, not just a word.

I hopped out at the corner and ran to my cousins' house. The entire block smelled like *chollint* and chicken and sweet apple kugels. Everybody watched, disapproving but riveted, as I sprinted across front yards, a little destructive but relishing the freedom of being outdoors in daylight.

I disappeared into my cousins' house, where the women clustered in the kitchen, the stove already in overdrive.

* * *

Evie's limo pulled up to the house at 8:42, the exact end of sunset. I was waiting at the door.

"How was Shabbos?" she asked. Evie fiddled with the stereo as I hopped in. The sky turned a shade of opalescent, glowing yellow reserved for Saturday nights. I slammed the door shut and tinted windows dimmed the light to purple shadows. The fluorescent streetlights of Pico Boulevard went from intense to muted as the car swallowed up the outside world.

"Sucky," I said. "Imagine going to dinner with your family, and then not being able to leave for the next twenty-four hours."

"At least your parents weren't there," Evie said.

"Yeah." I stared out the window, thinking of where my parents were. Probably asleep by now.

"I had to go to this awards show. The Teen Independent Spirit Awards, which are, like, *the* most self-obsessed awards out there. All the TV cameras were from local affiliates — I mean, *local*!"

"Mmm," I replied distantly. Sometimes when Evie talked, I had to zone out or I'd start caring for real. "So, anyway, what's on the agenda for tonight?"

In a snap, Evie was all business. She looked displaced for a second, startled to find herself talking — *complaining* — about something that wasn't perfect.

"Tonight?" Evie combed a stray lock of hair from her eyes. "Oh, I thought we'd do the beach."

For a few weeks in junior high, it was lame to be *shomer negiah*. The first rush of hormones catapulted us into this whole new life, receiving new bodies and wanting to try them out. I was always one step behind everybody else, tripping over myself, the girl at sleepover parties who always brought up *shomer negiah.* I told everyone it was *osser* to touch boys, and so I never would. One night it reached the boiling point, all the other girls laughing at me like a bad dream, they started singing, *I get so* shomer, *baby, I get so* shomer *I could crrry . . .*

I *did* cry that night, hysterically, so isolated and stifled in that room. I hid with my sleeping bag over my head till everyone dropped off and fell asleep. Then I walked out on the back porch and fell asleep in a chaise lounge. I *knew* the other girls were feeling the same things I was. I didn't understand why they didn't talk to me, too. I was frustrated, thinking we could figure the world out together, wondering why nobody would.

Shortly after that — a few months, at most — the tide switched. We developed a sense of responsibility for observing the laws, and the promiscuous girls who'd taken their sexuality for a spin quietly slipped that sexuality off the table and into their back pockets, hiding it from the world. All of a sudden, they stopped being rebellious, and being Orthodox was cool again. Even then, some girls would still fool around with their boyfriends. We were a little awed. Mostly, though, we were grossed out.

That Saturday night, I felt so lonely. I wasn't sure how much of it was horniness, and how much was needing someone to understand and feel lonely, too, wanting that person to need me and ask me and beg for me.

Of course, Evie had programmed the night's agenda in advance. One of the teen stars on her old soap opera, *Inhibitions,* was having a birthday party. On the ride over, Evie gushed. His name was Russell Jake Hanover. During their time on the show, Evie had a monster crush on him. Only, he was out as gay. Since Evie's departure from the show nine months ago — her character, Adela Anna Mae, was sent to boarding school after sleeping with her stepmother's ex-boyfriend — bisexuality had become acceptable in Hollywood, and Russell Jake Hanover was embracing it fully. ("If it's a trend," I asked, "why aren't you part of it?" Evie shook her head exasperatedly and said, "Hava, I've *always* been bisexual," and I couldn't tell whether she was lying or not.)

"So are you excited?" I asked Evie. We climbed out of the limo in the parking lot, removing our sandals. I wore a three-quarter-length silky skirt that let the wind breeze through, a Thomas Pink man's paisley dress shirt that I got at a thrift store near my house, and a denim jacket. Evie had on a see-through polystyrene miniskirt and shirt with a bikini underneath. She looked like a person from the twenty-second century, if you count the future predictions in men's magazines.

Evie rolled her eyes again. I don't think she ever got excited.

When we arrived, the beach was already crawling. The party was by Santa Monica Pier, the carousel high in the air, lighting up the night sky as humanity's last foothold before the coast faded into the blackness of the Pacific Ocean. Every few minutes, a lost balloon soared into the air. Teenagers kicked up sand, running past us, flocking to cars to grab drinks, to find a forgotten stash of pot, or to hide and make out. Their faces were blurs of familiarity from Evie's magazines and other circuit parties. Everyone seemed as beautiful and doomed as the characters they played. I dug my hands into the pockets of my jacket and breathed the salty brine air. A foreign-looking guy with wavy, manicured hair was running the other way. He slammed into my shoulder. He didn't apologize. He didn't turn back.

Evie glanced over her shoulder.

"Fuck him," she said. "He's *so* not even a seven. You're an eight and a half, easy. Come on. Let's go."

Her skirt shimmered and blurred as she walked to a cooler propped up in the sand, removed a bottle of beer, and cracked it open with a nail. She gulped it down easily, like Coke, and vanished into the crowd.

I knew she expected me to follow her.

I stood before the throng of teenagers. Every girl here shared the same age, dress size, and personality type. If you believed in Nielsen ratings, this beach held most of the top 100 most sexually attractive teenagers in the United States.

I found Evie. She was laughing hysterically in a circle of other kids. They listened to a smart, evil-looking guy with pointed eyebrows. He was telling a story about some acting job. His face looked familiar. I watched him hard, trying to place him. It hit me in a flash. One of his current roles was in a very dark, very moody drama aimed at teens, but more intelligent and thoughtful than most teen shows.

He played a teenage vampire.

Not like I ever watched any of those shows. I mean, I did sometimes. I might have seen it at friends' houses, in the background. Meira had a crush on the guy who played the bad-boy glam-rock Egyptian mummy. He was probably somewhere around the party.

On the show, the vampire — this guy — was sensitive, brooding, withdrawn. The first time I'd seen the show (at

Meira's house, it was playing in the background, and then we all glanced at the TV at the same time, and eventually we got drawn in and we watched the climax and the conclusion) he was on-screen. He was sitting with his victim, blood already dripping from her neck, but they'd started having a conversation. He talked about how nobody understood him. I remember his character talking about vampires the way I talked about Jews. "Just because you look one way doesn't mean you have to act that way," he had said.

I imagined that capes and fangs were a lot like long skirts and yarmulkes.

It was like everyone here knew the code. Or maybe they'd all just grown up better than I did. I felt a connection to this guy, the sensitive vampire who I'd seen monologging once. It was all I could do not to run up to him and start bonding. We had a history together. He just didn't know it.

I listened to the story. I laughed when everybody laughed. I cast appropriately passive expressions during the lulls. Loud trance music played from a speaker system somewhere. The tide rolled against the sand. Other people interrupted, but this dude was resilient, he kept telling the story. It was okay. People still listened.

I don't know why it took me so long to realize his story was about the gay character on the vampire show. I remember being turned off by the way he said "like" so much and cackled at his own jokes. Nobody should ever laugh at their own jokes. For a second I thought he was Russell Jake Hanover but then somebody called him Mike.

"And shit, man, dude always calls me Michael," he said. "Michael, can you *helllp* me *lifffft* this *draw*bridge?" His gay accent sounded about as authentic as a pet rock. He was pathetic. Evie and the teen stars set loose another burst of laughing. I felt pathetic giving him an audience.

I turned to walk away. I didn't stop till I was ankle-deep in ocean. The party wasn't crowded, and the beach was huge and dimly lit. Stars formed a giant bubble over us, stretched out so far it felt like being inside a snow globe. The stars were so close to the horizon, the way they only are on camping trips. It was this weird autonomy, boy-band stars and WB icons, walking around like we were invisible.

Back on the beach, I walked through another big circle of conversation (this one, about *Cosmo*'s latest fashion flaws page) and thought about splitting. I wanted to. I didn't know how successful I'd be at finding a ride, and hailing a cab near a beach late at night was impossible.

So when this guy started talking to me, I played nice and answered.

His name was Jake. I wanted to ask, "Are you *that* Jake?" but there was no reason. He flaunted his control of the party. Like most of the boys there, he wore khaki shorts with no shirt. His build was skinny, but athletic. He looked strong, but not threateningly.

He asked to fix me a drink. I told him what I was allowed to drink.

"Diet?" he guessed.

"Why not?" I answered. I smiled mischievously.

Jake fished a shaker, some vodka, and a flask of orange juice from a driftwood-shaped cooler. I blinked.

"Clever, isn't it?" he said. "It's my parents'. I never really know what to do with the money I make when I act. It makes me nervous to have too much in the bank, like I'm just asking to be manipulated. So I tell my parents to have a ball. They have extravaganza parties like this all the time." He walloped the shaker three times with his palm and poured into my outstretched martini glass with a steadiness that surprised me.

"Martini glasses for a beach party?" I asked.

"Sand is nothing but ground glass. Give that drink in your hand two thousand years, and it'll flow between your toes like the tide. When you think of it that way, martini glasses are more disposable than plastic."

"You've obviously thought this out." I smiled as I sipped.

"I think a lot."

"You don't find that very often around here," I said.

"It's hard to find anything new around here. Especially if you're not into the regular dance-and-grind routine."

"I *know*. Like dancing and grinding is the only way to have fun in this town," I said.

"Do you want to fool around?"

Vodka spurted from my lips.

"What did you say?"

"Sometimes it's better not to think too much," Jake said.

Heat flooded my forehead and my cheeks. I was about to tell him off. My mouth roared and flamed and, after a second, the fire dissipated.

Jake stood there, not disappointed, still curious. He looked like he could really listen. I wanted to tell him about waiting for the right moment and about not touching boys and how sex was like a secret, and you wouldn't tell your biggest secrets to somebody you just met.

Jake watched me patiently.

And then I thought about how it made sense. A party like this, everybody else was trashed, and I'd only had one vodka cocktail. Nobody but me would remember. It was the perfect opportunity for a kiss-and-run.

Sometimes it's better not to think too much.

He was right. No matter what I was thinking, I was thinking too hard.

I breathed deep and long, let all the air rush out of my lungs.

"No," I said. "Thanks, anyway, though."

I drained my drink. Jake poured me another. This time he made me hold a second glass for him. He made a face as he poured. We both laughed without really knowing why.

Jake was a good sport. "Since I'm not gonna get you drunk," he said, "I might as well wonk up myself, too." We sat by the driftwood cooler, spooning our bare feet into the sand at the tide line, talking about nonsensical shit.

"How did you get invited here, anyway?" he asked, turning on his side to face me.

I still faced the ocean. "Evie Cameron," I said. "We work on a show together."

"Your name's Hava, right?" he said. "Damn, you *are*. I saw your cover. You got lucky. *Everyone* on that magazine cover looks washed up."

"Lucky, meaning I've never done this before, yeah."

"So you're really an Orthodox Jew?" he asked. "That's cool."

"No, I'm not," I said. "That's just a vicious rumor."

The night crawled by. Evie came over on some guy's arm, asked if I was okay, because she thought she was going to leave. Evie lived all the way in Beverly Hills, which was close to my cousins' house, but across the city from my Hollywood pad. "Don't worry about it," Jake said. "I can give her a lift."

"Are you sober enough?" I asked.

"Does *anyone* in this town drive themselves?" Jake smirked.

He tried asking me about being Orthodox, but I wouldn't give in. I told him that Evie told the press I was really Jewish, but she was a notorious liar and actually she was seeing two secret therapists for kleptomania and chronic dementia.

"Then what about your hair?" he asked.

"What?"

"Baby," Jake said, "you can't fool me. My mom plays mah-jongg with Madonna. Short hair hasn't been hip since last fall. Orthodox women have short hair so they can wear wigs; that's how I know you're a Jew."

I flushed. *That's only married women*, I was about to say, but that would spoil everything.

"I cut my hair the night before rehearsals started," I said. "I was drunk. And irrationally affected by punk rock music."

He believed me after that.

Jake showed me his car, a sporty little Mini that he drove himself. He flung open the driver's door, slipped in, and asked me again if I wanted a ride. I asked him again if he was sober.

"Sober enough," he said, tapping his nose with a finger.

I giggled.

I decided to believe him back.

We talked all the way home, through the five-minute lights that never changed and the slow, sleepy neighborhoods. When there was silence, it was an easy, friendly silence, as we racked our brains for another subject to introduce. He pulled onto the sidewalk in front of my apartment building, stopped the car, and gazed at me as I fumbled with my knapsack.

"Hava," he said, "it's been great meeting you. Thanks for an incredible night, okay?"

Jake's eyes rolled over me, lazy and happy. I knew that the proper decorum for saying good-bye, for kids who weren't Orthodox, included giving each other a hug. That's the language that secular people spoke out here.

I knew he didn't expect anything.

And I knew, if I wanted to, I could kiss him.

I reached over. My fingers touched his jawline, delicate, warm to the touch. Small, invisible lines of hair on his chin rubbed against the raised lines of my fingerprints. His jawbone was strong under his skin. Tight, too. His chest was still bare, breathing heavier with every second that my fingers lingered on his face, entirely still. Skin stretched against his jawbone. Tiny veins pumped his heartbeat, fast. I lay my other hand on his chest. I could feel his nipples harden, blood coursing through, building up. I felt my own breaths. They were short and tense.

"Thanks," I said. One hand shot to the car door, coolly manipulating the handle.

I dashed, almost jumped through my door and into my apartment complex. The metal door clanged shut behind me. In the center of my complex, the pool trembled, microscopic vibrations of the earth's surface. Tiny circlets jerked into being, spattered, and spread to the edges of the water.

00

HAVA NEGIAH

Ian was coming.

You know when you get really excited about something, so excited that it can never measure up in real life when it finally happens? Everything worked that way. This was going to be my first summer really alive. The first summer since I started taking the subway every day by myself. I had a date with a brick wall every night, my shoulder shoved into it, cocked steep so I looked like a slutty East Village piece of trash. Only, you know, with better self-esteem. I loved imagining myself trashy.

This summer I was supposed to try out the person I always wanted to be, take her for a test drive. Instead, I was actually turning into the person I always wanted to be, and portraying someone completely different on a television show eight hours every day.

It was enough to drive a sane girl schizophrenic.

Yeah, I told myself. *It's a good thing I have friends in the outside world.*

* * *

Evie strolled into my dressing room nonchalantly Monday afternoon.

"Hava, did it weird you out last weekend when I told you I was bisexual?" she asked.

"No," I said. "Anyway, I figured you must have been."

"Oh!" Evie said brightly. She reflected for a moment, deciding whether or not it was a compliment. She shook her head and let it drop. "Well, how about you?"

"Me?" I said. "No way. Last November I thought I might be, but in the end it was definitely too trendy. And I don't like girls."

"*Haaa*va," she moaned.

"Why?" I asked.

"You know how I've been developing an uncontrollable crush on Charles?" Evie said. "I think that, if he catches us making out in his dressing room, he'll become jealous and aroused out of his mind and he'll want to date me."

"How do you know he won't want to date *me*?" I asked. I felt a little offended.

"Oh, Hava. You're too *old* to be an illicit fantasy. I mean, you're practically *legal*. Anyway, this doesn't go against your Orthodox Jewish oppressive anti-sexuality principles because you wouldn't have to touch Charles. Only me."

I shook my head. "Evie, this is *so* not a workable plan."

"We can practice first, if you want."

"Maybe I can write you a love letter or something."

Evie, weighing her options, considered the idea. Her chin dimpled. By now I knew that meant that her brain was in overdrive. "I'll let you know," she said. She got up and left my dressing room.

* * *

That Thursday, I finally stopped being afraid of Ian's wrath and called him.

"Ian, baby," I said, "where the hell have you been?"

"Nice to hear your voice," Ian remarked dryly. "What have you been up to? I grew a goatee, shaved it, and my band's been through two bassists."

"You were supposed to be mad at me."

"Christ, Hava! That was like, what, a month ago? They must have you on more Hollywood drugs than I thought."

"Ian, every day here feels like a century. It's like I'm stuck in a time warp. Every word I say, I know I'm going to repeat it twenty times before it's out of my mouth for good."

Ian's petulant sigh sounded distant and mechanical, a buzz on my phone. "Humor me, Hava," he said. "I'm the poor, unfocused, unsigned one. You've got a Fortune 500 corporation telling you that you're a worthwhile human being. All I have is your phone calls."

"When do you get here? I'm really not feeling the argument right now."

"Next Sunday. I found a cheap flight online. I got tired of reading the same journal entry on your Web site a million times and wondering which lines I'm supposed to read between."

"It's about to be Shabbos," I said. "And I still have no idea where I'm spending it. Probably sitting by the windowsill in my cousins' apartment. Again."

What I meant to say was, I have no friends.

"Don't worry," Ian said. "You're all over those G-d-type things, you know? So G-d is bound to send something your way."

* * *

I was going to end up with my cousins for Shabbos again. It was an easy niche to fall into. They cooked for me, invited guests that I should be interested in (they were all either too old, too boring, or too straight-up *weird* — like the college biophysics major who was attempting to prove that Jews had a superior gene for intellect). For a safety net, my cousins were a horrible choice. But I could be Orthodox in peace there, and I could sit on the balcony and flip through books and spit cherry pits in the street late at night. My cousins were mellow, laid-back, a California flavor of easygoing. But they always let me know what they thought of my thrift-store clothes and my punk rock lifestyle. It was never anything I wanted to hear.

"Hava." Evie caught up to me in the dull khaki lobby after shooting had ended. There was a wide smirk across her face. I felt background music coming up.

"What up?"

"Charles wants to talk to you. He's in with the Producers right now but he said he'd just be a minute." Her voice lowered, and she glanced behind her back. "I think he wants to ask you about me."

"Evie," I started, "haven't we had the this-isn't-the-best-thing-for-you talk already?"

"Twice," she chirped. "You came to realize that I was more advanced about relationships than you are and it was your duty to help me. Make sure you mention how full my lips are, 'kay?"

"Evie . . ."

"*Please?*"

"Evie!"

"Here he comes. Look chipper!"

"You bet!" I said brightly, loudly, smiling a big fake smile. I could hear Charles's footsteps coming from behind me. Evie took off down the hall, missing her chance to revel in my glorious sarcasm.

I continued walking in the other direction, rounding the corner just as Charles left the Producers' office. I acted like I hadn't been looking for him. I brushed a strand of wig out of my eyes. "Oh, hey, Charles. I heard you were looking for me?"

"Hava!" Charles's deep-throated voice boomed, warm. "What are you doing tonight?"

"Calling in sick. I'm about to run to my fam — to Pico Robertson for Shabbos." I sighed. "You know, where all the Jews live. It's just like on TV."

"Of course," he said. "Well, what about tomorrow night?"

"Who wants to know?"

"Would you like to do dinner?"

I looked at him, surprised. "You mean — at a kosher restaurant?"

"The theory was that we'd both be able to eat, yes."

"Are you sure you're asking the right Goldberg girl?"

"Hava," Charles said, almost reprovingly. "The girl I'm asking is not named Goldberg. And I'm positive I'm asking the right person to dinner. You're the only one I would want to spend it with."

I wrote out my cousins' address on a wad of paper, along with the time Shabbos ended and the names of two or three kosher restaurants I knew. "Don't worry about that part," Charles said. "I'll get my assistant to work out the fine print."

"Umm, right," I said.

"Sorry. If you'd rather, I'll tell you that I used the yellow pages," Charles offered, winking. He wound down the corridor.

I was excited.

Shabbos had never moved slower. There were sixteen people at the dinner table and my cousins made everybody go around and introduce themselves. As was their custom, you had to say your name and how you got here and one thing about yourself.

As was my custom, I lied. The father of the family stopped the cavalcade of clever impromptu answers ("We're Chezky and Chani, and we got here by walking!") to point out that my name was *not* Ethel Lurleen Fuckovsky. I sighed and told the crowd my true, hidden agenda: that I was working on a sitcom about Orthodox Jews.

"Oh!" everybody cried at once.

Now they recognized me. The rabbis at all their synagogues had referenced the show in their sermons the week that it was announced. Each guest had something different to say about *that*.

I watched the hours tick on.

I know there are people who don't like being Orthodox and do it anyway. I hate those people. Some are afraid of Divine Retribution. Others live in Orthodox ghettoes, and they're afraid of losing all their friends. Some people just don't want that much freedom, and they like following the Commandments because it's a regimented routine.

I never subscribed to that. I want to be happy about the things I'm doing when I'm doing them. I want to believe in every song when I sing. When I'm miserable about Judaism, that just means that I still care enough to hate it.

And it was a good thing I didn't have Charles's phone number, or else I might have been tempted to call on Saturday afternoon and tell him to get me out of there.

But that's not how Orthodox Jews work. We do things without passion all the time. I mean, otherwise it would be like cheating on your husband every time you saw another hot guy. It makes sense to me, and I follow the Law, but that Shabbos afternoon — halfway through lunch, with six hours of sunshine before any Lincoln Town Car rolled up to rescue me — I thought about walking out. I really did.

That night, we stood out in the backyard to watch for three stars to appear and Shabbos to end. Flames curled around the husband-cousin's beard, and we made Havdala with the smell of acacia branches and cinnamon cloves. I felt a little bit trapped in the moment. I never wanted it to end, how some moments are just perfect, standing still and focused. But I also felt how I was so much bigger than that single moment, and I wanted to break out of it. I wanted a whole life filled with great single moments.

After Shabbos was over, I sat on the stoop and waited until my cell phone buzzed. Charles stayed in the car when he picked me up. He dialed my phone instead of ringing the doorbell. I jumped up, tossed my knapsack over my shoulder, kissed the wife-cousin good-bye, and climbed into his car.

The car was a battered Volvo, brown, solid, and bricklike. It was in fine shape, and the paint wasn't peeling or anything, but it was not the ride you'd expect Charles to have. Hell, he could probably get cars free on promotion. But he chucked me a folder of CDs, mostly hard-edged classic rock bands, and told me to choose one. The car's CD player was brand-new, hi-tech, and had an array of buttons that looked like the car's hyperdrive controls. A man who paid attention to music. I approved. The seats were also fresh, redone in slick black leather. From the inside, the car looked like a Mercedes.

"Where are we going?" I asked innocently, sliding in some Rolling Stones.

"Where do you want to be?" Charles said. He was wearing wraparound shades. When he smiled, his face looked aerodynamic, like it could cut the wind in half.

An hour later, we pulled up into the parking lot of the nicest kosher restaurant in Los Angeles. Spotlights swooped over the entrance, the windows, the wood slate siding that lined the building. Inside, every woman but me was wearing some fancy type of evening gown, and I tugged on my cargo skirt nervously. Charles waltzed past them, straight up to the hostess's podium. An instant later, we were being escorted to a table.

"You just cut in line," I protested to Charles. I watched as the hostess folded a cool Franklin lengthwise and tucked it smoothly into her breast pocket.

"You wouldn't?" The corner of Charles's eye was playful, jubilant.

"Not that way. It's —" I fished for a word.

"Bourgeois and brutish?" he finished for me. "But you would duck and shove and push your way to the front of the line without thinking."

"That's different," I protested.

"Because you're an underdog?"

"Because it's style."

I folded my arms confidently. I sighed and strode over to the table with a swagger in my step. I could feel heads turn. I liked thinking that I could control the turn of heads, that I had that kind of power. Of all the eyes on me, I could feel Charles's the hardest, piercing through the turn of my hips and the bounce of my hair, looking at me deeper than anyone else. He watched me taking in the dining room, and he smiled, like he'd learned long ago how to be a movie star in a restaurant, and now was just a spectator of the sport.

How did Charles and I get this way? Less than a month into filming, and I felt like he had me figured out. My own parents didn't have me figured out. And this man — who's twice my age and says "*ba-rook*" instead of "*baruch*" — had me down cold.

"Charles," I murmured, "tell me how I don't fit in here?"

I stretched my arms luxuriously across the table, sliding my hand to the edge of the white linen tablecloth. I etched my fingernails beneath Charles's knife and picked it up. I ran the blade through my fingers, twirled it like a baton, touching the serrated edge to the webbed indentations where my fingers meet my hand.

He watched me contentedly.

"You *do* fit in, Hava," Charles said. He folded his hands above his plate, tremulously close to where I held his knife. "This business isn't about climbing totem poles. It's about outshining. The minute you start thinking, *How can someone else be on the cover of that magazine instead of me?* you've lost, because you're acknowledging there *is* someone else. Not you, Hava. That's not the way you work. You don't even pretend. In your twisted little universe, you're the only person who's popular."

"I never *used* to question whether I was punk enough," I said. "I always thought it was so lame to worry how many records you owned or what store you bought them at or whether you memorized the liner notes. Because I always had Judaism as a backup culture. I always used to worry I wasn't Jewish enough."

"Admitting your faults is a dangerous thing to do, Hava. Saying anything aloud that you actually believe in. People can use that sort of thing against you."

I twisted the knife so two fingers wound around its handle and the other two stretched out straight, like an appendage to the knife in the shape of a scythe.

Charles reached over to touch the knife's point with his finger. The tip of his finger was thick, stiff, calloused with thin veiny white lines that ringed the edge of his finger to the topmost border of his nail. The edge of the knife sank into his skin, gently, bending a valley into the skin, not even close to breaking it.

"Can I take your order?"

The waiter hovered over us.

My knife clattered to the table. The expensive china rattled and spun.

The waiter's pen stood in midair, poised to fly down onto paper with our order. I hadn't even looked at the menu. Bad form. I usually need an hour to decide.

I slid up in my seat like it had just occurred to me that we were in a restaurant. I unfolded the menu cautiously. I glanced at the gatefold at light speed, found the entrée list — "Sautéed portobellos and rigmarole," I said without hesitation. "Potato leek soup. And French fries, please, if you have them."

Charles hadn't even touched the menu.

"Steak, rare," he said, cocking an eyebrow at me. "And a bottle of Cabernet. Whatever year your cellar master recommends."

"Steak?" I inquired. Steak was dangerous. I was a vegetarian. So were Ian and Moish and Meira. Evie wasn't, technically, but she only ate salads. The thought of someone being so brash and insensitive and singularly selfish to eat meat regularly — the thought of an ego that big — did more to pique my interest than anything.

Charles read my disgust as amusement. "It's the safest thing to order," he said. "Little-known Acting Fact Number 37: Looking at a menu makes you look indecisive. Go with the guaranteed specialty."

That made me more suspicious. I *liked* the way Portobello Rigmarole sounded. So what if I had to discover it on a menu?

The wine came quickly. The server poured it high into the glasses, splattering droplets on the inside rims, letting thin rivers run down into the soupy dark body of wine at the bottom fulcrum of the glasses. He held out the cork for Charles to smell.

Charles took it, held it under his nose, and held it over to me. As I leaned over to smell, I could feel Charles's eyes instinctively fall down the simple sheer neckline of my button-down shirt. I felt myself blush resoundingly. I closed my eyes, inhaling the cork vapor slowly through both nostrils, staying in that position for several long seconds. I pushed my shoulders back. Tonight, the world could stare.

The wine settled comfortably in my empty stomach. The rest of the night was padded and pillowy, conversation dropping like a blur on my ears and passing through me like water. I had something to say about everything, but I didn't share it. I nodded, calm, assured. I could feel Charles's interest so strong on me. It felt like a gift. I stared back and I saw everyone else in the studio who resented me or reprimanded me or just plain avoided me, and I felt the attention solidify and multiply, flowing into me by way of the intensity of Charles's gaze. It made me feel like I could do anything. I felt so attractive, like any way I moved was a different position that professional models would be jealous of. The way I slouched on the armrest of my chair. The posh smugness that I brought my knees up to my chin with. The pudgy-nosed, cheeky wholeheartedness with which I chewed my food. Charles's words felt like wisdom in my head. Maybe he was right. Maybe I was the center of my own universe.

My phone rang. There's nothing as embarrassing as a stupid vanity phone ringer in a fancy restaurant. Mine was a beepy Muzak version of "Sheena Is a Punk Rocker." I bit my lip hard, cursing myself for not switching to vibrate mode.

I checked the display. It was Moish.

I jammed my thumb on the power-off button.

"My agent," I told Charles, rolling my eyes.

I don't think he believed me. But he smiled indulgently, as though I deserved to be believed.

The meal was nice. It had been so long since I'd sat at a restaurant with another person that I'd forgotten how to eat and be social at the same time. Food these days was divided into two categories — when other people ate nonkosher food in front of me, like the Fairfax punk rock kids with their inevitable burritos ("Aren't you hungry, Hava?" — shrug — "Well, um, if you say so") and when I ate, usually alone, from a microwave or sitting at the counter of a lonely kosher restaurant.

I tried to explain to Charles. My words came out slurred. Drinking so much kosher wine was also an uncommon occurrence for me. Usually I could only drink beer or mixers. I wasn't ready for the wine dripping into my brain, running my thoughts together in a way that made perfect sense to me but translated to a gloppy mess for the outside world. I smiled broadly at Charles. I was still in the power position, but I was drunk.

My drunkenness hit midway through the meal. It surged through my head, threw me off balance completely. My stomach wobbled. I tore slice after slice from the loaf of pugilese bread on the table. I could feel the lack of food in my stomach. Once the bread soaked up the wine in my stomach, I would be less drunk. Of course it made sense. I didn't bother with margarine and oil. I watched Charles dig into his steak, and I stuffed myself with vegetables and bread.

The bill came and Charles paid, which was a courtesy because all of a sudden I could afford meals like this and any transaction involving money seemed ridiculous. Like, if Moish and I wanted to order a pizza, and Moish wasn't making anything and I had an extra hundred bucks in my wallet, of course I was going to treat him. I guess that was the way it always worked in Hollywood, and since Charles had a series of sci-fi blockbusters under his belt, not to mention a buddy-cop film that costarred David Lee Mitchell, I let him foot the bill.

Outside, the stars glittered like skyscrapers and the air smelled like the ocean and Chinese food. "Where do you want to go now?" I asked. I made a point of sounding excited and giddy, watching Charles out of the corner of my eye.

"I don't want to disappoint you, Hava, but I might have to call it a night. My dog needs to be walked exactly at midnight. If I don't take him, he starts crapping everywhere. I guess that's what I get for being an insomniac."

He said *insomniac* and my bones chilled. I felt a flurry of recognition.

"Unless," Charles said, "you'd like to come and say hello to Bolshevik?"

"I think I'd like that," I said.

Charles handed our claim check to the valet. As we waited in the scratchy warm night, watching the valet cross the parking lot, I smiled naïvely at Charles, thinking if I acted normal, he wouldn't notice how drunk I was. "Don't you take a limousine to work?" I asked him.

Charles laughed. "Not even David Lee gets limo service," he said. "That's the studio deal. You're fresh off the boat from New York, so you can get away with being chauffeured around this year. But if, G-d willing, we go into a second season, there's no way they'll spring for a limousine again."

"Are you serious?"

"Dead serious." He cocked his fingers like a gun. "No limo for you."

Cool.

Charles was so mysterious. We hadn't even had the whole G-d conversation yet, and I knew he understood why I believed. I don't know why my usual guard against trusting people never got raised with him. But I guess it was just natural. My mind had typed him so naturally as a stay-away, as someone that I'd intrinsically have nothing to do with, that the more we talked, and the more I realized I had in common with him, the more comfortable I began to be. I once read an article in *Punk Planet* by this death metal girl in Ohio or Idaho or something who dated the quarterback of her school's football team. The quarterback said he got tired of everyone trying to look alike. I read the article to Shira and Meira. I told them I'd say *no* if a popular guy tried to ask me out. I wonder if Shira and Meira saw through me with the same transparency with which I saw through myself.

The car wound around slick, steep turns, snakelike roads. Deep trees brushed the roof of the car. It felt like a forest, but when I pried my eyes away from Charles and the conversation and stared out the window, I was looking out on a golf course. Los Angeles, man. This city had a jungle inside.

Charles's house was nothing like I imagined. He lived in Beverly Hills — "a few blocks away from Evie," he said nonchalantly, pulling the car into the driveway — and when I flinched, he laughed and told me to relax.

"Nobody ever walks around this neighborhood," he assured me. "There's no way she would see you."

I think he thought we were still mad at each other. "Oh, no, Charles," I told him. "Everything's fine, honest. Evie and I are friends again."

He started saying something, but swallowed it.

We pulled into his driveway. Compared to other houses on the block, Charles's place was modestly mid-size, but it was still huge. The exterior was wooden, the most masculine of the mansions on his street. It looked like a Texas steakhouse, beige and brown, with overlapping slant-paneled wooden roofs and log cabin windows, like Davy Crockett's. It was surrounded by a stake fence that towered way above my head. There was a big yard with grass that was unnaturally groomed, level like Astroturf. Spotlights illuminated the windows and cast long, lonely shadows around the house.

Inside, everything was comfortable, almost to a fault. The sofas were square-shaped, utilitarian and new. The rooms were twice as big as they needed to be, and the furniture sat away from the walls like it was too small for the house. Tables and chairs seemed to exist more for show than for actual use. The television and kitchenette looked like display models, just out of boxes.

As we walked in, a huge, lumbering ball of shagginess ran up to us and leaped on me. Its tongue slurped at my face like a tentacle. I fell against the wall, losing my balance, choking and laughing. My hands rose up in balled fists, automatically, the way yours would if a three-hundred-pound monster dog bounced up on you — but his body was soft and warm. Nappy knobs of fur clumped against my skin. The dog felt comfortable, like a human body against mine. I lifted up my chin and he swaddled my face with that monster tongue, warm and wet.

Bolshevik bounded down the block. Massive tubby paws catapulted him high in the air, more frog than dog, unrestrained by the leash. Charles and I strolled behind, the leash leisurely affixed to his wrist, our pace brisk. Bolshevik was our entertainment. We followed his path, went down the streets of his choice.

I liked to walk briskly. I knew Charles would, too. It was totally unrelated to my fearful glimpses at every window we passed. My stomach turned knots, fueled by stray thoughts of Evie, waiting for a ride on the street, or coming out of her swimming pool, in a bikini, frozen outside her front door. I tried to focus on the dog. Three hundred pounds of furry fast-moving meat. He should be able to hold my attention.

I was more transparent that I thought, because as soon as we stepped back onto Charles's house, he locked the gate, tossed Bolshevik's leash to the ground, and ran inside his house. I ran with him. We threw ourselves against the foyer wall, next to each other, panting.

The outside world disappeared, lawns and houses and all. Every trace of Evie was gone. We stood uncertainly by the door. On the other side of the door, Bolshevik yipped happily. The chain of his still-attached leash rattled.

"We're safe," Charles said.

I knew we were. Inside the house I felt comfortable. I pushed the weird furniture, the unnatural sparseness, out of my head. The only thing in my head was Charles.

"Now that we've got that out of the way . . ." I murmured.

In the window, palm trees flopped lazily in the night breeze. Bolshevik rolled around in the yard, his white coat sharp against the green grass. The windows were wide, but nobody could see in. There was enough space between his house and the main gate to hide an army. It felt like the world was a TV on in the background, and we could tune out everything but ourselves.

I was acting another role. With every person I hung out with, I became another person. With Moish I was self-assured and editorial and motherly. With Evie I was slow and prudish and uncivilized. I liked the character I played around Charles best of all. He was always stepping back to watch.

Across the room, Charles put his wallet in a drawer. He threw his house keys into the air, caught them, and jingled them in his hand.

"Ready to call it a night, Aaronson?" he asked. "Or do you want to go out and find another adventure?"

I was next to him. I gave a start. Time hiccupped and suddenly I was standing next to him, breathing down his collar, seeing his nose and his left cheek in microscopic detail. My hands wrapped around each other, nervous and clammy. They dropped to my side, calm and collected. They interfolded behind my back so I looked docile and schoolgirlish.

"No," I said. "No, Charles, I think I'd like to stay here."

In that next interspersed, spliced-out moment, everything around me stopped. Charles's lips were still, the hairs on his mustache frozen in perfect icicle rows. The palm trees outside tilted in the breeze and didn't spring immediately back.

I didn't have to kiss him. I could stop everything, freeze it forever. I didn't even have to run away. I could change the subject. I could say a word, any word at all, instead of moving our lips together and ending the conversation. I could tell everyone in the world that we had kissed, and nobody would be the wiser.

I could tell absolutely no one and still know that I could have done it, that I could have started a perfect affair with my television father.

I could get out of this world, close my eyes and be back in yeshiva. I knew this was wrong. It wasn't the way of my people. It wasn't what I wanted. It wasn't what G-d wanted. I shouldn't be doing this.

I could say it was his fault and he coerced me into it and that it wasn't a violation of Jewish Law at all.

I leaned forward.

I kissed him.

12

WAKING UP FROM TINSELTOWN

I mean, I didn't *sleep* with him.

I ran to the bathroom and peed. When I came out we sat on Charles's bed, the only comfortable room in his house, the smallest in a wing filled with empty rooms, undecorated walls, and lavish mahogany hardwood floors. His room seemed to have been squeezed in at the corner. It enclosed a queen-size bed, a night table, a bare-bones dresser, and a bookcase of biographies of American presidents. I asked him what that was about. I lay on my back, on his bed. My breasts rolled to the sides, their weight shifted off my lungs. I listened to his voice fill my head as he talked about Jefferson, Cleveland, Ulysses S. Grant. His favorites were the Expansionists, early- to mid-nineteenth century, when the country was still getting on its feet and the very rich and the very poor lived more similarly than they do today. He talked about Cleveland's staunch working-class sensibilities, how he was raised rich but still had to make his own money. He talked about Jefferson's lifelong ambition to be a religious scholar. He never did. He was great at having ideas and terrible at explaining them to other people, the one reason he kept losing the presidential election to John Adams. Charles told stories of the presidents like soap opera sagas, and I guess they kind of were. Of the presidents together, Charles said: "You'd never meet a more lovable gang of assholes."

I was so drunk.

I kept feeling like I was going to throw up and then Charles kept asking me if I needed to throw up. I yelled at him, "*Do NOT say that WORD aGAIN!!*" and he said, "Which word?" and all I could do was laugh. I said I didn't know why the wine took so long to hit me. Charles said, that was what wine *did.* He put me to sleep with a jug of water by my side of the bed and told me to keep drinking from it.

"Don't worry about me," I said, "I'm not gonna drink anything. I'll be asleep in twenty seconds, flat."

And then I was.

In the morning I woke with the sun.

I had gotten notoriously bad at sleeping a full night since I moved to L.A. I found myself fully clothed with the exception of my shoes, a light mesh comforter draped over me.

Charles was sound asleep next to me, far on the other side of the bed, under a different blanket. His arm stretched out toward the center of the bed, but not even close to touching me. I slipped off the bed without disrupting his comforter and gathered my knapsack off the floor.

There was a towel and toothbrush ready for me in the bathroom. I didn't question why Charles had a supply of extra toothbrushes. I just liked that he put in the extra effort. I washed my face, brushed my teeth, combed my hair back with my fingernails. The judicious red block numbers stared at me from the clock in Charles's bathroom. I closed my eyes to shut out the sunlight.

Through the crack in the door, the room looked the same as it did last night, barren and presidential and unruffled. The bottom blanket was even tucked in. Charles lay there, still asleep, chest rising and falling. His eyes were closed and his posture was balled up. Everyone looks like a baby when they sleep.

I reached for the towel to dry my face. My eyes grazed the red-block-number clock again.

9:38.

Oh, shit. My brain did the arithmetic.

Ian's flight had just landed.

I couldn't pick up Ian at the airport because I didn't have a car, but I told him I'd pay for his Supershuttle. He was due to arrive at my house between ten and eleven that morning. I hustled to find a taxi. It pulled in at 10:42.

Ian's Supershuttle got to my apartment building ten minutes later. Count on Ian to be late when I needed him to be. I ran back out, settled the account with the shuttle driver, picked one of Ian's guitars off the foamy Sunday-morning grass, and lugged it to my door.

Ian was wearing tight ripped jeans and a girl's skinny V-neck soccer shirt in luminescent red and blue. He'd dyed his hair platinum blond and cut it haphazardly so it looked cutting-edge. The soccer jersey was number 13. That was Ian's lucky number. He was always trying to look badass. Really, he never would. He had too cute a face for it. He might be able to play the evil nemesis on Hello Kitty, but even that was stretching it.

G-d, it was so good to see him.

Ian's clothes were tussled and ransacked from the nine-hour flight (New York, 6:32 a.m. takeoff, plus a two-hour layover in Salt Lake City). His bags were dusty and so were his cheeks. He sleepwalked into my apartment like he owned the place. He threw his bags on the bedroom floor and collapsed straight down on my bed.

I hopped on the comforter next to him.

I propped up my head with an arm. He smiled at me, giddy. I laid my hand on his hip and ran it up his side to his rib cage, exploring the unfamiliar sensation of touching another person's body, my fingers against the warmth of skin that was not my own, prickly masculine hairs, so different from touching my own arm. How I only felt *touching* and not the *being touched* part.

I could only trust he was feeling it back.

It was warmth and unexpectedness. I could feel Ian's pulse and his lungs breathing. I could feel the tremors as my fingers lay on his skin.

"Hava," Ian said.

I licked my lips. My fingers lay directly over his nipple.

And then he said, his voice lilting higher and shaking, "Are you trying to do what I think you're trying to do?"

"I want to."

"Why?" Ian said.

"Be*cause*," I murmured.

"But I like *boys*."

"I know."

"You do?" Ian gulped.

My face glowed hot and red. I struggled to make the lie sound right. I cleared my throat and tried to act natural, like I'd known all along. "Of course I know. I mean — I'm your best friend, right? I mean, I've always known. But it doesn't matter. You're a guy. Guys get aroused by anything."

Ian held my hands still. He cradled them between his.

"Hava, is that what this is about?"

I relented. I nodded wearily into his chest.

In a split second I got a flash, an out-of-body experience, like I was watching myself in a movie, every word and gesture something to be watched instead of acted out. I heard the echo of my words in my head. *I want to.* Cliché after cliché.

I felt absolutely awful.

Then I was back in my body, slammed to earth. Ian looked on patiently. That look in his eyes that made me start talking. The gates opened and it spilled out, everything, up to and including this morning.

"Oh, Hava," Ian said, running his hand up and down my shoulder, like he was cooling me off, slowing my pulse down, "It's okay. Really it is. None of this matters, remember? It's Tinseltown."

"But I thought I'd be like that forever. I thought I was unflappable."

"It's okay, Hava. It was only one night. You have a million nights left on this planet, and each of them is gonna get better and better. You know? None of it matters. There isn't even a word in Hebrew for 'virgin.'"

I looked up in surprise. Then I remembered helping Ian on

his religion paper for World History class last year. He was writing about the virgin birth that Isaiah predicted, and I showed him how the word *virgin* in Hebrew meant "young woman" and, even back then, young women could get pregnant without much difficulty.

"At least you could have tried to do it with Moish instead. That boy has style like nobody's business." Ian grinned at me. He'd always been Moish's biggest fan. Moish always thought that Ian was teasing him, and, honestly, so did I. Now my mind was racing. Did Ian have a crush on Moish? Had he always had one? I could not be having this crisis right now. I was already in the middle of a crisis. I pretended my head was a computer and I performed a mental empty-trash.

"You should tell him," I said. "Moish could use the flattery points."

"No way. I have feelings, too, you know. I don't want to throw myself at someone and not get caught. You, at least, have guys waiting with open arms . . ."

"I didn't *sleep* with him, Ian. We only kissed."

"And you're this upset?"

I felt ridiculous. I felt like an utter virgin, every bit the way kids call you a virgin in school in fourth grade and it's supposed to be a bad thing and you deny it. In Ian Land, the only things you were held responsible for were the style of your clothes and the jokes you told. I knew that Ian understood why I was upset. It was that unspoken way that your best friend always covers your back.

The vision of myself earlier this morning, waking up fully clothed next to Charles, tiptoeing out, mentally begging Bolshevik not to bark as I unlatched the front gate, seemed like a million years away. That wasn't really me. Nobody knew but us. I didn't even need to acknowledge it happened if I didn't want to.

"Hava, baby — no offense, but *please* keep away from me on your wedding night."

I cracked a smile.

We ate a quick bagel and avocado breakfast and then we went on a walk. We started down Hollywood Boulevard, following the stars to Mann's Chinese Theater and the Egyptian and the space-age shopping mall with Indian elephant-g-d statues where we stopped to get Häagen-Dazs frozen sorbet. We put our hands in the cement to see which celebrity's handprints we fit most closely (me: Audrey Hepburn; Ian: Paul Newman). We went to the Hollywood & Vine farmer's market. We bought a five-pound strawberry box and gave strawberries to baby girls and old men. We tried on baseball hats and Cat-in-the-Hat hats and Rastafarian Afro wigs. We walked along the food booths and I bought Ian a plate of vegan wheat-free morel and scallion pasta, and even though I couldn't eat it, he seemed so happy with it that I didn't mind. The seared mushrooms sizzled straight off the grill, bleeding a meaty brown sweat, so juicy that I could taste them in the air.

In front of the Egyptian Theater, Ian and I held hands as we walked, and a man in a pinstripe vest and top hat stopped Ian and asked if he wanted to go to a taping.

"What show?" Ian said.

The man started his pitch. When he said "a normal American family, only Orthodox," we couldn't hold it in anymore and our sly sidelong glances erupted into giggling and the guy recognized me from the promo T-shirts and apologized profusely and told me how he was an actor, too, and did I think I could put in a word for him? I said sure and took his card.

Meanwhile, a herd of tourists overheard the conversation and came up and asked if they could take a picture with me. This kid tugged on Ian's sleeve. "Are you Ewan McGregor?" he asked.

Ian raised a knowing eyebrow at me.

We got back home at sunset. We stopped at a grocery store and Ian stocked up on tabloids so he could make fun of mainstream culture. We laughed and snorted and talked dirt about all the recent celebrity mergers and acquisitions in my social crowd. I showed Ian my private journal, the one that doesn't go online, and he read it with exaggerated interest and cooed like he was reading a fashion magazine. We fell asleep in the same bed, far on opposite sides, not touching at all.

"Ian," I croaked, nearly asleep, "are you sure you're gay?"

"I was afraid to tell you," he whispered. He sounded wide awake. "I mean — you being Orthodox and all. Are you still allowed to be friends with me?"

"Ian," I sighed, sinking my hair back into the pillow, "I'm just trying to get my own shit right. I'm so far from throwing the first stone. Like, light-years."

And when we woke up, the room was swimming in lazy morning sunlight, it was wicked early, and there was a limousine waiting outside.

I thought about Ian being gay. I considered the information. Could I picture him naked, having sex with Moish or David Lee Mitchell or Tom Cruise? *No.* I shuddered. That was gross.

Then I realized, no matter what, when you picture your best friends having sex, straight or gay, it's going to be gross.

I tried again. I imagined Ian holding hands with a young Tom Cruise and bringing him to dinner and introducing him to my parents, polite and nervous, like I always used to picture Ian doing with his new wife, one day, far in the future when we'd still be best friends but we'd both be about to get married and buy mortgages and watch Must See TV at night. I'd cook Ian dinner, and his fiancé would be nervous about me. "This is Tom," Ian would say, wringing his hands. "He's very special to me and I'd really like you to meet him."

Yeah. That made sense.

I'd asked if Ian could come on the set. First I asked Howard, who *hmm*ed and *umm*ed his way to oblivion. I thought about barging through the big black doors of the Producers' room and asking *them*. But, assuming the doors actually opened — I didn't test it — I would also need the chutzpah to intrude on their never-ending board meeting, whatever went on inside.

So I asked the director about Ian. "Why?" he said, irritated. "What does he do?"

I was puzzled.

"Writing, directing, lighting? Good G-d — is he an actor? Don't tell me he's an actor."

"No," I said, "he's in a band."

"We *have* a soundtrack producer, Hava. He can't just come on the set and start handing out demos."

I rolled my eyes. "He plays bass in a hardcore band," I said. "He *hates* Hollywood. He's my friend from home. That's all."

"Oh. Okay."

I don't know why I thought it would be fun to have Ian on the set. It wasn't like I was having such a blast. Moish had been in L.A. since I got here, and he'd never once asked to come.

Only, I knew Moish would act bitter and resentful toward the faux Jews of my TV family. Ian, though, would love them. Sitcoms were his kind of kitsch.

In the morning, Ian and I walked through the halls, whispering frantically about Charles and seeing Charles and any one of a million possible variations on what to say about Charles. I was worried that he would take what happened too seriously. I was worried that he wouldn't take it seriously enough.

We brushed in and sat in the conference room and flipped the new script open. It was another me-centric episode, a loose follow-up to the boyfriend episode where I go on a date and wind up at the same restaurant as my parents. (Paula: "Do you know how many kosher restaurants there *are* in New York?" Me: "Not enough!")

Which meant this new actor guy, Kevin Maximanoff (famous for bit parts in a few large films, teen gross-out comedies mostly) was sitting in the reading room that morning. I took it as a good sign. I hoped that Kevin's presence would overshadow Ian's. I felt increasingly guilty about starting my own version of Bring Your Kid to Work Day.

From the moment that he walked in and sat across from me at his customary seat at the head of the table, Charles played the role straight. No surprises, no hushed asides — no direct eye contact, even.

"Morning, Charles," I said evenly, my voice totally steady.

"Good morning, Hava." He returned the total neutrality.

Paula flipped open her script. Even the sound of her pages rustling was different. She knew. I didn't know how, but I could feel it. Evie poured coffee. The trickle of her coffee sounded different, purposely loud. Were they all watching me? Did they suspect something?

I played it cool. I avoided even looking at Charles. I focused on my script. I tried to follow the conversations going on around me.

Kevin actually was Jewish, I found out, which was surprising. He knew about as much about Judaism as a rock, which was less surprising. At one point, Charles leaned over and whispered to him that *k'vetch* only had one syllable. To have Charles Beaufort correct your Yiddish pronunciation — now *that* was embarrassing.

The script was a real doozy. In the first scene, one of my teachers notifies my parents that I flunked a test, and so my mother decides that we've been drifting apart and she needs to spend more bonding time with me.

"Bond*age* time is more like it," I said.

"Sho*sha*na!" Paula's voice cracked like a whip. We were only in read-through but her voice was sharp enough for an actual filming take. The table shook. Jamie and Corey jumped out of their seats.

I saw through Paula like she was made of cellophane. She wasn't just yelling about my test score.

How did she know?

How did they all?

I stumbled through the script read. I was good enough so nobody snapped about Ian's presence. That morning, Ian was my safety. I made eye contact with him whenever I felt like I was going to break down. With him watching, I could act my heart out, pretending all the words were secrets that I was whispering in his ear.

In the pauses between lines, I breathed slowly. I recited Psalms in my head, the ones I had memorized. Steadiness. Repetition. The smallest variations on a theme. Ian was in front of me instead of a phone call away, and G-d was in my head instead of in a prayerbook.

The dull white script sat in front of me. I read the words, and the emotions came, fast and cheap.

New scene. I was helping Evie's character with her homework. She asked how she was supposed to believe I knew what I was talking about.

An entire auxiliary script was being written in my head. I wanted to tell Evie that I knew everything she was going through, that I'd been through eighth grade and I'd survived. I focused on her, not as me focusing on Evie, but as Shoshana Goldberg focusing on *her* little sister. *I've lived my whole life alone so far, fucked up on my own. Now I'm showing you how to do it right.* I wanted to tell her how I'd tasted Charles in my mouth for hours yesterday morning, before the taxi brought me home and I could finally brush my teeth again.

Lunch break. I went to my dressing room to get freshened up. I told Ian I'd meet him in the lunchroom. My head was still buzzing, and I wanted to collect myself.

I passed Evie on the way out, scurrying along the hall. She walked so close that she bumped me. It was the lightest bump I'd ever received, her bare shoulder scarcely touched the fabric of my shirt. Her eyes skimmed over me with cold, mechanical perceptiveness. She knew.

"Hey." I smiled, ducking into my dressing room fast. I shut the door and collapsed against it. The wood paneling pressed into my skin. I wanted to change my clothes. I'd worn a bright purple shirt and a lime-green skirt today. I felt my colors clashing against the crew all morning. Only now did it start to bother me. I wanted to put on layers, shroud myself in sweatshirt after sweatshirt until nobody could see my breasts and I could hide my face like Obi-Wan Kenobi and be untouchably cool.

I shuddered.

You're out in the battlefield now, Hava. You don't get to decide when you can retreat and when you can't. All you can do is fight.

I felt super guilty about giving Ian so little of my time. He could insist that it was okay all the way till Tuesday, but he didn't fly out here to ride bitch and watch me hobnobbing it with more tedious actors. I felt a responsibility to entertain him. I felt a responsibility to justify my massive paycheck. Oceans clashed in my head.

I put on a stiff face, wished I'd remembered to buy a flask for my knapsack, and marched over to the cafeteria.

I found Ian sitting at a vacant table with Kevin, my fake boyfriend. Kevin was munching on a pork sausage. Ian was eating raw undressed lettuce. He had to be overdramatic and indie.

I flopped down next to him like I had no life left in my body.

"So what do you think, baby?" I asked. "Is this the time of your life or what?"

"I *like* it," Ian insisted. "All those old people and kids hunched over your scripts together. It's like the weirdest fucking study hall I've ever seen. I loved that one part where you went to the dance club with Kevin — I mean, with Yechezkel. Do I call them by their acting names in person?"

"I'm Kevin," Kevin said. "*Please.*"

He extended his hand. Ian took it graciously. He always shook hands like a British nobleman, surrounding the shaker's hand in a double-palm clasp.

"Working with actors is definitely weird," I told Ian. "It's like, you have a public relationship and a private relationship with each of them. You want to call everyone by their stage names on the street and their real names onstage. Eventually you build up a callus — like, whenever I'm talking about having a sister, I say *Hindel* and not *Evie.* But we slip up all the time."

"I'm not sure if I'm amazed or appalled, Hava," Ian finally managed.

"Be amazed, Ian. You're my guardian devil. If you ever disapproved of me, I'd never be able to live with it."

"Don't do *that*! Then *no* one in New York would want to date me."

"You're so much more . . . flamboyant, is that the word? . . . than you were back east," I commented dryly.

"It couldn't possibly be because I don't know anyone in this entire city, and I'll never see any of these people again after a week — no offense," Ian added in Kevin's direction. "No, that doesn't seem logical at all. Maybe it's the weather."

"Trollop."

"Hoosier."

"Blowfish."

"Tramp."

Ian and I stuck our tongues out at the same moment, and

then our hands flew out to grab the other's tongue simultaneously. Neither of us got caught.

I grinned wildly. Ian rolled his eyes. The cameras might be off, and it might be over a stack of lettuce and a half-cold plate of macaroni and cheese, but we were still Ian and Hava.

And this was our reunion special.

Kevin struggled to keep up with the conversation. I felt slightly ashamed of being such a married couple in front of him, but it felt pretty good to have the in-your-face-and-flamboyant routine active again. And, you know, not on the phone.

Ian and I chuckled self-consciously and brought ourselves down a little. We turned to Kevin. We were so aware of ourselves.

"It's still pretty cool," Kevin said, to me but mostly in Ian's direction, "you bringing your boyfriend on set."

"Oh, no." I laughed. "He's *so* not my boyfriend."

Ian's eyebrows shot up. He was laughing, too. I shot him a look that asked him to kill this quick, and then I remembered something. "Did you really come out to me yesterday?" I demanded.

"Maybe," Ian whispered softly. He looked unsettled for the first time that day. Maybe his brash tourist-ness was wearing off. No: I was calling him out.

"*Why?*" I demanded. "I mean — why now?"

"It seemed like the right time to tell you?" Ian said, more as a question than a statement. Kevin's eyes shot from one of us to the other in rapid-fire.

"Well, what about the past seventeen years of our lives?"

"There was always something going on."

"Like what?"

Ian sat back in his seat, raised a fist, and shot a finger up as he listed each item. "I was going to tell you after the Tartufi show last March, but you broke your arm falling into the stage. The next week, I bombed my American History A.P. test. Then you broke your leg biking the wrong way across Fifty-seventh Street at rush hour. You were making S'mores in my bedroom and the curtains caught on fire. We were going to stay up all night the night school ended, and then you had to catch this airplane to Hollywood."

I fished for a reasonable response. I came up with nothing.

Kevin, who by this time was far out of the loop, struggled for his reentry to the conversation. He shoveled nuggets of sausage into his mouth, using his fork like a spoon.

"And," Ian added, "may I say you're excruciatingly weird when it comes to flirting."

He shoveled a final forkful of lettuce in his mouth.

All afternoon we ran through the family-only scenes. The director wanted to keep Kevin on hand in case we came back to his scenes, but we never did. Instead, he sat on the sidelines with Ian and they talked to each other in hushed whispers. Eventually, they got bored with talking and there was a period of silence, during which I stopped eavesdropping and focused on my lines. The next time I looked up, they were making out furiously. Hands darted over chest and cheek like ice-cream scoops. It lasted through most of the afternoon. Nobody else seemed to be rattled.

Kevin's small fist closed on the collar of Ian's shirt, ripping him closer. When rehearsal ended, they parted seamlessly and walked away with a smile.

At that moment, I hated Ian. He even knew how to steal a kiss better than me.

I took Ian to Fairfax after work. We ate dinner at a Mediterranean-and-Chinese place owned by Israelis, so the falafel tasted like Chinese food and the Chinese food had a falafel aftertaste. They brought out a plate of sauces with the Chinese noodles. The hummus and sweet-and-sour sauce ran together like yin and yang on the plate. But it was easier than trying to scavenge for vegan food for Ian in my bare-bones kitchen, and also, we both wanted French fries.

It was still early. The place was empty, and we sat in the middle of the restaurant surrounded by empty tables. The TV had Hebrew cable on. Some Israeli awards show blared. Full-figured Viking blond models in golden toga dresses clapped at each other. The only sound in the restaurant besides ourselves was uninterrupted Hebrew syllables, flurrying through the mouths of announcers in a constant typewriter buzz. It was so hot that day.

"I don't buy this at *all*, Hava," Ian said. "I know you've got laws and all, but you hook up with some dreamboat actor guy and he's smart and funny, and you two just kiss and go to sleep?"

I shrugged. "Somebody said all Jewish women are doms and all men are subs."

"I'm trying to imagine you with a whip and flogger, dishing it out to crusty forty-year-olds. I'm failing."

"We fell asleep. That was it."

"Hava."

"You sound like my mother."

"*Ha*va."

"You're gonna say my name like that till I talk, aren't you?"

"Hava!"

I closed my eyes.

I felt my mouth move. I felt like I was performing a séance, only instead of a demon inside, it was myself. I told Ian everything, not holding back, the whole story of the whole entire night — from the island of boringness that was my cousins' house to the restaurant, to walking Bolshevik, going inside his mansion, waking up alone, sneaking out in the morning.

I snapped out of it and looked up at Ian expectantly.

Ian looked thoughtful and invasive. His eyes twinkled.

"He was really asleep?"

"Of course he was," I said. "Why? Do guys usually wake up earlier than girls? Do you think he was pretending he was asleep so he could spy on me?"

"He was probably waiting for you," Ian said. "He had one eye half-open to see if you'd peel off your shirt. He was probably waiting for you to jump on top of him and work the morning nookie."

"'Morning nookie'? Ian, you are shitting out of your mouth."

"It's true," Ian said. "He's old and creepy. You're young and nubile. You're supposed to savage him. Ravage him, I mean. G-d, I can't believe you, Hava. You hooked up with a man and slept with him in the same night, and there was absolutely no overlap."

"As opposed to you, right? Ian, you got play during my rehearsal."

"Well, there wasn't much else to do."

"But you didn't have to hook up with my *boy*friend," I whined, kind of as a joke, but not. Suddenly I was taking it more seriously than I needed to be.

Ian could tell. "Hava, he's *not* your real boyfriend. He's not even straight. Don't make me point out that, with that kind of logic, you just made out with your *father*."

Ian waited the requisite number of seconds. Then his eyes widened and he got all cutesy and said, "Do you think we could hang out with Kevin again this week?"

"Ian, *please*! I'm trying to deal with a trauma!"

"It's not a trauma, Hava, you just did something you didn't want to. I'm trying to get your mind off it. And it's completely all right. It's not going to happen again."

"Well, why not?"

"Because you're Orthodox! Because you don't want it to!"

"Maybe I do want it to."

Ian sighed. "Then you would have gone home with Charles today, instead of going out with me," he said. "You *don't* want it to. This is a man whose chief hobby is patriotism. And don't get me *started* about his hair."

Ian was right. I didn't want to hook back up with Charles. At that moment, I couldn't remember if I had even been thinking at the time that I wanted Charles, or whether I just wanted *someone*. His lips were in the right place at the right time.

And I trusted him.

"But I hate how you can do this so seamlessly," I said. "I wish I could live like that. You didn't even ask Kevin for his number."

"That's 'cause I know where to find him," Ian said. "Will you get it for me?"

I glanced at the time. "Come on, dude," I said. "We're meeting Moish at nine, and we have places to hit." And I needed the conversation to stop.

That's why I loved Ian. He was good at knowing things like that.

I took him to the Fairfax school yard. We sat there for a while, walked around, watched the boys skateboard. I didn't know how to introduce Ian to everyone since I didn't know any of their names. Ian asked if he could borrow someone's guitar and he started strumming it, playing a song with muttered lyrics that I recognized from him talking about it, but nobody blinked. Nobody even noticed. It was all pretty standard there, any guitar playing – whether standard or brilliant virtuoso New York slinkster-cool guitar phenomenon – was just another part of the background noise. We watched the sun go down and then we headed to Moish's, walking, until a bus passed us by and we beat feet to the pavement and caught it. In the backseat Ian said he didn't get why Fairfax was so cool, but I knew he did. It was the one part of town that he did get. It was just invisible to him, since he still had his own Fairfax back in New York. He didn't need to be constantly reminded that he still fit in.

I did.

At Moish's, we stayed in and sat around the futon and talked all night. Some nights it felt good to stay in and ignore the fact that there was a city the size of Creation outside the door. Some nights, just a big bay window was enough. I sat on the ledge as Ian and Moish traded stories about their summers so far, staring at the cars as they rode by, as if the boys' voices were a song and my eyes were filming the music video. All the slated rooftops looked empty and identical. All the cars were loaded with four or five people, rare for Los Angeles.

Moish had his camera on two strings, and he pulled them to rotate his camera toward any of us when we spoke. Somewhere around when Ian was grilling Moish about his interviews, I zoned out completely, started drawing pictures on the window with the smudges of my fingers. When I looked back, I saw that Moish had left the camera fixated on me.

Around midnight we went out on a walk, Ian's request. He said he wanted to see Melrose. It aroused a combination of his bourgeois repulsion/fetishism and his punk rock sympathies. We went to the store that sold only plaid clothes and the store that sold shoes with painted-on murals and the vintage T-shirt store where Ian found girls' soccer shirts in orange and blue, yellow and purple, and rainbow sherbet patterns. We stopped in front of the red neon glistening sex palace. Ian had been talking about it from three blocks away. He'd read about it in a magazine and then he spotted the display against the night sky. He begged both Moish and me to come in, but neither of us would. At one point, there were daggers in his eyes and I was sure he was about to say, *You would if Moish wasn't here* but you better believe he didn't. The store sign shone an oppressive red and I felt so small, totally dwarfed, like G-d had found out about my transgression with Charles and was calling me on it. But that's not how our religion works — when you fuck up, you don't spend time thinking about it; you get on with life and do good things from now on.

I kicked the gravel on the street outside while Moish ran across the street and filmed some wide-angle shots. Ian fumed about having to walk into a sex store alone. He said he didn't want people to think he was trolling for sex. I think he was afraid they would ask how old he was.

With Ian's big blue eyes, though, he had no trouble finding a straight couple to accompany him inside and show him around. When they came out, the couple was laughing tenderly with their heads tilted back, like a gum commercial. Ian held a two-foot realistic reproduction of a penis, wrapped with gold ribbon and a bow. "Use it in good health!" the male half of the couple called to Ian as they strode away, waving after him.

Ian held the package out to Moish as a present. Ian was big on giving presents. Moish was sure that Ian was trying to proposition him, and so he stormed ahead and ignored us for the next three blocks.

I looked at Ian exasperatedly. Ian shrugged, mystified. He held out the gift to me as an explanation.

I shook my head, disgusted. I would've been disgusted even if Ian wasn't shoving a neon-green larger-than-life replica of a male genital in my face. For all Ian's wisdom, when it came to flirting, he was just another two-year-old trying to get a rise out of a cute boy. I watched Moish half-jog, half-strut half a block in front of us.

"Should I try to catch up with him?" I asked Ian.

"Let him go. It's my only week in town, remember?"

I sighed. I ran ahead.

Talking down Moish was a mammoth job. He was so stammery and agitated. I'd been dealing with Ian for the past twenty-four hours nonstop, almost, and I was suddenly on this breezy, whimsical level. Around Ian, I was perpetually calm. Around Moish, I was always ready for an earthquake and an emotional trauma.

Moish kept on passive-aggressive blowing up at me. He huffed his breath. He made crude complaints that ended in questions like "Am I right?" or "Does that make sense?" At one point I realized, nothing I could say was going to make any difference. I shut up and zoned out and said yes when he took breaths, to make it sound like I was paying attention.

We walked in silence for a block or so, listening to night noises. The streets were still pretty busy. Snatches of conversation floated by us. I heard my name and froze before I remembered to ignore it. Then it came again, familiarly — "*Hava Aaronson*" — and that time, it was Ian's voice. In conversation with someone.

Moish sighed loudly and rolled his eyes.

I, however, was curious. Even if Ian was just using me to pick up boys, I wanted to see the kind of boy my name was worth.

It was a tall, thin, smart-looking man with perceptive eyes. It didn't look like Ian was hitting on him, so much as *being* hit. His voice rang in your head like a song on the radio, so familiar and so off-putting at once. Moish and I both recognized the figure at once. But neither of us believed it.

"Hava, Moish," said Ian. "This is Mr. Welles. He makes movies."

Moish and I shot glances at each other. We weren't sure whether to laugh.

"First names, please," said the man. "If we're all friends, that is. And I'd very much like to be friends, wouldn't you, Ian?" He smiled enticingly at Ian. I was feeling more fictional than ever.

In an unspoken exchange of glances, Moish and I decided to play along.

Moish was on him at once, like a predator. "You're — this is amazing," he stammered. "You're such an honor. I mean —"

The man laughed. Just like his voice, his laugh was larger than life. He was *so* not who we thought he was. But he was so good at the voice. *That* voice.

"Mr. — uh, Orson," Moish said. "I thought you were dead . . ."

He laughed again. "This is Hollywood, Mister Moish. No one ever really dies here."

Moish and Orson shot questions back and forth at each other all night, till dawn, almost. They talked about editing and writing dialogue for yourself versus writing for other people and how convoluted it can get to mix your real life and your fictional one. This guy, whoever he was, had his shit down pat. They got on like brothers. Better than brothers. They got on like different versions of the same person.

Orson had a screamingly overt fascination with Ian, whether sexual or social, I couldn't tell. Ian was a walking commercial for himself. He attracted everyone. He gently edged the conversation back to Moish whenever it faltered. And Moish was always ready to spout out more questions about imagery, dialogue, and the creative process. After a while the conversation became too intense and artistic, and I started thinking stuff in my head. I loved knowing creative friends like Moish with his scripts, and Ian with his punk songs. But I felt lost when they talked about the compulsion to create.

I just liked going out instead.

The sun was breaking through the clouds when we said good night to the man who called himself Orson. We all went back to Moish's place, giddy and sleep-deprived. "That wasn't really *him*, right?" said Ian. "Like, was that a ghost?"

Moish shrugged. “He put my number in his cell phone,” he said. “Ghosts don’t have cell phones.”

Moish opened the door, and we all tumbled in. We fell asleep on the couches, Moish and Ian on the big one, me on the love seat. When I closed my eyes, Moish’s head cradled on Ian’s shoulder. They both snored loudly. In the morning I brushed my teeth with my index finger, tiptoed out, and hailed a cab.

It was a good thing my day job came with a built-in wardrobe.

For the rest of the week, Ian helped Moish with his movie while I worried. Ian could find adventures like normal people found pennies on the sidewalk. One day Moish called me from Anaheim; this guy was trying to pick up Ian and had to run to work. He dressed up as Mickey Mouse at Disneyland and he asked, would they like to go with him? Another night I wanted to hook up with them after filming, but I was at home in Hollywood and Ian was going on a date with Kevin in Venice Beach and Moish was going to spy on him and whisper clever lines in a radio in Ian’s ear. I was going to tag along, too, but Ian and Moish both shot me a look, like I was trespassing on sacred boy space.

And besides, I had to deal with work.

Work had turned into this carefully practiced routine, an eight-hour-long knee-jerk reaction. I memorized my lines and recited them, more natural-sounding than ever. Lines like *Good morning* and *Excuse me* and *No thanks, I’m not hungry today.* I asked Evie if she wanted to hang out with Ian and me some time that week. She scowled at me like she was disgusted I’d even ask, and I thought, *Did I forget to say the right lines?*

I kept trying to get Charles's attention. Not for anything real. I mean, I just wanted to *talk* — or, not even talk, I wanted to know if he was okay and that we were still friends.

"Hey," I stopped him in the hall, pressing my hand against his elbow, "what are you doing this week? You want to hang out?"

"Oh," he said looking all distracted. "I'm sorry, Hava, I have to work on my Zen Kabbalah classes every night after rehearsal."

But when his gaze passed over me — or when, in rehearsals, his character had to address my character — I could feel his voice tremble.

That night before Ian was supposed to leave, he met me on Melrose Boulevard after work and we rode home together. We were going to stay up all night again, making Tofutti pizzas and trolling the Roxy for hot guys for him to dream about on the flight back.

And then we were at my house, microwaving our pizzas, and my skin crawled and I felt so unstable, like Ian was about to leave me forever and I wanted to hang on to him forever and that it was his own fault, and I hated him for abandoning me.

We ate in silence. Ian lay on the bed. I paced the perimeter of my room like I was stalking myself. Ian watched me calmly. He asked if I was okay. His decency made me madder.

The buzzer sounded.

"That must be Moish," I said.

"I'll get it," Ian volunteered.

The second he disappeared into the hall, my cell rang.

I jumped off the bed, ran to where my phone was plugged into the wall. "Yeah?" I spat into it.

"Hava, it's Moish. I just called to say I'm in traffic, I'll be there in, like, ten minutes, tops."

"Then who the fuck is buzzing —"

I froze.

"Hava!" cried the voice.

The Voice.

The voice that was creepier than Baby Goldberg's, more resonant and trademark-patented than Orson's, and more fear-inducing than anyone, anywhere.

"Hava, what room are you hiding in? Is this really where you live? You didn't choose this décor yourself, did you? It's *atrocious*. Come out and help me with my bags. The limo driver left, he said he had another appointment, if you can believe that, the ship they're running is so loose it's going to sink itself — Havaleh, are you in there? What are you doing? How are you?"

I froze.

"And, darling, what the hell did you do to your hair?"

It was my mother.

13

OEDIPUS WOULD NEVER GUESS

Let me tell you about my mother.

She was born in a tiny apartment in Bedford-Stuyvesant in Brooklyn, the youngest daughter of a Hungarian rabbi. She was one of eleven children. Her mother was also the daughter of a rabbi. Like many Jewish women raised in a rabbi's house, my grandmother knew Gemara even better than her husband, and she encouraged her daughters to study Gemara, too.

When she was little, my mother sat at the kitchen table, fighting with her sisters about Torah principles and medieval rabbinic arguments. Their battles would last for hours, unresolved until my grandmother stopped cooking long enough to rebuke them all and snarl the answer. She yelled at them to go look it up. "Teach yourself!" she kvetched at them. "You want to be self-sufficient? The buck stops here, kids." If her husband the rabbi was in the room, he'd blink, startled and self-aware, and watch his daughters return to dissecting his Talmud books.

That didn't last. My mother grew up in the generation of secular Orthodox professionals. She was raised in the same neighborhood as non-Jewish kids, the first generation of our family to do so in a thousand years. She went to public school, where her third-grade teacher discovered my mother's prodigal ability to complete advanced computational equations in her head.

Even that early in her development, my mother was turning into a hardcore, better-than-everyone-else math nerd. Her old tests were still framed on the kitchen wall of my grandmom's brownstone in Park Slope. When I graduated from junior high school, I stopped being a perfect straight-A student and started getting angry and bored. My grandmother finally gave up, moved the tests to the back room, and stopped referring to my mother in every conversation we had, idolizing her.

But my mother never stopped idolizing herself. She was the biggest nonpresence in my life. She worked twenty-hour days so frequently that sometimes the only times we'd communicate all week were by phone.

She was a financial planner for one of the biggest banks in New York City. After a year running numbers for the corporate office, she was placed in a special division, as top secret as it got in the banking world. She predicted the future of money.

She was the real-life equivalent of a creepy science fiction movie where credit cards control your life. She theorized the different ways that money would evolve. My mother had calculated the exact month that the penny would become obsolete, the weight of paper currency for colonies on the moon, and whether implants beneath our skin would ever replace credit cards.

My mother took off work for the first two years of my life, to the day. She read every child-rearing book studiously, methodically, patting me on the back exactly three times when I needed to burp. She rejected breast-feeding after deciding that a plastic nipple was more hygienic than her own pimple-framed breast. According to my father, she walked right back in the office on the day after my second birthday. She even got there ten minutes early. She was so organized, she only needed ten minutes to bring all her files up to date.

Being three thousand miles away hardly affected our relationship. Her voice on my cell phone sounded exactly the same in Los Angeles as it did in New York. The only difference was, here I never had to worry about her barging into my room on a whim.

Once I asked my father if my mother's bulldozing people skills ever bothered him. He looked surprised. He told me my mother had a strong personality. After twenty years of marriage, most people lose every trace of personality. They become like robots, he said, agreeing automatically, having dull conversations that read like *Family Circus* cartoons.

My father was the kind of person you'd want to take along to the doctor's office. On the way he'd find the coolest parts of any New York block, the hundred-year-old pharmacy or the celebrity in normal citizen drag or the crazy homeless person wearing rabbit ears and a medieval jester's costume. Then he'd wait for two hours while you had your surgery.

My mother was the kind of person who should run for president, but who you'd never want to actually meet. At a hospital, I'd trust her to be the surgeon, to plan everything, and to be there in case the machines fuck up. She has the kind of hands that are lousy for hugging, but perfect for slicing a person open.

I mean, I loved her, but I'd never want to hang out with her.

* * *

"I thought I'd surprise you, honey," my mother said.

My living room was small, but it led to a corridor that funneled into an even smaller bedroom. Only because of my meticulous attention to detail and my New York every-inch-counts design sensibility did my bedroom qualify as a room and not a closet. The queen-size bed filled most of the available space. A stack of books and zines lay by my bed. There was a small lamp in one corner, and the smallest file cabinet–size bureau you ever did see wedged between my bed and the wall.

At this moment, my mother's nebulous presence was taking up the rest of the room. Short, skinny, and spiky, she had hair pulled back tighter than a spring, and rigid posture. I sprang up, instinctually feeling the need to hide my private space from her.

"Mom, it's a surprise when you show up to *dinner.* When you come across the country without telling me — that's not a surprise. That's un*fair.*"

G-d, I was so mad.

My mother's eyes moved from Ian to the still-active cell phone that lay in my hand, then to my burning red eyes. "Honey, are you sure this is a conversation you want to have with other people around? Why don't we go freshen up a bit and go catch dinner?"

I stood facing her, hands at my hips like a Texas Ranger. Our eyes narrowed. She was prepared for this. I knew she was prepared for this. Why fly three thousand miles to see me when you know you're asking for a fight?

"Mom," I said, through gritted teeth, "Ian is leaving in the morning. Give me one last night for him."

"But —" She looked horrified. "But I thought maybe we could *all* go out. Together. Please?"

"Mom."

"I could treat you to dinner. Or maybe a movie?"

"*Mom!*"

"I'm a responsibility, Hava. Like your job. You wouldn't skip work because your friends were here, would you?" she said.

For someone whose job it was to calculate human nature, my mother knew depressingly little about how I functioned.

I looked over my shoulder at Ian, stirring in the living room uncomfortably. Moish stood in the doorway, looking tremendously unsure whether or not he should enter my apartment. "No," I said. "Mom, you can stay here. I'm going out with the guys. I'll be back around five or six a.m. There's blintzes in the freezer, if you want."

"Empire?"

"Tofutti."

And we were gone.

Once we were outside, Ian gave my elbow a squeeze. I knew, in the wake of my mother's whirlwind of craziness, the weirdness between us was over. We went straight to the Roxy. Each of us carried one of Ian's suitcases. Moish wanted to walk, but the club was six or seven miles away from my house. We had to catch a cab. I said I'd cover it. We walked down Hollywood Boulevard so we had something to do instead of standing still. We checked at every corner to see if a taxi was coming. Moish twisted his head every few steps because he was neurotic like that. To his credit, he successfully hailed the first cab to come our way.

I tried to have fun that night, but it was hard. The first band we saw was a teenage punk rock boy band. All their songs were about their parents or how nobody understands. I shook my head furiously. This wasn't supposed to make me feel like a bad love song. This wasn't supposed to make me nostalgic. I gripped the balcony handlebars harder. My knuckles were turning a brilliant shade of red. "Are you okay, Hava?" Ian asked, touching my shoulder the tiniest bit. He lay his hands on the fabric of my shirt without pressing.

"Oh, Ian," I said. "I'm sorry I'm such an ass."

"You're not," he said, still watching the band. "You're just full of yourself."

I opened my mouth to argue.

"It's okay," Ian said. "So am I."

Those times we spent together on the roof, we never talked that much. I just needed to know that Ian was there. Tonight, it felt like the same thing. We pushed our way around the barricade of nervous-looking couples who watched the band studiously, like they were putting on a modern dance performance, and pushed into the pit of gnashing teenagers. We danced our ridiculous dances and hopped our ridiculous pogos. Between songs, we screamed our terrible screams. Ian and I both felt giddy and we danced wild and flamboyant, like we weren't aware of our own bodies. We took turns leaping up and punching our fists in the air and yelling "YAY, metal band!" If they had thrown us out for public drunkenness, it would be entirely understandable.

We went to Canter's Jewish Deli because, although it wasn't kosher, we had all read about it in books. Ian ordered a New York chicken salad without the chicken ("and without the New York, too"). Moish and I got egg creams that came furry, drenched with drizzles of chocolate syrup and foaming over. The sugar energized us through a few more hours of conversation, and before we knew it, the pink Coca-Cola clock on the wall struck six a.m. We picked up Ian's suitcases and loaded him into a cab. I smacked some bills in the driver's hand before they smoked away. Moish's camera followed the trails as they sped off, then panned over to my crumpling face.

"Your best friend in the universe has left the building," he voice-overed, zooming in on my head. "How do you feel, Hava?"

"Come on, dude," I said. "Where do you want to go? I'll hail you a cab."

Moish looked at his watch, then at the sky, streaking orange and cardamom with morning clouds. "The ocean," he said. He didn't take my money.

We walked to the subway instead.

Nobody in L.A. actually rode the subway. Neither of us had ever tried it. The station was paneled in a bright mosaic. The walls were sanitary and pristine, freshly polished. It was enough to make New Yorkers like us suspicious. Moish said he'd take it as far as it went, and he'd see where that got him.

I ran back upstairs and caught a cab to work. It seemed like the reasonable thing to do. There was a car showing up at my house in a few minutes, where my mother was staying. I was sure the cab wouldn't be wasted.

A feeling of dread started to fill me.

Regulations and reservations were not things that a person like my mother worried about, I figured, and I was right. The studio smelled like coffee and sticky buns. The fluorescent lights hummed with bright Monday energy. A big easel announced that David Lee was filming *Mega Force III* and would not be in this week's episode.

Great, I thought, starting to feel even more alone.

My mother passed through my dressing room as the stylist was fucking with my face. When I walked onto the set, my mother had a paper tray of Starbucks Grande Caramel Macchiatos and she was passing them around to the crew.

"Mom!" I screamed. "You are *not* allowed to be here!"

"We let your friend come all week," said the director. "And *he* didn't buy anybody lattes."

"That's different," I said. "He wasn't related to me."

The director sipped his own Frappucino gratefully.

My ears burned. I could feel them burning up. Even worse were the scenes we were acting out today. It didn't seem so bad to read all these meretricious flirting scenes on paper with Kevin three seats down, but onstage they were positively embarrassing. We sat on my bedspread and traded witty banter. I smiled shyly. Kevin raised his eyebrows suggestively. On the cutaway shots, Evie chased Baby Goldberg around the house and then got chased around the house by Baby Goldberg. If I didn't catch myself, my eyes would be rolling constantly all morning. It was impossible to take this stuff seriously. And I was flirting with a boy whose last movie had been *Altar Boys 2: The Revenge*.

At lunch, I went to grab my special meal and ate it on my own. I took my time. I paced nervously before I finally left the kitchen with my tray.

My mom waved me over. As if I could have missed her. Floral dress, straw hat with a mile-wide brim, and big circular leopard-print sunglasses. Indoors. She waved with one hand

and gripped Paula's wrist excitably with the other. "Oh, Hava! We were just talking about you!"

"Hello, Hava." Paula smiled.

In Paula's sly glance I saw a CIA spy cam, slick and merciless. She was hypothesizing every sordid detail of My Night With Charlie. She smiled patiently at my mother. This could only mean the worst. Paula was my mother's age, had my mother's shrewd plotting intellect, and she appeared to be my mother's new best friend. There was no way that could be good for me.

My mother's cell phone rang. She went to get it, gesturing at me to sit down. She held up a finger, mouthing the words *I'll just be one second.*

I whispered at her: "Mom, do you want me to see if they can heat up another kosher meal?"

She covered the phone. "We'll share. You're not going to eat all that, are you?"

I sat. Paula and my mom gave each other conspiratorially friendly glances.

My mom, still on the phone, said *yes* a few more times, hung up, and turned to me. She had that self-satisfied expression that she always got after a successful business transaction.

"Hava, dear," my mother said, "you've hardly told me anything about Paula. We've only just been talking since your bedroom scene, and already we've got so much in common."

"Hava, dear, your mothers are joining forces," Paula said with an air of subdued evil. "It's so ironic, don't you think? No, it's not ironic . . . what's a better word?"

"Oedipal," I snorted.

Paula's eyes registered amusement.

The smell of the kosher meal hit my nostrils. Mixed vegetables and that slimy mushroom wild rice. It was the grossest meal of the rotation. There was utterly no reason for me to stay and have lunch. I stormed into the writers' room, logged in to my online journal, and breathed as my fingers got kinetic, spilling my secrets in a haze of fake names and places.

I wrote about Ian's visit. I wrote about sending him and Moish off, and I wrote about sitting onstage in my bedroom with Kevin about to kiss me and how I felt absolutely nothing, and then my night with Charles.

I wondered if they would fire us.

I wondered if they would encourage it.

If they discovered it.

"I wonder what G-d would say when you tell *him* about fucking Charles."

The voice gave me a jolt. It was warm and moist against my ear, so close it was almost in my head.

"Will he throw lightning at you at once, do you think? Or will he wait until you're absolutely finished explaining? How it wasn't your fault, how Charles invited *you* to dinner, how your body was so horny for a man's hands on you that you weren't even in control? I could sell your secrets on eBay, Hava. Maybe G-d will want to hear the details. Maybe G-d gets horny, too. What do you think of that, Hava?"

"Evie," I said. "Aren't you over Charles Beaufort? What happened to your slash-and-burn boyfriend lifestyle?"

"I'm over him, Hava," she said. She hovered over me. I gripped the ends of the armrests. I was petrified with anger. I couldn't move. "Charles. Kevin. Even G-d, Hava — I'm over him, too. Maybe you can tell him when you pray to him."

"Can you *please* stop saying 'him,' Evie?" I said. "Jews don't believe G-d has gender. Hebrew has a gender for every word, even tables and napkins. They just translate it as —"

"*I'm not talking about fucking Hebrew!*" Evie screamed in my face.

"Then what do you *want*?" I yelled. "A confession?"

Evie paced back and forth, walking around me. She leaned over the chair from behind. She drummed her fingers on the armrest, deliberating. I shuddered. She had never seemed so dangerously unpredictable.

She stroked my hair.

"I don't believe in G-d," Evie whispered. "If there is a G-d, he's probably watching Italian women bathe naked right now." She walked toward the exit, lay one hand on the doorknob. Her hand was so small. She could get breast implants and collagen in her lips, but her hands were still childlike, small and grabby like a baby's.

"I wouldn't waste my time telling G-d, anyway," Evie said. "Not when your mother's right here."

At the end of rehearsal that day, we did a final run-through of the entire episode. Usually it was a dry run, with empty, silent pauses when the audience was supposed to laugh. Today, my mother was the soundtrack. She cackled madly at all the jokes, even the sexually tinged ones.

"Hold on, hold on," said the director, conferring with the crew. Evie and I were frozen onstage, me on my bed, her hovering above it. Her eyes met mine, then flickered for a second over to my mother, in the audience, sipping yet another Starbucks coffee drink.

"I'm sorry," I hissed at Evie. "I really am. I didn't even have sex with him —"

"Give me a hundred thousand dollars," Evie said. "I know you have it. Or else I tell your mother right now."

"What?" I whispered. "You don't need money! Your parents are rich!"

"Your parents are *here,*" she hissed.

"Why are you doing this?" The horror in my voice grew.

"Because I can."

People watched from afar, idly fascinated.

The anger surged within me for a second, and my body jolted, almost fell off the bed. Then, just as quickly, it dissipated. I felt calmness flood through me like water.

Like water.

"Evie," I whispered, quick and harsh, "do you see that woman out there?" My mother sat in a corner, on her wireless Palm Pilot, tapping out stylus codes to G-d knows who, keeping up with her business life. "She means nothing to me. Less than nothing. My number one wish is for her to be disappointed in me. So go on. Tell her."

"*Action!*" the director shouted.

Evie and I snapped to attention. We recited our lines with such gusto that everyone earnestly believed I had an uncontrollable crush on Kevin, and I honestly couldn't decide whether or not I should make out with him.

Mom had meetings all the next day, the "other" reason for her being out here. She didn't even tell me about the meetings till after rehearsal that day. I decided not to tell her off. Instead, I called my father. He was about to run out for a double shift on the ambulance. When I heard his voice, I got warm chills. The good kind of chills. I felt flattered; my dad was taking five minutes out of saving the world to talk to me.

"Hava," he said. "Please. She might be unreasonable now. But one day you'll get along again, and you'll be glad she flew out to see you."

I didn't have the heart to correct him.

"I wish it was you out here," I said.

"It's better that it isn't, Hava. You and me, we're fine. We can pick up whenever you get back. But your mother and you are holding on by a thin strand."

I grumped.

"I hate it when you're wise," I told him. "I'd rather you were selfish."

There was a pause so long, I thought one of us had gotten disconnected. Tonight I wanted him to be here so bad. I wanted to crawl on him and hang on his shoulder. I wanted him to be the only man that I touched. I wanted to have his raw honesty backing me up. I missed his warmness. I missed *him*.

"I know, *meidele*," my father murmured, sounding every inch of the three thousand miles between us. "I wish that sometimes, too."

My mom was taking a red-eye flight, but she wanted to get to the airport something like five hours early. She scheduled me in for an early dinner and quality time before her flight, ninety minutes. Her last meeting ran an hour late, though. We met at the same restaurant that Charles took me to, the only fancy kosher place in town. I had three bowls of French onion soup while I waited for her. The waiters were coming by the table to talk to me and kid around. The kosher supervisor brought a deck of cards. I wanted to tell them all to go away so I could use my cell phone, but I didn't. To tell the truth, I kind of liked the attention.

Finally she showed up, clothes magnificently unwrinkled, but her face in a flurry. She sat down, and the first thing she did was glance at her watch. "*Jee*sus," she said. "I didn't even realize the time."

"That's hardly surprising, is it?" I said. "You'd better order something to eat. I might grab dessert."

She looked like she was about to say three different things. Instead, she stood.

"Come on," she said. "Let's go somewhere."

"Where?"

"It doesn't matter." My mother threw her platinum card at the waiter. He caught it in midair. She stopped at the maître d' booth to retrieve it, signed the bill for my bowls of soup, and led me to her rented Lexus outside.

We drove in silence. Meaning, I was silent, and she glared at me any time I was about to say something.

"You know," my mother said, "we have it so easy. People like television because they really don't have any problems that can't be solved in half an hour. We just prolong them. Because we, as a society, are neurotic. The last time I remember someone having a problem they couldn't solve, it was 1983. *And* it was cancerous." She stopped the car. We had just crossed Hollywood Boulevard, a bastion of lights, and were heading for the dark Hollywood Hills. "Do you want to see a movie?"

"What movie?"

She shrugged. "Just a movie."

"I *hate* movies. I can never sit still that long."

"Well, *I* have a flight to catch. We won't have to see the whole movie. We'll watch till we get bored, how about that?"

My mother had a ridiculous smile on her face. We drove down Sunset to a theater, left the car, and walked to a theater. We stood in front of the marquee, deliberating.

My mother said the name of a movie. I shrugged amiably. It was tame, a legal thriller, a few guns, probably no sex scenes. I would've picked something funny, but she didn't ask. She paid for our tickets, bought Cokes — no popcorn, cause they probably sprinkled it with lard, and no candy because it was bourgeois — and sat a safe distance from the screen. The tension was palpable. We kept a safe distance from each other. Neither of us used the intermediate armrest so we didn't have to touch. The sex scene came about an hour into the movie. My mother was uncomfortable. I was uncomfortable. She asked a question with her eyes.

"Let's motor," I said.

We listened to my favorite radio station on the ride back. She dropped me off at Moish's house. She walked me out of the car, up the path, and paused before the main gate. For a moment, I thought we were going to hug. But her hand darted out, and I noticed her check her watch out of the corner of her eye. She smiled hopelessly. "I'd better run," she said. She gave me a parting smile and ran to the car. I stuck my hands in my pockets, rang the doorbell, and settled into the night. That was pretty painless.

Moish was doing confessionals, facing his camera and narrating straight into it. I told him to move over. I wanted to talk.

Moish left the television on while he was filming — "background noise," he called it, even though the outside crowds on Melrose a block away were loud as fuck. Television announcers were better, Moish said. Their voices were always modulated. They never got too excitably loud or confessionally quiet.

"Then why are you watching entertainment news?" I said.

"It's Hollywood, babe," Moish said.

I don't know where this "babe" thing came from. Right before my eyes, Moish was evolving into a real Hollywood *mensch*. Every conversation you had with him felt like a script, like he didn't trust me to speak my own words right.

I stared at Moish's big glowing eye through the lens of his camera. "I don't know why we feel the need for all these confessionals," I whispered. "Your film. My online journal. What kind of people watch imaginary families on TV every night, anyway?"

"My film isn't confessional," Moish said matter-of-factly. "I never have confessionals. I always tell everything to everyone. I haven't needed to keep a secret in almost a year."

I cocked my eyebrow. "Really?"

"I swear."

Moish was the kind of person I always wanted to be. Honest. Singular. Solitary. We were both the outcasts of our school. Only I toned my punkness down, alienated it, ridiculed that side of myself when I hung out with Shira and Meira. Moish flaunted his intellectual dorkiness, wore it proudly. And that's why he never had to keep secrets. Because nobody wanted to hear.

I blinked into the camera. "Moish, baby, you're absolutely stark raving mad. . . . So where was I? Right. So, I call Ian after every minuscule development in my — I call him whenever something happens on the show. Any time there's any kind of drama, I feel the explicit need to tell him about it. Details and names and everything. But people like Evie and Charles, people who are around me every minute of the day, I can't talk to them. I don't know why we feel the need for all these confessionals. I mean, when we can't even talk to the people around us."

I trailed off, not because I was done but because I heard my name. I was trying to ignore the white noise, play it off as people talking across the room.

But Moish heard it, too. His head jerked away suddenly. The camera jerked with him. Both swung over toward the TV.

"Hava . . ." Moish murmured. He pulled away. Startled. Disturbed. Disgusted.

I knew what was happening. But, like a fictional character two feet away from the movie monster, I couldn't move. I felt my destiny coming on me and I wanted to run away.

"Hava Aaronson, the actress who plays Shoshana Goldberg on the new fall series *The Goldbergs,* is the only member of the show's cast who is actually an Orthodox Jew," the smartly dressed woman anchor was saying. "But, as this recent video from a Friday night West Hollywood punk rock house party shows, Hava has taken her own summer vacation — from the rigid rules of Orthodoxy, that is."

On television, I crowd-surfed over the hands of dozens of waiting punks. I felt my stomach drop. It had been all day since I'd eaten. Including the Starbucks lattes that my mother brought for everyone but hadn't given me. Not that I would have drunk anything from Starfucks, anyway. Not like any of it mattered.

"For further details, you can read Hava's own account on her secret anonymous Web page at www dot —"

Every word fluttered out of my body, curses and all.

That was it. I had nothing left.

14

THE BEST BAD TRIP

"I need to take a road trip," I said.

"What?" Moish looked bewildered.

"I need to get out of here."

I rubbed my palms against the fabric of my skirt. The TV cut back to the image of me dancing, moshing, flickering like a bad flashback.

It was Wednesday night. Hump day. The first night of the Hollywood weekend, millions of parties, even all-ages ones. Outside Moish's window, the Melrose clubs bustled with a kinetic frenzy.

"We *can't*," Moish said. "I hate to be the bad cop, but we've got G-d to consider. Your filming wraps up Friday at five. Even if it ended on time — which it doesn't — we'd only have three hours, at most, before sunset."

"Fuck that." I leaped up. I ran behind the couch, over to my backpack, throwing in a couple of clean shirts.

I looked at Moish wildly. My eyes burned. "Moish, you saw the TV. I have to leave this town."

Moish's face contorted, his mind wrestling with questions about the videotape. I knew what he wanted to ask. I knew he'd understand, once I explained.

"Fuck Shabbos? Is that what you mean?" Moish said. His voice trembled.

"No," I said. "Fuck everything else. Everything *but* Shabbos. Fuck Friday. Fuck filming. Fuck the *world*, Moish. Don't you want to get out of Los Angeles?"

"Uh. Umm. Maybe. Sure?" His face went through a confusing series of expressions.

I glared at him.

"Yes," said Moish.

I grinned. "Okay. Let's drive."

One summer, Moish's uncle got him a job at a kosher cattle ranch in Iowa. For two months, Moish learned how to ritually slaughter cows. Moish also received instruction in the secular aspects of Iowa living. He learned to ride horses, play darts, grind cattle meal, and chew tobacco. He learned to taste the difference between twenty different varieties of beer, which astounded all the kids at Rashi High for about two weeks before they all decided that Moish was a dork again.

One more thing. In Iowa, Moish also learned to drive.

The insurance premium was high, but I put it on my credit card. It was pure black magic, how you could make any expense evaporate if you had a credit card. And now that I was a television star, I had the magic to back it up.

* * *

We stopped at a roadside store in Coalingua Junction and bought slushies and Fritos. “Get one of these, too,” Moish said. He tossed a gossip magazine on the counter.

The sad girl behind the counter looked at me questioningly. Her hair had blond streaks and her eyes, cloaked with mascara, had a quietly desperate glaze that was asking us to take her out of there. I felt so responsible. Like, if anyone could, I could.

“Sure,” I said. I shot Moish a look.

“It’s about your family.” He held up the cover. Sure enough, the headline read PARTY ON, JEWS!

Underneath was a collage of photos of Paula, David Lee, various models, and a close-up of a bottle of anonymous pee-colored booze.

The cashier was a shy girl with symmetrical piercings in her lip, labret, nose, and between her eyebrows. You could tell she was trying to look out of place. Her eyes darted from my face to Moish’s yarmulke and back.

“Are you one of them Goldbergs?” she said. “I read about that show in *TV Guide.* It sounds okay. I dunno, I just can’t get excited about sitcoms anymore.”

“Yup. That’s us.”

She grinned a little. “That’s cool. I mean, it’s cool that you’re doing it and all. It might be good. You never know, there’s always a few shows that turn out okay.”

“Yeah, we hope so, too.”

“Well, take care.” The girl rang up our purchases, counted my change, and waved good-bye as we walked through the parking lot.

“Do you think we should have offered to take her with us?”

I asked Moish. The wind blew in our faces. I waited for it to calm down and repeated myself.

"Nah," said Moish. "I think we made her happy as is. She'd only freak out about meeting movie stars and getting back to work before she ran out of sick days or whatever."

"Do you think they give vacation days at this kind of job, though, Moish?" I asked. "I mean, working right on the highway, she's, like, *asking* for salvation. They should give her a five-day vacation every month for the explicit purpose of going off with rock stars or actors or whoever offers her a ride." I thought of all the clauses in my own contract, about kosher food and all. I thought clauses were a pretty good idea.

"Or we could just baptize her and make her Orthodox," said Moish.

"Now you're not being serious," I said. "I'm serious. We could have changed her life."

"If she really wants her life changed," I told Moish, "she'll find a way to change it."

We climbed in the car. The coast poured by. Plains that stretched for miles, plots of grape bushels and fields of yellow mustard seed and pink carnations to be harvested for midsummer dances. We fought over the first CD to listen to. Moish wanted *Also Sprach Zarathustra*, the theme to *2001*. I rolled my eyes. "We're on an *adventure*, Moish," I kvetched. "Classical music is *lethargic*."

The camera in Moish's hands shot from my face to his in quick, jarring motions. "It's good," he said.

Ultimately, since Moish was trying to film with one hand and drive with the other, I could snatch control of the CD player. I put in Hole, *Celebrity Skin*, which always made me think of Los Angeles and adventures. So many of the songs had quick, drumroll-like beats and fast upswing guitars. When you played it in the background, your life felt like an action movie. I rolled down the window and flattened my palm against the wind. My fingertips blew back, struggling. My hair whipped around. It was the first time that my hair was long enough to blow.

I strained my eyes against the horizon. There was a blur of fog and monoliths. I imagined it was San Francisco.

Three hours later, I was still trying to make out San Francisco in the distance. The music had long since become grating, both of our send-off CDs were exhausted, and Moish's weird Sonic Youth twenty-minute-long screeching experimental rock projects were the only thing we could agree on. Neither of us spoke. The road was giving both our brains freezer burn. I didn't have to pee but I thought about asking Moish if we could make a pit stop, just to induce a change of pace.

Instead, I whipped out a pad of paper. "Okay, dude," I said. "What do you want to see in San Francisco? Give me a list."

Moish closed his eyes. The road was so straight and flat that there was no need to keep them open. He scrunched up his mouth and thought, and then he started listing.

"Fisherman's Wharf. Everyone says it's boring, but I want to get footage of tourists buying I HEART SAN FRANCISCO shit and some fat old sea lions sleeping on the dock, and maybe cut back and forth between them. And maybe there will be some cool performance artists doing shit on the street for change. I want to see City Lights Bookstore. And I want to go to some sort of poetry event, even though there's no way it will be good. Chinatown. The building that Francis Ford Coppola owns. The

Archer Detective Agency from *The Maltese Falcon.* And I want to see the ocean from up north. I want to see if it looks different."

I nodded. Right now on the radio there was a dog barking in what might have been a syncopated drumbeat. I didn't know. I was busy listening.

"What about you, Hava?"

"I want to see the Golden Gate Bridge," I said. "So I can stand on the edge with my head against a beam and look down and have nothing beneath me. I want to feel what it's like to jump."

I looked dead-on at Moish. I waited for him to react. The corners of his mouth struggled, trying to force words out. I liked being around somebody who was usually extreme, so that I could top his extreme.

I wasn't sure if I meant it. I was feeling pretty dire these days.

A hill came up, and Moish focused on the road as he swerved. I stared at the road, too. Some of the hills were charred, like a forest fire had recently hit.

The dashboard clock flashed the time in pale green digits. If I was in L.A., we would have just wrapped up the final rehearsal before filming.

"Or maybe I'd just like to spend an afternoon drinking coffee," I said. "And maybe for someone to sit down next to me and not know who I am and still be interested in me."

"I'm interested in you," Moish said.

"I know," I told him. "But only 'cause you haven't found anything more interesting yet."

Twilight started early. When you're on the road, it takes a while for the sun to set. We were still coasting through industrial parks of bland Silicon Valley green-windowed office buildings at sunset, and we hit rush hour traffic as the pointy, cathedralesque suspension bridge (the dull gray Bay Bridge, not the bright and tacky, postcard-ready Golden Gate) popped into view.

On the other side was San Francisco.

The cars stood bumper-to-bumper for half an hour. The screaming dogs CD whirred to a stop. Neither of us made a motion to change it.

"Sun's goin' down," Moish remarked.

"That it is," I agreed.

"Have you done afternoon prayers?"

"Nah," I said. "You?"

"Nah. Want to?"

"I'm down," I said. I yanked my prayerbook out of my knapsack.

Moish slid his laminated pocket prayer sheet out of his wallet, flung open the door, and climbed out.

"Moish!" I sirened. "What are you doing?"

"Traffic isn't going anywhere," he said. "And I'd like to."

He jumped onto the hood, and stepped from there onto the roof. I listened to the tinny clang of three steps backward, then three steps forward. I heard the mumbled Hebrew of his prayers.

I rolled down my window, climbed out, and joined him.

When we finally rolled into the city, neither of us knew where to go. Moish had bought a guidebook, but neither of us wanted to be stuck in a mid-range Holiday Inn chain with little kids who ran the ice machine early in the morning and families who went to bed at seven-thirty. That left the really nice places and the really crappy hostels.

Hostels it was.

The few hostels we could find, though, looked seriously druggy. Moish and I were from New York, and not ones to make generalizations, but we had to step over a man sleeping on the doorway of the first hostel and we didn't. In the second hostel, the desk clerk's arm looked like it had been through a sewing machine.

And so, at around midnight that night, we found ourselves pulling our rented red Corvette into the portico of the Fairmont Hotel.

The woman at the front desk, a squirmy little goblin whose name tag said MRS. HUMPHREY, scowled at us like stains that won't come out. "Do you have a reservation?" she enunciated. "Are you absolutely certain you're at the right hotel?"

"Honey," I said to Moish, "this *is* the hotel that the Bushes spoke so highly of, isn't it?" He pretended to study the brass logo behind the desk, and shot me a thumbs-up. I turned back to Mrs. Humphrey. "I believe I *am* absolutely certain, thank you."

She raised one eyebrow contemptuously. "We *do* take a credit card impression upon check-in," she informed us. When she spoke, she only used her bottom lip. It reminded me of evil Muppets.

I slapped my hologram-accented AmEx Platinum on the counter. "Just ring it up, bitch," I said.

And, as an afterthought: "The penthouse, if it's open."

Moish jumped up and down on the bed, trampoline-style, leaping on his feet and landing on his ass. I tried to plug his laptop computer into the phone line to check my e-mail, but I wasn't having any luck. I think the main reason people stay in five-star hotels is to call friends from the hotel room and say, "You'll never guess where I am."

The wall-length windows showed off the San Francisco skyline. It was prim and brief and colorful, but it looked like a CliffsNotes version of L.A. Also, we hadn't been anywhere in San Francisco, so the lit-up hills didn't signify anything to me. They could be wild amazing parties, but they could also be families watching TV on a boring old La-Z-Boy sofa.

We went to sleep with the lights on, surrounded by Romanesque pillars and fireplaces and squashy plush sofas. I pulled the dividers shut, waved good-bye to Moish, and fell asleep staring at the nymphy Cupid statue by my bed. Gray clouds encased the window.

The room looked the same when we went to sleep and when we woke up. I stretched, crawled out of bed, checked on Moish through the glass doors that separated our rooms. Then I eased the screen doors open and climbed out to the balcony.

The morning was foggy and tepid. The fog was so thick I could see a gray blur in front of my face. I reached out my hand. It felt like touching a cloud of steam above a teapot. In one direction I saw narrow rows of miniature pastel houses on a hill. There was grass on the far side. It boggled me that there were cities that just *ended* like that. As if the city got tired of growing.

In the other direction, I saw the ocean, the sun's reflection narrow on the glittery surface. It was hella early for a vacation day, seven or eight at the latest. I'd been waking up so early lately, alert and primed as soon as I leaped out of bed.

"Come on, Moish!" I thudded my palm on the glass panes of the separator. "It's Friday."

I heard him moodily grumping through his morning prayer. "*Haaaaa*va," he groaned. "Go back to bed. It's still legally last night."

I ousted him from his room. I opened the entertainment system, popped in a Liz Phair CD, and blasted it to the sound of sunrise.

The weather cleared by mid-morning. We checked out of the hotel (service: [*x*] Unsatisfactory, reason: Mrs. Humphrey), stowed our clothes and toothbrushes in the car, and grabbed beverages at a café in the Mission. I drank coffee and orange juice; Moish took straight espresso. We sat on a sleepy corner of Valencia Street, watching frumpy-haired art school types rub the sleep out of their eyes and step into the sun.

I eyed the art kids as they walked by, guitars strapped to their backs. Moish sat across from me, facing away from the street, thumbing through his guidebook frenetically.

"Hava," Moish shrilled, "what are you thinking?"

"How lucky we are not to be in L.A.," I said. I meant it, too. I hadn't felt a breeze in *months* and this morning, it felt great.

"Get serious, Hava. If only momentarily. Shabbos is this afternoon. We still don't know where we're staying or eating or anything."

"Relax," I said, grabbing the guidebook from him. "We'll find a Chabad house somewhere, just like we did in L.A. They'll let us sleep there. And if there's no room, I'll rent another hotel room nearby."

"Not with these hills," Moish snorted, snatching back his guidebook. "Driving up them is bad enough. Without wheels, forget it, we're goners."

"Moish. There is a whole indigenous culture in this city. Generations have grown up with hills like these."

"Have you read the guidebook at all? I mean, have you ever seen *Vertigo*? Nobody is *from* San Francisco. Everyone moves here. We are gonna starve. Just like Pico Robertson, only without a jolly Santa Claus Hasid like Yossi to save us."

"Fuck, Moish! Look up 'Chabad' in the index. Does it say anything?"

He flipped and shook his head.

And then, like manna raining down on the Children of Israel in the desert, I caught sight of it.

"Hey, you!" I leaped out of my seat and bolted. "Jew! Wait up!"

The guy was wearing a big floppy knit hat that could have been a rainbow hippie-Jew bukhari yarmulke, but while people watching, I had automatically filed the hat as a Rastafarian Jah-love beanie. Only my last-second glance at the guy's ass made me realize what was going on.

Tzitzis, those pale white fringes that looked so obvious and flammable on Moish, almost camouflaged into this dude's Hawaiian shirt and khaki corduroys.

He turned around at once. Big opaque sunglasses and a short, doggy beard smiled at me. "Whoa whoa whoa," he said. "Hang on there, girl. This is the land of left-wing activists. But not everybody around here who calls you Jew wants to be your friend."

I stammered.

"C'mon, come on," the guy laughed, "this isn't *so* Middle America. What's your name? What are you doing here? And who's the goth boy with the yarmulke?"

Sruly, our new friend, introduced himself and seated himself at our table. He ordered coffee and orange juice, the same as me. I liked alternating sips — something bitter, something sweet — and I'd never seen anyone who did the same thing. Sruly noticed the confluence of our habits and just nodded, pacifyingly, as though it wasn't actually the cosmic coincidence that it felt like in my brain. Sruly treated everything with understated coolness. He'd noticed Moish sitting there — Moish's yarmulke was, after all, turned out to the street — but, he said, he'd figured we were just more summer tourists.

Moish and I exchanged nervous glances. We admitted that we were in high school and on a road trip.

Sruly was really into that. He laughed at everything we said, even the things that weren't funny. He told us that we needed to stay with him in Berkeley for Shabbos. Moish hesitated, but I was prepared. I seized the moment and accepted, nodding furiously.

We left the rental car on the street. I was dubious. Sruly gave me a look that said to stop being so East Coast and relax. He led us to his car and we all climbed in.

Over the bridge, the houses grew shorter and more suburban. We pulled into a side street and walked through a narrow corridor of wisteria and vines. The house was big and rickety, painted a bright shade of aquamarine. It was somewhere between makeshift and beautiful. The house, Sruly told us, was called the Blue Hebrew.

Two guys ran around the kitchen in a frenzy. Stubble-filled faces dated them, college age maybe, a few years older than us. The air smelled like buttered onions and stewed tomatoes and avocados and carrot juice. Sruly ran to a boiling-over pot and stirred, spooning in flecks of thyme and cinnamon. Moish and I, backpacks in hand, stood in the center of the kitchen. We were like the fulcrum of the room, and they orbited around us.

Sruly glanced at us and grinned. Moish and I gulped back, waiting for him to direct us or say we could help or show us where to drop our stuff, but he was back on the boiling kettle, stirring in powder that looked more like potions than spices.

Eventually, this girl appeared in the doorway. "What are you doing?" she exclaimed. "Are you visitors? Did you just get into town? Come with me. The boys really will help you out, but you have to bully them into doing it. If you're hungry, grab some cookies from that tray. Follow me. I'll show you where you're sleeping."

I shrugged. Moish and I followed her out.

"I'm Rivka," she said, as an afterthought.

She walked us out to the garden backyard. She unlatched the door to a hut out back, an old maid's quarters with walls covered in ivy. Small square windows poked out from the mossy mesh. "The boys inside were Hagai and Ari and Sruly. You don't need to remember any of their names. Just keep asking. We're informal around here, so you shouldn't feel bad being informal yourself." Rivka rummaged through a ring of keys that she wore around her wrist. "Now, are you two together? Did you want to sleep in the same bed, or in the same room, or separate?"

She turned the handle and pushed open the door.

"We don't —" I began, and immediately fell silent.

Moish's jaw dropped dislocationally low.

The little house was filled, floor to ceiling, with film equipment. Cameras and monitors and thin long strips of spent film, reels and reels of new film. In one corner sat a pyramid of reel-to-reel canisters beneath a dominating poster of Alfred Hitchcock and a montage from *The Birds.* It was like someone had opened the door on Moish's deepest fantasies. It was a total bona fide film director wasteland.

We both got bug-eyed. Rivka tucked her hands behind her back and leaned against the door, swinging with it.

I was the first to recover.

"Oh," I said, "we can sleep in sleeping bags anywhere. Separate. I mean, we're not together. I mean — we're friends, but we're not *together* together."

Rivka grinned, shrugging. It was a friendly shrug, not dismissive. She treated us nicer when she knew that Moish and I weren't hooking up. Or at least (I thought, with a flurry of guilt) that we weren't hooking up with each other.

It was a Jewish thing, I guess. Finding out someone really *is* Orthodox, and not just mostly Orthodox, or Orthodox-style.

"This is Sruly's studio," Rivka, warmer, told us. "Sorry about all the electric stuff lying around. Just ignore it, if you can."

"I don't think Moish is able to ignore it," I said. "Is Sruly a film director?"

"You could say that," said Rivka.

We reentered the house through the kitchen door. Rivka and I moved furniture around the living room while Moish helped Sruly cook, all the while asking him questions about filming.

I think Moish was a little disappointed to learn Sruly's movies were mostly independent. He made one movie about getting ready for Shabbos and another about a drive-in marriage booth where you and your boyfriend spoke to a rabbi through a fast-food window and then he performed a wedding ceremony on you. Most of Sruly's actors were his friends, housemates, some local actors from across the bay in San Francisco. Their rabbi friend, one of those old people who never seriously matured past the emotional age of a schoolboy, played the rabbi.

"And who exactly *sees* these movies?" Moish asked skeptically.

"Mostly, Sruly does," Rivka called from the living room.

"Lots of people do," Sruly said. "Not *loads.* But everyone in the movie got a copy, and they show their friends. The Saturday night after I finished editing, we had the biggest party ever and we projected the movie on the side of the house."

"Did you just film with a video camera?" Moish asked.

"No way, dude. We started 8mm and then switched to AV digital polyfiber . . ." Sruly's voice faded off in my head as I screened out the technical information that I would never understand. Plus, Rivka and I were lifting a huge mahogany table from one end of the room to the other, and I needed to pay attention.

We set the room with plates and silverware and seat cushions for thirty. At home, we'd sometimes have large meals at the rabbi's house, but no regular families ever had dinners this big. I was starting to work up a sweat, shouldering four chairs at a go. I made some remark about estimating high when that boy Pinhas – a slouchy, shy cute kid who alternated between switching CDs and mixing up a jalapeño and tomatoey-smelling chili in a pot as tall as a child – looked over in my direction and said, "You think we're overestimating? You just wait."

Moish left to get ready and, when he came back, I took my shower. I took my time, staring at the tiles on the wall for the longest while. The tiles were a jigsaw pattern of forest greens and sandy beiges, so different from my pastel oranges and mints at home in Hollywood. Suddenly, there was another gravitational shift in my brain, not only from my parents' house in New York to my apartment in L.A., but to three hundred miles north. There was an hour left till Shabbos, and no way I could get anywhere by then, even if I wanted to. I felt more homeless than ever. My spine shivered, feeling the pangs of adventure.

I came downstairs, fixing the buttons of my shiny gold-and-violet checkerboard shirt. Kids were starting to arrive, gradually, in twos and threes. Some dressed in earth-toned hippie smocks, some in khakis and collared shirts, others in clubby rave pants and turtleneck tunics. Everybody's wardrobes were mellower than the stiff New York jacket-and-tie uniform, less formal than the Los Angeles synagogue-lite tie-and-sandals uniform. You could almost say they were individualist thinkers, except that we were at a communal Shabbos dinner. Rivka and Sruly and the kids seemed nice and playfully irreverent and all, but I was still wary. I'd never trusted large groups of Jews to be cool, hip, or even — except in the ironic sense — fun.

They were mostly college kids. Moish and I kept exchanging glances until I realized how much we were making eye contact, and felt lame for it. I let the conversations build. This lanky kid in basketball shorts and knee-length *tzitzis* flirted with me. I let him, for a little. Then I turned to my left. This Ultra-Orthodox-lookin' girl in a long skirt and form-hiding smocky shirt started talking to me immediately. She asked what I did. I tried to answer noncommittally. She looked skeptical.

"I'm in high school," I said.

She grinned conspiratorially.

I gulped, not knowing what to say next.

"What about you?"

"I'm a rapper," she replied.

Somebody banged on the table and the conversations fell. Glasses of wine were dispersed, flurries of hands passing them through the crowd. Rivka cleared her throat, raised a fiery wine goblet, and made kiddush.

Everybody hummed along. I broke my exile and shot Moish a confused look. I was so not accustomed to this. Not that women *couldn't* make kiddush. But they never *did*.

We washed, the line pouring out the door, and we ate challah. Salads and sauces sprung from everywhere. The ostensible rapper girl gripped my hand. "It's okay," she whispered. I could tell she sensed my culture shock. "Everything here really is Orthodox."

"Umm, thanks," I gulped.

"And hey, don't worry, all the food is vegetarian. Just in case you're worried about the supervision on the meat."

"Vegetarian?" My eyes gleamed. I felt like I'd found a hundred-dollar bill lying on the ground. I mouthed the word in Moish's direction. He'd lost the lonely, deprived, video cameraless look that usually plagued him on Friday nights. He was deep in conversation with a bunch of athletic-looking U-Cal girls.

I shrugged. He'd figure it out for himself.

After dinner, I could have sworn I heard a snare drum. I was about to turn to the guy next to me and say something about how the neighbors had no respect, playing loud music on a Friday night, but then I listened and realized it was coming from inside this room. Some kids began to drum on the table. I scanned the place, looking for the radio. Then I noticed Sruly, *shockeling,* swaying back and forth with his hand cupped over his mouth. He *shockeled* with the same rhythm as the snare drum. His fingers fluttered out when the high-hat cymbal taps came.

"He's beatboxing," Moish hissed in my ear.

"I *know,*" I said, more snidely than I should have. I was half mesmerized by the performance, and half annoyed at the presumption that Moish could cross the room to talk to me.

"Queen Malka," Sruly rapped.

– "*Malka,*" echoed the crowd –

"Is in the house. Let me hear you say Queen Malka –"

"– *Queen Malka* –"

"– is in the house."

People whistled.

The girl I'd been talking to stood. She levitated above the heads of the crowd. She licked her lips. She waited for her moment.

"Is Rebbe Yochanan speakin' the truth?" Queen Malka said. Her flat palm shot out and caught the beat. She swayed with the rhythm.

"*True!*" echoed the crowd.

"He's makin' *zivugim* to create *Yam Suf*!"

She broke out verses. Everyone sang the choruses by heart. By the end of the night, wine was flowing from pores in my skin, the room was bouncing, and I was in hysterics. Moish was drumming Sephardic beats on a table with two other kids, and his face was a roller coaster of giddiness. My brain spun. I was wild. I was delirious. I fell dizzily into Rivka's arms. She helped me to the couch, slipped off my shoes, and lay me down. My body was buzzing with sugar and alcohol and adrenaline.

"This isn't real," I murmured. "People like this don't exist."

"Somebody has to," Rivka whispered to me. "Why can't it be us?"

"Nnn," I moaned softly as she pulled a crocheted afghan over my body. I shut my eyes, and that was it.

By late Saturday afternoon, my neurosis was in remission. We flopped lethargically in the garden behind the Blue Hebrew house. A ring of tulips and wisteria crowned Moish's head, and his yarmulke flapped onto a patch of honeysuckle. I swung back and forth in a hammock, one hand dangling down, getting all Michelangelo with a magnolia.

"Tell me how I need to get back to L.A.," I said to Moish. "Tell me how I fucked up, and how Hollywood is out for my blood, and I'm a self-centered asshole and the weird-ass Producers are gonna hang me out to dry. Tell me I should run back right now."

"But, Hava. I think it was a good idea."

"Just tell me," I demanded.

"You should run back and apologize," Moish said dryly.

"Fuck that." I sighed, easing farther into the hammock. "It's Shabbos."

Sruly meandered out of the house, looking freshly awake. His Hawaiian shirt was even brighter than yesterday's. "Well, Hava," he demurred, "check out the ego on *you*."

I bolted up, sending the hammock into spasms. I grabbed for a post.

"It's true," explained Moish. "She's a famous actor."

"Despite the fact that we're Orthodox," I said defensively, "we have a life, too."

Sruly's toothy grin widened.

"Then what do you have planned for tonight?" he asked.

Moish and I exchanged remedial expressions.

"Well, come with us," Sruly said. "We'll hook you up."

The sun went down. We headed into the city, which, from across the Bay, felt too small to hold all the cars waiting to drive inside. Red brake lights sparkled like an airport runway along the bridge. We walked inside the club, dancing up a maelstrom at once, Sruly gallivanting monkily with the black kids, swooping arms and clunking feet. Moish shook his fists self-consciously, glancing around constantly to examine how everyone else danced. And me, I felt freer than ever, like all the other people were a backdrop instead of an audience. I could cut loose and nobody would notice. The few women there were so illustrious and decked out, dresses with millions of sequins, faces painted like skintight masks. And, when I did cut loose and dance, the room felt like camouflage, like I wasn't trying to blend in. Like I was playing my own game.

"Is this a gay club?" I yelled to Sruly over the music. "Are you guys really down with that?"

He grinned conspiratorially.

"We like the gay clubs best," explained Rivka. "Being gay is, like, the closest you can find in the secular world to being *shomer negiah*. The boys never try to bump and grind with you."

"Yeah!" I exclaimed.

"Hava," said Moish, his face scrunched up in confusion. "I think you have officially found your people."

I opened my mouth to reply, but then a drag queen in four-inch stilettos grabbed Moish and swept him into a tango dip.

My eyes sparkled. *I* sparkled. Not that I was comfortable. But I finally felt *un*comfortable in a way I could deal with.

"*That's* the reason?" I asked Rivka.

She shrugged her shoulders. "All our rules about sex," she said. "How we have to wait. Who we're supposed to desire. Being Orthodox is the ultimate queer. More than anyone at my yeshiva would admit to, anyway."

That night, as Sruly pulled Moish and me to a table for drinks with a bunch of brightly colored dancers, I wanted Ian to be there for every minute of it.

"Omig-d! Is that Versace?" squealed the woman sitting next to me. She was tall, painted in pastels and florals, taller than me or Sruly or Moish. Long blond hair cascaded to the small of her wistfully proportioned waist. She fondled the sleeve of my dress between two four-inch lacquered nails.

I shrugged. "I dunno," I said. "I get all this shit at work. I just wear it when I need to look nice or something."

"Versace," she whispered dreamily. "Baby, I would give *any*thing for someone to stuff my ensemble full of Versaces."

I turned to her. I opened my mouth, then closed it again. I couldn't tell her this was overrated. There was a reason that she would never get asked to play the Angsty Teenage Daughter, even on a non-Orthodox sitcom. Nobody made TV shows about the way she grew up.

Maybe this is why all the great artists and writers and everyone were alcoholics. Because alcohol opens you up and it makes you permeable and more open-minded. "Shit," I exclaimed. "I need to call Ian."

I raced outside. Ian's number went to voicemail on the first ring. It was late where I was, and it was three hours later in Manhattan. Ian was way asleep.

So I went back in and danced.

Before long, Moish and Sruly and the drag queens found me on the dance floor. They joined in. We swung our heads and slurred our asses against the air. Our shins twisted and our knees clanked. None of us were prepared to drive back to the Blue Hebrew House that night, so we all ended up crashing at a swank, futuristic pad that was owned by a dot-com vice president whose job had outlasted the city's crash.

In the morning, we all woke up early, the alcohol turning to sugar, racing through our blood. I wanted us to start back to L.A. as soon as possible, after breakfast, if there was a kosher restaurant around. I was feeling antsy and remorseful. Moish looked put out. "We haven't even *seen* the city," he kvetched.

"What do you want? A guided tour? We could go back separately. I can pay for everything," I said.

Moish refused. "That's not what this was about," he said.

I felt bad arguing. Especially when I knew he was right.

Sruly was still asleep, swathed all over in blankets, like a Jewish guru. He struggled to sit up. He croaked a hoarse *Modeh Ani*, the prayer that you say when waking up, and rubbed the crust from his eyes.

Moish and I did that day on autopilot. Tumbling out the front door of the apartment building, we were surrounded in a haze of Chinese signs. We were in Chinatown. Moish remembered from the guidebook that City Lights Bookstore sat in the middle of Chinatown, and inside, I bought a journal and spent an hour scribbling while Moish read every beat poetry book in the whole entire attic. From there we walked to Fisherman's Wharf, got run over by mobs of grandmotherly tourists, and quickly headed back downtown.

Moish was mellow about the absence of his video camera. I was scared to ask, but I finally did. He shrugged. "It's in the car. I'll get to it," he said. "I'm still recording every moment I can. But I don't need to sacrifice every moment I have."

I didn't totally buy it. But I didn't push the point. It was Sunday and we were happy. I sighed, snapping a picture of Moish in front of the Golden Gate Bridge.

Moish and I took pictures of each other all over — Alcatraz, Ocean Beach, the Sutro Baths, and pushing a cable car, both of us grinning stupidly, like a sitcom family. With a shock, I realized, that's what we *are*. We tell bad jokes, we fight over nonsense, we pose for cheesy pictures, and we love every minute of it. Moish and I had become what we most dreaded — zany icons of twenty-first-century American life.

That night, we went to a poetry reading. Moish got up, started reading Yiddish proverbs in a whispery deathlike voice, and got booed offstage. We ran out of the club, laughing our hearts out. The car was already loaded and waiting outside.

We hadn't gotten to say good-bye to the other Jews, Rivka and Pinhas and especially Queen Malka. It didn't bother me. Queen Malka's hip-hop melody from Friday night was still stuck in my head.

I hoped it stayed there forever.

15

INVITATION

The studio felt familiar when I ripped through the doors Monday morning, bristling for the new script. I was ready for the new day. I was ready for whatever punishment, mysterious or otherwise, the Producers were ready to mete out.

To my surprise, nobody said a word.

I walked in, fresh out of Moish's car, combing my growing-in hair with my fingers to a respectable standard of straightness. The light fixtures glowed chalk-yellow. The rugs were still that shade of shit-brown. None of my fellow actors, histrionic drama queens that they were, said a thing. I passed Paula, David Lee, even Evie. None of them seemed to care. Evie looked a little self-satisfied, a swagger in her hips.

First thing was the morning meeting. Shira O'Sullivan was there, preparing coffee for everyone. Howard was on the phone with someone, apparently having some sort of argument about lunch. The kids, Charles, and the director were already seated. So was Kevin, who sat with the rest of the cast this morning.

David Lee came in, and everyone was instantly warm — "Hey, we missed you, how was the film shoot?" David Lee answered with his characteristic reserve — short, courteous answers that didn't say anything, but made you feel somehow grateful that he wasn't ignoring you.

David Lee blew on his coffee. A silence set over the group.

"So," I said nonchalantly, "are we going to have to reshoot the episode this morning or what? I still remember all my lines . . ."

"No," said the director, "we gave your plot to Evie. Hindel stole Kevin from you, and now they're going out. When you took off, the writers made some readjustments. Fortunately for us, Evie already had your part completely memorized."

I was silent.

Howard, still on the phone, murmured something about *only the rest of the season . . . then we can reevaluate the cast.* Evie, giddy and giggly, rubbed her palms together.

I dug my nails into the bottom of my chair, holding myself steady. Really I was keeping myself from leaping up and tearing out Evie's short-but-girlish hair, follicle by follicle. I grated my teeth. I watched the other actors hedge and look bored until Paula, dressed no-nonsense with an alligator-skin purse, entered. She strode through the doors, shot an icy glare at me, and swished into her seat.

"*Hem, hem,*" Howard coughed. He finally hung up his phone. "Now, shall we get to work on the new script?"

"With *her* here?" Paula, digging through her purse, indicated me by a curt dart of her miniature nose.

"Ms. Oxnard, we told you, we're not firing anyone," Shira O'Sullivan said calmly.

"*I* told *you*. I'll quit."

"Please, Ms. Oxnard," said Shira.

Paula shut her purse with a decisive *snap*.

"Paula, please," Charles pleaded, softly.

"*No*. That's *it*. I am *through*," she said, raising herself out of her chair. "This is so. Fucking. Ludicrous."

Everybody else froze. Except for Howard, fidgeting with his phone, there was dead silence.

Then Paula froze.

Howard's fidgeting sounded suspiciously like a number being dialed.

We all waited, afraid to breathe.

"Casting?" Howard, in that wheezy testosterone-depleted voice, said, "Can we have Mrs. Goldberg 2.0 come to the reading room?" He hung up without so much as a thank-you.

We heard a knock on the door.

It was a shrill, short, no-shit knock, sudden and loud. It was exactly the kind of knock that Paula would use. By some unspoken consensus, it fell to Paula to answer the door. The weirdness of the morning was wearing on all our psyches. Paula opened it wide.

A woman in her upper thirties, hair pulled immaculately back, wearing a black business suit, stood poised at the door. Her fist was frozen in the air, ready to knock again.

"Hello," she said in a pleasant, musical, slightly unsure tone of voice. "I'm Mollie Steinsaltz. I'm Mrs. Goldberg."

Paula's features changed. For a single, split second — and only if you were looking at her eyes, like I was — you could see her features change. Paula became every bit a forty-something woman, middle age and wrinkles and varicose veins around the temples, sleep-deprived, squinting, the trauma of indecisiveness leading to more scrunchy wrinkle-inducing indecision.

Then Paula's regular, unmarked skin and unbreakable facial strength came back.

"Get out," she said.

"Excuse me, I'm sorry?" said the woman at the door.

"I'm Mrs. Goldberg. Get *out*."

Paula slammed the door in the other woman's face. Then she smoothed out her skirt, combed one strand of hair back with a fingernail, and took her seat.

None of us felt entirely comfortable. We shifted in our seats.

Presently, scripts were brought out. We took them eagerly, a little too fast. Even Baby Goldberg, in his booster seat, gnawed with vigor on the corner of his copy.

Charles said, "Good L-rd, do they have duplicates for all of us in there?"

"Not all of us," I said. "Just the expendable old dime-a-dozen bitches."

"Hava!" Charles snapped, in a voice that my father would say belonged outdoors.

"I'm sorry," I murmured. "Is that what you want me to say? I'm sorry that it's true?"

"Hava, you're acting like you're about six years old," Charles scolded.

"Give children an inch, and they take a mile," said Paula. She picked her script off the table and flipped through it like a week-old magazine, barely paying attention. "Especially the underage hussies."

My nerves flared up. Half a dozen retaliations fired through my head, from *You're acting like you're FIVE* to *That's not what you thought last weekend.* I knew that Charles still had it for me. I could feel his eyes lingering on my body when he spoke and when he looked at me in rehearsals.

And maybe it was just Berkeley swimming around my head — me getting a little bit older, less confrontational and more reserved, and possibly just a little more civilized — but I didn't say anything. I flipped open my script to the first page. I tried to watch everyone without being obvious. They were all nervous, docilely flipping their scripts open, too.

I breathed easier. I didn't have any lines on the first page. Less to worry about. More space to lie low.

An hour later, I still didn't have any lines and I was breathing less easy. Call it kismet, but I wondered what exactly Paula's purpose in walking out was. Howard said they weren't going to can me. But we were halfway through the show, the writers had stopped only twice for corrections, and the only appearance I made was incidental — Page 7, *The Goldberg family sits around the television.*

My speaking part could have had Helen Keller doing over-dubs.

Kevin fell into the role of Evie's on-screen boyfriend easily. I started to wonder if I was a ghost. The only person who paid any attention to me was Charles, who glared at me between reads, looking at me like I was a five-year-old who peed her pants once too often. I could feel the director and the other actors and, from some hidden camera, I was sure the Producers were watching me, too. I was afraid to speak at all.

At the end of the episode, I had two lines. Both were my signature catchphrase, "*Oy vey*, dude!" When I said them, the air around the table froze, and everybody stopped breathing. Both times, I said my line emotionlessly, boringly.

The director didn't even bother telling me off.

The minute rehearsal was over, I stormed into my dressing room. I slammed the door shut, folded my arms on the table, dropped my head in the middle, and cried.

I was frustrated and angry and ineffective and a total loser. I wanted to do things my own way, and they'd been humoring me the whole time. I kept telling people I was a star.

I was such an asshole. You don't *tell* people you're a star. You wait for them to tell you. The world was such an evil fucked-up place. I thought I could bite it, and it slapped me away like a gnat.

There was a knock on the door.

"Go away," I called.

I turned around, expecting to have to repeat *go away* until Charles left. The door creaked open narrowly, and — looking a little sheepish, a little self-consciously intrusive — David Lee swung his skinny body inside.

"Sorry I missed all the drama," he said, grinning sheepishly. "You know, I had the new movie shoot. Evie filled me in. I can't believe, the one week I take off is the week all the action happens."

I tried to wipe my eyes clean without being too obvious, which is never a successful move.

"Don't take it too hard," I said. "I missed most of it, too."

"When I was sixteen, I was shooting *Riverdale High Blues*. This one weekend, I convinced Christina Applegate — you probably wouldn't know her, she's this other Hollywood person — to steal the director's car with me for the weekend. We drove straight through the desert to Vegas. We had the wildest weekend ever, Hava. We put the movie 2.6 million dollars over budget. It was the best time of our lives, though." He shook his head. "I can't fuckin' believe I'm telling stories from my youth. I swear to you I'm not that old. Hey, who left you the TV?"

I looked where he was pointing. A small, seven-inch television sat there, wired and pointed in the direction of my chair.

"No idea," I said. "You don't usually get rewarded for running away for the weekend, do you?"

"Maybe it's a message. Like a letter under your door?"

"Maybe." I shrugged, taking it off the desk.

"Turn it on," David Lee said.

"What?"

"Turn it on. If someone left you a letter, you'd open it, wouldn't you?"

I pressed the power button. A white dot appeared on the screen, and then the picture sprang on.

The angle and blurriness looked like a closed-circuit camera, the kind they use in banks and 7-Elevens. The room it showed was small, though, and you could almost see the whole thing. Harsh fluorescent lights. One big wall mirror, a desk, and a canvas chair. As the picture fuzzed into focus, Paula strutted into the changing room, puffing on a cigarette and then extinguishing it on the table. She undid the buttons on her shirt and pulled it off. She wore a shiny padded bra underneath. She shook out her hair and it was longer than you'd think it would be. There was a residue of curls.

Paula went to answer the door. A deep, satisfied smile crossed her face.

She reached one hand out to grab her visitor's arm and, fluidly, naturally, she placed the newly fetched hand on her breast. Paula's other arm shot up to her visitor's hair and pulled him in — though, it's only fair to say, he leaned in symphony with her — for a greedy, harsh, full-mouth kiss. It lasted several minutes. I stared, transfixed, unable to break my paralysis. Charles's hand slid under her skirt. Paula moved into it. She shifted her weight into his palm. She wrapped her legs around him, fencing him in, unwrapping his belt and zipper with a single motion. Her hips buckled. His pants dropped. They bumped together awkwardly and excitedly, at first surging fast, then slowing, yogalike, in a single, synchronized motion.

It occurred to me that I had never actually seen people having sex before — not so clearly.

I mean, I'd thought about it constantly. Actually seeing it — and seeing it in a weird, voyeuristic way — felt like a moment of revelation. Like solving the last clue in a crossword puzzle. Human bodies intertwined so bizarrely, almost not at all.

They were moving so slow, now, almost the exact same speed together. One of her hands massaged his back, gently, lovingly, with her long fingers and short, sharp nails. The other held his head tight, fingers clamped into a fist. Paula brought his head down on her neck, which he sucked on, softly.

Paula, though, stared straight into the camera. A look of triumph was painted dead across her face.

"Maybe it's a tape," David Lee said. "Maybe it's from years ago."

I shook my head. "That's her dressing room now."

Her lips were shaped in the sound of heavy, heavy breathing, about to scream in fury. She gripped her feet tighter around Charles's body and lunged herself forward, slamming him against the far wall and off-camera. The wall of my dressing room, the wall we shared, shuddered. I pressed my palm against it. You could feel the pounding.

"Nope," I said. "Not a videotape."

David Lee reached over and cut the power. He yanked the plug straight out of the wall. "What do you say we take a walk?" he said. "Looks like it's going to be a long lunch break, anyway."

Outside the studio, he lit a cigarette and offered me one. I shook my head politely. We turned west on Melrose, walking toward the factories and warehouses. David Lee took one strong drag on his cigarette, then pulled it from his mouth immediately.

"Did I ever tell you I'm Jewish?" he said.

"Are you fucking serious?" I exclaimed. "I have been living my life thinking I was the only alien here. No, David Lee, I don't think you did."

"David Leibel Miller," he said. "My mom's family was old school. Some of them even wore the hats. They don't anymore, some kinda family battle where half of them followed *this* rabbi and half of them followed *that* one and nobody could agree to disagree. My dad wanted me to change my name. He grew up in the Bible Belt and still thought that Jews never made it in show business. It's never been a big enough scandal for the tabloids to report; just a little quirk nobody knows about. Anyway, just thought you might be interested."

"And I thought you were just some Luke Skywalker master-race poster boy. Mister tall-dark-and-handsome."

"You really think I'm handsome?" David Lee sounded surprised.

"Puh-*leeze*. I think you're hot, but you're *so* not my scene.

And I think I've had enough of relationships to keep me quiet for the next lifetime."

"Charles?"

"Charles."

We made a right, turning between two warehouses rickety enough to be condemned.

"He's like that, though," said David Lee.

"Like what?"

"Soft. Sensitive. He always falls for honest women, and he lets himself get used by the tough ones. He can't say no, you know. Most men can't."

"How do you know?" I demanded. "He and Paula dated for a while."

"They *slept together* for a while," David Lee corrected me. "I know you're Orthodox and all, but there really is a difference. Charles doesn't go for difficult women like Paula. But *they* go for *him*, and like I said, he can't say no. The kind of drama that Charles goes for is all old-fashioned, women who don't say much and who he can trust. He likes dominant women, in control of their own lives, who don't mind taking control of his life, too."

"But how do you know all this?" I asked.

David looked down the street in both directions. It was pretty deserted.

"Look," he said. "Have you ever known someone who always got themselves into tricky, screwed-up situations more than their fair share, like they were purposely trying to make their lives harder, or something like that?"

I thought of my mother, her sudden whirlwind tour into

town like a corporate takeover of my sympathies. "Yeah," I said. "I could think of a few."

"Well," David Lee shrugged, "that's the way Charles is. He subconsciously needs to test the emotional bonds between himself and the people he cares about, partially as a traumatized, dramatic plea for help, and, on a deeper level, as a reaction to his own constant portrayal of characters engaged in dramatic relationships."

All this time I'd thought of Charles as the cool older guy, mysterious and distant. Now I pictured him as a little brother, geeky and greedy.

I closed my eyes. I sank back against that warehouse wall. I breathed.

"Oh," I said. "I get it."

We had gone to the end of the block, and David Lee was standing on the corner, staring into the next neighborhood over. Sirens sounded in the distance. No matter how long lunch break was, I was sure it was over by now.

"Come on," he said. "We should get back."

"David Lee, you are amazing," I told him before I had time to think about what to say. "I had no idea you were that perceptive."

He looked almost embarrassed.

"If there is ever, *ever*, anything I can do for you . . ." I wrang my hands in gratitude.

"Absolutely nothing, Hava," David Lee said to me. "Although, if that boy Ian ever comes back to town, you could slip me his number."

There was a twinkle in David Lee's eye all the way back to the studio.

* * *

We got back late and the director was ready to yell all over me, but Charles tapped his elbow and said *"I don't think that's a good idea"* — Charles, who never said a word about anything on set; Charles, who was twice as big as the scrawny mock turtleneck director. The director backed down, and the rest of the afternoon went just fine.

More to the point, Paula's smug, self-assured look evaporated after I kept clearing my throat — I had a coughing fit during my second "*Oy vey*, dude" line — and Charles ran to get me a glass of water. He came back with a vase of sparkling S. Pellegrino and an empty glass. I gulped it down nervously.

"Um, thanks," I said.

For the episode's climax, Evie introduces Kevin to the family over dinner. At one point, Baby Goldberg is screaming "*Osser!*" in the kitchen so loudly that everybody runs in from the dining room, except for Kevin, bewildered, and Evie, who's trying to tell Mom and Dad about Kevin and stuttering all over herself. As soon as everyone leaves the room, the script calls for Kevin and Evie to turn to each other and start whispering clever one-liners about the family.

On cue, Baby Goldberg stopped teething on the script and yelled "*Osser!*"

Charles: "Why is something always *osser* with that kid?"

Me: "*Oy vey*, dude!"

"The family runs out," read the director.

We looked expectantly at Kevin and Evie, because the scene belonged to them now. They were grinning at each other from opposite chairs. I don't know who twitched first, but in a moment's breath, Evie leaped from her chair onto Kevin. He was already reacting.

They met halfway, their mouths fell open, and they grinded into each other, groping and pawing and kissing.

My gaze caught David Lee, who rolled his eyes. Jamie and Corey started giggling. Under the table, Paula nestled her foot between Charles's legs. He cradled the ball of her foot with his hand, not pushing it away, but not letting it make contact with his crotch.

Baby Goldberg began to scream, totally uncontrollably this time, "*Osser! Osssssseeeeerrrr!!!*"

But neither Kevin nor Evie had any idea what the word meant. Their chins dug deeper into each other, harder and harder as the minutes passed.

The director, meanwhile, scribbled down notes.

Howard raised an eyebrow. "You're not thinking of *using* this, are you?" he remarked. But the director shot a look that said *Why not?*, and we all felt a vicarious surge of financial horniness, thinking how our ratings would soar.

The day ended early, and there was nothing I wanted more than to get out of there. I ran to my dressing room, jammed a couple of things in my knapsack, and was all set to scram when Charles appeared in my doorway.

I wasn't mad at him. Okay, no. I was mad at him. But talking to David Lee had made my opinion of Charles plummet less than it would have, and the fact that I still let him talk to me was a miracle in itself.

Charles acted like he knew it. His voice dropped an octave

softer than it ever went. He looked entirely at me when I spoke, never drifting off or losing focus.

"Hi, Hava," he said, leaning against the side of the door. "What are you up to tonight?"

"You know. Popular people things."

"No way."

"Yeah, you're right. I'm going home, and I'll probably nuke dinner and spend a few hours on the phone until I pass out from sheer exhaustion."

"Want to go to a premiere?"

He held up two golden tickets.

I snatched them from his hand. I eyed the glistening hologram logos warily. "What, Charles," I said. "Are you trying to get on my good side or something?"

Charles looked caught. "Maybe," he admitted.

"Then come with me instead," I said, and whipped out two tickets of my own.

I kicked out Charles while I changed, and then we walked out to my Town Car and told my driver that I wouldn't need him. He actually looked kind of hurt. This was the same guy who, for two entire months of filming, I tortured by being late every day. I wondered if flaking on a hired driver who never spoke to you still counted as flaking.

But Charles had already contracted a limo for the night, and we cracked little-kid jokes, standing around, waiting for it to pull up. I asked him what you call a fish with no eyes ("Fsh!"). He told me the one about a man with no arms or legs in a pile of leaves ("Russell!").

His limo driver was kickass. He was this shriveled old Jewish guy, about ninety years old, who kept turning around and interjecting dirty jokes into our conversation. He didn't care about propriety. He didn't really care about anything. I guess when you get that old, you realize there's not much pomp worth pumping.

"That was Hymie Sirowitz," Charles said, climbing out of the car. "He's been working for the network for forty years."

We weren't going to the glitzy golden-ticket premiere, but we dressed up, anyway. Charles wore an Armani tuxedo and an old-fashioned bow tie. My skirt was a tight paisley pattern that cut into beaded strands at the knee. Half-tall go-go boots stuck sweatily against my legs, and I wore a white tank top with a denim jacket over it, covering my arms, but splashing more cleavage than I'd want to show in a society column.

Aw, I told myself — *get over it.* G-d was the one who hit me with these overdeveloped mammaries. G-d could shoulder some of the guilt, too.

We parked on the top level of a garage that looked like a prison and walked the slanting levels in silence. Charles paused in front of the elevator, but I ignored him. After a second, he followed me. It startled me that I could pull him like that. No, actually, it didn't — I had run away from rehearsal and not gotten kicked off the show. It was like I was finally starting to realize how much other people listened to me. I was finally starting to realize how much power I had.

Inside the theater, Charles was visibly thrown. No lights, no paparazzi, no Ashton Kutcher stepping out of a limo with cameras blazing. A small crowd of hipsters milled about.

"Would you like some popcorn?" Charles asked. "Are you allowed?"

I shrugged. "If you're not worried, I'm not worried."

We stopped at the popcorn counter and I asked to see the

oil. It was kosher. While Charles waited, I ran over the crowd with my eyes, checking out all the people I recognized and the people that I knew.

"Ooh, Charles!" I cried. "I'll be right back!" Through the bodies, I spotted a concession stand with a big printed sign that said KOSHER.

I kept looking around the lobby for Moish. I figured for sure he would be surfing through the meager crowd, dressed in a pure-black tuxedo and pulling all sorts of enigmatic stunts, but he was nowhere to be found. There was a small coalition of Orthodox Jews, identifiable by their yarmulkes and Dockers khakis. The lobby lights dimmed like a real theater. People scurried inside to find seats.

Charles showed up at my elbow. "Shall we?" he whispered. I shrugged again. He looked at me with big sad eyes.

I walked into the theater ahead of him. I could feel him scampering behind me. I didn't turn around. When we sat down, my eyes glued to the screen and didn't turn.

The title shots began at once. There were no previews, no commercials, no fancy animation, just black letters that flashed on the screen, one line at a time, in the foreground of the picture.

hollywood movie

by mosheh baruch resnick

starring moish resnick

and the rest of the world

The credits lasted exactly as long as the drive to Moish's cousin's house. We watched L.A. come into view through the window of Moish's Supershuttle, pueblo houses turn into shopping centers and then the wide horizontal pale-colored homes of the white sections.

I shivered. The sudden explosion of blue, from the white-and-gray puritan airport colors to the rainbow-blast lens of sunlight as Moish stepped outside, it felt like something big. Like the inaugural splash of your skin into a swimming pool, that first moment of summer. It took me a second to realize how vividly it reminded me — not of my own limo ride from the airport, but of the drive back home from San Francisco. When the hills separated and the San Fernando Valley opened up below us, this lingering feeling started in my stomach, the same place where vomit starts, but it was the exact opposite feeling.

It felt like coming home.

We didn't actually get to *see* Moish until a good hour and a half into the film. There was this really interesting conversation with his superintendant, whose bald, shiny Indian head bobbed up and down on the screen like a tugboat and who took any opportunity — glasses in the sink, an overhead light that took minutes to flicker on completely — to dish about his wife, pregnant for the fourth time with twins. She refused to get a job because it wasn't their tradition. "Shit, man, you want to go for a beer?" the dude asked Moish. "I'm a super. It is a weird thing. I am paid to live here. All I really do is, I collect checks from other people who live here. I start to distrust myself. I ask myself, what the hell do they pay me for?"

Moish held the camera at his waist. We saw the upper half of his super's body. The keglike outline of his belly hung over his belt, vibrating when he talked. I liked him and felt repulsed by him at the same time.

Finally, the super left and Moish set about arranging his room. I don't know why this was all so compelling, but it *was*. I broke my eyes away from the screen and looked around at people.

Everyone in that audience was glued to the film. They laughed quietly when they laughed at all, sat in utter, expectant stillness when they weren't. We stayed honed to the sound and the flashes of movement and the details of Moish's disembodied voice.

After trying to unpack his suitcase one-handed — and here Moish's ghost hand folded into view, and the entire audience of actors and musicians and studio honchos sat forward, breaking their perfect *Playboy*-model postures, to see what sort of clothes, books, or other implements Moish would remove from his suitcase — he looked around the room. We looked around the room, too, a dizzying 360-degree spin of the camera. Then he set the camera on a table, lens pointing into the doorway of his room, and walked out.

As an audience, we experienced the moment in parts.

My head spun when, after an hour and a half of vicariously walking around at a steady level, in a straight Moish's-eye view of the universe, the camera disjoined itself from Moish's shoulder, pivoted, and spun around.

Then we saw Moish.

He stepped out nonchalantly from behind the lens, first his almost-not-there black-swathed butt, his legs and torso, his whole body.

He kneeled down to face the suitcase. In doing so, for a single solitary second, he faced the camera directly, eye-to-eye. His eyes glinted. He was smiling. *Holy shit*, I thought, realizing for the first time what everyone else in that room had been feeling all night.

Moish is a rock star.

The audience roared.

I wasn't sure whether Moish's smile was a wink at the camera, or a residual smile from moving in, or Moish's shivery thrill at thinking that, one day, his funniest home videos might be seen by millions of people on thousands of screens across America.

The applause died down fast. Moish was stacking his clothes in piles on the floor, each looking like a big bar graph. He sat down on the monitor. He gazed into space for the longest time. Five minutes passed. I found myself studying the nearly still motion picture image, spacing out just like Moish, the world beside me slipping away. I moved my head slightly. Everyone around me was enraptured, gazing, zombielike. They made grocery lists and boyfriend lists in their heads. They wrote stories. They imagined their own lives up on a screen like Moish's.

It was unbelievable. Reflexive escapism. Abruptly, Moish stood up. He strode toward the camera, wrapped it on his hand, and left the apartment building.

Moish moved on, walked down Melrose Boulevard, the blocks around his house. He started talking to people he didn't know. He kept the camera running. Strangers, some unbelievably beautiful, some hideous, stared straight into the camera lens. Everyone smiled.

I felt such a bizarre interest in characters I was never going to see again. I kept wanting them to come back, just to find out they were still there.

I wondered if this was the way people were going to feel about me someday. Or Shoshana Goldberg. Or both of us? That calculatedly detached look I plastered on my face when I was trying to be typical-teen Shoshana — were people going to believe in that?

Suddenly — *wildly* — I prayed that they would.

The audience was really into it. They were laughing when they were supposed to, whispering enthusiastically when the scene called for it, snickering at every opportunity.

And then, at some point, people started talking to each other.

Not in that whispered, middle-of-the-movie way. They spoke in a normal coffeehouse volume, eyes fixated on the screen, as though they were watching a cabaret show.

As if imprinted to the audience's thought patterns, the lights rose the tiniest increment, from theater black to mod bar muted. The film continued for a while. I looked at Charles, raising a questioning eyebrow. He leaned over to me and whispered, "I don't know if anyone in the world will like this. But I do." Hearing him say that — someone who was wise and knew the ropes — made me feel better for Moish, wherever he was. I scanned the audience. A few coiffures and mohawks stood out from the crowd. No berets.

Charles looked at me questioningly. I shook my head. I'd find Moish later, after the movie. Or, maybe when the onscreen Moish went to sleep and everybody took a coffee break.

He turned back to watch the movie, and so did I.

Five minutes later, I could feel Charles again. He looked at me expectantly, as though we were actually going to have a conversation during the film. I raised my eyebrows and fixed my eyes on the screen.

His head took a hint from mine and rotated in the same direction.

"I'm sorry," he whispered.

"Mmm?" I asked.

"G-d, Hava. For today. For everything."

"Charles," I whispered. "*Charlie.*"

"Have I told you, you can call me whatever you want?"

"You have," I whispered, traces of a smile creeping up my face.

He breathed in a moment of silence.

"I didn't want to do it," he offered at last.

"Then why did you?"

"It felt . . . I don't know. Because I'm an asshole, I suppose."

"That's an excuse, not an answer," I pointed out.

"Hava," he murmured my name like music, regretful and

sad and breathy. "Hava. You're so perfect. Half of me is afraid I'll spoil you forever. The other half of me is screaming, I want to hold on to you before I lose that chance."

I blinked. I sat still although I could feel my body shivering. In the film, Moish was trying on clothes in a Melrose vintage store. It was a little bit painful without all the quick camera cuts, but everyone was getting a playful rise out of seeing his disembodied feet hop into jeans and dresses from behind the curtain.

I dug my nails into my knee. I breathed harder.

"I don't want to lose this, Hava," he said. "I don't want to lose *you*. Even if you call me into your dressing room and kiss me once. We can kiss whenever you want."

I don't know why I'm still Orthodox. It's not because my community expects me to be Orthodox. It's not because my parents expect it from me — if I broke Shabbos, my father would love me, anyway, and my mother wouldn't notice.

Only, I really do believe in G-d. Put aside all the other shit, and that's the one thing I can't get past. When I look at food, I know someone made it. When I pull the blankets over my head in the morning, I know that someone created the fibers. When I get drunk and every star feels like a song, that feels like G-d. As cynical as I am, I'm grateful for what I've got.

Shomer negiah was never like that. It didn't make sense that G-d didn't want me to fool around with guys until I was married, and then after I was married it was a biblical commandment to fool around. Okay, it made a little sense. But I could ignore it. Hell, I might be the only person in my whole entire day school who wasn't ignoring it.

But this whole thing, not touching guys, it wasn't for G-d's sake. It didn't feel like it was for G-d at all. If someone asked me — well, if someone asked, I probably still wouldn't tell them. But, to myself, I said I wasn't doing this for G-d. I'm doing this for a husband that I haven't met yet, that I might never end up meeting. I really do want to fall in love. And if the guy I fall in love with has been *shomer* his whole life, waiting for me, I'll feel like such a jerk. I'll feel like I've been cheating on a lover that I've never met.

"We can kiss whenever you want."

Charles's voice was so close to my ear that I felt the words instead of hearing them.

"No," I said, mopping up sweat with the collar of my shirt. "No, Charles. I don't think we can."

Charles looked like he was about to say something, then thought better and hushed himself. Then he opened his mouth again. "Hava," he said, "you are an incredible young woman. I think I wish I could hug you."

Without waiting for an answer, he gathered his coat, rose up, stood by my seat for a minute, and exited the theater.

Actors. They always need to have the last word.

By the fourth hour of the movie, Moish had found an all-night restaurant and was writing in his journal. The camera followed each brush of his handwriting in long, curvaceous strokes that looped across his Moleskine notebook. Reading the letter was riveting, just to see what he came up with.

But people had begun to drift off half an hour earlier, during the much more exciting Will You Be My Friend? spontaneous interview segment. By the time Moish's letter began, the theater was almost empty.

I gathered my things, walked five or six rows back to the last row of seats, and planted myself next to the most beatnicky shadow I could find.

Moish's face, bright but uneasy, flashed the ghostly white teeth of a smile in the darkness. "Hey, Hava," he said. "I'm glad you made it."

"So am I, dorko."

I noticed his face was gleaming red, even in the movie-screen light. It felt like we were sitting around in his room, watching DVDs, shooting the general shit. Apropos to nothing, we burst out laughing.

I changed the subject. "Does this mean you stopped filming?"

He pointed to a camera on the floor, positioned between our laps. It was pointed up at our faces, flashing an infrared light in our eyes.

"You wanna get out of here?" Moish asked.

I was baffled. "Walk out of your own premiere?"

"I can come back," he said. "Besides, there's three weeks' worth of filming to do. You didn't think I'd spend it resting on my laurels, didja?"

On the way to the all-night kosher pizza palace, Moish filled in the blanks. This ultra-small distributor found him. They wanted to release the film as an art piece in upscale bars and clubs. The idea was to charge one admission for the season — kind of like, you pay one cover, you come back and have the movie play in the background all season. "They're going to get sponsorships by all kinds of alcohol companies, then we'll refuse to do product placement because I'm underage. They'll sue. The distributor says it'll be huge."

"Moish, how the hell did they find you in the first place?"

He shrugged. "The guy kept saying something about Orson Welles. Or a guy who sounded like Orson Welles. I couldn't tell."

He had that knowing glint in his eye, though. Like there was more to the story than I knew, more than I would ever know.

"You're insane." I sighed agreeably. "Oh, Moish. What would Jesus do with you?"

The pizza place was sparse, dirty, and hot. It looked like a ghetto Kmart after closing time. An ancient couple leaned on the counter like a cane. I ordered slices with green bell peppers and pineapple for Moish, and mushrooms and red onions for me. Moish washed his hands while I ordered. He ran to a table and plopped himself under a picture of Mount Carmel, took out a folder, and sketched new storyboards.

"Look at you," I said when I sat down. "Getting together that snazzy little premiere."

"Yeah, right," said Moish. "Now the only question is, do you think they'll show it at Rashi High for a special assembly?"

I chewed on a slice of pizza, crust first, the premiere still swimming in my head. It swam together with filming, and with going back to school, and with the giddiness I was still feeling from Berkeley. I remembered the first time I heard secular music that I loved — I mean, really *loved.* It was Ani Difranco, singing this song about buildings and bridges and how nothing is impermeable forever, not even steel. I remember thinking how I had to hide that album from my teachers and my friends, to not talk about it, because secular music wasn't supposed to be as piercing and holy as, say, Rabbi Carlebach's music or the ben Dovid Band.

But it *was.* That's what I wanted to tell Moish. That was the genius of his film, that it wasn't about an Orthodox boy or an art boy or an alienated poetry boy — it was *him*, all together and unique, just like I was Hava, all together and unique. Maybe I was more like the people in Berkeley than home. But I still didn't know how to take it with me — how to, you know, fit myself into my life.

I might be a celebrity in the secular world. But still, in the Jewish world, nobody cared.

"Mind if I take one?" said a voice beside me.

I looked up. Facing me, with his signature impish smile, black-button eyes, and shaggy sheepdog hair, was the face that smiled down from a zillion posters in Meira's room at home, the face that sporadically appeared on posters in the windows of every kosher coffee shop and pizza dive in Manhattan. My gut instinct, to pull the cell phone from my pocket and call Meira and Shira immediately, was stifled only by my immediate inability to breathe.

"I'm kidding. Really, that much grease would kill me," he said. "I'm Yosef ben Dovid. I sing with this band, the ben Dovid Band. I'm sorry for interrupting like this, but are you Hava Aaronson? My wife and I have been trying to track you down for months. If you're not busy, we'd love to invite you for Shabbos."

16

THE LIGHTS COME UP

Howard nervously licked his lips.

"The Producers are a bit upset with your, shall we say, acting. Or, rather, the lack of it. They'd like to see you pay more attention to your lines, your dramatic personage, perhaps believe the words a little more than you currently do."

Howard shot those words out in a wheezy, nasal declaration, twiddling his thumbs like speeding bullets. Beads of sweat fondled his forehead. His face swelled big and red. It matched his maroon-and-beige-striped tie a little too exactly to be coincidence.

Howard was a professional at being diplomatic. But I hated being diplomatic with a passion, and so, I suspected, did the Producers.

"A bit upset? A little more? Perhaps? Howard, you qualify things more than a prescription drug company. Just say what you mean."

He sunk into the chair in my dressing room, his sizable bulk filling most of the space in the room, rolling into the chair's wooden frame.

"The reason you haven't gotten any lines the past few weeks," Howard said, "is not only because you're unreliable. You can't *act*, Hava."

"Well, *duh.*"

I hadn't been hired to act. I hadn't told anyone I could act. I got hired because I had some acting credentials. Well, I had one credential. And because I was Orthodox and feisty and all that stuff. I was the last person on earth who would lie about my acting ability, real or imagined.

Evie was standing in the hall behind Howard's back. She weakly suppressed a giggle, making eye contact with me and then breaking it in favor of watching Howard stammer himself into a further mess.

"So . . . being as how the next few scripts are, uh, have been written with you in one of the, errm, in the major role, the Producers wondered if you could possibly . . ."

"Spit it *out*, Howard."

"Take acting lessons."

My mouth dropped.

"*Me?*"

"That was, err, that is my understanding of what the Producers wanted." Howard squirmed, bracing for a tantrum.

"But if I didn't," I said slowly, like plotting chess moves, "they couldn't really do anything about it, right? Except maybe give the bigger parts back to Evie."

"They can do plenty of things. Two weeks is more than enough time for them to make your life comfortable, or to deplete it of such comfortability. And, if the time comes for a second season, if you would like to ensure Shoshana Goldberg's role as a character . . ."

"Maybe you *should* just give my part to Evie."

"Evie's part is big enough for the episodes. There's plenty of interaction, and the last episode needs someone of your age and . . . uh, your maturity and . . . your . . ." He floundered. "Your vocal abilities."

"You mean because Evie and the rest can't say *schlep* without making it sound like a sneeze?"

"Well, yes."

"Fine. You win." I folded my arms across my chest. "I'll take acting lessons."

Howard looked like I'd just cut him down from a noose.

"Thank G — I mean, that's great, the Producers will be pleased to hear it," he said. "And you can, of course, charge the bill to Goldbergs Productions."

"That's fine, I'll be able to cover it. I should have started taking them much earlier in my professional development, in any case." Now he looked positively delighted to be there. "And thank *you*, Howard. You always know how to make a girl feel better about herself." I squirmed convincingly in my chair, like I couldn't *bear* not to hug him on his way out.

By this point, Evie was in quiet hysterics in the hall, barely able to hide. She ducked out of sight as Howard left, and a second later she slipped into the room and snapped the door shut behind her.

"Damn, Hava. You're actually going to take acting lessons?"

"No way, dude."

"But Howard said —"

"Just watch me." My eyes glimmered with the sort of mischievous spark that I would expect from Evie.

Only this time, it was mine.

Once Evie scored in the ratings points with her new on-screen boyfriend — Kevin was now a recurring character on the show — things got better between us. I finally realized that, whatever I did, nothing would change in my "friendship" with Evie. It was all about keeping her satisfied — or, more accurately, about keeping her from getting angry. The first day I saw her with Kevin around her wrist, she'd never been happier with me. And when it became public knowledge that I wasn't going to fight her to get my lines back, I might as well have been her own guardian angel.

The next day, I let the melodrama flow.

I mean, I *acted.*

I gave just a little. It was enough for them to notice a difference. My scene called for a temper tantrum.

Normally, I would yell as loud as I could, and back it up with some severe foot-stomping and flailing hands.

Today I lowered my voice. I shifted my eyes. I kept my hands in their regular position, on my hips or by my side, and only moved them when needed. I held my movement to a minimum. The director didn't stop rehearsal on my account at all. Corey and Jamie were less frisky with me, sensing the start of a new, professional acting persona. Even the baby, when I forgot to say the blessing over my string beans at lunch and he fixed his evil glare on me, hesitated before he leaned his head back and flipped his mouth open and cried "*Osssssser!!!*" into the air.

The next day, I was even better. I read my script through during both car rides, that night after work and the next morning before it. I tried memorizing not only my own lines, but the lines before and after mine. I closed my eyes and imagined Charles and Paula and David Lee saying those words to me, and then I scrubbed them out and replaced them with Mr. Goldberg, Mrs. Goldberg, my elder brother.

My mind spun when I thought about having an older brother. I thought of David Lee's weird, unconventional advice; the way he gave it over, conversationally, but with a hint of dipping into the pool of our ancestral wisdom as fuck-up teenagers. I started from there. I swallowed hard, tried to focus my eyes on him. I tried to become his sister.

I was turning into a real celebrity around the studio. Paula argued that I didn't need a scene alone with Evie. "Nothing important happens," she said, "and it doesn't help the plot." The director, afraid that he might lose a scene with his two almost legal actresses in exchange for losing his leading actress — an ex-model whose popularity in the 21–34-year-old male demographic was certainly considerable — was about to concede the battle and drop the scene. As he was about to tell Paula *yes*, they both heard strangely poetic voices coming from the stage. They turned around. It was me and Evie, playing the roles with more meaning, more tenacity, and more hot oozing sexiness than real life.

```
                SHOSHANA
My friends are not full of themselves!
You have no right to make judgments
about my friends!
```

HINDEL

You have no right to tell me what to do!

SHOSHANA

Well, maybe you should just come to the Ben Dovid Band concert with us and see for yourself!

HINDEL

Fine, I will! (HINDEL *stomps away*)

SHOSHANA (*to camera*)

Oy vey, dude.

My burst of acting energy was contagious. I thought I was only holding myself back. But when I said the words like I meant them, Evie's voice and her anger and her chutzpah went up a notch, too. By Friday, I was giving it everything.

"Wow," Evie said, loud, so the director could hear it. "Maybe I should take acting lessons, too."

"Maybe we'll get a group discount."

"Is your teacher hot?"

"She's a babe," I said. "She's smart, too."

Howard didn't even pretend to understand.

Even Charles remarked on it, late one evening, when everyone else had already cleared out. I was staying behind to avoid as much last-minute cleaning as I could. I'd just finished afternoon prayers, standing up and facing the wall. I took three steps back, three steps forward, bowed, and sat to recite the last psalm when I felt like someone was watching me. I spun around.

"Charles!"

"Sorry to interrupt. I just wanted to say, Hava, your acting is . . . it's really fine. After this season, if you don't get offered a spinoff show, I'd be very surprised."

"Well, thanks."

I turned around, started screwing with the piles of clothes on my dresser. Combining things. Separating them.

Charles was visible in the mirror. He stood still, watching me, a faraway look in his eyes.

"Do you think I'm disgusting?"

I didn't hesitate. "No. *Disgusting* would be if I was underage by years instead of months, or if I had a sickly body and no chest, or if you wanted me to do creepy things," I said. "I just think you need to get out more."

"Yeah," Charles echoed weakly. "Yeah, Hava. You're probably right."

"I'm sorry."

"It's okay."

"Umm." This was suddenly awkward, like I was absolving Charles of blame. Our whole period of knowing each other — okay, our whole *relationship* — I felt like we connected eye-to-eye on everything. Now there was this whole fog around him. For the first time, I really was about thirty years too young.

"Are you . . . holding up okay?" I asked.

Charles looked startled.

"Me? I'm fine. I'll probably spring right into a rebound. Probably with some model who wants to start acting. She won't know how to do anything that doesn't involve using her body to manipulate people. I think I'm about due to be manipulated, though. It'll be a good ride."

"Oh, Charles." I wanted to run to him.

I dug my nails into my palm. I wouldn't let myself.

"Hava."

"You deserve someone better than that. You deserve someone who understands."

"No," Charles said sadly. "Thank you, but no. Right now, I think I just deserve to fool around. Don't lose respect for me, okay? Really, I never stopped being a twelve-year-old boy."

I nodded glumly.

"Chin up, soldier. And don't even think about not speaking to me."

I opened my mouth. It quivered wildly. I don't know what I wanted to say. But it didn't matter, because suddenly, Charles was gone.

That Shabbos, finally, was brilliant.

I was ready to leave this town behind, with only two episodes left before we broke for the school year. Except for last week in Berkeley, Shabbos seemed to be about surviving instead of celebrating, enduring the rules until we could use electricity again.

The ben Dovids' house was a vivid Technicolor brilliant after those pasty-white Shabboses at my Pico Robertson cousins' conservative manor house. Last night on the phone, I told my cousins where I was headed. Their response was subdued. They displayed a brief flurry of excitement, glad that I had found my place and that my place did not involve them.

Moish and I got there an hour before Shabbos. Yosef ben Dovid and his wife were subdued, but they were just about the coolest people I'd ever met. They dressed in street clothes that were so hip they almost looked like Gentiles, and they said "yeah" and "cool," unlike normal Orthodox people, who were so robotlike they didn't even use contractions. We sat and waited for the ben Dovids to finish cooking and they let me play CDs on their stereo from their gargantuan record collection. I played some obscure Pearl Jam import singles, the Nields, Radiohead. I started soft, but built up to furious, concentrated jam songs. Different friends of theirs arrived, all in couples, and I turned off the stereo. Yosef knocked on the wall to fetch us, and everyone prayed together in the living room.

Mendel, Yosef's brother, started each prayer with a dirge melody and we all chimed in, like campfire songs, the words flowing into each other. It was simple to ease from praying into talking, and the ben Dovids and their guests fired questions at me, some disbelieving, some cynical, some a little intrusive. I blushed, which seemed to relax everyone, since Modern Orthodox people can be unhesitatingly prudish about the modern world, and we all secretly suspect that other Modern Orthodox people are serial seducers and have secret lives.

In some ways, these people were like new hang-outables, but they were also sort of like my parents. Over dinner, I told them about the Fairfax kids and they frowned in disapproving recognition. But I started talking about my adventures onscreen, and avoiding hugging my fake TV father and the baby who only said *osser*, and everyone was rolling on the floor. I talked big, with enthusiastically overdone gestures and imitated baby voices.

Yeah, I had some gifts.

In the morning we walked to synagogue, just Moish and me. We got there early, and I sat with one of the guests from dinner.

She smiled at me politely but then, when I tried to catch her eye, she was just, like, *what?* It was like we had a one-night stand of friendship.

And I prayed. I *prayed.* I shut my eyes and shut out the world, pretending I was praying alone in my chauffered limo, pretending that I was alone on the roof of Rashi High — and I yelled, my voice searing out, being swallowed by the chorus of a hundred women around me and the entire congregation and the Torahs in the Ark and Pico Boulevard, and somewhere far away, out to the ocean — I prayed like I was singing out to everything. And I prayed loud, loud enough for everything to hear me.

By the time Shabbos ended, though, the good things were the ones that spun around in my head. I sat outside the synagogue, waiting for the sky to cloud over and for evening prayers to start. Moish was shmoozing it up with a movie producer, who loved the nonstop reality concept, loved Moish, but dismissed the two together. "You got a good mind," he was saying. "Good minds look horrible on camera. You think too much. You need to filter it out. You do that when you tell stupid people what to do."

I sat on the patio stoop outside, gazing at the stars — or, rather, the lack of stars. Shabbos was over when three stars shone, although big cities gave off too much light, and we went by the time printed on Jewish calendars instead. I thought I spotted a star above the redwood tree in the backyard, but it turned out to be an airplane.

Mendel loomed in a deck chair behind me. His tall, lanky body sat like a praying mantis. His chin rested between his thumb and forefinger, looking thoughtful, but forced. I shook my head. How was I somebody who would make snap judgments like this?

"Your television show," he said. "What is it like?"

"You mean, the plot?"

"Everything."

I gulped. Not this again.

"It's easy," I said, and suddenly, it wasn't so easy. For the first time, I wanted to really tell someone what this TV show was *about*.

"It's a bunch of people pretending to be something they're not. The other actors pretend to be Jewish. I pretend to be upstanding. I'd rather talk about my favorite bands and wear clothes I like and bring my friends on the show, but it's another way of being disciplined. It's just one more thing I have to sit through. It's like going to work, and then six o'clock hits and I get to be me again."

"Don't you hate reading other people's lines and suppressing what you really want to say?" Mendel asked.

"I figure, saying their lines is the mode of communication, not the communication itself. Just being there is all I really want to say."

"Hmm." Mendel stroked his chin.

"I mean, I don't know if I want to say anything at all."

"So why are you doing it at all?"

I shrugged indifferently. "It's a job."

Mendel didn't say anything, and I knew that wasn't the reason. Everyone had a balance between the amount of time they worked and the amount they played, brain-on time and brain-off time. My mother spent all her energy working and none of it on human interaction. My dad was a madman paramedic, but he exhausted himself trying to live a normal life in the hours outside, going to morning prayers at synagogue and talking to his friends and hanging out with me. For me, hanging out with my friends *was* work, keeping track of everyone's drama and channeling sexual energy and watching Shira freak out and Moish make his movie and Ian be a glam drama queen. That was my real art.

And in the in-between time, I just needed to kick it and play around.

"Okay," I said. "You know on your album, when you do that cover of Mizmor L'David? Yosef is singing it, then you come in with a guitar solo and rip that shit off the roof. Like, you really tear it up. That's what I want to be like. Taking those ass-stupid lines that some Hollywood hack wrote, that I don't even know what they mean, and making them sound like gold."

Slowly, Mendel nodded.

"And 'cause it's fun," I added.

"Really?"

"Really."

The sky was discernible from the treetops only by a darker shade of black. The North Star gleamed like a faraway spotlight. Somewhere, geese were honking, and there was a rustle of wind.

"And what are you going to do tonight?" Mendel asked.

"I don't know," I said. "Go dancing. Or to a concert. Maybe see the ocean."

"And after this week?"

"Moish and I go back to New York," I whispered.

"And . . . ?" Mendel prompted, whispering even quieter.

"And then we rock the twelfth grade," I said.

Mendel started abruptly, as though someone had just called his name. "I see three stars in the sky," he said, standing. "Looks like Shabbos is over. You want to do havdalah?"

Havdalah was an event. People had been trickling into the house since I'd left, and now a mass crowded around the table, singing wordless dirges. Some of the men held hands and swished back and forth. One boy with curls of dreadlock length vibrated when he sang. A guy in a rainbow vest and yarmulke moaned the notes deeply, like sex. Somebody held a candle over our heads. A voice cut sharply through the singing, "*Hinei ail yeshuasi!*" The air smelled of mint and myrrh. The candle had five wicks. They climbed against one another with a fury, hugging one another and pulling angrily away. The moon rose and filled up the window. Yosef's long hair flew into a frenzy.

The wicks of the candle plunged into a cup of wine. There was a loud, sudden sizzle. The room plunged into darkness, lit only by the now-dim shadow of the moon, far away through the living room window.

As suddenly as it started, people began to drift away. The yeshiva boys filed past the wine cup in a line, dipping their pinky fingers in, placing drops of wine behind their ears and in the corners of their pockets. Couples said their good-byes and vanished to their own houses, like bears going into hibernation.

Evie picked us up at the house. She introduced herself cordially to Moish, who she realized at once was weird, but her eyes widened when I mentioned the name of his movie. "You're Moish Resnick. You were in *Variety* last week," she said. "And the *Times*. You made that movie about yourself. G-d, that's so cool and postmodern. You're kind of cute."

"I'm hands-off too," Moish said. "Just like Hava."

I watched them talk like I wasn't even there. I could feel my instinctual self tensing. This was the point where I said something obnoxious to make Moish hyperaware that he was flirting and make Evie feel like an outsider.

My fingers twitched. I felt the urge to jump out of the car, run to the nearest all-night internet café, and write the longest fucking journal entry ever. I would tell everything.

I caught my breath.

I was having a regular night out with Evie and Moish. Watching them flirt, laugh at themselves, test the boundaries of their sexuality like I'd done. Maybe Evie had more history than me and Moish was more pious. But, sooner or later, we all make the same mistakes.

There was the telltale cell phone bulge in my pocket.

I could call Ian and bitch.

But I knew what he'd tell me. *You need to commit to your life in Los Angeles.*

Shit, who was I kidding? I'm glad Moish was finally going to get his groove on. And, in this twisted, older-sisterly way, I was proud of Evie for being the one to do it.

"You absolutely suck, you two," I said. "Whatever we do tonight, you're paying."

Evie wanted to go see a movie. Not a premiere, not anything special — just a movie. It had Harrison Ford in it, and an explosion, and this guy playing the President of the United States who didn't look at all like the President. I sat between Moish and Evie for the film and, as soon as the previews ended, I tried to start up a conversation with Moish.

He *ssh*ed me.

I lost track of the film quickly. I swear I have ADD. I even took the tests. The only thing that kept me from being diagnosed positive is, you have to have bad grades to have ADD, and even after I stopped getting all A's in junior high, I was still pulling good grades.

Only, I could never concentrate long enough to care.

I was still staring at the screen, thinking, when Moish and Evie walked out. Moish bumped me on the arm with the popcorn bucket.

I looked up, startled.

"Come *on*, Gipper," he said.

"Are you okay?" Evie asked disapprovingly. She frowned at me, taking a sidelong glance at the brightening light fixtures and at the people exiting the theater.

"I'm — I'm fine," I said. Evie's voice was a jolt back to reality.

Evie's voice. In a second, I saw Evie — quizzing Moish, acting barely interested in his answers, really using him as a sounding board to obsess about herself — Evie, this whole time, had what I was looking for. No matter who she hung around, it was her pulling the ropes, making her own world turn.

And I realized, *I can do that.*

In eighth grade, Fruma and I stood downtown, shivering, in a part of the city that neither of us recognized. Fruma looked up the place in the Yellow Pages. I trusted her, but not entirely. I kicked up snow with my boots, furious at the miserable weather, furious at Fruma for going along with this plan. She marched along as though the snow wasn't even there, her feet barely sinking into the puddles, her shiny white jacket unfettered by the snow and sludge. I was wearing a canvas army peacoat that, until that day, seemed like a great idea. Fruma kept saying over and over again what a shame that my parents didn't buy me something nicer. It was true. They would, if I'd let them. But until this year, Fruma never let her parents buy her ostentatious shiny coats, either.

Fruma marched in first. She placed the permission slips, the ones we'd signed with each other's parents' signatures, on the desk. She double-checked the cost, the license, the safety precautions. When it came time to choose nose rings, Fruma picked out the perfect models for both of us.

Then it came time to sit in the chair, and Fruma told me to go first.

I did.

It didn't take long at all. There was a sensation of cold steel pressed against the outside of my skin, then suddenly I could feel it on both sides. The absence of a hole's breadth of skin on the wall of my nostril, that tiny eight-millimeter void, was now filled by a tiny circular piece of metal. My nerves shrieked pain louder than a bomb, but only for a second. My eyes popped open and it was over.

In that second that I'd shut my eyes, the world became a different place.

Maybe I felt something, my parents' influence suddenly nonabsolute, or the fact that, now, I automatically fit in with a group of people besides Jews. Maybe I saw the rest of my life opening before me, right up to the point where I'd play the rebellious teenage Orthodox daughter on TV sets across the country.

But it wasn't any of that.

When I opened my eyes, Fruma was gone.

I walked home alone. I took the expected heat from my parents, who finally caved in and let me have dinner at around midnight. It hurt to eat, like every time I moved my mouth I was pulling on the fibers that held my nose together.

I didn't see Fruma again until the next day at school. She stared at me, unblinking hatred burning in her eyes, locked like a target on the left side of my nose. She jammed her hands in the pockets of her sweater.

"*Osser,*" she spat. Just that single whispered word.

That was the last word we ever said as real friends.

I was extra vigilant when we filmed the next-to-last episode, pinching myself to pay attention, making eye contact with everyone, including the director, including Paula, including Charles. I wanted not to be noticed. It wasn't a measure of wanting to be noticed, or proving my future, or even of measuring up to the rest of the cast. My acting career was a game, no more. I knew that much. And I wanted to win, just to prove to myself that I could.

As improbable as it seemed, I was getting to *like* Shoshana Goldberg. You could tell in a second why they cast me to play her — half 'cause I'm Orthodox and half 'cause I'm pretty, but I'm too punk rock to make it a weapon — but in the course of my reading Shoshana's lines, I began to realize our differences, too, the parts of us that didn't overlap. Her cloyingly chummy retorts. Her habit of, like, *living* for boys to date. Her sickeningly sweet deference to her mother in the last five minutes of every episode. Those were the steps I had to make in the beginning. At first I hated it. Then I started liking it a lot; too much. It wasn't hard to pretend I was wholesome. But now it's getting hard to pretend to be wholesome in real life.

I was worried that, with half as many lines as I used to have, I wouldn't stand out as much now. But I owned these lines, recited them with vigor, and I stayed in the background so well that, when the spotlight was on me, I really took it. We came out to take our bows at curtain call, like we always did, and the studio audience clapped as loudly for me as they did for the real actors, Charles and Paula and David Lee. Evie got the loudest applause of everyone, from the grandmothers who still recognized her from the soap opera. She curtsied daintily, something I've never seen an actual Orthodox girl do with an ankle-length skirt. Evie also made sure to undo the top buttons of her shirt for the curtain call, so all the men in the audience could appreciate how far she'd progressed from child-acting. I'd never seen an Orthodox girl do that, either.

We walked off, totally spent, stinking like perspiration and burning-up makeup from the lights. Evie asked me about getting a beer, and with the crisp assurance of someone with one foot in the adult world, I said I'd love to. She smiled, and I turned to go to my dressing room and wash up.

And who should be blocking my path but the lumbering, roly-poly Howard.

"Miss — Miss Aaronson," he stumbled. "Hava, I mean. How are you doing. All that. I've got rather, I've, errm, received a message for you."

"What is it this time?" I snapped. "Were my lines slow? Did I face the wrong left? Was I not showing enough cleavage? Did I act too Jewish? Or not Jewish enough?"

"It's not that at all," Howard said, quickly for once. "It's the Producers. They'd like to have a word with you."

17

THE PRODUCERS

The heavy wooden doors opened into a hallway. The corridor was long and dim, fluorescent lights clipped to the walls like torches instead of the overhead light fixtures like every other hallway in the studio. There was a deep, undulating feel to the modern art that hung in the hall — all abstract — and when I stopped walking, it sounded like there was music being played, although what music, or even what kind of sound exactly, you couldn't tell.

The floor sloped down, so gradually you almost didn't notice, except that I kept tripping over my own feet. I could feel the elevation decreasing. My ears popped. There were no doors, no adjacent hallways, nothing.

Frosted glass obscured the room where the Producers worked. You could see silhouettes. The room glowed a bright definite white, like Heaven. Shadowy forms rose and fell through the windows. I expected a receptionist or a servant to come up and meet me. At least for my name to be announced.

But everything was quiet, eerily quiet. No one to tell me when to enter.

I took a breath. I reminded myself, I was punk rock hardcore. Nothing fazed me. Especially not social conventions.

I put one hand on one glass pane. I flung both doors open at once, swept through, and I strode broadly into the Producers' inner sanctum.

It wasn't at all what I expected. A small black card table sat in the center of the room. Four bridge chairs surrounded it. Stacks of leather-bound books clung to the walls in cases, and faint glints of sunlight shone through from slits high in the air. The room was shrouded in darkness. One solitary candle, fat, drippy, and long-wicked, sat at the center of the card table, flickering left and right. The books' spines glinted in gold, the words embossed in some forgotten, forbidding language.

The plastic bridge chairs looked comfortable, but cheap. Made in a Target factory, sloping on a generous angle to soothe and appease the generic human backbone.

Behind a bookcase, I saw a pudgy, bearded Santa Claus–like face peek out. The head was framed in a black hat. Hasidic side curls poked out from beneath his hat. He did a double take when he saw me.

"Herschel!" he whispered loudly. "Yitzie! She is here!"

I glanced at the golden book spines again. If I tilted my head, I could understand the titles perfectly. They were Jewish books.

A minute later, I heard the other two voices, Three Stooges–like, "She is here? Is she here?" The voices sounded echoey and distorted and strangely comfortable.

Something old and familiar nagged at the back of my head.

It hit me: They were speaking Yiddish. But I understood every word.

"Uh," I said, "am I supposed to be in here? Am I . . . am I allowed to be?" I spoke loudly, so there was a metallic echo in the room. I also spoke in English. If I spoke back in Yiddish, the conversation would be about five words long.

The three rabbis emerged from the bookcases and wiggled over to the table. They wore shiny black *bekesha* coats tied at the waist, foxtail hats, and white knee-high stockings that made their legs look unnaturally skinny, like chicken drumsticks. Each walked to a chair, sat down, and folded a brittle pair of hands on the table. They gazed intensely at me.

"Sit down, Hava," one of the rabbis offered.

I pulled out the chair, slipped into it, and placed my hands on my lap. "What's up?"

They spoke like they didn't even hear me. "It's been a good season," one mumbled, mostly to the others. "A very good season. Television is like wine. Some years, the air's just sweeter."

"Are you the Producers everyone's talking about?"

"I still think it was a mistake," another rabbi said. "To cast an Orthodox actor on a show about Orthodox people? It certainly didn't help Hava. And it's not like she was a positive influence on the rest of the cast."

"And she dances in mosh pits on Shabbos," the first pointed out.

"She didn't do anything *osser*. Even when we tried to make her kiss Kevin, she refused and ran away. She made it through the season, and she's still *frum*," noted the second rabbi.

I thought about mentioning my kiss with Charles. That didn't seem like what anybody wanted to hear right now.

"All I'm going to say on the subject," the third rabbi said — his beard was longer and whiter than the other two — "is that she's still here. And I think that this young lady's behavior has been consistently impressive."

"Even with Charles?" I retorted.

Shit.

"My dear," the third rabbi turned around, looking at me directly for the first time, "who do you think stopped the tabloids from running wild with *that* sordid tale?"

He turned back to the table and folded his hands.

My mind raced.

"It wasn't that sordid," I mumbled.

We all baked in the silence for a moment. Then I heard a rustling of curtains from behind the bookcase, and we all looked up.

An even older woman hobbled into the room. A silver-and-blue scarf encased her hair. Wispy white clothes hung over her body. She emerged, maybe from the same spot as the rabbis, but she didn't enter the room so much as she *appeared.*

There was no chair for the old woman. She didn't need one. She stood with preternaturally good posture, one hand leaning on a cane, the other clutching a Hebrew book that was bigger and thicker and heavier than any of the other books in the room. She walked like the tide coming in. When she reached the table, she came to a stop, opened the book, and read to herself. Even when she talked, her eyes never left the page.

"Hava," said the old woman. "We're down to the final episode. We have something very special planned for you. I'll warn you — it's arduous and unprecedented and it might not pay off. But we think it's right up your alley."

The rabbis listened acutely as she detailed their plans for me. When she had finished, the rabbis nodded spastically, heads on springs, as if they'd been trying to say the same thing themselves. The woman looked me in the eye.

"Tell us what you think. Can you do this?"

I swallowed. Her eyes were small and beady, sunken into the back of her skull. But when we made eye contact, and I looked into them, I thought I could see something golden.

"I think I can," I said.

The studio was buzzing. Scripts were passed out. We'd condensed the regular five-day schedule. It was late Tuesday morning when we got the scripts, and filming needed to be finished by Friday. We had even less time than usual to record. Everyone stood in the set, thumbing through scripts, memorizing their lines scene by scene.

Jamie and Corey, Ritalin-deprived as usual, dashed in. Their identical bob-top haircuts bounced when they ran. They ran straight to me.

"Hava!" the boy called. "Check out this week's *Enquirer*!"

The girl thrust a newspaper in front of my face.

"Jeez, Corey." I grabbed the paper from her, exasperated. I realized that I'd just called the girl *Corey* straight to her face, and I still didn't know which of them was which. I recovered after a second. My face flickered emotionlessly. I hoped they didn't notice.

They didn't appear to; they stood by with identical curious faces, watching me take in the newspaper cover.

The headline read SHOSHANA'S UN-ORTHODOX FASHION SECRET: Hava Aaronson Wears Pants —

LEADING ORTHODOX RABBIS CRY "OSSER!" There was an unflattering page-tall picture of me in a trench coat and an Ornj band T-shirt.

I flipped to the story. It was a tell-all exposé about the rave pants in my dresser.

I lowered the paper. Jamie and Corey were standing with identically eager expressions.

"Are you going to sue?" the boy asked.

"Everybody sues," the girl explained.

"It's more press if you do," he said. "Of course, you've got a better case than almost anybody — religious reasons and all. Then again, we *have* seen you in some pretty brief Hilfiger digs."

I tossed the paper in their faces. "Didn't I tell you two not to touch this shit?"

"Yeah," said the boy. "But you also told us not to curse in front of the wrong people."

I spun around. Howard was sauntering up, less than pleased, a leery expression spreading across the gulf of his face. "Were you talking about me?" he demanded.

I looked behind me. The twins were nowhere to be seen.

"It doesn't matter, anyway," Howard said. "Come on. Rehearsal's starting."

Now that I knew who the Producers were, I felt curiously better about acting. Like, there might be a million Jews who thought I was a heathen, but now there were at least four who were rooting for me, investing in me, hoping I paid off. I said the lines with a renewed confidence, pretending they were written especially for me, and written by people with the same power-charged faith that I had. Even though I got cold shivers whenever I encountered black-hats in Jewish circles, in the greater context of the outside world, I felt connected to them, like fighting with your brother until a bully shows up. I felt a drive when I studied my lines, *shockeling* back and forth like I was praying. And when I slammed the script shut and left for location filming, the typewritten title stirred something inside that made me feel wild and crazy and superstar and, also, vilified.

THE GOLDBERGS

Script #0113

"RUN SHOSHANA RUN"

SCENE 1

(SETTING: *A subway car.* SHOSHANA GOLDBERG *and her two best friends,* CHAIM *and* CHAYA, *sit on either side.)*

SHOSHANA (*voice-over*)

It all started like a normal ride home. Friday afternoon. You couldn't get us out of school fast enough. . . .

CHAYA

I can't believe Shabbos starts so early this time of year!

CHAIM

Yeah, only thirty minutes for you to put on makeup. How will you ever survive?

SHOSHANA

Makeup?! How very 2002 of you, Chaya.

CHAYA

Would you look at that, it's our stop! We'll see you on Sunday at the class picnic, Shosh. Have fun with the fam . . .

(CHAIM *and* CHAYA *get off*)

SHOSHANA (*voice-over*)

Sometimes your life was moving so fast, and everything was so confusing, and you wish it would all just stop.

(*The train SLAMS to a halt.* SHOSHANA *gathers herself. She looks baffled for a moment, then says* —)

SHOSHANA

I wish a million dollars fell into my lap.

(*She looks eagerly at the sky*)
(*opening credits*)

The episode was going to be in real time. It was a thirty-minute slice of Shoshana Goldberg's life. Her friends get off the subway, Shoshana stays on, and the train comes to a sound CLUNK. The subway is stuck. Shoshana looks at her watch. Shabbos starts in twenty-nine minutes.

Without hesitating, she throws open the subway door, jumps onto the track, and runs down the emergency stairs to the street. Close-up of the street sign. Shoshana lives five neighborhoods away.

"Damn kids," says an old lady on the subway car. "Can't even use the same subway exits as normal folks."

Cut to the Goldberg house. Hindel lifts a charred, smoking chicken out of the oven. She fans off the smoke. In the background, Jamie and Corey are throwing challahs at each other. "Twenty-six minutes till Shabbos!" one yells.

The other one shrills, "Shoshana's gonna be in *sooo* much trouble. . . ."

Cut to Shoshana, dashing through streets. A Hatzolah Yiddish Neighborhood Ambulance almost runs her over. She jumps onto the crowded sidewalk. Four hefty construction workers swing around a huge plate of glass. She ducks underneath.

"Be careful!" Hindel says. She's setting the table at the Goldberg house. She swipes a fancy plate from the baby's high chair as it squeals, "*Osser! Osser!*"

Shoshana jumps back up from the sidewalk. She trips one of the construction workers and they all tumble over. The glass breaks resoundingly. Shards shoot into the air. Shoshana does a double take, runs down the street, and through the Fulton Street Market, avoiding booths, newspaper vendors, groups of dancing school kids, and bums. Out of the corner of her eye she spots a shortcut. She dashes through a clothes store. She makes a wrong turn. She stumbles into a bar.

Fifteen bearish men in burly leather look up. It's a biker bar.

She giggles. "Hey," she says. She backs up against the doors. "Sorry about that. I'm kind of, uh. In. A. Hurry."

The Goldbergs' dinner table is half set, clock frantically counting down the minutes. Fourteen minutes to Shabbos.

"Hindel," Mrs. Goldberg calls, "have you seen Shoshana? Her Shabbos chores aren't done yet."

"She's such a slacker," Hindel says. "She's behind on, like, *every*thing."

Shoshana, somehow, has acquired a motorcycle. She speeds down Lennox, Mason, turns onto Flatbush Avenue. Her long skirt flaps loudly. "*Oy vey*, dude!" she shouts into the wind.

In the tracks of dust behind Shoshana, a huge, burly biker is chasing after her, shaking his fist. He gives up after a block. In a gruff, ogre voice, he grumbles: "It's gonna be a real schlep home tonight."

"Did you hear something?" Mr. Goldberg asks Hindel.

She looks up from the table, glances around, and shakes her head. "I think you're losin' it, Daddy," she says. She goes back to folding napkins.

A Hebrew textbook flies into the camera. We spin around. It soars down the street. Shoshana's eyes follow it. She swerves, narrowly missing an oncoming tractor-trailer. She hears the Hebrew book smashed to bits.

"Lost that one." She grins, revving the motor back up. Her gaze flashes to a street sign. She's five blocks away. She zooms down the street. Everything's a blur.

Everything's quiet. The family is still, sitting in the living room.

"Oh, well," says Mrs. Goldberg. "It's time for Shabbos."

The family stands, stretches, walks into the living room. The women stand in front and get ready to kindle the Shabbos candles. The men stand in the shadows.

Shoshana, knuckles ripping on the handles, swings a narrow U-turn.

"*Boruch atoh Ado-nai,*" sing Mrs. Goldberg and Hindel and Yacheved.

Shoshana jumps off the motorcycle, flips her knapsack on her back, and takes a valuable one-minute breather to adjust her bangs.

"*Elo-heinu melech ha olam,*" harmonize the Goldberg women.

Shoshana runs across the school yard. One basketball shoots by her head. Another bounces into her stomach. She stops and shoots it. Three points.

"*— asher kidshonu, bemitzvosav —*"

She's running through the houses, backyard to backyard. Leaves whip her face.

"*— vitzivanu, lihodlik nair —*"

Shoshana hits the Goldberg front yard. You can tell by the toys strewn over the lawn: toy cars, Yoshie and Yacheved's laser guns and basketballs, a baby-size swimming pool, and a stuffed Torah-shaped pillow.

"*— shell Shabbos,*" the Goldberg women sing.

The moment is still, tranquillity. The pale calm yellow radiates off the children's faces. Mr. Goldberg crosses the room, folds his hands, kisses his wife on the cheek.

Noises of cars screeching, children yelling, and the inexplicably chaotic sound of Canada geese hooting.

The door slams open. Shoshana drops her bag and brushes her hair out of her eyes.

"Amen," she says hoarsely, collapsing against the door.

* * *

Filming wrapped, and there was a huge party at Canter's Deli, the capital of Jewish-style nonkosher food, to celebrate. Waiters in 1950s tuxedo vests swirled around me. Still exhausted, I let myself flail around the party aimlessly. I took ten minutes trying to hail a waiter without any luck. Evie sighed, reached out, put her hand on the chest of a scurrying waiter, and ordered for both of us.

The waiter nodded swiftly and vanished to the bar.

Moish looked at Evie in admiration. "You know how to play this game," he observed, glowing with reverence.

"Finally, somebody notices," Evie remarked. "You would not be*lieve* how many times Hava and I have been out, and she ridicules me for ordering her some kind of drink with pig's blood, or wine that isn't Manischewitz, or some G-dforsaken shitsicle."

Moish laughed, folding himself against Evie's lithe body, the perfect piece of arm candy for her to have tonight.

Tonight, for our victory dance. The string orchestra at the bar stopped tuning and launched into a Tommy Dorsey number, and the crowd started twirling off into paired duos. I spotted David Lee enfolding Paula between his arms in a waltz, Charles and a faceless blond model, Evie and Moish, even Howard and Shira O'Sullivan. Now *there* was a couple that deserved each other. I could read their lips; they were talking about contract negotiations.

A waitress passed by, offering me pigs in a blanket and spinach rolls. "No thanks," I said automatically, "I keep kosher."

I leaned against the counter of the bar, watching Moish and Evie spin each other into a dip. Evie leaned back a step farther than was necessary, her meager cleavage almost spilling out of her mini-dress crop-top. Moish looked a cross between appalled and enticed.

To my surprise, I felt proud. Moish's behavior appealed to me in a been-there done-that way. A new, as-yet-undetermined wisdom that resonated when I saw Moish in the exact same place I'd been at the beginning of the summer, suddenly touching somebody without any of the *shomer negiah* automatic pilot electrocuting your brains, seeing yourself in a third-person kind of view and realizing that, although your loyalty was still to G-d, you had the power to do literally anything in the world.

The bartender slipped me the drink that Evie had ordered, a shiny orange-and-green concoction with olives floating like lily pads. "Thanks," I murmured, sipping tentatively.

Charles came behind me. He leaned on the bar, gave his drink order, a vodka tonic and a pear cider. My eyes remained focused on the bartender. I tried to keep my breathing steady.

"Hey, kid," Charles said. "I guess congratulations are in order?"

I watched his date. She struck up a perky conversation with David Lee Mitchell, who looked vaguely disinterested. He made a brotherly, tortured kind of eye contact with me from across the room. Charles's date giggled amiably.

"I guess so," I mumbled.

Charles's eyes followed my gaze. I wasn't being subtle, and my mood wasn't that hard to decode, anyway.

"You know, they're already talking about having us come back and shoot more episodes."

"I know. I'll miss half of my senior year."

Charles shifted uneasily when I mentioned high school.

"Yeah. So," he said, "any chance of persuading you to apply to schools out here?"

"I doubt it."

"Where are you thinking of?" he asked, in this ridiculously helpful tone of voice. "UCLA? NYU? Or are you thinking of a specialized acting school?"

"She's not as pretty as I am," I said.

The band cut out at that exact moment.

Several people looked at me, then pretended they weren't.

A second passed. My blushing subsided. The band eased into another number, something loud and raucous and Duke Ellington.

"You're right," Charles said. "She isn't."

"Whatever."

We sipped our drinks to get out of talking for a second.

"Oberlin, Sarah Lawrence, maybe Smith," I said. "As far away from here as I can get." When I registered his shock, I added, "It's only Los Angeles, baby. I've already done my run-away-to-California thing."

Charles took his drinks, which had been sitting on the bar for a while.

"Besides," I added, "there are too many Jews here. It really devalues the currency."

"So, we're okay then?"

"Fuck yeah. Just don't expect me to rebound with Justin Timberlake or anything."

"You could," Charles said.

"No. I couldn't," I replied, pointing my finger up at Heaven.

I spun around and walked away. The crowd parted for me like the Red Sea.

Evie and Moish were still dancing. It was kind of fulfilling to see Moish getting it out of his system. I went over, whispered in Evie's ear, cocked an eyebrow at Moish, and then I passed through the frosted-glass doors into the night.

I hailed a cab.

I wasn't going far. It pulled up in front of the Goldbergs lot at Paramount. I stuck a bill through the front-seat valley. The driver waited for me to ask for change. I didn't.

The guard on duty was the same one that had been there my first day. This was the first time I saw him on the night shift. He didn't look quite so tired or quite so cranky. He was cackling maniacally to an episode of *Full House.* I smiled indulgently.

He nodded, as if he knew exactly where I was going.

The doors to the studio were unlocked. So were the doors to the long Gothic hallway. I wondered if they'd been unlocked the whole time. I wondered what would happen if I'd gotten so fed up halfway through that I'd demanded to see the Producers then.

Probably nothing.

I'd been getting the feeling, lately, that I was bigger than any sort of change. I'd always come out on the other side, but I'd never be too different from me.

As I stormed into the Producers' office, a nervous, skinny man brushed past on his way out. He carried a burlap sack full of posters and charts and test models. I could swear there was a picture of a rabbi that looked like Ronald McDonald.

Two of the rabbis sat at the card table, poring over documents. The old woman watched them. From time to time they would ask her a question. She nodded or shook her head accordingly.

The two black-bearded rabbis flurried over the papers, not even noticing the sound of the door.

The woman looked up.

"Hava," she said, smiling.

"What gives?" I said. "You can't even have the closing party at a kosher restaurant?"

"It's good publicity," said one of the rabbis. "In L.A., nothing says *Jewish* like a non-kosher deli."

The papers scattered across the card table looked like plans for a kosher restaurant chain. The logo on the design schematics said GOLDBURGERS.

"Yeah, well, I'm fucking starving," I said.

"*Lan*guage, Hava," urged the other rabbi. "And we got you kosher food on the set, didn't we?"

"It only took a month of fucking making myself peanut butter and banana sandwiches," I retorted. I put a subtle accent on *fucking*.

"It's not like *we* get catered lunches every day," the first rabbi shot back.

"The paperwork was a bureaucratic nightmare," said the other rabbi.

I opened my mouth to let the other curse words fly.

The woman turned. She fixed her solid beady gaze against me. I considered throwing a fit, but my words froze before I could launch them.

"Religion is a relationship," said the old woman. "And any relationship is a test of faith. If we handed your Jewishness to you on a silver platter how long would you stick with any of it?"

There was something in the way she spoke — a tone, the mismatched antiquity of her words, her calmly meditative voice —

that made me question everything. From the composition of the cast, and Shira O'Sullivan's curious passive-aggressive anti-Semitism, to the Broadway show, to the freak meeting when I body-slammed that Off-Broadway producer on St. Mark's Place.

I brushed my hair out of my eyes. I had to dismiss it. If that was all true, then none of this would be a wild ride. And I needed to keep believing I was wild.

The third rabbi emerged from behind the bookcases, carrying a large, luxurious spread of bagels and cream cheeses and olives and tomatoes and whitefish. He placed it atop the paperwork, plopped into the remaining chair, and they all began spreading themselves sandwiches.

"Sit down, Hava Aaronson," the old woman offered. "Your stomach must be growling all sorts of things at you. It's kosher, I promise."

I glanced through the narrow slits of window. The moon that night was full. It cast bronze shadows across the table and the bagels and it sliced the rabbis' faces into shards. I took it in, breathing heavily.

I knew I could learn so much from these people. If I stayed, this room might be like my own yeshiva. I could learn all sorts of things about G-d. I could learn all sorts of things about myself.

If I stayed.

"Maybe I'll take one for the road," I said, grabbing slices of tomato as I spoke. "I've got an appointment to make."

The taxi pulled up at the beach, let me off a narrow strip of the Pacific Coast Highway. The moon filled up the sky. I hefted two huge garbage bags on my back, staggering past the stone barrier, walking between dunes. The sand crept into my shoes.

Stray fires burned in small patches along the beach. A few of them still had people, huddled close and hugging each other, playing '80s songs on acoustic guitars. For a second I was afraid Evie had joined one of the crowded ones. Then I spotted her behind a small, deserted patch of flame, head lolling lazily on Moish's shoulder. Moish looked so uncomfortable and excited that I wanted to tell him everything, all the secrets. I didn't. Sometimes, silence is the best advice you can give.

Evie's eyes popped open wide as soon as she saw me. She pulled herself up on Moish's arm. "Did you really get everything?"

I threw down the two bags as an answer.

Evie's eyes got even wider. "Holy shit, baby," she whispered.

"I, uh," Moish stammered. "I think I'm going to go take a walk."

We watched his black-shrouded form vanish quickly into the night.

"Did *you* get what I told you to?" I asked Evie.

As an answer, she brought out a huge bottle of nail-polish remover.

"Nice," I said. I took it from her, unscrewed the lid, and emptied it onto the fire. We both flinched as the flames tripled in size and exploded, shooting into the sky. Sparks licked at our knees. I could feel my face, and even my brand-new hair, now the length of my fingers, sizzling. The ocean surged calmly in the background.

Evie peeked into a bag.

"This one's yours," she said, passing it to me. Then she dug through her own bag, removing a handful of clothes. "What do you think we should do first?"

"Polyester," I said. "It keeps the fire going."

She fished out a blue plaid miniskirt, a pair of thigh-high stockings, and red ribbons that no one above the age of ten would ever wear in their hair. I remembered the second episode we filmed, where Howard said she needed to wear those ribbons to look more wholesome. Evie dumped them all on the fire at once.

There was a furious sizzle.

"Now you," she said.

I dredged out a push-up bra, a baby tee that said KOSHER MEAT across the boobs, and a pair of short shorts that were in my wardrobe from day one but that I never wore. I tried to imagine myself as an Orthodox fly girl. I shuddered.

I hurled it all into the fire.

Clouds of smoke flew up, climbing into the sky until they mingled with the distant fog. Noxious fumes poured out, and Evie and I made disgusted faces at each other and laughed. We sank into the sand, our backs propped against the log that we were originally sitting on. Our hands wrapped into each other. She grinned at me and I grinned back.

There went our wardrobes. There went our pasts. It was like we'd come to the end of our board game and remembered for the first time that it was only a board game.

"I'm glad you didn't turn out to be a stuck-up bitch," I said.

"I still can't believe you got the last episode like that. After you ran away and everything."

"Yeah, well, I still have to go back to *living* like that. That whole fucking sitcom world. It's more fun when it's over in half an hour, isn't it?"

"You should try movies," Evie said dreamily, looking at the stars.

I looked at her sharply. I don't think I realized until jerking my head like that how drunk we were. They'd mixed stiff old drinks at the party, with fancy mixers that my body wasn't used to, and it was only starting to hit me now.

"I don't have to go back to school in the fall. I got cast in this teen comedy flick. It starts filming with five weeks in Aruba, and then Colorado Springs, just in time for the first snow."

"Jesus," I whistled. "They pay for vacations like that?"

"Vacations are what movies are about. We take them, the world watches us and lives vicariously."

"Since when did you become a philosophy major?" I asked, only halfway teasing her.

"I'm a lot of things," Evie said softly. Her eyes glowed with a depth I hadn't noticed before.

Evie's birthday was coming soon, in early October. She was turning sixteen. She told me yesterday that she might come out to see me in New York. I felt a surge of excitement at the thought of it.

By the time Moish came back, Evie and I had fallen asleep, her head on my shoulder, and the tide rumbled like an old man snoring. A soft wind was blowing the sand out to sea, and our legs were buried beneath the level of the ground, enveloped by sand.

Moish spoke to us in low, rhythmic murmurs. If we were awake, his voice would have put us to sleep. Since we were asleep, his voice stirred us, easing us gently into awakeness. I blinked several times. I watched his head shift into focus.

"Moish," I said. "You are be*yond* insufferably lame."

"I know," he said, grinning. "But I'm not going to let you freeze to death on a California beach. Now, *move*."

He had a taxi waiting for us on the highway. He walked me slowly toward the car, bracing his arms in case I fell over, but not touching me the whole time. Then he wrapped his coat around Evie's shoulders and, her factory-showroom clothes beneath Moish's stained black peacoat, he walked her to the taxi and planted her beside him. He dropped me off at my front door, unlocked it for me, and tucked me into bed. He pulled the covers over my shoulders. I raised my arms so he could tuck the layers of blanket securely under me. I was barely awake when the blankets rustled the hair on my neck. I heard the door lock, and I went out like a light.

My brain folded over and I started to dream.

I dreamed I was a girl.

My name was Shoshana Goldberg. I went to high school in New York, lived in a neighborhood where everyone was Jewish. My parents were crazy, my friends were one-dimensional, and no one really understood. I lived two floors up from my gay best friend, who I was a little bit in love with. I went to high school and hated it. Everybody saw a piece of themselves in me, but nobody got me completely. My friends loved me, but they didn't understand me at all. I knew artists, writers, and moviemakers, but when I made my real art — dancing to loud music, praying in words that other people wrote — I was the only one who heard it, singing myself lullabies against all the other dreams that came, against the night.

18

HEAVEN TONIGHT

I pounded my fist against the locker, twice to lock it, once to open. Shira and Meira stood in the background. They were giggling about the note I'd just gotten from Shimon Lackman, which didn't straight-up ask me out, but implied exactly that.

I switched the subject back to graduation plans. Shira was going to Israel. Meira wanted to apply to a liberal arts college in Ohio. Her parents weren't speaking to her. They both wanted to wear sunglasses to graduation, "just be*cause*," Meira told me. I said I was going naked beneath my robe. I waited for their eyes to roll, then winked, *gotcha*.

The bell rang.

My head swirled around like a camera zooming from chaos to my locker. Doors clicked open. Four hundred teenagers at Rashi High poured out of their classrooms and swarmed the halls like hungry muskrats. From down the hall scurried Fruma and the band of freshmen wannabes who followed her around, wearing identical jumpers, their hair in buns. From the other direction came the basketball team, laughing about a joke nobody else would understand. I caught the tallest guy's eye and laughed along, just because I could.

I slammed my locker door shut and thumped it twice. I tucked a calculus textbook under my arm, spun around, and walked toward my next class.

Rivkie Gutstein-Gruber, my parents' best friends' kid, ran up to me. She'd just started ninth grade. Shira and Meira and I couldn't get over how small she was. "Hey, Hava!" Rivkie exclaimed, bubbling with enthusiasm. "I just had to tell you — I can't wait till tonight!"

She bounded off toward a group of other kids, boys and girls together, each as diminutive as she was.

"G-d," said Shira, shaking her head, "they make them shorter every year."

Just then, Saul Horowitz, the hottest guy in our class, walked by. Meira bit her bottom lip hard. Shira latched onto my wrist and dug her nails in deep.

Saul stopped in front of us. He leaned into my ear and whispered to me, confidentially: "I can't wait for tonight, either."

Between classes, I slipped into the girls' room, hid in the farthest stall where I used to go alone and perch on the toilet seat and write poems during classes. I slipped my Discman out of my bag and unwrapped the headset. My boots straddled the toilet seat. I sat in the air with my back against the wall, and cranked the Hole CD up past ten, banging my head and shaking my grown-out hair and gripping my air-guitar wrists in the air. I skipped through songs — "Awful" was too fast and "Malibu" was too slow — until the opening chords of "Heaven Tonight" came and I rocked out. Courtney's singing sent a premonitory shiver up my spine.

I guess I couldn't wait for tonight, either.

In Prophets, Rabbi Greenberg passed out textbooks, the Sforno commentary on Job. Nimrod Mandel groaned. Rabbi Greenberg silenced him with a single death-eater glare. He let the next book drop from his hands, slamming to the wooden desk surface with a dull, resonating thud.

"I'll tell you what, Mr. Mandel," he said, avoiding Nimrod's easy-to-jerk-around first name with a cruel humor. "*You* can pretend to take the commentary of Rav Shimshon ben Sforno with the same levity due any revered Torah scholar. And *I* will pretend to give you a fighting chance of passing."

He thudded the heavy volume down on the next desk, which happened to be mine. He raised his eyebrows questioningly toward Heaven.

"Hava Aaronson," Rabbi Greenberg murmured treacherously. "How gratifying that you decided to return to the unsophisticated East Coast for one final season."

I squirmed in my seat. "Thank you, Rabbi," I said.

"I trust we can rely on you to keep the pages of your Sforno straight and uninterrupted for the remainder of the period."

"I'm fine, Rabbi, thanks," I said, sinking lower into my chair.

"And may I just say, I trust that tonight's television entertainment will be of a higher standard than the network's usual sitcom fare," Rabbi Greenberg said. He thumped one final book on the desk behind mine and cleared his throat again. "I look forward to seeing you as the butt of someone's jokes beside your own."

Rabbi Greenberg retreated to the desk at the front of the

room. He opened his book straight to the correct page, as usual. "Now follow on page seventy-six, where the Sforno addresses the Adversary's running commentary on the misery of Job's existence. Mr. Horowitz, if you'd like to start reading aloud."

At lunch, I slid down the bench till I reached Moish and pulled a brown paper bag from my knapsack. The cafeteria tables were a set of three big-slat wooden boards, two thin boards for seats and a wider board for a table. I dug out a peanut butter and banana sandwich.

"My life is already over," Moish said as soon as he saw me. "Our Talmud prof assigned a paper about last year's classwork. I didn't even *go* to class for half of last year. NYU Film School is going to laugh at me and spit on me and hang me on the gallows to dry."

"I, uh, don't think they use gallows at NYU anymore," I said. "Besides, they're smart people. Talmud has shit to do with film school. They'll just look at your other grades and love you for that."

"There's not too much to love. My English class is all British classicists. Math is Mrs. Edelstein, who hates me. We don't even *have* film classes. It's like, flip the pages of your Talmud and see the Hebrew letters in animation."

"You got me, Moish. I guess you really have nothing to put on your college apps but a nationally syndicated feature film."

"Nepotist," Moish spat, and kept on kvetching.

Moish's voice dropped to a whisper in my head. I looked around the cafeteria at the other students, all my age or younger. I was a senior now. I recognized them all, and somewhere in the past four years, I had a story about almost every one of them. Stuck amidst the normal students, like wild cards, were freshmen. They looked like caricatures of our class, smaller and more Japanimation versions of us. I looked for a lonely girl in a Metallica shirt.

Fruma sat at the head of a table of mostly girls, gesturing wildly with her hands, as everybody erupted into identical laughs. Meira and Shira were at a quieter table, all of their friends exchanging rosters and comparing textbooks, weighing their lives one against the other. Rivkie Gutstein-Gruber sat by herself in a corner, scribbling madly in a wire-bound book. I wondered if she was doing classwork or writing curses in her journal. If she'd turn out to be one of the nerds or one of the rebels.

Then I kicked myself for thinking that. Maybe she'd be someone else entirely, writing anarchist diatribes to hand in for Bible homework, poems at the end of an equals sign in algebra.

Moish looked at me like something was the matter. "What's up, Hava?" he asked me. "Are you listening?"

"I'm sorry, Moish, I'm not all here today," I told him, wrapping the knapsack strap around my hand. I kicked away from the table and stood. "What do you say we go out on the roof and pick the buildings for our corporate headquarters?"

"My corporate headquarters are going to be on Wilshire Boulevard."

"Well, fine. Then you can pick which parks to use for location shoots."

"Deal."

We raced each other to the roof. We gripped the wire fence, pointing at buildings and meadows and riverside observation points until we heard the distant, muted sound of a bell ringing inside. I stood with my feet in the woven-wire grooves and leaned my upper body over the railing. I looked directly down at our neighborhood, beneath the taller buildings. I saw Gottlieb's, the kosher rib place, the Jewish gift shop with all the menorahs.

Moish's bangs blew furiously at his eyes. I don't remember Moish's hair ever being this long. I stared at the landscape of buildings, closed my eyes, tried to turn everything to nighttime and convert the buildings into a sea of gleaming yellow lights.

"Moish," I said. "Do you remember being in L.A.?"

"Were we there together? Like, at the same time and everything?" He stretched his arms, leaning over the side more precariously.

I opened my eyes. It was day again. The buildings washed back into their dull red New York selves.

"We were," I said.

"There and back again," Moish repeated, dizzily.

"It feels like such a time warp. One day you're in front of a million cameras talking to an imaginary America. And the next thing you know, Mrs. Edelstein is in front of you and it's like nothing has changed; she still expects you to hand in your homework on time. And it's like, what the fuck, why can't I act my way out of this like everything else? It feels like I learned to speak another language, and now I'm the only one who speaks it. The only thing different is that Fruma's not teasing us constantly, but that's probably 'cause she's scared of us now."

"Fruma's not teasing *you*," Moish corrected me. "She still thinks I'm an ass. This morning she called me the Yiddishe Dracula. I told her that didn't rhyme. She didn't even answer."

"Don't worry, Moish, babe," I said, getting that 1950s pinstripe tone of voice that Moish used to use. "As soon as your movie comes out, she'll be kissing your feet just like Evie Arling Cameron."

That lit up Moish's face red as Christmas.

But only for a second. "That reminds me, Hava," he said. "Am I still invited to your house tonight?"

"You and the rest of the world," I groaned. "Miss it, and you might be the only Jew in New York who does."

"I can't wait," said Moish, grinning.

After school, we strode past the row of Jewish stores on West Seventy-second Street. In front of us, Rivkie and a few other freshmen, friends of our families, flew ahead.

"This is senior year, isn't it," I said to Fruma. "When everything is so temporary, you need to hold on to whatever you can."

"As *if*," she said. "I can hold on to whatever I want. I'm just being charitable, is all."

We entered the pizza place, just down the block from our school. G-d, it felt so surreal to have everything this close together again.

The freshmen already seized us a table, a big circular one back toward the kitchen. Shira made sure to order mushroom pie for me. But after sitting still and being lethargic in class all day, my stomach felt moldy and full. I missed the ideological Californism of starchless, salad-inflicted meals.

I picked at my pizza nebbishly. Everyone else ran away to wash their hands. They returned in a thunderous wave, digging into the pizzas like madmen.

"What's wrong?" Shira crunched at me. "Did you get a new favorite kind of pizza?"

I struggled with words before deciding not to respond. I wanted to tell her, I've changed, but I didn't even know if it was true. Everything I do differently, they kept saying it was California. But it wasn't. It was me.

"Hava," Rivkie's voice floated down from the far end of the table. "Tell us again how you almost got kicked out of school."

One or two of the freshmen kids, hearing my name out loud, stopped stealing sidelong glances and now stared at me unabashedly. I grinned. Young Jews were so fickle. Next week, their cousin who played drums with the Ben Dovid Band would be in town and I'd be old news. But today, I was big.

"Not right now," I said. "But did I tell you about Queen Malka, the Orthodox woman rapper in Berkeley?"

One of the freshman boys guffawed. Another elbowed him in the stomach.

"Yes, twice," said Rivkie. "But tell me again."

When everyone was good and stuffed with pizza, somebody finally checked the time. It was six-thirty, half an hour later than anyone was supposed to be there. Stomachs heaving, everyone ran home to dinner, hoping that our digestive acids would dissolve the pizza into some saucy excuse for our parents.

I walked through the front door of our apartment and I couldn't move much farther. Tables were wedged against all the walls, and a couch was blocking the entrance. I hopped onto the sofa from behind, kicked my feet atop the upturned coffee table, and collapsed into pillows.

"Hey, old man," I said. "You need some help lifting that?"

My father shot a G-d-save-me look.

"Don't worry, I got it." He waved me off. "You're a woman. You shouldn't do such heavy lifting."

"All righty," I said. "You asked for it." I slid off my ass and grabbed one side of the coffee table.

Once upon a time, that would have gotten my buttons pushed for real. Between my parents, my father was always the one who was designated homemaker. When I grew old enough to help with chores, I was totally lethargic. The one thing that could always get me to help was suggesting that I wasn't up to it.

"There's my little whippersnapper," said my father, gripping the other side.

We huffed and puffed and rearranged the tiny apartment into the biggest vault of empty space we could manage. The couch and chairs squeezed artfully against the far walls. Our big recliner took up the corner usually reserved for Mom's cactuses. In the outside hallway, our neighbors passed by and wondered why the building manager had thought to adorn the hall with such bizarre vegetation. Grasping a cactus firmly enough to move was a bitch. I spent valuable furniture-rearranging minutes tending to my pricks.

At eight-thirty, people began drifting in. First, my relatives, the aunts and uncles from New Jersey, who always planned to spend an hour parking and always found parking immediately. Then came Rivkie Gutstein-Gruber and her parents. Mr. Gruber wobbled in the hall. On his back sat an elephant-size television, old-fashioned, with fake mahogany panels and knobs the size of a fist. He lowered it to the ground with a resounding *thwump* that they heard three floors down. Mr. Gruber and my dad and I had to turn it on a three-quarter angle to fit it in the door.

When we finished, my aunts were in the kitchen, arranging the melons and pineapples into platter formation. My girl cousins, in their matching dresses, sliced cheese cubes and arranged pickle slices and pretzels in circles around them. Yiskah, who was four, arranged them into pyramids.

That was my New Jersey family — xenophobic and patriarchal. They lived in a small town whose population was almost exclusively Jewish, and regarded the city as a necessary evil, good only for Broadway shows and bagel deliveries. I plopped down next to Yankie on the couch. "What's up, Yankie?" I asked.

"Nothin'," he said.

"You know," I offered, "I got interviewed on this talk show last week. They asked me to list my ten favorite songs and then introduce each one —"

"Did you go into the radio station?" Yankie asked.

"No, they do everything by phone now."

"Oh," he echoed emptily.

"*Hava!*" A new batch of family.

The door flung open with alarming regularity. Relatives entered in a steady flow. Ten minutes before showtime — on the television, the reality-show contestants were wrapping up this week's terse emotional conflict — my friends showed up, all in a huge confederation, just as I had begun to worry.

Shira, her misgivings about my debut in the secular world now evaporated, ran to hug me. Meira and Fruma and one or two other girls from our class piled on. Bodies crushed me.

"Shira wanted to get you that book *Kosher Sex* as a gift," Meira whispered. "But I said it was in bad taste. And besides, you can always borrow my copy from the bottom of my mattress."

"Shmuel sends his regrets," Fruma said, courteously if not warmly. "He says television is *osser.* If he *did* watch any one television program, he said it would be yours, if that's any consolation," she added.

I group-hugged them all again.

Through Shira's meticulously sprayed hair and everybody's shoulders, I got a camera-cropped view of the crowd that had assembled. My old teachers, downstairs neighbors, virtually all the kids in my grade, some of my parents' friends that I only vaguely remembered. The same crowd would reassemble here again in a few months, for my graduation party. But it wouldn't be quite the same. Tonight felt tentative and ephemeral, a recipe you'll never duplicate.

We separated. In the far corner, Moish leaned against the doorpost, hands in pockets, chewing on a toothpick. He wore a black collared shirt with a beige-and-white tie. Things were changing, I thought. We were changing.

The television volume shot up, an uncle bent over the controls. The end credits to the last show were spiraling by. "Next," said the announcer, "they're so unorthodox, they're Orthodox! The series premiere of *The Goldbergs* after this break."

"Oh my G-d!" shrieked Yankie, tackling me at the waist with his little body. "Hava!"

I let out a yelp.

On the screen was a montage of my summer. Me and Evie fighting. Charles and Paula hugging. Jamie, Corey, and me sneaking into the synagogue with all the lights out. Baby Goldberg chasing Evie around the house.

I cringed.

Hesitant fingers touched my knocking knees: Shira, Meira, my father.

I looked around the room. Rivkie and the few other freshmen were clustered by the sofa, eyeing one another with the tentativeness of freshmen in a coed environment. My black-hat family, the men standing behind the women, petulantly stroking their beards. Moish was still by himself in a corner.

I offered a weak smile at my father. The network's theme chimed. A hokey animation gave way to the studio kitchen. I shuddered. It was every hackneyed line I had to repeat a million times.

Paula stood in the kitchen, mixing a kugel. Evie sat at the kitchen table. She was complaining about her Talmud homework.

"But where's Hava?" one of my cousins chirped.

"Yechezkel, *quiet*!" his mother whisper-yelled.

The conversation between Paula and Evie had run its course. Just as the studio laughter was dying out, I walked onscreen and plopped down on the couch.

Instantly, everyone in the house fell silent. Fifty pairs of eyes were riveted to the screen.

Out of everyone there, I alone had the power to turn away. Even if other people in the room didn't feel like watching, or were afraid to watch secular television, or even wanted to blink, they couldn't. In a sort of horror, I realized that everyone here was watching this like it was the most important monologue of my life.

Me, I let my head loll into my propped-up hand. The bright TV flicker on my cousins' impressionable faces. The cynical expression in Fruma's eyes. The envy in Shira's.

Of everyone, my father was the most interesting to watch.

He sat next to me on the couch — like guests of honor, my father and I were on the couch — his body perched on the edge, hands folded between his knees, face intently forward. The blue glow reflected off his tautly trimmed beard, his angular jawline. His eyes were alight and intelligent, not like how most people's eyes zone out during a TV show. He was alert, kinetic in the most with-it way. I reached up and touched his hair. He didn't move. At breakfast today, his only day off for the week, we got through almost the whole meal without an allusion to this moment. I mentioned it and he looked surprised. He looked up from his spinach-olive omelet and remarked how excited he was. "I'll be able to see the months I missed" — that's how he put it.

Yankie slipped an arm around his infant sister. I turned back to the television. Like an old '80s love song, I recognized Evie's line. On-screen, I was about to say my first "*Oy vey*, dude!"

In the corner of my eye, Meira slid off the couch.

"You can't go now!" I hissed to her. "I'm about to —"

Then I saw why she was standing.

Briefcase still in hand, my mother smoothed down her skirt and took the seat that Meira had vacated. Meira, meanwhile, sat uncomfortably on the arm of the sofa. My mother crossed her legs, arranged her posture, and settled into watching the television.

From the corner of my eye, I saw her smile at me.

I stiffened. My eyes held tight to the television. There was quality entertainment on. No way was I turning away to ask how her day went.

"Oh, my, now look who's home from day care!" Paula was

saying on the TV. David Lee emerged from the living room, carrying Baby Goldberg, bundled in a swath of blankets.

The baby's cute little paws reached out. Paula leaned down to kiss him.

"*Ossssser!!*" he screamed.

We laughed, and they cut to a commercial.

Instantly, everyone began to talk. Fruma complained that everyone pronounced Shabbos wrong. The aunts and uncles, in loud whispers, remarked how it wasn't as offensive as they thought it would be. Like one uncle said, his beard flip-flopping, "It's not evil. It isn't *good*, but it's not evil."

On the floor, Yankie sat and watched his baby sister. Every time she stuck her thumb into her mouth, he yelled "*Osser!*"

"Well, Hava," my father said, tapping my knee, "I think you did it again."

"What do you mean?" I asked, perplexed.

"Everyone is confused and astounded and amazed. And it's all your fault."

"You make it seem like I should be proud or something."

"Oh, Havaleh," he said, "of *course* you should be proud."

"Everybody *loves* you," my mother added.

I felt a chill.

"I think I'm going to fetch a beer," I said, heading off to the drinks table.

"Apple juice or soda!" my father yelled after me.

Meira, Saul Horowitz, and a few of the kids in our class were standing around the drinks table, looking mischievous. Rivkie Gutstein-Gruber was there, too, holding a cup and trying to blend in. "Dude," Saul grinned at me, "your show rocks."

"Um, thanks." I grinned specifically at Shira. "Hey, are you digging it?"

"Oh. Yes. Digging." Shira raised her glass and drank. I'd never seen her so self-conscious. I wondered what kind of stories she had from this summer. I wondered if she'd still let me hear them.

I poured myself a glass of apple juice with just a splash of vodka. I'm pretty sure I caught my father watching me. I'm pretty sure he grinned.

I took a gulp as I walked back to the couch. The vodka bitterness ran up against the clean sweetness of the apples, forcing a gag. I recovered naturally, all my acting skills at work. I planted myself back on the couch, between my father and the robot, just as the second act was coming on.

I made it through the rest of the show uninjured. Cringed during one of the conversations between me and David Lee about having a crush. My grandfather cleared his throat when, on TV, I said, "But I want to see him and be around him and be his eye candy!" Several of the uncles looked over, too.

Shoshana Goldberg felt like a totally separate human being on the screen, isolated from myself by time and geographic distance and immaturity. This girl I used to be was pretending to be another girl, saying words that somebody else had thought of.

And I thought about how Jews never talk to each other when we pray, how it's such an individual thing, and even after praying we pretend that it never happened. If I'm wiped out, if it was that intense, I need to act like it wasn't. And when you see someone else praying beautifully, eyes shut, mouth like a heavy-metal singer, *shockeling* back and forth with such devotion like she's afraid for her life, you never tell that person how amazing she looked. If anything, you file her away in your brain, making a mental note that maybe you should try to catch up with her later, some group conversation sometime, see if she's a friend of a friend or something.

I said good-bye to everyone as they left, hugging my female friends from school, kissing my girl cousins' cheeks and smiling meaningfully at the male cousins.

When everyone had left, I rolled my eyes and sank against the door.

My mother stood up abruptly. She stacked dishes, threw them into the sink with a clatter, and walked out without a word.

"Well," I said, "I think we pulled that off hitchlessly, wouldn't you say?"

"Hava," my father said.

My father was never someone for many words. He was an uncomplicated human being, joyous, kind, easy to please, and easy to understand.

He looked hurt. I knew what I had to do to make it better and I knew I didn't want to do it.

"Why does it matter?" I said. "She missed the show. She got here late and she didn't apologize and she didn't even help set *up*. She doesn't *care*."

"Yes, she does," he said softly.

No arguments. No logic or reasoning. My father was the only one who knew me this well; I hated fights when it got reduced to "Yes!" "No!" and back again. I struggled with just being there. I wanted to run off the fire escape. I looked at my father, so small across the room. Even the kitchen cabinets were bigger than he was. And his full-moon eyes, bright and pleading.

"Go talk to her."

I shuffled down the hallway.

My mom was sitting on her bed, back facing me. The door was open. I knocked on the doorway.

"Don't come in."

Her voice was forceful. My mother never sounded forceful. Even when she yelled at me, there was always the illusion of charisma. I hated this quietness. I took a step forward, into her room.

She could hear me walk.

"*Go away!*"

The words came out all muffled and distorted, barely human. Her throat was clogged with phlegm and she sounded like cellophane stretching.

I didn't go away. I listened to her cry.

"*Huk, huk, huk. Huk, huk, huk.*"

I winced. I felt like I'd been punched in the gut. She sounded so pathetic when she cried. My stomach felt big and hollow.

I cringed. It was like watching bad acting. Only, it wasn't.

"Mom —" I started.

"*Don't!*" she screamed.

I took two steps back. The hardwood floor creaked.

My hand was still frozen in the air, hovering two steps back from my mother's shoulder, where I had been about to rest it.

"I spend my whole life trying to make it better for you, Hava. Every hour I spend at work is five hours you won't have to work when you're in college. You never realize how much I do for you. And all you do is yell and scream and embarrass me —"

She flicked her wrist open to show an empty palm.

I don't know what gesture she was trying for. It failed. She batted her eyes, filtering tears. Her state was all my fault, and I felt powerless to change it. The complexity of my paradox made my stomach turn.

"Mom," I said, "I love you."

"No you don't," she said. She was cool, like stating facts.

I froze, not knowing how to react to that. *I love you:* humanity's secret self-destruct code to make everything better again.

"How can you *say* that?"

"You embarrass me in front of your friends, Hava. You ignore me and pretend I'm not a part of your life and then, when I want to be, you *ridicule* me for it. You spent three months barely checking *in* with me. I can't remember the last time you asked me how my *day* went."

"Maybe that's because I'd like to be a *part* of how your day went someday."

"When have you made the effort?"

I opened my mouth and closed it.

"When did you make the effort?" Her mouth filled with mucus again. The words stuck like paste.

"I'm sorry, Mom," I said, shaking my head. "I thought you were the adult. I thought you were supposed to show me how to do all this."

G-d, I thought. I could go in for major escapism right now. When I was little, I used to contemplate running away all the time. Only, I never actually did.

I walked over to the window. I pushed it open with one

hand. I used the other to boost myself on the sill, jump over the wooden plank and onto the rattling fire escape.

I stayed there, crouched. I thought of all the unspoken stuff going on as we all watched the show, the disapproval and questions, the things we never say. So many things we never say aloud.

The sky was alight with glowing gray clouds. Stars peeked through the cloud cover. It reminded me of California, how it felt to be that close to the clouds. Roofs spread around us like tectonic plates. I could hop on any of them, float away until the earth had separated miles away from my old apartment building.

Gravel crunched. My eyes shot over to the other side of the roof. I noticed a tiny black hemisphere behind the greenhouse-like hatchway, visible slightly against the less-black sky. I ran over to the hatch, pitched my body across it, and looked down.

Lying in the gravel, head propped against the hatch, was Ian.

His eyes vacantly watched the sky. When I sprang into view, a grin popped across his face.

"Hava," he breathed. "It's fucking good to see you."

"Goofball," I said. "Why didn't you come to my party?"

"*Your* party?"

"It was *for* me. It can be my party." I slid off the hatch and landed on the gravel with a *crunch*. My ass smarted. Small puddles of stones, caught in my skirt, rumbled against my shins. "So why weren't you there?"

"Your parents invited my parents. They didn't want to go. They said it sounded like a — well, a Jewish thing. They were afraid they'd be trespassing."

"The *show*, maybe. But all the other neighbors were there.

Aw, well. I don't know if I'd actually have wanted you to be there."

Ian shot a look at me. "Hava, I'm feeling delicate tonight. Jimmy Auten and I made out in the bathroom and I don't know *what's* going on with us. Say you're kidding fast, okay?"

"I'm not. Tonight was just more performing. When I'm with you, I like that I talk and you listen and we always keep it real."

Ian got it. I knew he would.

"Yeah," he said.

He pushed himself away from the hatch so he could lie down all the way. The back of his head sank into the gravel. His dirty-blond hair fell away from his eyes, and his nose pointed directly at the sky.

I lay myself down beside him. I blinked at the stars. There were a million of them. Just like Hollywood.

I opened my mouth, about to ask Ian if he thought we'd ever die. But that wasn't the question. What I meant to ask was, *Do you think we'll ever change?*

I wanted him to tell me *no.* Ian, so beautiful and perfect, making snow angels in the gravel when he moved. I remembered in California when we stayed up all night watching bands and had Italian sodas at Canter's as the sun was coming up. If I could act that moment a hundred times, record it for the network and replay it forever, I would. How do you freeze a moment? Easy answer: You don't. That's why it takes us so long to die. So we don't have to spend the rest of our lives chasing the one perfect moment that we wasted. You never realize something's perfect until it's gone, anyway.

"I'm listening," Ian said. "You can talk if you want."

"It's okay," I said. "Talking's lame. Just be here."

In Judaism, you never atone for sins by saying a million Hail Marys or anything. You suck up the damage, realize you were wrong, and live each moment like it's your first moment ever. If you suddenly decide to keep kosher, it's as if you've done it your whole life.

I reached over, took Ian's hand. I could feel where it was without looking. I squeezed it and it was warm.

The night got cold, the way nights do when it's about to turn to autumn. The city was settling down, growing into a silence. Eventually, Ian brushed the stones off his corduroys to leave. Above us, a shooting star arced across the sky and fizzled. The star didn't look like it exploded, the way you learn about them in school. It seemed more like it dropped out of sight and hid.

I could be that kind of star. For a while, at least.

Ian made a move to hug me. At the last second, he didn't go in for the kill. He wrung his hands together and looked at me across the way, hugged me with his eyes, gave me a look that was meaningful and mournful and satisfied and unfulfilled.

It didn't matter. We had forever, I was sure of that much.

Ian, two floors below my feet, scampered into his window. Between the rungs of the fire escape, he was small as a bug. I heard the distant clank of a window and he disappeared.

I climbed back inside the same window I'd left by. Streetlights and the neighbors' stray television sets bathed my parents' room in purple and green, everything a velvety shade of night. I tiptoed across the floor. My shoes were still on the roof. The space next to my mother was flat, conspicuously vacant. Dad had left for work some time between when I'd run out and now.

"Beryl?" my mother moaned softly in her sleep, reaching

over to touch the space where my father slept. I wondered if still, now, she woke up thinking he'd be there on the nights that he worked. I wonder if his night shifts affected her the same way her overtime affected me.

I froze on the carpet.

For the barest fraction of a second, my mother appeared to sigh back into her pillow and sleep. But I saw her elbows struggle up and down like the last Twix bar stuck in a vending machine. She pulled herself up on a pillow and opened her eyes to narrow slits.

"Hava?" she murmured. "Is that you, Hava?"

I tried to leave soundlessly. I took two steps before I hit the loose board and the floor creaked like New Year's.

"Hava," she murmured. "Don't go. I lied to you before. I do love you."

"I know, Mom," I said.

She looked so vulnerable and undressed in that bed. I touched her cold, smooth cheek. It thrilled and terrified me that she had a body that could still be so young. I used to think — venomously — that she should be punished for working so much. The corners of her mouth didn't even wrinkle. Only her faraway sparrow eyes looked old. For a second, free of my body, I pictured my father coming home to her, to this bed. It was so safe. I thought about running to my own bedroom, digging out my cell phone, and calling Charles ("Ring me any time, Hava — I'll need your call more than you will, I assure you") and then, with a little shiver, I decided not to. Not because talking to Charles would make me uncomfortable. It would make me *too* comfortable. Right now, I needed to be uncomfortable.

One day, I'll settle down, find a boy to make me feel safe, laugh at all my jokes, to be alternately ridiculous and sublime with. I'd already made the world's biggest personal ad. It airs every Monday night.

Now I'll just see who shows up.

In New York City now, it's four in the morning. In Hollywood, it was one o'clock — the night was just beginning. My body never settled back on East Coast time. I kind of hope I never settle. I roll into my bed, but there's an itch under my skin that sleep won't sedate.

I grab my notepad and my knapsack. I climb out the window and down the fire escape. I take the stairs past Ian's lightless window and twenty-seven floors down. I jump the final ten feet to the ground. My feet smart, but the world swirls around me and suddenly I'm there, everything is an adventure, lights camera action and I'm gone.

CAST & CREW

Many thanks, appreciation, goodwill & more love than some ink in a list can convey to Douglas Adams, Claudia Alick, Sini Anderson, Cristin O'Keefe Aptowicz, Eric Axelson, Gertrude Berg, Berzerkeley Slam, Jello Biafra, Darren Blase, Blue Hebrew House, Cooper Lee Bombardier, Lynnee Breedlove, the Butchies, Clint Catalyst, Phred Chao, Steve Chbosky, the chomosexuals, Maxine Clair, Sherilyn Connelly, Doug Coupland, the Crown Heights Hasidic Underground, Dennis Dalrympole, Mos Def, Deep Dickollective, Sandi Dubowski, 1853, Beth Everheart, Kristen Freeland, the Freundels, Dan Friedman and Ali G, Kamilah Forbes, Temima Fruchter, Yoshie Fruchter, the Fruchters, Daphne Gottlieb, Rabbi Steve Greenberg, Pinhas Grossman, Mary Harper, HBO, Cara Herbitter, Michaelryan Hicks, Bob Holman and the Bowery Poetry Club, Wylie Huey, Rachel Israel, Dan Kaufman, Kris Kovick, Ben Krevitz, K'vetch, Devora Jagoda, Katrina James, Marek Jira, Dominique Johnson, Coltrane Johnson, Jen Joseph and Manic D Press, Juez, David Kasher, Katastrophe for the ladies, the Langers, Jason Lieberman, Audre Lorden, Bonfire Madigan, Rabbi Chaim Mahgel-Friedman, Moshe Mandel, Jake Marmer and Mimaamakim.org, Kristen Martin, Itza Martinez, Matisyahu, TJ Michels, the Millers, M.G. Room, MJ, Lady Monster, Faye Moskowitz, Jonathan Oringher, Alvin Orloff, Stephanie Pell, the Pragers,

Yoav Potash, the Potashes, Queen Ester and MC Jen Miriam, Kirk Read, Haggai Resnikoff, Riot a Go-Go, Shauna Rogan, Carlos Santana, Cynthia Saunders, Mary Schroeder-Blumke, Sara Seinberg, Maurice Sendak, Sharon Senser, Adam Shapiro, Shotwell House, Erez Shudnow, radice Sidonové, Russell Simmins, Yudi Simon and YAM, Bucky Sinister, Andy Sinton, all the amazing Sister Spit chycks, Carolyn Slutsky, South Lawn at Central High, Anya Stone, Suicide Kings, radice Svabové, Michelle Tea, Jenny Traig, Buddy Wakefield, Megan Warnick, David West, Aliza Wasserman, Ronika Rakhel Weber, and YIDcore. Thanks to everyone who's ever lived or stayed in the Blue Hebrew House for making Shabbos what it is. Thanks to my parents for believing that you can pay rent with poems, to my sister for explaining WB plots, and to the rest of my family for not disowning me yet. And to my grandmom, for never once telling on me. Thanks to you, for reading and listening and giving me the chance to write. It's the only thing I ever wanted to do and, knowing there's someone out there listening, you saved my life.

David Levithan	**director**
Liz Matusow	**producer**
Harbeer Sandhu	**director of photography**
Keren Sussman	**grip**
Ani Difranco	**appearing as herself**
Sarah Lefton and JewishFashionConspiracy.com	**wardrobe**
Aaron Streiter	**gaffer**

a PUSH production